JEWELS OF ASTERIA

TO BREAK A CURSE

J. D. PIERCE

First published by Twilight Muse Publishing, LLC 2024

First edition

ISBN (paperback): 979-8-9915085-0-6 ISBN (hardcover): 979-8-9915085-1-3 ISBN (Ebook Kindle): 979-8-9915085-2-0

Edited by K. F. Starfell; Proofread by A. E. Taylor

Cover designed by Getcovers

NOTE ON CONTENT

Your mental health matters. There are things within To Break A Curse that may make you uncomfortable. It is up to you whether or not you choose to read it. Please see the below list and make the best decision for yourself.

This book contains:

- Adult language
- Sexually Explicit Content
- Abuse
- Parental Death
- Sibling Death
- Death by illness/disease
- Confinement
- Forced Marriage
- Torture (on-page)
- Underage sex (off-page)
- Sexual harassment (off-page)
- References to cheating (off-page)

JEWELS OF ASTERIA

To Break a Curse is part of a series of fairy tale retellings, each taking place in a different kingdom in Asteria. Each kingdom's book(s) will be a separate story with interconnected threads.

See if you can spot the hints to what retelling and kingdom comes next before the end!

WELCOME TO THE RUBY COURT

BOOK ONE

Where fire runs through our veins and lights our souls ablaze

CHAPTER

ONE

Arabelle

The fire must have destroyed my hearing. There was no other reason for what I thought I heard my father say. I blinked down at the bandages covering fluid-filled boils from being dumb enough to grab a piece of burning wood. Fire seared up my arms at the smallest twitch of my fingers.

My head still swam in a fog of grogginess from being unconscious for so long, and I leaned back against the pillows.

My gaze darted back to him, standing in the door, wearing the same clothes I'd last seen him in. Odd. I couldn't remember ever seeing him wear the same thing twice, let alone for...however long I'd been asleep.

"I must have misheard you. What did you say?"

He closed the door behind him and leaned against it.

"I said I've accepted Louis's marriage proposal. You'll marry him once you're healed. Nine months should suffice, according to the doctor."

His face portrayed no emotion, none of the dread that pumped through my veins instead of blood.

My face contorted, and I wrinkled my nose. A steady thrum of my pulse pounded all the way down to my fingertips in a constant reminder of what had happened.

"You can't be serious. You've said time and again that he didn't have the position or power to marry me." Bile burned its way up my throat, but I gulped it back down. "You, yourself, said he wasn't worthy of our family."

If he wasn't worthy before, what could have changed to make him worthy now? It made no sense. How was this happening? Now, of all times? I swallowed the whimper when I accidentally flexed my fingers, and pain screamed through them.

"What about Ember? What about Garnet?" They were much better choices for a bride than I was.

The door groaned behind him as he shifted his weight. His countenance changed, and a muscle feathered in his jaw.

"Do you not remember the night of the fire?"

My eyes dropped to my hands again. I remembered little from that night. Only the scorching heat, the collapsing house, and my lousy attempt at rescuing Isa. Even though we were identical, she had an elegant grace about her I'd never picked up. I made up for it in other aspects, but I'd never compare to her.

"No. Not really."

He folded his arms across his chest, rumpling the already wrinkled shirt and jacket.

"Your brothers and sisters didn't make it out of the fire."

Hot tears burned tracks down my cheeks. "What about Isa? Did she...?"

A lump clogged my throat before I could finish the sentence. I was glad for the agony in my hands; it eclipsed the hollowing of my heart. In a single night, I lost almost my entire family. My tears stained the bandages when they splattered on them. I didn't know how to face a life without Isa in it.

"Isa's fine. Her face was badly scarred, but she'll survive.

Unfortunately for us, Simon called off their engagement when he saw her face was damaged."

"Where is she?"

Damaged? Shouldn't he have said injured? She was his daughter, not some old piece of furniture. But, then again, that was never the kind of man he was.

"She's resting right now. You can see her soon." He shifted from one foot to the other before speaking again. "We have no other prospects since Simon left her. That is why I've accepted Louis's offer."

My insides twisted up in knots so tight it almost made the pain in my hands disappear. He only saw us as objects to trade for his benefit. I accepted it long ago, but it still burned a part of my soul when I was reminded. I bit the inside of my cheek until I tasted blood.

"But you said—"

A vase of roses crashed to the floor when he flung his arm out to the side. He frowned at them before turning that irritation back on me.

"Things have changed, Belle."

"They can't have changed that much."

This time, I didn't stop my fingers from curling, albeit loosely, trying to let the sharp throb ground me. It failed. Panic was a living thing under my skin, and I couldn't quash it. Agreeing to a marriage without falling in love? *That* was the end of the little freedom I had enjoyed in my life. And to give it up for *Louis* of all people? Bile, again, burned at the bottom of my throat.

"Unlike Isa, you never made an impression on any suitors, not a good one anyway." He raked a hand through his shoulder-length chestnut hair – the same hair I inherited from him. "Your... behavior," he hesitated, eyes moving from my bandaged hands up to my unkempt hair and back again, "has left a bad taste in the mouths of many."

White hot fire seared through my arms.

"He only wants to subjugate me because I hurt his pride. Because *you* hurt his pride when you refused him before."

Focus on the pain; that's all I had to do. Stay focused on the pain and ensured my temper was in check.

"The reason matters little. He has gold and a better position than we now hold. The fire took everything."

The cold, scheming tone was one he always used when he declared what was best for us.

"He'll provide us a comfortable life."

Us.

"I will *never* love some...some *beast*. Someone who hurts others just to retain his power over them."

I didn't care about gold or comfort or station. I wanted the freedom to live my life as *I* chose. To be able to dance through a field of stars until dawn, to love someone with every ounce of my being, to sit and read a novel until I couldn't keep my eyes open any longer. Louis wouldn't allow any of it.

"Good thing love isn't a factor. I raised you to know better than that. And if I were you, I'd learn to keep that mouth shut and him happy." He dropped his voice to a harsh whisper as he stepped away from the door, as if he could be heard. "We all know what happened to his first wife."

Panic gripped my spine and held fast at the mention of his first wife. I knew the rumors, but they couldn't be true, could they? There was no way that the town would let him get away with killing her and not do anything. I swallowed around the growing lump.

I squared my shoulders and lifted my chin in a move I'd seen my mother use.

"I will *not* marry him."

I held onto the pain, leashed it to me as a crutch to prop me up.

It didn't matter what he said or what excuse he gave me. I would outright refuse Louis myself if he tried to force it. I could take Isa and run. *To where?* I didn't know, but anywhere was better than this.

He dropped his arms as anger flashed in his eyes.

"It is not *your* choice. *I* decide who you will marry, and you *will* marry him."

I held his stare with an inferno raging in my blood, screaming to be let out, to burn everything to cinders and leave no trace behind. He couldn't make me do this. But I knew better. Women never had a choice in these things. I counted my breaths to fight the sobs and distract myself from the stinging in my eyes.

A creak of hinges sounded, and the doctor cleared his throat in a hoarse rasp. I'd forgotten where we were. He laced his fingers together in front of himself and rocked back onto his heels.

"I don't think now is the right time for this little chat of yours, Henri. Arabelle has only just awoken from such a tragedy. She needs to recover her strength."

My father clicked his tongue in a sound of annoyance.

"Louis will be here in a few days with an official proposal. I expect you to give him a favorable answer."

He left.

"I'm sorry, doctor."

I couldn't bring myself to look at him, to let him see the shame in my eyes for being such a disobedient daughter. Men never understood.

"Now, now. There's no need to apologize. Let's change those bandages, shall we?"

He pulled up a stool next to me and carefully turned my hands over to undo the wrappings.

The same breeze that set my dressing robe fluttering played with the blooming tulips in the doctor's private garden. Despite the doctor's protests, Louis had insisted on bringing me out here. I knew why. I fought to keep my face neutral from the cringe that enveloped every part of me.

"I know you're probably opposed to marrying me," Louis finally broke the silence. "I'm sure you've heard the rumors." He took my hands in his and turned me to face him. "But let me assure you, there is no merit in them. I would never harm you."

I forced a smile onto my face and hoped to God that it reached my eyes. The press of his grip sent ripples of agony up through both of my arms and though I wanted to rip my hands from his, it might have caused even more pain.

"That's not the only reason, Louis," I paused, clenching my teeth through the pain that screamed and threatened to buckle my knees from his grip.

I had to be careful what I said to him.

"We have nothing in common. And my family has nothing to offer you anymore." I let my eyes drop from his. "Why would you want to marry someone with nothing?"

He was not unattractive; women in town swooned after him. With his broad chest, sculpted muscles, tall stature, gorgeous green eyes, and long black hair, he was too perfect – disgustingly perfect, as if he had something to hide under it all. That wasn't my problem with him. There was something rotten inside him that set my teeth on edge.

"It was never about what your family could offer me." He brushed a stray lock of hair from my face. "You are beautiful and unique and headstrong. Lesser men may shy away from that. But I love a challenge."

A challenge. That's all I was to him.

He took my chin between thumb and forefinger and raised my face to his.

A familiar disgust bubbled up from the bowels of my being, and the control I had over my tongue slipped.

"Louis, I'm not a—"

"I'll take care of Isa, too. See to it that she wants for nothing."

That gave me pause. Reason enough to slip the harness of self-control back on, keep quiet about every deplorable thing about him, and consider his offer. Simon dumped Isa because she was scarred – *damaged,* as my father put it. She might never find someone who would accept her.

Taking this offer meant I would give up everything I wanted; my future, my freedom, a chance at love. I didn't deserve any of that if she couldn't have it, too. The sister I couldn't even properly save. It was my fault she had the scar, my fault that she wouldn't find her happily ever after. And this was the price for it.

"Alright. I'll marry you."

"Excellent choice, Belle."

I cried out from the burning pain when he tried to drag me by the hand. I hit my knees, holding both to my middle and fought to hold tears back as that pain fully eclipsed my being.

"Forgive me, my excitement got the best of me. I'll see to it that you and your family's remaining belongings are brought to my estate."

He stared down at me, and I could have sworn he had a smirk on his face.

"No. We shouldn't live together until we are wed," I said through gritted teeth. "Think about what people will say."

If all I had were these few months of freedom left, I wanted to keep every last second.

"Come now, Belle. Where will you go? Your home burned down. You have nowhere. People will praise me for being generous enough to allow you and your family to stay with me now."

He was talking down to me, literally. He didn't even offer me a hand up.

"We'll manage. Please, Louis. My reputation is all I have left."

I didn't care about my reputation, but I prayed he didn't realize that.

"Fine. But I won't pay for you to live somewhere else. You're on your own until you're mine."

"That's fine. I'll see you in nine months."

When Louis turned to leave, my breath came easier. Surviving a marriage to that man would take a miracle, but I'd have to, for Isa's sake.

The agony burning in my hands made it a chore just to get back to my feet, let alone back inside the doctor's house.

That's how we ended up in an old cottage that a strong wind might topple. My father was furious that I declined Louis's offer to live with him. But he backed down when Isa took my side and chided him for the impropriety of it. We were crammed together in a room with two tiny cots while my father slept in the main room. It was a far cry from the comforts of our old life, but something about being here *felt* right.

CHAPTER

TWO

Lucien

The twin gold statues clanged against the stone floor when I threw them across the room. It failed; the ritual that was supposed to break this gods' forsaken curse utterly failed. I raked my hands through the fur matted over the top of my head, and I spun to my friend, the only person I had spoken to in nearly twenty years.

"You said this would work, Elie, that these hideous things would break any curse." I slashed my clawed hand through the air. "But I'm still a beast!" my bellowing voice rang against the walls.

This curse was set by a witch, but I knew the truth about who was really behind it. And I had half a mind to go into Hesnen and rip Aamon from his Obsidian Palace with my own claws. To curse me was one thing, but my kingdom? The coward hadn't even bothered to show his face and claim his wrongdoing.

The knot in Elie's throat bobbed when he swallowed.

"I thought they would, Lucien. I'm sorry."

We'd both spent years scouring every book in the library containing even a modicum of information about curses. When

9

he came across the statues in one of the oldest tomes, he set straight out and spoke with a merchant about finding them. To think they'd be nothing but some old wives' tale. Or maybe the magic holding my curse in place was just too strong for such artifacts to touch.

"Now that this has failed, will you please let me find someone to bring back here? It's the only way."

He spoke with tentative care, no doubt remembering the times he'd brought the subject up with me in the past. The only method all the books agreed would break any curse was a road I wasn't willing to travel.

"You already know my answer to that."

I didn't want someone else here, didn't want to be seen by another soul. They would run screaming, and I couldn't blame them.

Elie raked his hands through the red curls of his hair before splaying his arms.

"We're out of time, Lucien." His golden eyes swirled with a desperation I'd only ever seen once before. "If you don't break this curse, you will die."

"We've been over this before, Elie. I'm not allowing anyone else in this castle. I will not allow myself to fall in love with another person."

"You don't have a choice if you want to live—"

"I would rather die than go through that pain again," I bit out through clenched teeth, fighting to hold the restraints of my temper in check.

Why couldn't he drop it? He knew what happened the last time and why I was so against this. Yet, I knew why. I saw it in his eyes; we drew nearer to the end every day.

My duty to my kingdom should overwrite any desire or emotion I had about it, and maybe it made me a wretch, but I didn't care. They were better off forgetting my existence and living their lives as they were now. Agony clawed its way underneath my ribcage and wrapped around my heart.

This was why I was cursed.

My selfishness.

Grienia would be better off without such a king to rule over it. I ground my teeth together and turned my back on Elie.

"Get out."

"Please, Lucien, just let me help you. We can't give up yet."

His steps sounded from behind, growing closer.

"It's too late. Even if you found someone today, they couldn't possibly fall in love with me before time runs out."

With the face of a monster and a temperament to match, it was an impossibility I didn't want to take a chance on. It was better this way. Elie would be free this way. He just needed to accept it.

"Please, Luce—"

"—I said leave!" my voice boomed from my chest and echoed down the empty hallways. There was silence, then his footsteps as he walked away.

Arabelle

Tongues of fire licked at my arms as I rushed past them, shielding my face as the screams of familiar voices called to me from further inside the inferno. I choked on the smoke blackening the walls, reminding myself not to brace on any as the flames crawled up them. Wallpaper bubbled and split open; paint melted.

"Isa," I called out into a house that swallowed every sound with the roaring of burning wood.

"Isabelle!"

Soot stuffed itself down my throat with every breath. I needed to turn and run, but I couldn't leave them, couldn't leave her.

"Isa. Please answer me," I cried out again.

The stairs to the upper floor lay in a heap of burning wood. I couldn't get to the others. But Isa's room was on the same level as mine. I needed to get to her; I needed to save her—at least her.

"Where are you?" I croaked, my voice weakened from the smoke. "Please..."

My vision blurred, and my eyes stung enough that tears prickled at the edges of my lids.

A faint cry, carried on some phantom wind, finally sounded over the creaking of the scorching beams. I moved toward it, through fallen debris and opened holes, until I found my twin. Breath stole from my lungs. A thick, fallen chunk of wood trapped her.

"Belle!" she cried out, her hand reaching for me.

"Hang on, I'll get you out of there."

I rushed to her, grabbing hold of the broken debris and reeling back with a hiss. Red, angry welts formed on my palms from the heat.

God damn it. I wouldn't let her die here. I took a deep breath, bit down the fear of hurt, gripped that piece of wood, and lifted.

"Hurry, Isa, I can't hold it for long."

She started to squeeze out but winced when my strength faltered, and the debris shifted toward the floor.

"Sorry."

I heaved it up again. When she was clear, I dropped the wood and grabbed her hand, pain screaming in my nerves at the touch as I led her out of the manor. Tears streaked my face. The screams of my other siblings filled every inch of air left in the burning house. Arms wrapped around me as I stepped back toward the manor.

"Stop. I have to go back; I have to save—"

"Belle?"

Isa's voice jolted me from the memory of flames and death, sweat rolling down my cheek and neck, soaking the edges of my night dress as I stood before the clouded mirror. The images of that night started coming back little by little after I woke.

My eyes drifted to her, to the scar slicing down from temple to jaw. The scar I hadn't seen until I woke days later in the doctor's home, hands bandaged and throat still raw.

The clatter of my brush on the floor lurched me from my thoughts. I bent to snatch it up, wincing at the swirls of healing skin on my palms. I took a deep breath, held it for a few seconds, and released it. We were safe. That was six months ago. Yet I still couldn't tolerate to have a fire burning in the hearth or stand next to a bonfire outside. Even the small flames of candles set my body trembling now.

"I'm sorry. I was lost in my head again," I said and mussed Isa's braided, chestnut hair—the same as mine. She shooed my hand away, and I sat the brush back on the table.

"Thanks for snapping me out of it." I unscrewed the lid of the healing ointment the doctor gave me. It smelled of peppermint, with a hint of lavender, as I dabbed it on the burns.

"Are you alright?"

"I should be asking you that..."

In these past six months, we lost everything except each other and our father. He'd been away when the manor burned. And now, I glanced around the small hovel of a home; here we were.

"Do you still think about..." I swallowed, the name more difficult to say than anticipated, "...Simon?"

Her eyes sharpened with an anger so rare that I had only seen it a few times before the fire. Her expression turned to one my mother had worn.

"Why should I think of him? He was too shallow to stay after what happened. Clearly, he was only after our gold."

I winced at the harsh words. I thought she had been lucky enough to fall in love with the man she was to marry. And, though I still caught the sadness in her eyes from time to time, she did her best to hide it. But that anger...It was quick to surface.

She frowned, the scar pulling taut on her skin. The bastard had taken one look at her after the fire and ended things. He said wouldn't marry someone with a marred face. It'd taken everything in me not to hold him down and drag my knife across *his* face.

"I'm fine. Father will find a match for me eventually." Even as she said it, the words rang hollow.

My heart plunged down to my stomach as my eyes traced the pink groove in her cheek once again. My insides tightened, and I swallowed hard, fighting back the bile that rose in my throat as I forced the memory back into a dark corner of my mind.

"You know you don't have to avoid the subject, right?"

Her question grounded me against the spiral my mind wanted to cast itself into.

"What?"

"The fire. You can talk to me about it. I won't break if you bring it up."

My eyes caught on that scar once again. "How can I burden you with my problems? You lost more than I did because of it."

I followed the direction of her gaze in the mirror and my breath hitched as she stared and stared at that scar.

"Instead of looking at it as a loss, maybe we should be thankful for what we gained because of it." And it was then that I noticed it; a small, almost undetectable, glimmer of guilt flashed through her eyes.

Muffled voices pricked my ears, and my attention snapped to the door. My father was out there speaking with someone.

Isa followed my gaze.

"A man from Starside arrived to speak with him a few moments ago."

"About what?"

She gave a shrug of her shoulders and walked to the tiny bookshelf tucked in the corner of our room.

"He told me to go back inside, so I did."

But I knew her, knew she wouldn't just leave without *something* of use.

I studied her. Our father had treated her like nothing more than a mangey dog to be rid of these last few months. She no longer smiled or laughed when she had once been all that and cunning, to boot.

"What?" She caught me staring.

"You know what it's about, don't you?"

"I have no idea what you're talking about."

It was to be that kind of game then.

"You mean to tell me you didn't listen on the other side of the door?"

There it was—that clever, calculating mind.

"One of his ships came back."

If a ship came back, there was a possibility that it brought valuable cargo with it, cargo that could be worth a fortune. I worried my thumbnail between my teeth. If someone from Starside came this late at night, chances were good that it, indeed, carried such a boon.

"Do you know anything else about it?"

"No."

If her short answer wasn't enough, she slumped into the blankets and opened her book. The conversation was over. I ground my teeth and walked to the front door, pressing my ear to it to listen to the distorted voices.

My father's voice sounded from the other side.

"Are you sure it's one of mine?" he spoke in his usual heavy cadence. "I was told they were all gone."

"Yes, the captain's name is Callum. That's one of yours, no?" another male voice asked.

Moments of long silence passed before the stranger spoke again. "Henri, you need to get to the port. As fast as you can," he paused, "since you live in the middle of this forest, it'll take almost an entire day to get there. And you'll want to leave before the snows come."

"What am I supposed to tell my daughters? I can't just leave them alone here. What if someone comes by to harm them?"

"They'll be fine. No one will come all the way out here."

I sucked a shaky breath in, placing a hand on the door and whipping it open to see my father standing with another slightly younger man. The pale light of the full moon flooded the dark crevices of the small cottage until I stepped out into the cold night.

"You should go, Father. I can look after the both of us until you get back."

If he didn't go, he'd take out his frustrations on us, and that wasn't something I was willing to allow.

"It's only a day or two. We've been safe out here; you don't have to worry."

The serenity of the forest brought me peace of mind after everything that happened. My father's ships had been lost, and not a full month later, our manor burned down. But this place... it was quiet. It didn't have people staring at us. I could forego all the riches in the world and live a happy life here with Isa. My father had never accepted it, though. He wanted to regain what we lost by *any* means necessary.

"Go get Isa. I'd like to say goodbye before I'm off."

His face relaxed, and the corner of his mouth edged up in a crooked smile.

Strange. He never asked to see Isa anymore. My gaze slid to the stranger on the other side of him. He must be doing it for the sake of appearances, to still look like he cares.

I left the door to swing shut behind me as I stepped back into the ramshackle old cottage, boards squeaking in protest as I padded to the bedroom I shared with Isa. She was still right where I left her when I came back in, and for a brief moment, I reconsidered disturbing her.

"Isa, Father wants to speak with you."

"Why?"

She didn't lower her book; she barely glanced up over the top.

"He means to go into town tonight. Come, let's tell him farewell before he goes."

She was colder to our father now, but I prayed she wouldn't

make me drag her out. He might well beat her again should she refuse to see him off.

She closed the book and set it on the small table between our beds. I offered a hand, and she took it, leveraging it as she pulled herself from the nest of blankets, and we went outside.

Our old steed gnawed on the bit between his teeth as Father draped a blanket over the dip of his back, saddle resting on a stump nearby. He wasted no time in readying himself for the outing to Starside. I had no doubt in my mind that he was eager to return to our previous lifestyle, the very thought of which turned my stomach leaden.

"You're going into town, Father?" Isa's tone changed from the cold one of seconds ago to something with a bit more warmth clinging to the edges.

"Yes, Isa. I need to find out if the ship that came in is truly mine. And if it is, we can leave this old cottage behind and buy a better home."

The muscles in her nose twitched, in her cheek, what emotion was she fighting to keep from her face? When it was just the two of us, she showed no sign of fear of him, but I couldn't help but wonder if she remembered the impact of his fists.

He came to us, placing a hand on either of our shoulders with a gentle squeeze.

"Is there anything you need? Or maybe something you want?"

He must have felt generous to offer us anything.

"No, we have everything we need here," I paused, hoping my words reached him. I'd tried these past months to tell him we didn't need the decadent lifestyle he'd been so desperate to win back for us.

"Just come back home safe."

I didn't want to think about what would happen if the snows came while he was away.

"A rose," Isa said, lifting her chin even as gooseflesh prickled her skin. "I would like a rose."

I glanced at my sister. It was a test. Roses at this time of the year would be near impossible to find, and expensive.

"Of course." He pulled us both into a tight hug. "Arabelle says she can look after you both while I'm gone. Stay safe. And if someone comes here, do not trust them. Go into the cottage and lock yourselves inside."

"We will," I said with a nod. "Don't be reckless if you can't make it back safe. Stay in town if you have to. We'll be fine."

He gave me a curt nod and hoisted the saddle onto the horse's back, buckling the thick leather straps.

"I'll be back soon. It's only a day's ride. I'll have to find buyers for the cargo, but I'll come home as fast as I can."

He put a foot through the stirrup and grabbed the horn, pulling himself into the saddle.

I gave him my most reassuring smile as he wheeled the horse around and dug his heels into its flanks. It set off into a light canter down the dirt path.

As I watched the horse disappear into the trees, my stomach tied in knots. The last time I was in town, I heard whispers of all the ships being destroyed and the cargo lost. How did this one manage to make it back into port?

Unease swirled in my chest, and I pressed my palm there, trying to will it into calm. If the chatter was to be believed, my father's crews hated him. I had no idea if he knew about them or not, but I never told him the rumors I'd heard. Guilt still weighed me down, even now.

I turned back to Isa. "Let's go back inside before we catch our deaths out here."

Could they be playing him for a fool? He rushed to the conclusion that the ship held valuable cargo without so much as inquiring about the ship – desperation blinded him. I let out a long sigh.

"Are you sure you're okay, Belle?" Isa asked as she held the door open, that ice in her veins melting with our father no longer around.

A cold breeze played with her braided hair.

"Yes, it's nothing." I couldn't burden her with these worries. "Why don't we pick up where we left off in the book?"

She studied me, her amber eyes staring into mine for the briefest of seconds before turning back inside.

"Alright."

The rusted springs slammed the cottage door shut again when Isa let go of it, and I grimaced at the resounding echo in the night. I hurried back inside as a shiver raked over my too-exposed skin.

There was no trace of Isa in the small living space, but a faint glow flickered against the wall from our bedroom. I relished these moments when we could just get lost in one of our books; they provided such a beautiful escape from this harsh reality.

When I walked into the bedroom, Isa had already crawled back into her bundled blankets and hunkered down to combat the cold seeping in through the cracks. I grabbed the book off our shelf, crawled into my own mountain of blankets, and wiggled until I was comfortable enough.

I flipped the book open. It was one of our favorites, a tale of a princess who had to win the affections of her prince. The catch? Her voice was stolen by an evil witch.

"Once upon a time…" The words flitted away in the night like wisps of smoke in the wind. Images of twirling nobles and desperate royals played like a living painting in our heads until Isa's soft snores filled the room.

Grey swirled into clouds in the sky, blotting out the stars and moon. Winter waited just over the mountains like a prowling cat ready to pounce. Snow would fall soon, and if my father didn't make it back before then...I closed my eyes against the thought.

CHAPTER

FOUR

Arabelle

When I stepped outside, the bite of air against my nose and cheeks was quick to chase away the remaining dregs of sleep pulling at me.

Isa kneeled in the vegetable garden, pulling up the dead weeds from their roots and clipping the remaining tomato vines to make room for the winter crops. She had laid a tarp aside to prepare for the colder months. A basket of mulch we gathered yesterday sat next to her.

I passed by Isa.

"Morning," I said, heading for the stump between the stable shack and cottage.

We'd need a backstock of firewood to get us through the winter. Father refused to chop the wood, and Isa – well, she wasn't great at it. The last time I let her, she nearly took her own limb off. That left me to do the wood chopping from now on.

Keeping my hands busy was the best way to stop my wandering mind; it gave me something to focus on. I slid on a pair of worn leather gloves. They offered next to no protection from blisters anymore, but they were better than nothing. At least they kept the cold at bay.

I placed a log upright on the stump and stepped back, angling my body just so before lifting the axe above my head and swinging down.

As I chopped the wood, Isa tended the garden. Dark clouds rolled in overhead, and when I stopped to wipe the sweat from my brow, the sight of them made my stomach tighten. It would snow tonight. I hoped and prayed to God that my father made it into town before it started.

Over the past few days, Isa and I had removed the bulbs from the soil, dried them, and left them inside the cottage, ready to plant in the spring. We left the hardy root vegetables that could survive the cold.

Isa worked on her second row, spreading mulch to keep the ground's temperature warmer for the carrots, potatoes, and onions.

My stack of wood was already large enough.

The garden was the more pressing matter to attend to right now. It provided us with food. It was the one thing I insisted on learning after we lost our fortune. I set the axe next to the stump and walked to where Isa knelt.

"It'll go fast if we both do it," I said as I crouched down in the new row, the soft soil shifting underfoot as I worked on pulling weeds.

We passed the shears back and forth, as well as the mulch. I placed it on the bare ground, leaving it loose enough so it didn't suffocate the roots. It was a repetitive process, but I was grateful because it kept my worry for our father at a minimum.

When I moved to the last row, Isa started at the opposite end.

"You pull up the weeds and take care of the tomatoes. I'll put down the mulch," she said and tossed the shears in the dirt at my feet.

I picked them up, shaking the soil off, and set to work on the vines and dead plants. My knees sank into the damp earth.

Truth be told, I preferred the itchy, woolen dress to the silk and chiffon gowns, as well as the smell of fresh soil to the cloying scent of perfumes.

Out here, I was free of the burdens society expected of me, and a part of me was glad our extravagant life went up in flames. I clipped a leafy, green spinach plant at the base, holes eaten through by some insect or another.

I preferred this new life; no worrying about impressions or being courted by some snobby man-child who would throw hissy fits about my love of reading or gardening. What was it the last one said? *Instead of reading, why don't I show you what men really want out of their wives?* I shuddered at the memory of those roving eyes.

Sweat beaded on my forehead and trickled down the side of my face. I quickly swiped at it with my thumb, noticing the smile Isa fought to keep off her face.

"What?"

"You just smeared dirt across your face." She mimicked my motion.

I raised my hand to wipe it away, and she let loose a hearty laugh this time. I realized why when I looked down at my gloved hand.

It was covered in dirt. Needless to say, every time I touched my face, I left a streak of it there. I laughed with her, a sound I relished – it happened so rarely in these recent days.

Winter hadn't settled in yet, not wholly. These last few days in the sun would pass too quickly, and then we'd be cooped up in this tiny cottage for months. I pointed at the tarp on the ground.

"It's time to cover the garden. We need to make sure it's secure before nightfall."

For if it wasn't, the snow would kill everything, and we'd have to start all over again in the spring.

I stood again, breathing in the musty scent of damp wood drifting over from the forest on the wind. It was one of my favorite smells – the dirt, decaying leaves, the animals, all of it. The thought of leaving this place for another mansion left a gnawing, churning pit in my stomach. I knew it was what my father wanted, but it wasn't something I ever wanted to go back to.

Isa rubbed her hands on the sides of her skirt as she stood. Together, we pulled the tarp over the garden, securing it in place with spikes and leaving enough room from the edges to keep the worst of the cold from it.

"What do you say to some hot dinner and tea?" she asked, placing the now empty basket upside down on the wooden post that used to be a fence.

"I think that's the sound of my stomach growling."

"Ah, there's my pretty future *wife*," the voice froze me in my tracks.

I willed the trembling of my body away as he approached from the opposite side of the house on near silent feet.

"Louis. What are you doing here?"

"I think it's high time you come back with me, Arabelle. This is no life for my bride to be living."

"I'll stay, but thank you for the concern."

Every utterance of *wife* or *bride* in reference to me made sick rise in my throat.

"Come now, surely you can't *enjoy* living out here. You'll stay at my home until the wedding."

He reached for me, but I leaned out of the touch.

"The wedding is still three months away, Louis. I'll remain here until it's time." I took another step back.

The crack to my cheek wasn't something I expected, nor was

the pain exploding through my skull as I crumpled to the ground. I grabbed my face and looked back up at the bastard. His hand was still outstretched from where he'd backhanded me. Tears stung my eyes, but I refused to let them fall, not for him.

"You agreed to this marriage, Belle. I agreed to take in your sister, too, because...well, with that hideous scar, no man will ever want her."

I could have sworn a growl slipped from Isa's throat as she crouched beside me, cold fingers digging into my arm. The same rumbled up from my own chest as I glared up at him, but I didn't dare speak, fear of him refusing the arrangement now tying my tongue.

"Don't give me that look, my sweet Belle. All you have to do is obey me, and she'll live a comfortable life."

His hand dropped to his side, and he gave me a deceitfully charming smile. "Come home with me and let us be done with this."

"I'll remind you again, Louis. It is not yet time for the wedding. You need to leave before my father returns. He won't be pleased to find you here."

I pushed back to my feet, Isa rising next to me. I shoved her behind me, so I was between them.

Louis laughed a dreadful, gut-twisting sound.

"I made sure Henri won't be back for a few days."

He snatched my wrist in his broad hand and dragged me toward the front of the cottage, where I assumed his horse waited.

I jerked against him, digging my nails into his flesh, but he wouldn't let go. Thoughts eddied out of my head. I leaned back, pushing my heels into the ground to stop him, but nothing did.

I didn't even hear the snap of the door, didn't know Isa had run inside until she'd returned. I did not see her until I watched as the black iron skillet met with Louis's skull.

She dropped it on the ground, tears running down her cheeks as I wrenched my hand free of him. He groaned, muttering curses under his breath. I didn't stay long enough to decipher them, not when I knew he'd lunge for Isa the minute he got on his feet.

"Isa, run!"

I grabbed her hand, and we both sprinted for the forest surrounding our home.

My dress caught on brambles and naked branches hanging low from trees. Thorns tore at my skin, leaving a trail of bright red across my cheek as I looked back to see if he was chasing after us. He wasn't. But we weren't slowing down. My fingers held tight around Isa's as I all but dragged her behind me.

"Belle, slow down," she panted, holding the hem of her dress in one hand.

"If we do, he'll catch us and *kill* you, Isa. I will not let him."

We ran deeper and deeper into that forest. I had no intention of stopping, not until I stumbled on a stone and saw a cave entrance hidden in the brush of some fallen trees. I shoved a panting Isa toward it.

"In here. We can hide," I said as I covered our tracks the best I could.

"Belle, I'm sorry, I—"

"Shh. Don't talk," I whispered, pushing her further into the cave and then crawling in myself and steadying my breathing, trying to quieten it back to a whisper of a sound.

Footsteps sounded right outside the cave. Only half a minute later, Louis panted a sound that made my body lock up. If he found us, if he found Isa, he would hurt her.

He might even kill her.

"Belle! Isa!" he bellowed into the woods.

Isa's fingers grasped the fabric at my shoulders so tight I thought she might rip it off.

I waited. Waited for him to move, to speak, to do something. He let loose a sound between a growl and snarl and moved away from the cave. When those steps were so far away I couldn't hear them anymore, we both loosed our breath.

"I think he's gone. Let's get out of here," I said, the dead leaves crunching under my hands as I crawled out of the cave.

When I turned back to help Isa to her feet, a gasp of cold air burned my throat, and I had to convince my knees not to buckle. A man stood next to the cave; her hand gripped in his.

The black armor he wore soaked up every bit of sun and left his pale skin standing out against it. But that wasn't what threatened to rob me of every bit of the relief I felt from escaping Louis.

No. It was the crimson horns curling out of his hair that made him look like he had stepped straight out of Hell. Fear rattled in my head like some forgotten instinct knew and understood what those horns meant. I swallowed, my mouth dry. This fear was ridiculous. The horns had to be some ornamentation he took from an animal. Humans didn't have them.

He wore twin, dual-bladed axes at his belt. Those, coupled with the armor, meant he must have been a warrior of some kind.

Steps sounded behind him, and my heart plummeted through my stomach when a second one, just as terrifying, stopped on his other side. He gave Isa a stomach-roiling grin that had me scanning the ground for anything I could use as a weapon.

"Look at the little pretties we found. I bet they'll be delicious," the first purred as he scanned me head to toe.

A creeping chill shuddered through me, and I swallowed the bile, itching up my throat. My eyes caught on a downed limb.

"Belle..." Isa winced as the man's hand tightened around hers.

I ground my teeth and slid my foot closer to that limb, unwilling to take my eyes off them or risk a sudden move. We ran out here to escape Louis. Was it only to fall into the hands of men far worse than him? I dragged my lip between my teeth.

The limb was dry, and a piece crumbled off when the edge of my foot touched it. I prayed it was thick enough and heavy enough to at least stun the one holding Isa.

He was two steps away.

I'd have to move fast.

I dropped down, and my nails dug deep into the cracking wood. I sprang back up, taking that first step before I was fully standing, and swung on the second step. The limb shattered over the man's skull. He let out a hiss and a flurry of words I didn't understand. He let go of my sister, and I interlaced my fingers with hers.

We ran.

"Where are we going?" Isa's heavy breaths were a sign she couldn't keep up for much longer; she barely managed now.

"I don't know. As far away from those two as we can."

"Shouldn't we go back home? If Louis is still there—"

"If Louis is still there, he will kill you for hitting him." I wasn't willing to risk it. "He'd never allow it to slide." And if he didn't kill her, he might well do something *far* worse.

Their footsteps were close behind us. Too close. I swerved behind a tree, dragging Isa behind me. A rogue branch snagged on the sleeve of my dress and tore the worn fabric from the bodice.

More curses sounded from the two men chasing us, but I didn't stop; didn't slow. We wouldn't be able to outrun them for long. Their strides were longer; their legs stronger – they were built to chase down prey.

The realization nearly took the ground out from under me. It must have done so to Isa because, one minute, she was running hand in hand with me. The next, she was ripped away.

"Isa," I cried out as I skidded on the grass.

She'd tripped over a stone, jutting up from the ground.

The two men were on us in seconds, before I could get Isa on solid footing. The second one grabbed for her, but I yanked her arm, pulling her behind me and toward the crumbling stone walls of some old building.

"We're trapped," Isa said, pressing her back to the wall and watching as the two closed in on us.

"Damn it."

A rotting, wooden handle from something I could no longer identify leaned against the inner wall. I grabbed it and brought it up in front of me with both hands squeezed tight enough for my knuckles to go white. I angled one end at the closer of the two.

"Stay back." My voice didn't command the authority that I wanted. My hands wouldn't stop trembling.

"What are you going to do with that, little pretty?" he sneered at me, eyes roving over my body in a way that left my insides twisting.

My fingers went numb from my grip on that handle.

"I don't know who, or what, you are...but stay away from us."

He snapped a buckle on his belt and lifted his axe out of it. He twirled it in his hand until the blade faced me.

"You're not even holding it right."

He lifted his weapon above his head and brought it down.

The wooden handle in my hands shattered. Splinters rained down between us.

If there was a god out there, I needed them to save us. Isa buried her face in my back, clinging to the fabric of my skirt. After everything we went through, after agreeing to marry that wretch, we were both going to die right here. I couldn't stop it.

I shoved the fear and sorrow down, refusing to give them that small satisfaction. He brought his axe up again, eyes wide, pupils blown, and a smile that showed a mouth full of fangs – fangs I couldn't help but imagine tearing into my flesh, into Isa's.

Before I could utter another prayer or drop to my knees and plead for Isa's life – though I was sure, somehow, that it wouldn't work – there was a flash of red. Both Isa and I hit the ground.

A horse stamped its hooves, and when I opened my eyes again, I saw that it was to the back of a third man. Metal clashed against metal, and the newcomer pushed the other back. I gawked at him, the fine cloak, shoulder length, slightly curled hair the same color as fire. I doubled over and hurled what little was left in my stomach.

He swung his sword in a wide arc. A thud sounded from the other side of him. The back of his cloak fluttered with movement, and then there was another thunk. I caught a glimpse of the first horned man on the ground.

I wiped the back of my hand across my mouth. It'd been a while since such fear tangled in my stomach to cause me to vomit. Tremors shook my body until Isa's hands rested on my back, rubbing small circles. We stayed like that for a long time. I didn't know how long.

The stranger turned to us.

"Are you two alright? Did they hurt you?" he asked.

"We're fine," I tried to push all the courage I had left into my words.

I straightened again, helping Isa to her feet.

"You're lucky, then. These...*men* are horrid creatures. They delight in ripping flesh from bone while their prey is still alive."

He wiped his sword on the pants of the closest one before sheathing it at his side.

"What are they?" Isa asked, her voice not quivering the way I expected it to.

His eyes narrowed on her.

"You should go home. It's dangerous in these woods. Especially after dark." He nodded to the sun disappearing behind the line of trees in the distance. "There could be more of them."

"We will." As I spoke, Isa rushed past me.

"A gentleman would see us home safe." Her voice held the sternness and command that our mother's once had.

When was the last time I heard that tone? I gawked at her, trying to recall a time I'd seen her show so much assertiveness to a stranger. She held her chin up, shoulders back. In the setting sun, that scar stood stark against her skin.

I glanced back to the man. A cloth mask covered his mouth and nose, but not the remarkable golden eyes. Curiosity and amusement waltzed together in them. I'd never seen eyes like that before.

He let out a huff, the mask billowing out. He grabbed the reins of his horse and turned back to us.

"I'll escort you back home."

Louis was nowhere to be found. Thank God for small miracles. The stranger saw us right up to the cottage, watching until we were both inside and had slid the lock into place. I waited next to the door until the rattle of reins and soft clomp of hooves told me he had left.

The dark, gloom of the cottage was not welcoming, but at least we were safe. I couldn't say the same for our father. If there were more of those men out there, he could run into them. He wasn't a warrior; he didn't know how to fight or even defend himself.

He may have treated us like no more than chattel to be traded for wealth, but he was all we had left. And if he didn't come back, we were at the mercy of men like Louis, or worse. I chewed my lip as I stared into the blackness.

I didn't relish the idea of going back into town, but if he didn't show back up soon, we might have no choice even if it meant walking the whole way there. The thought left a hole where my stomach should be as I remembered the eyes of those horned men on me and the utter helplessness that gripped me by the throat.

I shook off the memory and lit the small lantern on our table, taking care to keep the light low in case any more of those demons waited in the woods.

Henri

The sun hung low on the horizon by the time I reached the familiar town of Starside. Thanks to my ruddy horse needing to stop for so long, I arrived several days later than I anticipated.

I rode over the bridge leading to the stables and pulled back on the reins until my steed came to a stop. The stable hand shoveled rotting hay and horse shit, but it did little for the musky odor coming off in waves.

I slid off and handed those reins to another skinny stable boy dressed in raggedy attire, flipping him one of the few copper coins I had left.

"Feed and water him; I'll be back in a bit," I said, eyes already locked on the red sails bobbing and fluttering in the distance.

I closed my eyes and dragged a deep breath into my lungs as I stepped onto the dock, the sea salt and brine only being tarnished by the reek of today's catch. I opened my eyes, agitation furrowing my brow.

Those magnificent sails were in tatters, canvas hanging down and drooping onto the deck, the wood cracked and chipped as if it'd aged a hundred years in a few months. But this ship was The Isabelle; the black lettering on the back said as much.

It was tied up in the pier while repairs were underway. Some of her crew members were fast at work – shipwrights were on the dock shouting instructions and making lists of supplies. That damn captain was nowhere to be seen.

I stopped at the edge of the pier.

"Excuse me, sailor, where is your captain?" I shouted up at a man scrubbing the black railing.

"Callum? Last I heard, he was goin' to have a drink with the rest of the crew. Rough journey and all that."

He nodded toward the building behind me, a tavern frequented by sailors passing through to eat, drink, and whore around.

"Henri? It's been a while," a familiar voice rang out from the side, and I turned with a jovial smile plastered to my face.

"Louis, how nice to see you again."

His usual slicked-back hair was mussed, his clothes rumpled as if he'd been tossed about a training ring for an hour.

"You're just the man I wanted to see. I've been thinking. I'd like to move up mine and Belle's wedding. There's no need to wait so long, and with winter upon us, it'd be a shame for her to be stuck in that ramshackle little home of yours." Even ruffled, his appearance made the other townsfolk look like little more than beggars.

"I'll give it consideration, but right now, I need to speak to my man about some cargo," I said.

If Callum brought back the cargo I requested, I wouldn't need to wed my daughter to this lump of a man. No, then Adrian would be back on the table, and he was a much better match and came with an even better position for myself.

"I'll have your answer by the time I leave."

"Then I will await you outside."

"How generous of you, but you do not need to wait out here. I can come find you. I don't know how long this will take."

Perfect. The last thing I needed was for Louis to hound me about this.

"Nonsense. I would very much like an answer tonight. So, I shall stay."

"Fine. I will try to be quick about my business."

I turned toward the tavern and took a deep breath. Of all the ships that survived, why did it have to be this one? Callum was the one captain I felt didn't actually work for me, but I for him. He and his men were once pirates and were terrifying in every sense of the word.

The smell hit me first when I opened the door: stale ale, unwashed bodies, and sex. I coughed, almost choked, from the thick layer of smoke that cast a haze over the entire first floor.

A man with a raised flagon of ale stumbled back into me. The drunken slur he shouted in my face was as repugnant as the breath seeping from his mouth.

Wild moans and the wet slap of skin sounded from the level above, as well as the distinct *thump* of bedframes smacking into walls. I fought the instinct to wrinkle my nose or shrink away from any of it lest I be considered too soft.

I scanned the tables, trying to ignore the debauchery until I spotted the blond in a hazy sea of dimness. I weaved around tables and chairs strewn about the floor and took a seat across from him.

"I'm glad to see you made it back in one piece, Callum. The seas have been murderous as of late, I hear."

Callum looked at me through hooded lids, his turquoise eyes a muted blue in the dim light. A leather strip held his hair back in a sloppy mess of a bun. He leaned over and whispered something to the muscle-bound man on his left before he turned back to me.

"That they have, Henri. I lost half my crew on this little venture you sent us out on."

He turned up a flagon of ale, the amber liquid spilling down one side of his stubbled chin and dripping onto his stained white shirt. He wore the sleeves rolled up his forearms and collar unbuttoned to reveal his broad, inked chest.

A pad of paper sat on the table next to Callum, the top page revealing a charcoal sketch of the most beautiful woman I'd ever seen. He noticed what held my attention and snapped the cover over it with a murderous glare.

I swallowed and folded my hands on the table.

"I'm sorry about your crew," I paused, considering my words, "were you able to acquire what we discussed by chance?"

His eyes narrowed on me as sweat beaded on my forehead.

"We did."

"Great. Where are they? The gold I can get for them will be a fine start to setting my family right again."

My muscles relaxed in a wave of relief. Finally, no more living like peasants, and I could tell Louis what I really thought of his proposal.

"We sold them. Spent the coin on repairs to the ship. Split the rest among the crew, and here we are. Heard your house went up in flames not too long back. I assumed you were dead."

Did my heart stop beating?

The half smile he gave me set my bones rattling. He jammed the tip of his knife into the thick meat of a sausage and brought it to his lips. He tore through the morsel with slow, precise movements I had no doubt were meant to intimidate me.

"Y-you sold them?"

Those pieces would have secured my future.

"Didn't you ask around? Anyone could have told you I survived that fire."

It was as if Callum stabbed *me* in the spine instead of that sausage.

"Eh." He shrugged. "Maybe we did, maybe we didn't."

He stuck the rest of the morsel in his mouth, sliding the metal between his teeth in a vicious scrape.

"Captain, I need that cargo – I need the *gold*." I forced my voice to hold whatever steadiness and sternness I could muster in the face of the deranged stare he returned despite the growing lump clawing its way up my throat.

The coin I counted on was gone. I was ruined. I'd have to sell my daughters for the life I wanted. This man...my eyes bore into Callum; it was his fault.

The knife clattered on the plate after Callum lazily dropped it, his icy gaze unsettling my stomach.

"To be frank, it was just too much trouble to find you," he said with a shrug. "Besides, it's not like you have any power now that you're broke." A dangerous smile played on his lips.

"*You* work for *me*. That's all the *power* I need." I pounded my fist on the table, rattling the dishware and knocking over a drink or two.

The chair creaked as Callum leaned back and stared me dead in the eye.

"Not anymore. We've been feeling rather...exploited. So, we decided to keep everything that we found as back pay."

I puffed out my chest, my brows narrowing with anger, the vein in my neck pulsing with my heartbeat.

"You'll give me what's owed." My voice held a sharp edge to it. "Or I'll tell everyone here about your past."

"You know nothing of my past except what I allowed you to know."

The monster of a man next to Callum stood, towering over the table. His muscles bulged under a too-tight shirt, the thin material threatening to rip with even the slightest of movements. He grabbed the knife Callum had so carelessly discarded.

I stared up at the menacing threat, trying and failing to stop the blood from draining out of my face. My chest deflated with a wheeze as realization washed over me. I would die if I tried to go up against a man such as that.

"Yeah, no. You should leave. Now." Callum made it sound more like a suggestion than the command it was.

I shoved my chair back and stormed out of the tavern, making my way back to the stables. I couldn't afford to stay in town, not with the coin I had on me. And much to my dismay, Louis caught sight of me the instant I walked out. He matched my stride until he was side by side with me.

"Things not go as you planned?"

"No, they didn't."

"They sold the cargo I take it? Kept the gold?"

I froze mid-step and turned my furious gaze on Louis.

"How do you know that?" I had kept knowledge of that cargo secret from everyone, save for Callum's crew.

"Because I bought it. When I saw that ship come into port, I knew it belonged to you. I couldn't let you refuse me Belle's hand, so I immediately found Callum and offered him twice what you'd given him."

I'd known about Louis's obsession with Arabelle; it stemmed back to long before the fire. I refused him then. To go to this length to get his hands on her wasn't something I'd banked on. How could I have?

I gritted my teeth, the chill in the air sending a wave of shivers down my spine – or was it the look in Louis's eye as he spoke of my daughter? I was now stuck with this man.

Damn Callum. But all the cursing in the world wouldn't change things.

"I'll make arrangements and send her to you on the morrow."

"Excellent."

I hated the way he dragged the word out.

What I hated even more was that this man was always in the right spot to swoop in and save me and my family when we needed it. My teeth screamed their pain as I tightened my jaw.

It was almost as if Louis had orchestrated this entire ordeal for the sake of marrying Belle. He wouldn't go that far, would he? I sank my teeth into the meat of my thumb.

CHAPTER

SIX

Henri

The hoofbeats on the ground damn near lulled me to sleep. I huddled close to the body of the animal; any warmth on this frigid night was welcome. I pulled my cloak tighter around myself. The bite of the cold wind burned against my exposed face and neck.

The last vestiges of light glinted between the thick canopy of pines and skeletal oak branches. My insides twisted as a droplet of something wet landed on my cheek and stuck for the briefest of moments before rolling down. The first flakes began falling around me and quickly grew into fat crystals. I clung to my horse, pressing my legs harder into its sides.

In mere minutes, the snow was all I could see. The whipping wind howled in my ears, drowning out all other sound. Despite the dead, black night, everything was white – or rather grey. The horse neighed and stamped its hooves in the powdery snow. No amount of nudging with my heels urged him forward. He refused to move.

"Fine," I huffed out a breath that clouded in front of me as I slid from the saddle.

My legs were numb, and I stumbled, a burning rush shooting from my toes all the way up my thighs as the blood warmed from my movement. I snatched the reins and held my arm over my face, plunging into that dreary whiteness, feeling out the ground with each step before trusting it with my weight. If the whiteout cleared for just a few minutes, I could find shelter and wait it out.

A large tree trunk loomed into my line of sight. At first, it was nothing but a blur of dark grey, but the closer I came, the more I could make out of it. I knotted the reins around a branch and crawled into the hollowed trunk. It was better to wait out the storm and try to make it home in the morning.

Tree branches creaked and groaned with every gust of wind, but the thick trunk shielded me from the brunt of those frigid gales. I huddled in the back of the tree, as far from the opening as I could get, and stayed close to the ground. I pulled my legs in and pressed my arms against my shuddering chest, rubbing my hands against it to warm it with friction and movement.

Was this it? How I die? What of Belle and Isa? No doubt Louis would find his way to the cottage and take Arabelle for himself, but without my insistence, what of Isa? No man would take her, not with the scar now etched on her face. Maybe Belle could talk Louis into taking her in, too.

The wind carried a faint howl.

Great, just what I needed.

Wolves.

In the rare moments I actually found sleep, a cold breeze blew through and set my teeth to chattering again, and I snapped awake. What could I have possibly done to anger God in such a way? All I did, I did for my family. Every choice, every move, it was all to procure a better life for me and my children.

Sure, maybe I cheated some sailors out of their wages, maybe I sent them into dangerous places without so much as a warning, but that was what they signed up for. My children needed to eat and deserved every comfort I could afford to give them. *I* deserved it.

So why was I being punished for doing whatever was necessary to ensure that? I rubbed my hands across my chest in an attempt to warm my freezing blood. My eyelids grew heavy again.

The snap of a branch jolted me from an exhausted sleep I'd fallen into at some point. I rubbed my eyes and crawled out of the tree trunk, beset by the purest white snow I had ever seen. My horse broke free of the binds during the night, and I saw neither hide nor hair of him, not even hoofprints were left behind.

As I stood, I rolled my shoulders, a dull ache creeping across my upper back and down my spine.

I made it through the night – by some miracle.

I scanned the immediate area; everything was covered. I had no idea which way led back home.

"Am I even on the right path?" I muttered.

I could have easily gotten turned around in that blizzard. Whatever the case, I just had to pick a direction and follow it. But whenever I took a step, my foot sank into the snow to my mid-shin. My body roiled with shivers no matter how hard I tried to make it stop.

I forced myself to take another step and then another. The snow stuck in clumps to my pants, melting and freezing again, but I kept going. I couldn't allow myself to succumb here, not after everything. I didn't spend my whole life busting ass just to die in some ditch in the forest.

I planted my foot down but shifted and slid. I threw my hands out to grasp for purchase, grab anything, but the branches snapped because of my weight and the coating of ice. My body swayed forward, and the next thing I knew, I was crashing down a steep hill.

Nothing I reached for allowed me enough hold to stop, and I fell faster and faster. I thought I'd tumble forever, and that's when my ass slammed into the cold, hard ground. I let out a low groan and flopped back with snow sprinkling onto my face.

The world swirled around me as I lay sprawled in the ice and snow, panting puffs of frozen breaths into the chill air – air that burned in my lungs. I rolled onto my stomach and pushed myself onto my hands and knees, feet sliding beneath me until I managed to finally find traction to stand. I brushed the snow off my clothing.

"If I don't get out of this cold, I'm going to freeze," I said with my teeth clattering together.

But how? My god damned horse was gone, and I had no idea where I even was. Louis was waiting for Arabelle to come to him. Isa still needed to be matched. I had so much left to do. If I could just get my hands on a little bit of coin, I could make us rich again.

I shook my head and slumped to my knees. Nothing mattered if I couldn't find a place to warm up. Violent trembles racked my body, a cold wetness soaked through my clothes and settled into my bones. I tilted my head back and gazed into the cloudy morning sky.

"Please...let me live. I'll sacrifice whatever I have to." I sent up a prayer for whatever god might be listening.

As my eyes fell from the heavens. I noticed something not so far off.

What was that? A wall? The stone structure stretched into a mass of fog in either direction. I climbed to my feet once again, forcing my frigid body to move despite the screaming in my joints and the painful protest of my muscles.

The structure was massive; I wasn't sure how I missed it.

Maybe my prayer was heard and answered by the removal of the fog. I pushed through the snow, the arch of a gate visible through the hazy film. There could be people on the other side – people that could help me.

The portcullis had been left up, and the path was unhindered. A town, perhaps? I would have settle for a shack at this point.

When I passed through the gate, a rush of warm, gentle air greeted me like an old friend. Relief flooded through my veins as the cold ebbed away. There was no town; instead, an enormous castle dominated the expanse of land. I had to do a double take – there was no snow on the ground, anywhere.

How was that possible?

The grass was lush and green. Trees still had their leaves and bore delicious morsels of fruit. Birds bathed in a fountain of stone only yards away. Inside these gates, winter did not exist.

With a little bit of caution and a lot of desperation, I ventured further. I untied my stifling cloak and shrugged it off, hanging it over my forearm.

What was this place?

A citrusy scent wafted to me before I spotted the orange trees, fruit hanging from the branches just ripe for the plucking. I snatched one off the tree and ripped through the peel before devouring it.

The path curved and led to the castle doors, laden with every kind of flower I knew of – foxgloves, daffodils, larkspur, crocus, daisies, lilies, aster, irises, and more. Sitting within the vast floral scape were stone sculptures of angels, lions, wolves, cherubs, bears, birds, and fat-cheeked babes. The oak doors loomed large and plain by comparison, outside of the golden knockers in the shape of a roaring beast.

I lifted the ring hanging from its mouth, hammered it into the door three times, and waited.

No answer.

I moved to knock again, but the door creaked open. With a hefty push, I opened the door and stepped into the castle. The tiles and stone were crumbling, lines of them gouged out by...something.

The musky smell of dirt, dust, and damp rock filled my nose. The soft light of candles illuminated the hall with chandeliers and candelabras. Portraits of men, women, children, and families lined the walls as I moved further inside, though it looked as if some were moved because there were hooks and subtle, dark outlines where they once hung.

I stopped at a clear spot, my attention drawn to the four gashes carved into the stone and a knot twisted in my gut. I looked, listened, but there was no trace of whoever opened the door to me or whatever made those marks. In fact, there wasn't a trace of another person anywhere.

A low rumble vibrated the air, and my guard went up before I realized that noise wasn't from some animal but my own stomach. With the cold and snow behind me, my body was insistent on finding food. If memory served, the last time I ate was the night before I left home.

I slid into a small room to the side of the hall, a sitting room from the look of it, with two chairs set close to the hearth and a settee pressed against the wall behind them. All three matched with mahogany wood frames and dark crimson leather cushions.

Candles lit the dark room, a fire burning in the ornate stone fireplace. I eased my aching bones into one of the chairs and waited. Someone would come. Surely, they would. The fire was lit; someone had to be there. The warmth washed over me as tendrils of exhaustion snaked through my body, more insistent than the hunger.

My eyes fluttered shut, and exhaustion dragged me under without another thought.

CHAPTER

SEVEN

Lucien

How many long years had passed since I saw anyone outside of Elie on the castle grounds? Yet there someone was, strolling right into my castle like he damn well owned it. I'd long since forbidden Elie from bringing anyone here, much to my friend's dismal protests. I didn't want to see anyone. Didn't want them to see this...creature I was now.

I stood at the floor-to-ceiling window, the tattered remnants of scarlet curtains pulled back, and watched the man. Clouds choked out the light from the sun, and the color of the sky called for snow. Maybe it was already snowing outside the gates.

The stranger walked through the gardens in the front. He stopped to look at the flowers, at the orange trees my father had planted for my mother as a wedding gift.

I recognized that gait – the smell of desperation dripping from him like drool from a starved beast. It was something I was all too familiar with. The something that caused my little *predicament.*

Greed. Arrogance. Vanity.

My lip twitched up in a silent snarl. I didn't want him here. I

47

wanted nothing to do with the likes of him or those similar. I stalked through the halls, stone walls shredded from my rage and anguish after *that* night.

Moss and dirt peppered the walls and floors of every room in the castle now. I didn't care. There was no point in keeping up with it.

One good thing that came from this accursed form was how quick I was to adapt to the animal instincts. The enhanced hearing, night vision, and, my personal favorite, walking on feather-light feet to track down prey.

"Hello?" The man's voice was talons against my eardrums as I watched him creep further into my home.

The shadows at the top of the grand, sweeping staircase were a perfect place to hide as I tracked his every movement, from the flutter of his eyelids to the cautious steps. I wouldn't allow him to steal from me.

The witch's spell made the townsfolk forget all about me and this place. How did *he* find it? I even ordered Elie to shut and seal the portcullis that led inside.

I'd have to rip into him once this intruder left.

Which would be now.

I took a thunderous step toward the sitting room where the stranger ventured into, but fingers wrapped around my forearm and pulled me back.

My head whipped to the side, letting the rage that always burned just underneath my skin show in my eyes, teeth bared at the smaller man stopping me.

"What are you doing, Elie?" My voice held an edge that could slice through steel.

"It's my fault; I forgot to close the gate last night. Don't punish him for my careless actions." Elie's grip on my arm tightened as his eyes pleaded with me.

"He's trespassing in *my* castle. Why shouldn't I punish him?" A sound rumbled from low in my throat.

"You know as well as I do that it's winter outside those gates. He probably stumbled in by accident." Elie glanced back toward the sitting room, then back at me, those golden eyes asking for leniency as much as any words could. "Let me feed him while he warms up, and I'll send him on his way."

A tendril of panic slithered through my insides. If he stayed here, there was a possibility he would see me. I wanted to say no, throw him out on his ass right now, but Elie held his stance, and something inside me relented.

"Fine." It came out as a growl. "But if he does anything else, it'll be your hide that quells my anger."

"Whatever you say," he agreed as his lips curled in a sly smirk. "But we both know who'll kick whose ass here."

I snarled at him, then turned and skulked away, going back to one of the only places that gave me any sort of comfort these days. The doors to my chambers swung open with a heavy thud, hitting the walls on either side.

The place was a mess of shredded linens and chunks of stone torn from the walls and floor. I tried to forbid Elie from this part of the castle, but he never heeded my command. Every time I found him cleaning, I chased him away. He wasn't a servant and did a horrendous job whenever he attempted it.

Regardless, I didn't deserve to live in anything but this squalor. The witch may not have said it, but I knew that's what she wanted when she cast this curse.

As I walked into the room, I dug my claws into the stone of the wall, scraping and ripping chunks out and flinging them to the floor.

Elie wanted to let that intruder stay and feed him for whatever reason. I knew it couldn't just be the guilt that ate at him from leaving the gates up, there was more to it. How many times had I told him over the years that I didn't want anyone here? Yet he kept insisting.

His voice echoed in my mind more than I cared to admit. *If you don't at least try, you won't ever break the curse. Please, Lucien. At least try.* After the disaster that followed the first Blue Moon, he never spoke to me of it again.

I flopped on the remnants of my down bed, feathers and stuffing exploding out and fluttering to the ground. It was almost twenty years ago when the witch darkened the doorstep to the castle alongside that coward of a man, Audric.

Elie found out the man's name after a year. Audric went ahead with the marriage to Liana after he confronted me. That was how we found out my people had forgotten everything – he had no memory of who I was.

I gritted my teeth, jaw protesting. Nothing changed, yet everything had. We were stuck in a cycle of time. I had torn down the portraits of myself, even the ones of my family. I couldn't bear to look at them. What I once saw as perfection: the arrogance, the selfish smile, the glimmer of greed that shone so bright in my eyes.

I rolled onto my side, a stream of sun highlighting the dust particles fluttering about.

I closed my eyes against the thoughts, against the memories that I didn't want there. My body shuddered with the exhaustion of my anger, and I let the dreams take me somewhere far away, to a time of grand balls, beautiful women, and a handsome prince – a past I longed to forget because I knew I'd never lay an ugly, gnarled claw on it again. And yet, my mind tortured me with it every time I slept.

My hands held onto the narrow waist of a raven-haired duchess, Liana, Audric staring at me with those venom-tipped daggers in his eyes as we spun and twirled on the ballroom floor.

I wanted to tear the smirk off my face, even if it meant ripping skin from bone. I knew where this night led. And I couldn't do a gods damn thing to stop it.

Her sweet jasmine scent surrounded me as I grazed my lips over the delicate flesh of her neck, and the once pleasing gasp was now like grating glass.

I glanced around the ballroom, fire burning in my veins at the jealous stares from all those wishing to be the one in my arms – or to be me. I could have any one of them I wanted; all I needed to do was ask. They'd throw themselves at my feet and beg for it. But this night, I only wanted one.

My attention snapped back to the duchess in my arms, the need to devour her, taste her. The image of her on her knees shoved away every longing for anything else.

I whispered in her ear when the song ended, and I raged inside my skin, screaming and pounding fists against the invisible barrier of the past. I wanted to stop it, stop myself before I made that colossal mistake and doomed myself and my people to a cursed existence.

I left the warm embrace of her arms to let the cold air chill the boiling in my blood that wanted to claim her as mine for the night. Sweat turned to ice on my skin as the winter winds licked and lapped over the balcony. I remembered the thoughts I'd had while standing there, *ones of her body under my fingertips. The sounds she'd make when her body shuddered with orgasms.*

The castle was clean, and the walls were still intact as I walked through them, heading toward my chambers. My trousers fit a little too tight; my clothes scraped against my skin in a way that made me want to rip them off. The cold air did nothing to stave off the heat scorching through me. I stripped my tunic and shirt off. I bent to remove my boots, and that's when the knock on the door came.

Dark hair breezed past me as Liana walked into my room, the cloying scent of her perfume wrapping around me. The grin on my face was that of a predator that had lured my prey. I closed the door and made the biggest mistake of my life.

Henri

With unexpected swiftness, the next morning was upon me. I didn't intend to fall asleep, but I just couldn't keep my eyes open. I blinked until my sight adjusted to the dim light. With the warmth of the fire and soft cushions cradling me, I almost forgot about the blizzard and the unusual castle.

Breakfast sat on a little table in front of me without a soul to be found. The food was still hot; they couldn't have gotten far. But there was no one. How did they get in and out without waking me? Perhaps I was just that exhausted.

Trepidation triggered a need to glance around a last time before I ate the eggs and sausage links in silence, a twinge of unease slithering its way down my spine. Maybe I'd find someone if I looked around. It was a better use of my time than just sitting here.

I started my exploration.

I couldn't recall there ever being a castle in this part of Grienia. From the look of it, it was abandoned. Even though food was served to me, I still had yet to see a single person.

The foyer and hallways just beyond it were in shambles, dirt and dust caked so heavily in corners that plant life grew in it. Of all the questions plaguing me, one stood out above the rest: why wasn't this place gripped by winter's cold embrace like the rest of the land? I stared down the dark, empty hall. Silence – pure, unsettling silence was all that greeted me. No scuffing of servant footsteps, not even a hint of scurrying rats.

Each room I stepped into was either decorated with lavish furniture, window dressings, bedding, and area rugs, or serving as a storage space. Cobwebs swayed high on the walls from a draft, clinging to every surface. The metalwork in hinges squawked through the coating of rust.

Some rooms were locked or too dark to risk walking into. I didn't need to carry a lantern with me. The sconces lit of their own accord as I moved through the castle, but, for whatever reason, they would not light the rooms.

Flame flickered in the sconce on the stone wall as I stared and stared at it. Either the servants were excellent at their jobs, or something else was going on here. Or maybe it was both.

Unease prickled the back of my neck. Was the castle somehow enchanted? I'd heard stories of witches in my childhood. Perhaps I'd stumbled into one of their abandoned homes.

I creaked open the door to what appeared to be a bedroom themed in grey, gold, and silver. The frame of the bed looked metal at first glance, but it was made of beautifully carved wood and painted in metallic gold. Silver sheets and dark grey blankets made up the bedding, giving the room a sleek yet cozy feel.

An ottoman at the foot of the bed matched in color and style. Silver tasseled ropes held the charcoal canopy back, tying it in place. Gunmetal, velvet curtains were open only a sliver to allow a bit of sun in the room, gilding the silver chair set opposite the bed.

Dust particles danced in suspended air as I moved further into the room. Robes of the same dark grey lay atop the bed as if someone would walk in any minute and put them on.

The fabric was soft and smooth under my touch as I snatched it up and rubbed the material between my fingers. Spinning to a mirror, I held it up to my shoulders, staring at the reflection looking back at me – maybe these were left for me, just like the food.

If this castle was enchanted by witches, I would be taken care of, fed, and pampered. I could live like a king – well, except for the fortune. But I could get the gold back. I had two daughters that I could marry off. I just needed to find a match for Isa, then I could claim this place as my own—*if* the castle was truly abandoned as it looked. I tossed the garment back onto the bed.

The clomp of my boots echoed tenfold in the silence. I stopped in another room – an *enormous* room; a large chair sat on a dais toward the back.

Drapes of ruby red hung from the vaulted ceiling, separated by bronzed pillars. A thick, matching rug muffled my steps as I approached the chair. Not just a chair, I realized, but a throne.

I ran a fingertip over the intricate, woven bands of gold that made up the frame, dipping that finger down to trace the soft leather cushions. I circled the throne until I was back in front of it.

A layer of dust clung to my fingertip when I pulled it back. No one had sat on this throne in a long time, then. If there were people here, servants, they wouldn't have let this room – especially their sovereign's throne – be soiled like this.

The image flashed in my mind before the desire crashed down on me. I was a man of wealth and means once, a man everyone either feared or respected. I had dinners with the noble houses of Grienia and attended balls with the pinnacles of our society.

My fall from grace was nothing more than greedy vultures coming to claim what was mine, and the universe must have seen fit to reward me for my hardships, my patience, with an enchanted castle waiting for someone to claim it.

What would they say when they learned of it? Saw it? Those people who had denigrated me for these past months? In a place where wealth held sway, I would soon dwarf them all as their new ruler.

I lowered myself into the seat, digging my fingers into the ends of the armrests. Visions of courtiers flashed through my mind – people on their knees, kissing my feet, begging their new liege for forgiveness. The corners of my mouth turned up.

Atop a table next to the throne, nestled on a velvet pillow, was a crown. Golden thorns spiraled toward a ruby shaped into a blossoming rose at the front.

I placed the crown atop my head and straightened my posture, looking out into the throne room, picturing those faces. I would claim this castle; I'd be King. There was no one here. I was convinced of it.

I all but bolted from the throne, leaving the crown on the cushion as I near skipped to the door. Now *this*, this was the life I deserved.

The air outside was just as warm as it had been when I arrived, birds still chirping, flowers still in bloom, and the bitter cold nothing more than a memory. I followed the cobblestone path, hoping to find the castle stables. I didn't know how, but I could *feel* in my gut that there'd be a horse ready and waiting for me.

My steps faltered as bushes came into view – rose bushes. My lips curved into a smile as I remembered the promise I made before I left my girls. Isa wanted a rose, so she'd get a rose.

The crimson blossoms stretched along the side of the castle, a maze in and of themselves, with the entrance being a rounded arch that the roses managed to climb and cling to. I leaned over and inhaled the subtle, sweet smell of one as I plucked the flower from the bush.

I started to tuck it into my pocket, but a low, animalistic snarl sounded from behind me, sending a cascade of shivers through my body. What kind of beast made a sound like that? Nothing that I knew of.

The strange noise grew louder and louder. My hands turned clammy, and my heartbeat thundered in my ears. Heavy footfalls crunched the pebbles underneath. I spun around in time to see a large, fearsome animal barreling toward me on all fours.

As it approached, it rose on its hind legs, standing taller, taller, taller. It towered over me, reminding me of the stories my mother used to tell me of demon spawn from hell. Horns on either side of its head spiraled upward. Fury flared in its eyes as it leaned over me, yellowed fangs bared, shoulders drawn back, chest puffed out.

"I let you stay here, gave you food and a place to sleep, and you steal from me?" The growl sounded from his throat through clenched teeth, the deep timbre causing my knees to shake and buckle.

I dropped the rose as I fell to the ground. It rolled under the beast.

"I-I'm..." I stammered over my words as fear undulated through me, robbing me of the ability to speak.

What was this *thing* in front of me?

"I...I..."

"Spit it out, *thief*," he roared, the sound rattling my bones.

"I'm sorry, I'm so sorry," I sputtered as I threw myself forward and pressed my brow to the gravel at the beast's feet. "I'm glad of the hospitality, good sir." I prostrated myself and prayed that this monster wouldn't kill me. "I meant no harm in taking a rose; I didn't think you'd mind something so insignificant."

A low rumble radiated from the beast's chest, and I could feel that gaze burning a hole through the back of my skull.

"It's mine; it doesn't matter how insignificant it is. I should kill you where you cower for daring to steal from me."

"Forgive me my ignorance, my most generous liege. I just wanted to fulfill my dying daughter's last wish," I said with a forced waver to my voice.

I thought of losing my wife, my other children in that fire, of the losses I've kept experiencing, until tears came to my eyes.

"Excuses and flattery won't save you, *thief.*"

"I'm begging you: please, overlook this and let me go."

The beast fell silent for long moments as if considering me, then it spoke again. "Fine. I'll let you go."

I breathed out a sigh of relief.

"In exchange for your daughter."

I sucked it back in.

I sat bolt upright as my gaze shot to his. "My...daughter?"

What kind of request was that? I was prepared to have to negotiate for my freedom, but he only wanted a woman? This was perfect. My way to get rid of Isa with no man willing to take her. If I gave her to this monster, she would no longer be my problem.

"How can you ask a father to make such a decision? How am I to trade my life for hers?" I held my gaze down, hiding any glint of excitement that might shine there.

"And if I could, what would I even say to convince her to come?" A shadow of a smirk tried to play at my lips, but I willed it away before staring up at the beast, hoping my eyes shone with the silent plea and not the elation buzzing under my skin.

"What you say is up to you. Just make sure she is here within a week."

The beast turned to leave but stopped.

"Oh, and if she doesn't show up by the end of that time...I'll hunt you down and tear your throat out with my teeth," he said, baring them at me.

A droplet of sweat slid down the curve of my nose in a long glide that made me want to wipe it away, but fear kept me firmly in place.

"How will I get back to the castle?"

He glared down at me, and I felt a mere insect in that gaze.

"One of my horses will take you home and bring you back when time's up."

"It'll be done."

I bowed my head. Convincing Isa would be a simple task; she trusted everything I said. Belle would be the problem. She'd always been protective of Isa. I'd have to figure out a way to work around her. The best answer might be to not tell her until it was done.

Fingers of dread slid their way up my back and wrapped me in a cold embrace while I waited for the beast to go on, but he lingered.

Relief flared inside me when he turned away and left.

The stone beneath me bit into my flesh as I knelt there, still too afraid to look up until the sound of footsteps had long faded.

This may very well be a blessing – if everything worked out how I wanted. I'd be back home in a few short hours and free of a burden I'd been trying to get rid of for months since Simon called off his engagement to Isa.

The rose garden before me rustled in the slight breeze, and I leaned into it and plucked another before spinning on my heel and continuing to the stable. A horse stood just inside, already saddled with reins dangling just above its hooves.

I grabbed the leather straps and threw them over the horse's neck, sliding my foot through the stirrup, and swung myself up onto the animal. As I settled into the saddle, I had so many questions burning in my head about this place and yet never got the answers.

The abrupt cold stung my eyes, and they watered as I passed through the threshold of the gate and back into the wintry forest.

Lucien

Damnable thief, did he think he could steal from *me*? To take *my* rose? I let loose a snarl that rattled the chains and jewels on the chandeliers as I scraped the claws of my hand down the wall, pieces of it clattering against the floor as I passed.

I should forego the arrangement and tear him limb from bloody limb.

An antique vase shattered on the marble floor as I shoved it off a table. I allowed Elie to give him food, drink, shelter, and he *stole* from me.

A growl ripped from my throat as I tore another chunk of stone out of the wall.

And not only that, his words reminded me more of a naga's slimy tongue than a parent's. The way they settled over me when he spoke...a twinge of disgust curled my lip.

A man who could freely agree to give away his own child was a man who deserved none. My claws bit into my flesh as I raked them down my face. I was a fool to make such a deal in the first place. The thought left a bitter taste in my mouth.

Why did I make him that offer? My jaw tightened to the point of pain. Elie's words rattled in my head; time was running out, and options were at an end. There was only one way to break the curse. But there were no guarantees with his daughter; she could be anything from an infant to a full-grown woman.

"Idiot," I cursed myself in the reflection of a window. I hadn't used my head at all. In the depths of the frozen thing, my heart still clung to the ridiculous hope that someone might love me. How moronic. Not a creature alive would love me as the monster I am.

It was Elie's fault. The bite of pain from my claws digging into my scalp pulled me back from the ledge. He insisted that man stay in the castle, and if he wasn't the only company I could tolerate, I'd throw him out too.

The bones in my hands creaked and groaned when I tightened my fingers into fists, recalling the thief planting his ass on *my* throne and wearing *my* crown. I'd wanted to charge in and rip it right out of his grubby little thieving hands then and there. If it wasn't for the abhorrence I held for being seen, I would have.

And now I'd have another person in my castle permanently. I raked my claw through the matted fur on my head, grazing the horn and recoiling at the touch.

There was a simple solution to this problem. I would lock his spawn in the dungeon as soon as she arrived. Save me the trouble of having to deal with another person with sticky fingers.

"Elie!" My bellow bounced off the walls of the empty hallway.

"Does this mean you're going to 'take it out of my hide' as you so delicately put it last night?" Elie asked, stepping out of a patch of darkness.

Bastard had gotten too good at hiding in the shadows now, even with that pale skin of his.

I growled, raising a clawed finger at him in accusation.

"This is your fault, Elie. That bastard tried to steal from me."

"It was just a rose," he said with a tentative shrug, golden eyes never breaking from mine.

"It was not *just a rose*." My growl turned feral as an image of my mother in that garden filtered into my mind. "It was from *her* garden."

Elie stayed quiet for a moment, two, lips pressed into a line. "I'll accept any punishment you see fit to deal out, Luce."

My body trembled as I spoke. "Get the dungeon ready for a new prisoner."

The color drained from his face. I knew what going into the dungeon would do to him and I still made the demand. I hated myself for it the second the words left my mouth.

"You're going to lock him up?" Elie's brows shot up toward his hairline.

"Not him. The daughter he traded for his life. She's probably just a child."

"He traded his child for his life...?" The look of disgust on his face matched what swam through my insides. "And you're going to put her in the dungeon?"

The question and inflection grated on the ends of my nerves like sandstone.

"Where else would I put her? I can't have a brat running amuck in my castle, now can I?"

I caught a glimpse of myself in the shattered remnants of a mirror and nearly flinched at my own reflection.

"Or do you think she'd want to experience the fear that comes with this face?"

Elie's eyes held a glint of sadness beneath the hardened gold as he stared at me for a long second. If he contemplated the words he was about to speak, that'd be a first.

"Do you not long for the companionship?"

"No. You prove more company than I can handle."

He breathed in and sighed that same breath out.

"Lucien, I'm saying this as your friend, but you need to take a minute and really consider what's at stake here. Maybe she won't be a child, but a woman, then you might—"

I snarled, a vicious, horrid sound. "Do not finish that sentence. I told you, never speak of it again."

Elie splayed his arms, that glint of sadness now etched into all of his features. "Luce, if you don't do something soon—"

My claws dug through the fabric of Elie's collar as I grabbed him and slammed him into the stone wall. I growled, my maw mere inches from his face.

"It's already too late."

Elie's calloused fingers wrapped around my wrist and dug in.

"It is *not* too late, Lucien. You still have three months before the curse kills you. You just need to get someone to fall in love with you and accept you as you are," he paused, and I would've sworn right then that those golden eyes could see into my soul. "It won't be that hard. You just have to open yourself up to the possibility of it."

I bared every one of my sharp fangs at him.

"You said those statues would break it, that they would break any curse. But they didn't."

We had performed the ritual perfectly, yet I was still this...animal.

"I'm sorry." His voice wavered when he spoke, and his fingers relaxed their grip on me.

A pang of guilt lanced through my chest at the defeat in his eyes. All these years he'd spent trying to help me. But every time, every single time, I snapped at him, refusing his aid.

I hated myself for it, just as I hate myself for what I did now. It wasn't just my life at stake, but Elie's – the entire realm's. If I didn't break the curse, I would die and damn my kingdom to this endless loop of time forever, living the same year, over and over.

I loosened my grip and let Elie slide back to the floor as I glimpsed a fire stirring in those golden eyes of his, a fire that would burn through me if he ever allowed it.

"Expect the prisoner within the week."

"Lucien..."

"I'm going back to my chambers."

I didn't wait for Elie to respond before I turned and left him standing in the hall.

Arabelle

The snow finally stopped after two days of on-and-off flurries, leaving a blanket of white over everything, and still no sign of our father. Isa and I dusted the snow from atop the garden tarp together in the early morning, then we set to shoveling snow to create paths to where our chores took us.

I chewed my bottom lip as I cleared the path leading up to the cottage door. He didn't send any letters or messages. It could've meant any number of things. Maybe he got lucky, and the cargo was sold for a valuable price. I prayed that's what it was because the alternative...I didn't want to think about it.

I rubbed my hands together in the threadbare gloves and warmed them with my breath, trying to return feeling to my fingertips when hoofbeats drew my attention to the forest. A horse I didn't recognize raced up the path leading to the cottage.

My chest tightened, and I readied myself to run inside and lock the door for fear it might be Louis. When the animal got closer, I squinted my eyes at the approaching rider.

It was Father.

"Isa, Father's home," I shouted over my shoulder into the cottage, where she was preparing a warm meal for us.

The door creaked open as Isa stepped out, bracing herself on the frame when her foot slid on the icy stoop. The hem of her dress soaked up water from the snow at our feet. The horse slid to a stop, slinging clumps of snow in front of us.

Isa didn't say anything, only watched him dismount as she wiped her hands on her apron.

I breathed in a sigh as I took in his appearance, noting the new horse and lack of injuries.

"I'm glad you're back home safely." I combed my hand through my hair and forced a smile to my lips. It wasn't a lie. I didn't wish him harm. "I was starting to worry with you out there in all this."

I glanced at the horse again.

"Does this mean you were able to sell the cargo?"

My stomach did somersaults.

"No." He stopped in front of Isa, reaching into the inner pocket of his cloak, and pulled out a beautiful red rose, offering it to her. "You don't know what this cost me," he said to her.

Isa's fingers wrapped around the stem. "Thank you."

A slight crease in her forehead was all that showed her confusion and shock.

I watched her for seconds until the words clicked in my head, then turned my attention back to my father.

"What do you mean?" My brows rose.

His face darkened as he gave me a sidelong look.

"I'd rather not have this conversation here."

"No, you don't get to pull that. Tell me what you meant."

I planted my feet and squared my shoulders at him, prepared to argue.

"Father's right, Belle. Let's go inside. Dinner is almost ready."

She didn't even wait for a response before the door slammed shut after she disappeared into the dark beyond it.

Our father nodded to the house, a silent command to go inside. I ground my teeth and did as he bid, the words burrowing into my mind.

My eyes fell on the rose, just discarded on the table, while Isa stood by the fire, stirring whatever stew she had prepared. The door squeaked and snapped as he finally joined us and sat at the table. A glance at that rose. How could a rose cost so much to warrant such a tone from him? They were harder to come by but not so difficult that he should act like this.

I took a seat across from him.

"Tell me about the rose."

I couldn't just drop it, not with the way he kept eyeing Isa and trying to hide the shadows of a smile. I knew him, knew the things he did, the schemes he wove to get his way, and all his tells. I noticed it all, from the slight curl of his lip to the subtle twitch of a muscle next to his eye.

It was the exact way he stared at her now.

"It's between me and Isa, not you." He tried to wave me off, refusing to break his gaze on her even when he spoke to me.

I bristled at the audacity. The least he could do was look at me. I grasped the reins of my slipping temper and held tight.

"What did the rose cost you, Father?" Maybe if I plied him with sweetness and charm, his lips would loosen.

In a slow glide, he shifted his eyes over to me. Unease prickled my scalp. Whatever this business with Isa was, it couldn't be good, not if he was this adamant about not telling me.

Isa remained quiet in her place by the fire. How she managed to stand being near to one, I still couldn't grasp. She was the one who had been trapped, yet she seemed unbothered at all.

For long minutes, the only sound was the howling wind and

the light clang of metal on metal as Isa's spoon hit the side of the pot.

I thought he wouldn't answer and opened my mouth to ask again.

"It nearly cost me my life," he said in a soft voice that I knew to be a lie. "But he agreed to take Isa instead." He gritted his teeth, the expression on his face immediately turned to one of regret.

"He who?" Silence sliced through my world, my head.

"Isabelle, you're going to live somewhere else." He didn't even acknowledge my question.

"What?"

My gaze snapped to her as my heart pounded a thunderous beat against my ribs. Her shoulders tensed, her entire body locked up. I didn't have to see her face to know that panic now coursed through her veins.

I wanted to rage, to rip this man apart for causing it.

"You're also to pack your things, Arabelle. You are going to marry Louis. And you're leaving first thing in the morning."

The ground shifted; there was no other reason for the sudden free fall that my heart went into as I gaped at my father.

"What have you done?"

"I did what I had to. There was no cargo." He shifted in his chair, the wood groaning underneath him.

"Louis bought it all out from under me. He wants you. *Now*, not in three months' time." He rubbed his brow between thumb and forefinger.

"You just...agreed?"

That was why he had come. Why he insisted I go back with him. He'd already taken measures to force me to.

"And what of Isa? What did you mean *he agreed to take her instead?* She's supposed to come with me. Louis promised to take care of her, too."

Panic seized my senses in a vice and refused to let go.

He growled a sigh through clenched teeth.

"When I found out about the cargo, I knew I couldn't stay in town. I thought I could make it back here before sunrise. I was wrong," he paused and looked past me, out of the small window to the massive forest surrounding us.

"It started to snow. I got lost."

My mouth ran dry. If he'd been out in that blizzard all this time, how did he survive? Where did he get the horse? He made some kind of deal. He must have sold Isa to some man he met along the way in exchange for shelter—and a new horse, from the look of it.

My chest hollowed out. How could he do such a thing? I wouldn't allow it. Pain thrummed in my jaw.

"I happened across a castle in the woods. It was big and beautiful and abandoned – or so I thought."

"It wasn't abandoned?" My voice didn't sound like my own.

"No. It wasn't." He rubbed his hands over the stubble on his face and closed his eyes. "There was this...this...monster..." He trailed off, brows furrowing for a moment before continuing, "A beast of a man, really. He lived there. When he caught me taking the rose, he was going to kill me."

The chair groaned as he leaned back.

"Can you imagine?" He laughed a humorless laugh that set my nerves on fire. "Killing someone over a single rose."

My fingers tightened into fists. If it wasn't for the gloves, my nails would have dug grooves into my palms.

"What did you do?" I knew the answer. Before he said it, I knew.

"Well, you see..." His eyes flitted about before settling on Isa. She didn't turn to face him. "He made a really simple demand. All he wants is some company, and since Isa asked for the rose..."

Fear and rage burned through my blood as my gaze shifted from my father to Isa and back again.

"You didn't..." My heart could've shattered the earth beneath my feet as it plummeted. "Father...please tell me you didn't agree to that."

"I had no choice."

Isa's sharp intake of breath tore through me, and I slammed my hand down on the table hard enough for the rose to roll off the side.

"You did! You had a choice!" I flung my other hand out to the side.

"What should I have done? I needed to get back here to the two of you." He slammed his own fists onto the table.

"You could've stayed yourself. I could've looked out for us. We don't need you here." The words were cold and hit their mark, his eyes betraying the hurt.

"You would prefer me leaving you both without a parent? What would you have done? You're a woman. You can't do anything to provide for yourself, let alone your sister." He grabbed my wrists. "You choose what's best for your children, even if it excludes you from the picture."

I ripped my hands from his grasp.

"You can't let her go. *I* won't let her go. She'll live in constant fear—"

"You will. You're going to marry Louis. She has no suitors and never will with that scar." He shoved himself up from the table.

"That horse will take me and Isa back to the castle in the morning, and *you* will go to Starside and stay with Louis until the wedding. All of this," he waved a hand in a vague gesture to the cottage, "nonsense is done. He's tired of waiting."

The words were like a blow to my gut, and I fought against the bile surging up. I wouldn't let this happen. I didn't care what he said.

"I'm going in her place."

"You will not. I forbid it."

"Belle..." Isa started, her back still to us as she clutched the ladle in her hand. I could almost see the fear coming off her in waves; the rigidity of her posture gave it away. "It's fine. I'll be fine."

It was a lie.

There was no way she was fine with this. The relentless tug in my chest told me as much.

I couldn't let her face whatever it was that waited at the castle. I wouldn't let her be someone's prisoner, not when she was already a prisoner in our own family, and if it meant disobeying my father and sneaking out, then I would.

"You see, even Isa herself understands the situation and has handled it with more grace than you." He clicked his tongue. "I don't know what I ever did wrong with you that you would be so selfish."

I fought against the tightening of my jaw at the words. Selfish? For not wanting to let my sister go to some unknown fate? I steeled myself for what I would have to do – that unyielding pull told me it was the right thing.

"Fine."

My mind was made up. If my father wouldn't do what was necessary, then I would.

"He just wants company, right?"

I'd wait until they fell asleep.

"That's not too scary."

I glanced out the window where the horse stood, stamping its feet in the snow. If it would take them back, then it could take me. Whatever the parameters of this deal were, I'd make him accept me instead of her.

"That's all he wants."

I steadied my heart. This would infuriate not just my father but Louis as well. I tried and failed to find it in me to care about what they would say. I would save Isa, and a small part of me was glad of the fact that I might get out of marrying Louis.

"Isa," I waited for her to turn around and meet me with intense amber eyes – a match for my own. "Everything is going to be okay. Stay strong. No matter what happens."

A flicker of understanding shone in her gaze.

Let my father believe I would go along with his plans, give into it, and go to Louis, quiet as a mouse. He could do nothing once I left.

"I'll do as you say, Father," I said and lowered my head in mock subservience.

"I'm glad you understand." His saccharine smile brought my blood to boil.

After eating in uncomfortable silence, I waited in our shared room until Isa's soft and steady breathing filled the space before sliding out of my bed. My clothes from the day lay in a pile. I tossed them back on, ignoring the dirt stains.

Through a crack in our door, I listened to the snores of my father before slipping out. I knew where to step to avoid those squeaky boards in the floor. The problem would be the door. My luck just needed to hold out until I got to the horse.

I pushed on the door, and maybe God did show me favor because that damn spring stayed silent for once.

The horse stood still in the same place that it stopped earlier, *still* saddled and ready. I clutched the horn of the saddle and lifted my foot to the stirrup. The horse shifted closer to me. I hoisted myself up, throwing a leg over and gripping the reins with shaky, stiff fingers.

"Alright, take me to the castle."

Without another word, the horse jolted at a speed that left my head spinning.

Arabelle

When my father said 'castle,' I didn't know what I thought it would be, but it was not the sprawling structure that loomed overhead as I approached a wall that stretched far into the distance. I bit the inside of my cheek as I stared at it, overwhelming and terrifying with towers reaching for the starry sky.

Cold iron settled into my gut. What did I get myself into? I thought I might be able to deal with this man myself, kill him if I had to.

I didn't think it through.

I just knew I couldn't let Isa come. I swallowed hard, almost painfully so, against the cold and anxiety. Icy fingers of fear crept over my scalp, or maybe it was the wind.

If he was expecting Isa, and I showed up in her place, he might be angry, might kill me the minute I dismount. But it was a little late for that, now, wasn't it?

I stared at the approaching portcullis as the horse seemed to fly over the ground – if we didn't slow, we'd slam into the gate. I grabbed the reins and tugged, trying to force the animal to stop and fighting the urge to squeeze my eyes shut. But, as if on cue, with a crack and shudder, the metal bars lifted from the slitted holes in the ground, the pointed ends skimming the top of my head.

The very air changed when I crossed the threshold, warm and buzzing with an energy I couldn't place. What was it? It was familiar but I couldn't place it. Warmth kissed my skin, and my muscles relaxed into it.

Sweet, fruity, and floral aromas assailed my nostrils. It was almost intoxicating. Even the castle, which projected an image of foreboding only moments ago, now welcomed me into its core.

Pops and cracks resounded in bursts of colors that lit up the clear sky, bright blues and reds, vibrant greens and purples, vivid oranges and yellows.

"What the hell kind of welcome is this?"

Was there some sort of celebration at the castle? Must be a coincidence. Unless it was a bell toll for dinner's arrival. The explosions of color lasted right up until I reached a grove of orange trees near the castle doors.

The horse slowed to a lazy walk as its hooves clacked over the cobblestone path leading away from the front of the castle. I paid no heed to where it went, only gawked at the lush flowers as it moved down the path. I'd never seen such colors. This garden made the one back home look like a patch of weeds.

My stomach gurgled, though I wasn't sure if it was from anxiety or the fact all I could do was push my dinner around the plate hours earlier. I wasn't alone here; I couldn't forget that. Somewhere in this castle lived that man my father sold Isa to.

I found myself staring at a wall of roses when I realized the horse made its way to the stables, a small wooden structure on the other side of the rose bushes.

When the horse came to a full stop, I slid off its back and led it inside. Other horses stood in stalls and neighed at the sight of me, hooves stamping.

But it was empty.

No one was here.

My stomach rose into my throat, and I forced myself to swallow it back down. I could do this, face this.

I waited, but there were no stable hands that came to help, no groomsmen in sight. The horses were cared for and cleaned up after, meaning someone had to be here. Father did say he thought this place was abandoned at first; now I understood why.

Did the man my father spoke of do all the work? I couldn't imagine someone who was no better than a beast would care to look after these animals.

I removed the saddle, unbuckled the leather straps, heaved it off the animal, and set it with the others. He may have had it wrong, misunderstood this man's demands. I removed the bit and hung it on the wall, taking one of the brushes hanging next to it. Maybe I could change my plan—just a little.

I couldn't believe that someone who would ensure their animals were fed, groomed, and in comfort would be a bad person.

Each stroke of the brush down the length of the horse's body ratcheted up the twisting in my gut. It leaned into me ever so slightly, tail swishing back and forth, as if it sensed the veil of dread hanging over me. The bristles tugged through tangles in the mane and rubbed bits of dirt and bugs off it until I was satisfied, and then I led it to an empty stall.

Then, a thought struck me: It might not be so bad living here. Away from my father, away from Louis, free from what was expected of me. I shoved the thought down so hard that it nearly took my feet from under me.

Isa was still there.

If I couldn't kill the man and return, what would happen to

her? A shudder raked down my spine. I knew. I knew what our father would do, the match he would try to make.

The grumbling of my stomach drove me toward the castle's heavy doors after seeing to the horse. There had to be something to eat inside. Surely whatever beast-man, man-beast, resided in the castle lived off of normal food, right?

My father said he only wanted company. Unless that was a lie. Maybe he had worse plans for me. I cringed at that idea. No time for second thoughts. I took in a sharp breath and held it as I pushed the door open.

When nothing waited for me on the other side of the door, I released that breath in a rush of air that flooded me with relief. The aroma of bacon and freshly baked bread slammed into me like a solid entity, the breeze from outside drawing it out from wherever it was.

With another deep breath in and then out, I stepped through the doorway and followed that delectable, mouthwatering scent.

The heavy door swung shut behind me on a phantom wind, waiting only long enough for me to be clear of it. I spun around, my heart in my throat at the sudden movement and sound. I only stared a moment longer before my stomach rumbled its protests for food, and I obliged.

Candles were spread over tables in the dim, dank foyer of the castle, a film of dust hanging in the air and settling over every surface. I traced the tip of my ragged boot over long gouges in the dirt-covered floor. I couldn't tell if it was stone or tile.

The chandelier hung unlit with cobwebs wrapped around it several times over. If the rest of the castle was in this amount of disarray, I didn't see how anyone could live here. My gut roiled at the thought of this being my life from here on. No, I wouldn't let that happen.

I turned down the first hall, the light of candles flickering and casting long shadows against the stone walls. I passed through a darkened archway into a sitting room full of red and black furniture.

There were two chairs by the hearth. My jaw tightened at the fire crackling in a soft cadence. A table sat between the chairs, with a plate waiting on top. My mouth watered at the sight. I hurried to it but stopped, hesitating as I drew close to the fire. Memories of that night pushed through to the surface, and I swallowed in a dry throat.

I grabbed the plate and sat on the settee against the back wall, putting as much space between myself and the fireplace as I could. I tore the loaf of bread in two and shoved one half in my mouth.

My eyes could have rolled to the back of my head from pure bliss. I couldn't remember the last time I tasted food so delicious. I plucked a strip of bacon from the plate and bit into it, savoring the salty tang on my tongue. I let a soft moan slip from my mouth.

The delicacy I devoured held me in a state of enchantment, so fully that I almost missed the heavy footsteps growing louder by the second.

Almost.

My heart pounded hard enough in my chest that I thought it might burst from me. A lump formed in my throat as cold sweat broke drenched my forehead. I wasn't sure I was ready for what came next.

I curled my fingers into tight fists, the nails biting into my flesh, knuckles whitening as those steps grew louder and louder.

That little voice in the back of my head screamed and lamented to run, but I shoved it down. I wouldn't let Isa face this kind of fear, not when I could barely face it myself. She had been through enough; this was the least I could do for her, the sister I'd scarred with my weakness.

My eyes caught the silver glint of light, and I snatched the knife from the table, tucking it into the sleeve of my dress.

CHAPTER

TWELVE

Lucien

I had no intention of greeting my new guest. I didn't even want to know when she arrived. Yet Elie, with his theatrics, had decided to make a grand showing of it with sky fire in every color possible.

Did he mean to make the castle seem more welcoming? My lip curled at the thought.

It drew my attention to the window, like he no doubt intended to do, and I saw the child arrive – no, not a child like I expected.

My stomach clenched and twisted in on itself.

A woman.

I raked both hands along the side of my scalp, claws catching in the clumps of fur that were a mass of tangles and knots. Why did the child have to be a woman? This would get Elie's hopes up, and I didn't want to see the disappointment in my friend's face when I inevitably failed him. Again.

My jaw tightened as I stared out of my windows to the stables, the memories twisting my insides even more. I should play the part of a gracious host, at least. But this was the child of a thief, a

80

horrible, terrible man who traded his child for his own sake. She couldn't be much better.

I paced in front of the window, hands clenching and unclenching at my sides as I threw a look out to the stables every few minutes, trying to quash the raging storm inside my head.

This could be an opportunity, my last.

I crushed that hope down.

It wouldn't happen – it was impossible.

I'd stick to my plan: have Elie take her to the dungeon and wash my hands of it. What the bleeding hells was she doing in the gods damned stables anyway? It didn't take that long to board a horse.

I stormed to the door, ripped it open, and stomped down the hallway. Elie better have prepared the cell like I asked. I wasn't expecting her *the same day*, but that was neither here nor there.

As I reached the bridge spanning the foyer and leading to the stairs, I slowed at the delicate trill of her voice as it drifted from the sitting room. The soft lilt threatened to pierce through the ice I'd built around my heart, and I hesitated.

I braced myself on the edge of the room entrance, my claws digging into the soft wooden trim like it was flesh. The last woman I saw invaded my mind – the witch as she laid her curse on me.

My insides curdled, and the room swayed. I didn't *have* to imprison her in the dungeon, but if she were to stay here, live with me in this castle, I needed to make some things clear to her.

When I rounded that corner, my breath caught in my throat at the sight of her, head bowed low, deep in a curtsy, and the pungent scent of fear rolling off her in waves.

My fingers twitched at my sides as I fought every urge to reach out and touch her. A woman, finally standing before me again after all this time. I'd nearly forgotten how soft their skin was, how sweet they smelled – even if hers was tainted by that fear.

"I know you wanted Isa, but I came in her place. I'll make a much better companion for you. She's…" she stopped speaking as if searching for the words. "…been through a lot."

She paused, almost as if she was hesitant to continue.

"Please accept me over her."

She kept her face down as she spoke, the plait of her hair lying over her shoulder.

"I'll do whatever you want."

Words didn't come to me as my mind swam through a murky fog of memory, trying to remember the way I used to speak to women. The thought of using such a method again left a bitter taste in my mouth.

Even without seeing her face, I could tell she was nothing like my previous conquests. Maybe it was because I hadn't seen a woman in damn near twenty years, but indecent thoughts inundated my mind.

Damn that incessant dream that haunted me. I didn't need to think of sweat-slick bodies, pleasure-filled moans, and the last woman who uttered those words to me.

Arousal sparked inside me for the first time in too long, and my chest rumbled with a low growl, praying to the gods that my eyes didn't betray it as I spoke, "Careful what you say to me, girl."

I let the edges of my fur brush against her bare arm as I passed, and I could feel the shiver slide over her body. I settled into one of the chairs nestled by the fireplace.

She straightened and spun to me, a fire burning behind those amber eyes that ignited heat within my long, cold veins.

"I'll say whatever I have to if it means you leave Isa alone."

My eyes devoured her with such greed as I took in the whole of her appearance now, from her dingey hair to the callouses on her hands to the boots falling apart on her feet. My eyes traced the lines of her high cheekbones, down the soft angle of her jaw, over her velvet soft lips. If she was this beautiful, looking much like something dragged out of a gutter, gods. I wasn't sure I could handle seeing her cleaned up.

"So, you'd take your sister's place, no questions asked?" I didn't need to ask who this Isa was; I knew that look in her eye. Had felt it once upon a time.

"Yes, I would."

"Even if my intention was to peel the skin from her bones in ribbons of flesh for what your father did?" I leaned on my elbow, noting the shift in her stance, her tightening throat, stiffening muscles.

"Yes. But I warn you, I will not make it easy for you."

"Oh?"

A thrill of curiosity bloomed in my chest at her words. Even though she prostrated herself when I walked in, she didn't seem the type to bend or beg; she was made of something sturdier.

She took a step closer to me, and my claws dug into the wood of the armrest; a chip dislodged and fell to the floor as her scent washed over me anew.

"I won't leave her at the mercy of this world."

She brandished a knife from the place setting and lunged for me, aiming to plunge that blade into my chest. I was on my feet with both her wrists in my hands before she could take another step, twisting until I heard the clatter of the knife on the floor.

"Valiant effort, but you'll have to try harder than that, girl. Did you think to kill me and return?" I snarled, my canines inches from her face.

She twisted away from me, her eyes screwed shut.

"Better than just letting you kill me. Or giving you Isa."

I let one wrist go, gripping her face with my broad hand, claw grazing the delicate skin beneath her ear as I forced her face back to mine.

"Killing you would be a waste." My words came out in a low

rasp, and her eyes snapped open, her nose wrinkling in what I presumed was disgust.

"And I never specified which of you was to come. If you're here, then the bargain is fulfilled." To admit her father only mentioned one would make me look a fool – not something I would allow here.

All at once, I released her and bent to pick up the knife. Striding back to my chair and sitting. I twirled the blade in my fingers. She straightened her dress as I watched, eyes never leaving me.

"Give me your word that she will remain safe."

"Would you trust the word of a beast?"

A long moment of silence passed as we stared each other down. Would she even answer? Anxiety roiled in my stomach, and I clutched the knife in my hand.

"Do I have a choice?"

A smirk played at my lips, and I pressed them together to stifle it. So long had it been since I felt such a spark with someone.

"No. You do not."

I pointed to the chair next to mine with the tip of the knife.

"Sit." I winced internally at the gruff command.

A glance at the fire left shadows in the wake of all that fierceness from moments before, and I arched a brow. She moved with a stiff gait and sat in the chair, hands clutching the arms.

My breath hitched at the sight of her face gilded by firelight.

Fuck.

My eyes fell to her supple lips – lips that looked soft and kissable – what I wouldn't give to feel them on my... I shook my head as if I could rid the thought that easily.

She was a breathtaking sight to behold. And the fire burning within her matched my own. Thoughts once again swirled in my head against my better judgment. What I'd love for her to do with that fiery mouth.

But not before bringing her to the brink of ecstasy and denying her release over and over until she fell to her knees and begged me to forgive her attempt at killing me.

Begged me for that delicious release.

With a steadying breath and another shake of my head, I captured her with the iciest stare I could muster while that heat burned beneath my skin.

"It's obvious that you came here of your own choice, given what you've said." My claw tapped out a rhythm on the wood of the armrest. "That old man of yours is a real bastard."

Her mouth opened as if to say something but snapped shut again as her brows knitted together and her head tilted.

"What do you mean by that?"

I forced my gaze to remain cold, fighting back the heat threatening to empty my head of any rational thought. The sweet smell of her filled me with a warmth I'd forgotten so long ago, even before that witch showed up on my doorstep.

Her father gave her to me so I wouldn't kill him. The thought filled me with rage for her.

"Nothing. It's not important."

I peeled my eyes off her, feeling much like the ravenous beast I was.

"There are two trunks in the next room. Send whatever you want back to your family. I'll make sure they get it."

Silence settled around us, and I bristled. That stare of hers was going to burn a hole in the side of my head. The seconds stretched on into eternity before I finally had to break it.

"The only rule I have is that you stay out of the north wing. You have free roam over the castle otherwise."

"Do you have a name?"

My heart stuttered at the question, at the decency she showed me. I snorted, despite my rapid pulse, and rolled my eyes.

"Of course, I have a name."

Silence. Then, "Well?"

"Lucien."

She stood and circled around the back of her chair, eyes never leaving me as she moved toward the adjacent room where the trunks awaited her inspection.

I waited, but she didn't offer me hers. She wanted to force me to ask.

"Your name?"

"It's Arabelle."

And then she was gone.

Thank the fucking gods. My claws scraped against the wooden armrest, leaving grooves in the grain. I needed to get far, far away from her.

THIRTEEN

Arabelle

Bright silks in every color were draped from a wooden bed canopy. Jewels hung on chains from intricate carvings. Golden coins, cups, and gemstones spilled from open chests and hung over the edges of drawers.

My stomach twisted into a knot. These could belong to those who passed through before. Did Lucien kill people and hoard gold and jewels and finery like some kind of dragon of lore? I ran a hand over the loose strands of hair hanging from my braid.

I had fought the trembling in my knees when he first walked in. I even thought I might kill him and go home, but with his speed and strength, there was no way. I was his prisoner – for however long he found amusement in my company.

When my father had said monster, I never expected him to have a name, or to speak...or have any sort of humanity for that matter. I don't know what I expected, really. He didn't fit any expectations I had. Yes, he was a beast, but when my father said monster, this wasn't what I'd imagined.

That initial fear faded away somewhere in the midst of our conversation, and it felt almost normal. But that name. There was something familiar about it, something that tugged at threads in the back of my mind as if it was one I *should* know.

The candlelight glinted off something silver and drew my eye to it: a dress. My chest tightened, and I placed my palm flat against it. Isa would love it, the way the light reflected in an iridescent rainbow of colors, and the size was near perfect for her.

I ran my fingers over the delicate fabric of the bodice, my rough skin catching on it.

"She'd love this..." A sob lodged itself in my throat.

I left whatever gold and jewels were in the chests alone and dumped gold in them until they were full, laying the dress at the top of one. The flames of that inferno licked the back of my mind, and I shuddered. Nothing could ever replace what we lost in that fire, but maybe my father and sister could have a comfortable life with this.

With a silent prayer, I snapped the lids closed and hoped against all hope that they would understand and not try to force me to trade places with Isa. I wasn't sure Lucien would even allow it.

He said with my presence, the bargain was done.

Good.

I hoped I was right about him. I agreed to marry Louis, and I was prepared to. Up until I saw Lucien. Louis could go to the deepest level of hell with his proposal. Lucien didn't frighten me. I had seen plenty of men more terrifying than him, but he most certainly *would* frighten Isa.

Weariness overtook me, and I blinked sleepy eyes at the window. The sky was still black and bedecked with starlight. I had left the cottage late in the night, staying awake so I could leave without being spotted.

"What time is it anyway?" I rubbed my eyes and wandered back into the room where I thought Lucien would be waiting.

He wasn't there.

I sighed at the empty chair. The least he could have done was show me to a bedroom so I could settle in for the night. Prickly bastard. I shuffled further into the castle, following a path of candlelight until I opened the door to an empty bedroom.

Moonlight poured in through half-open curtains, and the door snicked shut behind me.

"I should get some sleep."

I brushed my hand over the top of my head, sliding it down the back. I massaged a sore muscle in the back of my neck.

"It's been a long, strange day."

I opened the rosewood wardrobe and if my jaw wasn't attached, I'd be picking it up from the floor. I'd never seen such fine clothes, even before the fire claimed everything. These were fit for high nobles or maybe even royalty.

My fingers danced over the assortment of expensive fabrics until I found a sleeping gown that I liked. I changed into it before crawling into the massive down bed and collapsing, too tired to even pull back the covers.

Orange light tinted the blackness behind my eyes, and I raised a hand to shield my face from the bright beams shining down on me. A gentle tang of citrus filled my nostrils, and I sat up, blinking my eyes open to the ocean of red surrounding me.

My arm dropped to my side as I stared out over the fully bloomed amaryllises stretching to the horizon in every direction. I pushed onto my feet, the hem of my dress grazing over flowers and stirring up more of that delectable scent.

"There's so many of them."

I spotted the tip of a black boot just above the flowers, and when I got closer, it was propped on the knee of someone lying in the field. Who was it? The amaryllises rustled with my every step as I moved toward the strange person. But who was I to really think them strange? I woke up in the same place.

An intense gaze fell on me, sending a tendril of warmth spiraling up my spine and back down to settle in my stomach when my eyes met his. I took in the square jaw, porcelain skin, mess of long blond hair, and back to those eyes, the color of a clear morning sky, yet rimmed with gold.

I had no clue who this man was or why he was lying in this field, but despite the silver and black masquerade mask hindering half his face, I knew he was a breathtaking work of art. I opened my mouth to voice the question burning in my mind but couldn't force even a squeak to grace my lips.

"I don't know why you're sad. You'll have everything you could possibly want."

My knees damn near buckled at the sound of his deep timbre. I tried to swallow, but my throat tightened almost painfully as I scoured my brain for two words to string together in a coherent sentence.

"I-I'm not sad." I cringed when my voice came out an octave higher than normal, and heat tinged my cheeks.

My eyes lingered on that mask, the sunlight catching in the blood-red rubies curving around the outside of his eyes. He pinned me with those blue eyes of his, unmoving from the spot he lazed in.

"You can't hide it. That face of yours shows every emotion." He finally broke the gaze and cast his eyes skyward once again.

A muscle in my jaw ticked as anger flared beneath the surface. I stomped right up to him and pointed at the glittering mask covering his features.

"I'm not the one hiding anything. What's with the mask?"

The corner of his mouth turned up in a smile that sent my heart skittering across the field of flowers, and his eyes found mine again.

"If you want to know, you'll have to find me."

"Huh?" The word tumbled from my mouth before I had the good sense to stop it. "You're right here, though."

"Am I?"

My brows furrowed, and I tilted my head.

"Yes, you are." Great. I find a beautiful man, and he's out of his mind. "How else would we be talking?"

"But are we really talking? Or is this all in your head?" His feline grin tugged at something low in my belly.

"I—"

"Find me, Arabelle."

My eyebrows shot up.

"How do you know my name?"

His only response was to smirk and look to the sky again. I took a tentative step toward him.

"How do I find you? If this is, as you say, in my head?" I wasn't sure he'd answer the question after shirking the last.

"Don't trust your eyes; not everything you see is the truth."

I narrowed my eyes and dragged my lip between my teeth. What was with this cryptic way of speaking?

"What does that mean? Speak clearly."

He vaulted to his feet in a single, smooth action and I retreated that earlier step, but he grabbed the back of my neck, pulling me so close that his breath ghosted across my lips.

"Don't desert me, not until you've saved me."

The blush that heated my cheeks spread across the bridge of my nose and to the tips of my ears as I dug my fingers into his forearms. His breath hitched under the touch, and, for a moment, I could've sworn something akin to hunger danced in his eyes.

"Save you? From the beast?"

Instead of an answer, his soft lips covered my own for such a brief time I wanted to cry out when they left me cold and surrounded by darkness. I wrapped my arms around my middle at the missing warmth.

A female voice sounded from all around me. "Don't let appearances fool you, young Arabelle."

Warm fingertips brushed against my jaw, turning my head.

I couldn't tell if it was the brightness of the gown or her entire being that lit up the room we now stood in.

"Do not regret what you've lost. You have far better things coming to you, should you only have the courage to reach out and grasp them for yourself." The woman's golden hair billowed behind her as she bent to press a gentle kiss to my brow.

FOURTEEN

Lucien

Was I really so ensconced in loneliness that any woman who darkened my doorstep was enough for my mind to come undone? I pressed the heels of my hands into my eyes as a growl emanated from my chest.

I swore I wouldn't bother with her, but my gods damned heart held onto that sliver of hope, and she was already in my head.

"There's only a few months left. What are you doing?" I didn't want to cling to the last dregs of false hope.

An unfamiliar warmth unfurled in my chest, and I touched a fingertip to my lips, the ghost of a sensation I'd long forgotten lingering there. I stared up at the strips of cloth hanging around the sides of my bed, barely skimming the floor.

Those initial days after the curse took hold left scars on more than just me. Every corner of the castle was marred from my unleashed rage. I rolled off the bed and stared at the claw marks carved into every surface of my room. I yanked the curtains back.

The gentle morning sun lit up the wreckage of my chambers as I gazed out of the window, peering across the beauty of my lands, and my heart squeezed. It wouldn't be long until my home crumbled.

That nagging, gnawing glimmer of hope sat at the edge of my mind. If I could really break this curse and free myself and Elie, my only chance would be nigh on three months from now. The one night I wouldn't be a beast – the night of the Blue Moon. We were so close to the deadline I shuddered to think what would befall us should I fail.

A knock sounded from the door, and I didn't bother turning around as it creaked open.

"What do you want, Elie?"

"I take it you decided not to throw the child in the dungeon after all?" The amused inflection in his voice made me grind my teeth.

"Obviously."

"What changed your mind?"

I didn't have to look to know there was a smirk plastered on that damned face of his; the smugness was alight in his voice. I shot him a glare anyway. He stood just inside the threshold, hands tucked into his pockets, and yep – a shit-eating grin split his face.

"I didn't feel like it."

"Must have been quite the looker if she changed *your* mind."

"Her looks have nothing to do with it," I snapped.

"Ah, so the daughter *is* a woman?" He stalked a few steps forward but stopped again as his eyes slid over me.

My face heated. I fell right into his trap.

"I know where you're going with this."

"Do you?"

"She'll never accept me. There's no point in trying."

He arched a crimson eyebrow at me, the gold in his eyes shimmering in mischief just like when we were younger.

"You know this for a fact?"

"She tried to stab me. So, yeah."

This time, both his brows shot up.

"And you *didn't* put her in the dungeon? Huh."

I loosed a growl and stomped toward him, straightening to my full, towering height.

I annunciated each word as if they were daggers to be thrown at him. "Say what you mean to, Elie."

An easy smile spread across his lips, and he rocked back on his heels.

"I think you might have a little hope left in that black heart of yours, after all."

I asked myself the same question: why didn't I just throw her in the dungeon and forget her existence? I came to the same damn answer every time. It still pissed me off. My lip curled up in a snarl, and I dragged a claw down the wooden banister of my bedframe.

"No. I don't."

"Then why demand her in the first place? Why bring a stranger here? If not for a last-ditch effort to break this gods damn curse?" It was Elie's turn to growl, and a fire I long thought stolen burned in his eyes.

My lip twitched as I fought down the rage. It wouldn't do me any good here.

"Her father stole from me. It's that simple. Someone had to be punished."

"You demanded his *child*, not him. Punishing her for his mistakes is cruel, something your father would have done." He chose those words with intent; they were meant to rip open old wounds.

"Why do you think she's not in a cell?" I leashed the temper that would have had me tearing my closest friend limb from limb. "I am not my father."

Elie's eyes fell from mine, and something like remorse shone there.

"No, you're not." He met my gaze again. "But you should give it a chance, Luce. She could be the one."

I dragged a deep breath in through my nose and forced it out through my teeth in a hiss.

"Fine. I'll try. Tell her we'll be having our meals together."

A smirk played on my friend's lips. "It's a start at least."

I waved him off as I let out a huff, dust flitting through the air in a cloud of particles that lingered for far too long.

"Might I also suggest a bath?"

I whipped my face back around to him, grinding my teeth together.

"Why do I need a bath?"

He just grinned.

"Women like a clean man, one that doesn't smell or wallow in his own filth, or have you forgotten that in your years of solitude?"

That grin turned feline, and I wanted to throttle him.

"Are you saying I smell?" A dumb question; I knew that.

Elie wouldn't shy away from the truth of the matter. I could feel the mats and tangles every time I touched my fur. My clothes hung off me in scraps. I couldn't even remember the last time I bathed.

"Yes," he said simply, spun on his heels, and walked out of my room.

"Bastard."

I walked to the fireplace and ran a finger over the mahogany wood, leaving a clean streak in the dust. Perhaps it wasn't just me that could do with a good scrub down. Did I have enough for that? I only had scraps of magic left, but I should be able to use it to clean the castle. It wasn't until now, having a new guest here, that I was suddenly, immensely aware of how bad I'd let it get.

I stalked into the connected bathing chamber and turned on

the water, the pipes groaning from disuse until the water started to fill the tub. I ripped the tattered rags from my body and left them on the floor, stepping into the bath with a shudder. Dirt came off me in drifts, darkening the water while I soaked.

I let my mind wander while I sat there, Arabelle's face coming unbidden to my mind, and the image tightened my chest. I leaned my head back against the rim of the tub.

Almost twenty years had gone by since I'd even talked to a woman. Liana was the last unless I counted the witch – I never counted the witch.

Regret tinged my tongue, and I crinkled my nose. This long celibacy of mine left me hyper-observant to everything about her. From the messy hair, disheveled from the ride, to the dirt under her fingernails. Every curve of her body. The sweet jasmine scent that filled my nose when I was so close to her.

A long-forgotten desire burned through my veins as I remembered the feel of her skin in my hands. I frowned as I grabbed for soap pearls and lathered myself up. I needed to be rid of this arousal before I saw her at breakfast, or I might take leave of my senses.

FIFTEEN

Arabelle

My eyes snapped open, and darted around the unfamiliar ambiance of the room, panic dancing across my skin until I remembered last night. I came to the castle. The pearl white canopy drapes shielded the bed from most of the light seeping in and pooled in the floor on four sides.

I rolled onto my side as light poured into every dark crevice. I exhaled and leaned onto the pillow.

Images of a handsome, masked blond swept through my mind as I brushed my fingertips over my lips. Who was that? And the lady? It was only a dream, but I still felt his lips on mine. I shook my head and threw back the covers. When did I get under them? I dragged my bottom lip between my teeth.

"Best not to think too hard on dreams." Not when the reality of my situation was much different.

Soft fur slid between my toes when I got out of the bed, the rug protecting my feet from the sudden shock of cold stone underneath. Sunlight leaked through dark curtains. They weren't the black I had thought they were in the dead of night, but with the light on the other side, they were a deep, royal purple. I flung them open, and a sharp breath shuddered from me as I looked out over the vast grounds.

Cobblestone paths led through mazes of gardens. Fields of grass stretched to forests on the inside of the wall. I spied a pond with some kind of fish sculpture in the middle, spouting water from its top.

"Maybe I'll explore today. He did say I'd have full reign of the castle."

I turned to face the room. Aside from the wardrobe and bed, there was a fireplace with two white chairs settled next to it, a vanity with an intricately carved thorn and rose pattern surrounding the mirrors, and a matching stool.

The curtain for the bay window hid a table with two chairs on either side. What I noticed more than anything else, though, was the absence of dust and claw marks. The room was immaculate.

A glimmer of red caught my eye, and I turned to see a crimson dress laid out on a valet chair – an expensive dress. My breath hitched.

"I see the sleeping beauty is finally awake," a male voice said from the doorway.

My eyes jerked up to meet his, the red hair sparking a recent memory.

"You..." He was the one who'd come when Isa and I were cornered by those horned men.

"Me?" His head tilted ever so slightly, and the loose curls of his hair fell around his face and to his shoulders. The corner of his mouth twitched. "Do you know me?"

"You don't recognize me?"

"Should I?"

"The horned men... My sister and I were cornered by them." How could he not remember something like that? Those men were monsters.

He held up a finger.

"Ah. So, that was you? Funny you should end up here." He made no move to come any closer.

With every jostle of his hair, the sun shining through it looked as if fire blazed atop his head, and I had to swallow the bit of awe creeping up.

"I didn't realize anyone else lived here."

"Someone has to take care of him. And see to the grounds. I don't think he could survive without me." He rolled his shoulders in a shrug.

"Someone has a high opinion of himself," I said in a wry tone before adding, "He seems pretty capable to me."

He gave another shrug with an accompanying smirk.

"Does he?" He arched a brow at my statement. "Because really, he's pretty hopeless. Always has been," he said with a chuckle that tugged on the corners of my own mouth and made me to want to join.

"You know him well." It was a statement, not a question. The softness in his eyes when he spoke of Lucien conveyed volumes.

"Yes," he paused, as if to consider me, "we grew up together."

"What was it like? Growing up with someone like...that?"

He remained silent for moments, golden eyes boring into me in a way that made me writhe in my skin.

"That is...a story for another time. I came to tell you that you'll be eating meals with Lucien while you're here."

My eyebrow twitched. Why did I have to eat with him? Wasn't it enough that I was just here? My father's words came back to me then; *he just wants company.*

"And if I refuse?"

A wicked grin split his pale face, and he leaned back against the doorframe.

"I can always throw you in the dungeon."

I pressed my lips into a thin line.

"Fine. Anything else I have to look forward to? Any other demands?"

"That's it. For now." His grin gnawed at my stomach, and I fought the desire to throw something at him. "I'm Elie, by the way."

"Belle – Arabelle," I corrected myself, manners forgotten with just how easy it was to talk to him.

"You should wash before getting dressed, Belle." He nodded to the dress laid out for me. "I can see the layer of filth on you from here."

My face heated, and I was sure it matched the color of his hair. I bristled under his stare. He laughed and slipped out of the door, leaving me alone again.

What a prick.

I didn't need someone to tell me what I should or shouldn't do. I ground my teeth together as I scanned the room until my eyes fell on another door. I stomped toward it and yanked it open. It was a connected bathing suite.

The porcelain tub was situated in front of a mirror, the golden claw feet keeping the base just above the stone floor. Sconces held burning candles and lined the walls. Vines carved from the pillars appeared to wind around them and up to the tall ceiling. A window with a view of distant mountains sat at the opposite end of the chamber.

I stopped at the edge of the tub, water already filling it. I skimmed my fingertips over the surface, leaving small ripples. The warming embrace begged me to step into it. I pulled my nightdress over my head, dropped it to the floor, and obliged the need that would pull me under if I didn't.

I sank in until the water kissed my jaw. Glorious heat worked into my muscles, and all the pent-up energy seeped away.

My body turned to jelly. Somehow, the water leaked into me

and turned my insides into nothing but mush. I could stay in here all day.

"If only I didn't have to eat with him."

I let out a small huff of disappointment before I found a sponge and the scented pearls of soap along the slim table between the tub and the wall. I scrubbed my face, neck, and shoulders, working my way down my arms, chest, and stomach.

I undid my braid and washed my hair, threading the oil that gave off a sweet floral scent through it. I leaned back in the tub for a bit longer.

In the cottage, it was all pails and cold, sometimes dirty, water. Of the few things I missed from my old life, pampering myself in this way was one. Okay, maybe living in a castle with a beast wasn't so bad. Irritation clawed at the back of my mind as I remembered the order to dine with him.

Water sluiced off me as I stood and stepped out of the tub, grabbing a thick cotton towel from the rack nearby. I let it absorb the moisture dripping off my body before squeezing my hair out with it and draping it over a rod.

I donned a dressing robe that hung from a hook on the wall and went back into the main room. I stared at the red dress Elie pointed out for me to wear. Was it Elie who chose it? Or Lucien? My coin was on Elie, but why? If he was as blasé toward Lucien as he was to me, then he might've picked it for a reason.

Curiosity pricked at my mind as I walked by the dress and opened the wardrobe; the finery sparkled and glittered in the sunlight. What if my wearing that dress irritated Lucien? Elie seemed the sort to do just that, given our limited conversation. A smile curved my lips, and I closed the doors again. I dropped the robe and slipped into the red dress.

SIXTEEN

Lucien

I found myself in one of the only rooms I would never destroy, one that burrowed into a deep place in my heart, along with memories I locked away. My fingers ran over the cold keys of the piano, the melody of songs long quiet playing through my head.

"I miss playing with you, Mother."

I sat on the bench and stared at the black and white keys, bringing my hands up into the position that was so natural for me. So long. It had been so long. I played one note, and the feel of the keys was different in this form.

Relearning the instrument with these claws had been tricky, but I finally mastered it. I played another, not stopping until my hands moved along the keys and soft music filled the air. I closed my eyes, letting my instincts and honed skills take over as I played. My heart quickened. How I missed this.

My mind drifted with the sound. I promised Elie I would make an attempt to break my curse. We both knew what it required now. It should have been easy, but how was I to put that on someone else?

And now Arabelle was here. Beauty aside, she had chosen to come in her sister's place. Something inside my chest warmed at the thought. The fear in her eyes had leeched out the longer she was in my presence last night, and by the end, it was completely gone. Elie had said she could be the one. Maybe he was right.

I opened my eyes again, fingers and feet moving in a rhythm that was like breathing to me. I glanced at the black case leaned against the wall and longing lanced through me. It wasn't the piano I truly wanted to play. But with these gnarled, clawed fingers, I'd never be able to play it again.

The door opened, and footsteps sounded from across the wooden floor; the sound of the piano almost drown them out. They stopped just before the raised platform. An emotion I barely recognized flickered on Elie's face before he schooled it, though a hint still lingered in his eyes as he watched.

Waited.

After the last note died out, Elie cleared his throat and spoke. "Breakfast is ready. Just waiting on you." His voice was strained with the hopefulness he tried to stifle. "You're playing again."

I dropped my hands and stared at the keys.

"I thought it might help clear the storm in my head." I stood, pushing the stool back. "Let's go."

Arabelle sat at one end of the table in the dining hall when Elie and I strode in. I cut a glance at him when I saw the dress she wore, cursing under my breath.

That damn dress brought out the color of her freckles against the pale skin. The deep red was a sharp contrast to her natural colors, but it looked too good. The bodice hugged her in all the right places to accentuate every curve. My eyes dropped to the bare tops of her breasts, pushed up by the corseted top. I fought to swallow as my mouth dried.

I had taken to eating my meals in my room. Elie sometimes joined me, but now I had a guest that I needed to entertain. How exactly did I do it before? No. What I did then wouldn't help me now. Butterflies fluttered around my stomach, and I hesitated in my next step.

Elie jabbed his elbow into my ribs.

"Relax," he whispered, passing by me and taking a seat next to the head of the table on the opposite end of Arabelle. He raised his eyebrows at me and nudged his head toward the chair next to him.

I shoved the anxiety out of my head and sat on the end seat next to Elie. It was just a meal. A normal, everyday meal. I could do this. But what should I say to start a conversation? What did one usually do in these types of situations? Maybe not this exact situation since I demanded she be here. And no woman had ever tried to kill me before.

"What do you think of the castle so far?" Gods bless Elie, breaking the silence as he started serving himself food.

"I haven't seen much of it," Arabelle paused and took a cue from Elie on the food, "but what I have seen has been...old and musty. Except for the room I slept in."

Elie choked back a laugh, coughing into the back of his hand while I clicked my tongue against my teeth.

"You're not wrong; this place could use some cleaning up," he said, shooting me a pointed stare, which I answered with a roll of my eyes.

Every muscle in my body went rigid when Arabelle's eyes met mine. I tried to serve myself food like any sane normal person might, and not like someone whose veins turned to stone.

"I was planning to explore a bit today. Any places you recommend?" She looked at Elie first, then at me.

My heart thundered at such a simple question. Or maybe I just wasn't used to anyone else looking at me. I took a bite out of my biscuit as each of the rooms in the castle filtered through my mind. How was I supposed to tell her where to go if I didn't know what she liked?

"Anywhere but the north wing." I was an idiot. I'd already told her not to go there. That wasn't what she asked. Elie's sidelong glance said he agreed.

"I know that already," she huffed and smeared jam on her own biscuit before taking a bite.

A look of pure bliss flashed over her face. Her knuckles turned white with the grip she held on the knife.

"It's a tough question to answer." Elie glared at me, and I couldn't blame him or the daggers in that glare. "There are a lot of places to see around the castle. I doubt you could visit them all in a day."

"Then what's your favorite place? Where do you go when you want to unwind?" Her focus shifted solely to Elie, and I couldn't help the small twinge of jealousy fighting its way to the surface.

"Me?" He cocked a brow at her. "I'm not sure you'd really enjoy the same places I do," he said with a half-smile.

She smiled in return, and the fork in my hand groaned as my fist clenched. This was so much harder than I thought it would be. Part of me wanted to shove her out the door, while another part knew that I needed her here, I needed to *act*.

"We won't know that unless you tell me."

Elie conceded with a halfhearted shrug.

"I like the training grounds." He rubbed a hand over the side of his neck, fingers catching in his hair. "I like keeping in shape, and feeling my body move." A feline grin crossed his lips. "You know, for the ladies. They like a man who can handle a sword."

"Elie..." I didn't mean to say it, not with such venom laced through his name, but the warning in my tone was enough.

Elie straightened as all that amusement dropped from his face. I gritted my teeth at the foreign twinge of jealousy that managed to override my senses, my rational mind. I'd never been jealous of anyone a day in my life, but here it was, seeping into my blood in a way that made my stomach curdle.

"You unwind by training?" Arabelle lifted a brow, finishing off the last of her biscuit and taking a sip of water to wash it down.

A twitch of his lips had Elie smirking, and he gave her a nod. "Training and soaking in the hot springs."

"There are hot springs here?"

Her gaze jumped between Elie and me, a smile playing at her lips again.

Elie jammed his elbow into my ribs, in part because I snapped at him, and in part because I knew he wanted me to make the offer.

"I can take you there. If you'd like."

She considered me and said, "That'd be fantastic." She shifted, wiggling in her chair before letting her eyes settle on me again. "Elie answered my question, but you haven't."

My favorite place in the castle was the music room. It was a place where I could find the peace that seemed so rare these days, the only place that wasn't soaked with vile memories of betrayal or pain. But what would she think of that? What if she preferred the hardened warriors like Elie? I glanced at him, eyes pleading for any kind of answer that would help, but he just gave me a curt nod.

I breathed in.

"The music room." Being honest was the only way this would work.

I waited, trying to read the expression on her face, but I couldn't.

"I wouldn't have pegged you for the type to like music."

"Why not?"

"Because you've been nothing but surly and serious since I got here."

I bristled at the comment. I wasn't that type at all. What was she even talking about? I made to look at Elie again, but he was shaking with laughter, and I glowered at him.

"You'll have to excuse him. He hasn't entertained a young lady in quite some time," Elie managed around snickers.

"No one asked you, Elie." Every word I spoke was sharper than the bladed edge of a sword.

"That was pretty evident last night. He threatened to torture me." Those amber eyes bore into me, and my skin could have caught fire.

"And you answered by trying to stab me," I bit back. Fuck, this wasn't how I wanted it to go. I needed to turn it back around, or we'd end up at each other's throats.

"Can you blame me? I'm your prisoner for a crime that I didn't even commit." Her knuckles whitened around the fork in her hand.

"You're not a prisoner," I growled. I could have locked her in the dungeon, but I didn't. I could do so much worse, but I wouldn't. Why was she being so difficult? My heart dipped into my stomach, and rage simmered in response.

"Then I can leave the castle grounds?" Arabelle splayed her hands on the table, fork still under her palm.

I gave her the freedom to go anywhere in the castle except my wing. Why couldn't she just be happy with that?

"No. You're to stay here."

Invisible fire burned at my fingertips as my temper rose with every word she spoke. I needed to leash that anger, shove it back down. But she was bent on prying it out of me.

"Then how am I not a prisoner?" Her shoulders tensed as the flare of temperament in her eyes met mine.

She was no prisoner, she wasn't locked up, she was not in chains.

"You're not in a dungeon cell, are you?" I placed my own fork on the table, claws digging into the wood.

I could do worse. I could do what my father would have. But I didn't. *Keep it under control. She has every right to be angry with me, to resent me.*

"Dungeon cell or extravagant room, it's all the same if I'm not allowed to leave." She shoved back from the table, slapping her napkin down over the plate, and stood. "If you'll excuse me."

She turned to walk away.

"Fine! If you want to be a prisoner, I'll make you a prisoner and lock you in your room!" I bellowed at her, pushing to my feet as the chair clattered on the floor behind me.

With a step back, I leapt over the table in a single bound and landed in front of her, grabbing her wrist and throwing her over my shoulder with a yelp from her. I stomped toward the doors with Arabelle pounding her fists into my back and kicking her feet. I hooked my arms around her knees and secured them to my body. If she wanted to act this way, she could deal with the consequences.

"Let me go!" she screamed in my ear, and I had to fight every instinct to dump her on the floor at my feet.

Elie was at my side in an instant.

"Lucien, don't do this. Please calm down and think it through."

He made no move to grab me, to get in front of me, or to stop me in any way.

"She wants to act like a prisoner, so I'm treating her like one."

I ignored the bite of pain in my shoulder when she hit it just right.

"I'm not acting like anything! You're the animal here. I'm not a bag of barley for you to just lug around. Put. Me. Down."

Her hand closed around one of my horns and she yanked my head to the side.

I let out a roar that reverberated through the entire castle, tearing her hand from my horn as I kicked the door to her room open. I dumped her on the thick down mattress and slammed the door shut behind me when I left, locking it from the outside and taking the key.

He leaned back against the wall, his arms folded over his chest, a displeased look on his face. I let loose a snarl and dragged my hands over my face. This was going *so* fucking well already.

"Good job, Luce. Way to win her over."

"Oh, like you could've done so much better in that situation," I growled, meeting his eyes as he leveled me with a stare.

Elie arched a brow, and a smug smirk inched the corner of his mouth up.

"I sure as hell wouldn't have fumbled it like you just did."

I ripped my claw through a tangle of matted fur on my head.

"I don't remember it ever being this hard."

"You're going to have to try a lot harder than that if you wanna get anywhere with her. Find out what she likes." He pushed off the wall. "I know it's not easy, but remember, it's not just you at stake here." He clapped a hand on my shoulder. "Maybe you should come back to training with me if you have such a hard time holding onto that temper of yours. At least you'd have an outlet again."

I damn well knew it wasn't just me on the line here. If I failed – gods – if I failed at this, everything would be lost. My fingers curled into fists, the claws digging deep into my palms as warm blood spilled between them and dripped onto the stone floor below. I didn't want to let them down, not again.

I swallowed hard. I was a fool. I thought I let go, thought the hope had withered and died but, just like a late blooming bud in spring, it refused to give up. My stomach roiled, and everything I had just eaten threatened to make a reappearance.

CHAPTER

SEVENTEEN

Arabelle

The mattress seemed content to swallow me whole as I struggled to get out of it and ran to the door. I yanked with all the strength I had. It was locked. I couldn't get out. My breath threatened to evaporate from my lungs if I didn't keep calm. Fear edged into my vision as I pounded on the door.

"Let me out! Please!"

I slammed my fists against the door until pain erupted in my hands. He couldn't lock me up in here. I wouldn't survive it. Desperation cleaved through me, ripping apart my steadfast will, my strength. It melted my anger into a puddle of fear and panic.

"Please, Lucien..." I hated the frailty clinging to my voice.

But there was no answer. I couldn't hold it back any longer. Anxiety coursed through me like lightning. The world spun, and oxygen fled from my lungs in rapid breaths. I sank to my knees and crawled to the bed, waiting for the attack to fade.

Walls weaved and swayed as I dug my fingers into the thick, soft blankets draped over the side of the bed. How could he lock me up like this? Nothing I said was a lie. I was his prisoner here.

Why couldn't he see that? I buried my face in the covers to slow the dizzying escape of air that made my head spin.

Once the world was no longer closing in on me, I pulled myself back into the bed and let oblivion sweep me under to a place far from here, from Lucien, from the castle, from everything I was.

I vaguely remembered the sound of the door opening and footsteps whispering across the stone floor, but didn't lift my head from the pillow, I didn't even crack my eyelids to see who it was. My stomach growled at the fragrant herbs and spiced meat, but I shoved it all down and ignored the part of me that begged to get up and eat.

How many times did the door open and close? I didn't count. A buzz in the back of my mind nudged me to just take one bite of food, and a sip of water, but I couldn't even bring myself to raise my head. It wasn't until the covers were ripped off of me and Elie stood at the foot of my bed that I tried.

"I know the situation is not...*ideal*...but you can't just lay in bed all day."

He clutched the comforter in his fist. His eyes burned into my flesh. I covered my face with my arm and twisted away.

"Get up, Belle." The tone left no room for arguing.

That wasn't going to stop me.

"No."

"You are not going to sit in here and waste away."

"And what would you have me do?" I snapped, shoving myself up to glare at him.

There was no anger in his expression. No annoyance or irritation. Only concern. A part of me softened.

"He locked me in here." The bite to my words died out somewhere along the way.

He sucked in a breath through his teeth.

"I'm sorry about that. He's got quite a temper. I'm trying to work with him on it, but it's not so easy." He eyed me. "Especially when you incite him like that."

I rolled my eyes and plopped back down onto the mattress.

"I've noticed."

"Will you at least eat something so I don't have to explain why there's a dead girl in the castle?" He tossed the covers back over the edge of the bed, out of my reach.

"Explain to who? I've seen no one else here." The place was empty save for the three of us.

"Touché. Then, for my own peace of mind," he said as he gripped the bedposts and leaned in. "Would it make a difference if I said 'please?'"

I couldn't fathom why he would care so much if I ate or not. We'd only shared only a handful of words.

"Do you really care if I do?"

"I care about how it will affect Lucien if you starve yourself on account of his rash decision-making."

Anger twisted in my gut, and I breathed it out in a slow exhale.

"It's all about Lucien with you, isn't it?"

"Yes. It is."

"Why?"

"Get over here and eat your lunch. Then I'll give you one of the many reasons why I care so much about him."

I held that vexing gaze of his, doubting that he would give me a simple, concrete answer to my question. If I didn't get up, he would just leave me to the torment that was my own mind in this haunting, quiet place. I got up and sat at the table.

"You should consider changing." He gestured to the red dress I still wore.

"Shut up."

My stomach deemed it necessary to imitate the sound of a dying animal the second the smells hit me. My cheeks heated, and I picked up the fork. I found those golden eyes again and never broke eye contact as I took a bite.

Elie's shoulders slumped, and he pulled out the chair next to me and sat.

"I told you before, I've been friends with Lucien since we were children. I've seen him lose a lot of people. I've seen him hurt in ways that would break most.

"And despite that, despite having every reason to hurt others, he never does. Not the innocent," he paused and ran a hand through his hair, "intentionally anyway."

The grimace on his face might have been intended as a smile. It was anything but.

"I know you see him as a monster," he continued. "One who's stolen your freedom. I don't know how to make you stop seeing him as that. But it isn't who he is. Not really."

"Why should I believe you?" I took another bite, and it took everything in me not to groan at the mix of garlic and onions. "Actions are what matters, not words. And his actions have spoken *very* loudly."

"That's fair. You don't have to believe me. But I will get him to let you out. And if you give him a chance, I think you'll come to understand that there's more to him than just what you see."

His lips tilted up, this time with a real smile.

I finished the meal and set my fork down. "I'm not inclined to give him a chance."

His eyes fell to my plate, then to my hand. His feline grin made me want to scratch his golden eyes out.

"I'll have to see what I can do about that. In the meantime, what can I do to make it more bearable for you in here?"

"Do you have any books?" Reading before bed was a ritual Isa and I had done since we learned how, and the few days without it left me with a hole in my chest.

"You like to read?" A flash of something lit up his eyes before he banked it.

"Yes. Is that a problem?"

"Not at all. I'll see what I can find in this dusty, old place."

He stood and gathered up the tray before leaving.

A trail of pale golden light snaked through the halls of the castle, casting no glow or shadows on the walls. I followed that line of gold as it led me up and up. A door creaked and swayed in a chilled breeze, leaving gooseflesh prickling my skin.

It was no longer the light I followed but a small voice whispering in my ear to see what was through the door. My stomach knotted and twisted with each step.

Moonlight gilded his pale blond hair in silver tonight as he leaned against the railing, back to me, and gazed out over the land. It tugged at a memory that wouldn't surface.

Dark clouds hung low in the night sky as a heart-rending backdrop to a sight that could have been from one of my romance books. Planters clung to the railings with anemones blooming inside. Humidity thickened the air; there would be a storm tonight.

The black of his clothes almost blended into the night, save for the dark red vest that hugged his waist. His long hair was pulled back into a low ponytail and sweat sheened off his neck.

When he turned his head at my approach, candlelight flitted off the rubies in his mask. Stepping closer, I could see more of him; the shirt rolled to his elbows to reveal corded muscle on his forearms and an unbuttoned collar.

My heart beat a thunderous rhythm while my hand shot to my chest to stop it from leaping out when those stormy blue eyes met mine. A buzz of lightning surged down the length of my spine and settled at the base of my tailbone. His beauty threatened to rob me of thought.

I tried to swallow in a rapidly drying throat. Heat rose up my neck and stretched along the edges of my ears.

Stop. I bit my lip, trying to regain that logical part of my brain that seemed to disappear every time he looked at me.

Who was he? And why did he keep showing up in my dreams? Perhaps it was out of loneliness that I summoned him or desperation for a savior from my current situation.

I wanted to speak, to say something – anything – but every word I'd ever learned eddied out of my head as he turned to face me.

"What are you doing up here?" It was all I could come up with.

His gaze swept out over the vast distance again.

"This is one of the places I can be alone. No one ever looks for me up here."

I followed that gaze and dared a step closer to the edge. This had to be one of the tallest towers in the castle to have such an unhindered and grand view.

"It's peaceful."

"Whenever my mind is a mess, I like to come up here and take in the beauty of the world." He rested both forearms on the railing again. "It puts things into perspective. Shows me what I need to do."

The cold railing bit into my palms when I stepped up beside him. "And what is it you need to do?"

Wind was my only answer as it whipped through my unbound

hair, danced with my night dress. I swallowed to calm the raging gallop of my heart. I'd be trembling if I didn't have a hold of the railing.

"I need to find a way to be free," he said at last.

"It's not that easy, is it?" I wanted to reach out and give him what small amount of comfort I could, but I refrained.

His mouth set in a straight line. "No, it's really not."

"If you figure it out, let me know. I'd like to be free myself."

I folded my arms over the railing and leaned onto them despite the screaming of my instincts. I tried to ignore the height.

"Maybe we can figure it out together." His eyes cut to mine, moonlight reflecting in a soft blue crescent.

The night faded into complete, utter blackness. I stepped back, stumbling over my own feet. Screams shattered the silence – men, women, children. Their fear permeated the air, soaking into me until tears dripped down my cheeks. I spun and reached into that darkness, but there was nothing.

"This is what awaits at the end." A disembodied voice spoke, void of warmth, of joy. It only held despair within it. And a cold so deep that I wasn't sure I had ever known what warmth was.

CHAPTER
EIGHTEEN

Arabelle

A cacophony of noise overwhelmed my senses in the ballroom, and I just wanted to escape it for a few minutes. What I didn't want was to get lost in this enormous castle that my mother dragged me to.

Every hall took me further and further from the chatter of courtiers and soft lilt of the orchestra playing in the background. Panic swirled in my head. How did I get back? Which way did I come from? I bit down on my lip until blood sprang up.

My slow stride turned quick until I ran down the dark, empty halls, the sound of my footsteps all that answered my calls for help. They would be so furious with me for going missing during this party – it was an event being hosted to introduce someone special, I couldn't remember who.

I looked behind door after door, yet there was no one who could help me. Mother and Father would leave me at the castle and go home. I was the difficult one. They'd be happy to be rid of me.

Tears welled in my eyes and blurred my vision as I sank to the cold floor. I gave up fighting the sobs tearing up my throat, leaving behind a dull ache.

"Someone please help me," I cried into the void of darkness.

And, as if it heard me, the void answered back.

A small hand appeared from beside me. I wiped my eyes with the cuffs of the dress Mother had to fight me into and looked up at the blond boy.

"You're here for the ball, right? I'll take you back."

Golden light surrounded him as if God himself sent me an angel to guide me home.

I took his hand, and he pulled me back to my feet. "You know the way?"

"We'll find our way together."

I blinked my eyes open, a sliver of light glinting off something golden on the bedside table. I didn't leave anything there when I went to bed last night. I sat up and leaned on my elbow, my fingers grazing the chain until I managed to grab it.

It was a locket. On the front, a tiny dragon roared, breathing fire. In its mouth was a ruby, and the flames bellowed from it, inlaid along the sides. I clicked the latch, and it opened.

There were two portraits on the inside of two blond boys. The one on the left was older, his features already losing the soft edges of youth. My breath caught in my lungs. He could almost pass for the man in my dream if it weren't for the too-yellow hair and missing bits of gold in his eyes.

My gaze shifted to the one on the right, a younger boy by maybe a few years. They must have been brothers. Who were they? And where did this locket come from? I scanned the room; nothing was out of place.

My eyes fell back to the portraits in the locket. Did Lucien have others imprisoned in the castle, too? I couldn't be the only one. The man that kept showing up in my dreams, he could be Lucien's prisoner, too.

"I have to find him." And anyone else that could be here and free all of them. Once I did that, we could all escape together.

Elie might have claimed no one else lived in the castle, but would he be honest with me if they held people captive? I doubted it.

A steady rap came at the door, and I put the locket around my neck, tucking it under the night dress.

Every day, Elie brought me a new book with breakfast; much to my surprise, they were always romance. He didn't seem the type to read romance, but then again, maybe he just assumed I was. I wasn't sure where he dug them up, but he had a new one for me each time. I devoured them one after another, sometimes staying up late into the night.

After the first few days, he asked about the peppermint scent clinging to me, and I told him about the fire and the burns to my hands. The next day, he'd brought me another tin of salve. *My own special healing salve.* I took it and was shocked that it did more for the pain than the one the doctor gave me. Even the scars seemed to fade after only a few days of use.

I'd have to get him to show me how he did it.

He sat with his elbow propped on the table, cheek in his hand as he watched me. I squirmed in my chair until I just couldn't take the staring anymore.

"What?"

"Nothing. Just wondering who this young woman in front of me is."

"I told you my name." There wasn't much more to know than that, not anymore.

"I don't mean just your name." He dropped his hand to the

table and straightened. "I told you something about myself. It's your turn to tell me something about you."

I raised a brow at him and set my spoon down next to the empty bowl.

"Like what?"

He tapped his fingers against the table and hummed. "Tell me about your family. Are they not worried you're here?"

I sank my teeth into my bottom lip. Elie had shown me nothing but kindness and a dash of playfulness since I got here. We had had a pleasant enough relationship, but to open up about my family…I wasn't sure that was something I could do with him. I could tell him a little, though.

"There's not much to say about them. It's just me, my sister, Isa, and our father. She's probably worried. My father, though?" After he insisted on the marriage to Louis, I disobeyed him. "I'd wager he is furious."

His fingers stopped their drumming, and his eyes hardened.

"Lucien told me about his deal with your father. How selfish can you be to do that to your child?" His words were a hiss through his teeth.

I shrugged a shoulder and slumped back into my chair. "That's the kind of man he is. He'd sell either or both of us to get what he wants. He brokered a marriage deal between me and a man in town with an awful reputation. A nasty rumor went around a few years ago. One that I now suspect might be true."

Nausea gripped my insides every time I thought about how Louis's first wife must have suffered.

"He only did it to regain some of his lost social standing."

Elie's stillness was preternatural. If I hadn't just been speaking with him, I'd think he was a statue.

"Your father wanted you to marry a man with a such bad reputation that it spawned such rumors?" Elie's rage was a different type of anger than Lucien's, and it was far more terrifying.

His words sent a rush of chill bumps over my flesh, and I locked my muscles so I wouldn't shiver.

"Yes, he did, but I doubt Lucien will let me leave to get married." My gratitude for it was a secret I'd keep forever.

"Do you want to marry that man?" He kept his voice calm and his tone neutral despite the anger radiating off him.

Hesitation trapped my words in my mouth. It shouldn't be hard to say. I was prepared to marry Louis for Isa's sake. But...

"No. I just wanted to keep my sister safe."

He draped his forearm over the arm of his chair and leaned back. I couldn't help but notice the easy grace with which he moved.

"I'm a bit familiar with arranged marriages myself. I've been in one since before I was born." He must have read the question in my eyes because he continued, "It's a tradition of my people. When my father retires, his title passes to me, and I'll be required to marry."

The smile on his lips didn't come close to lighting up the gold in his eyes. No, they were filled with a far-reaching sadness that I couldn't understand.

"You don't seem too happy about it."

He grimaced again, twisting his mouth to the side. "She's a nice girl and all, but not exactly what I want in a partner."

"You can't say something about it? Request someone else?"

Arranged marriages weren't unheard of. In fact, they were pretty standard, especially for those born into noble houses. But I'd never heard of one being arranged before a child was born. Even the highest of lords waited some time before betrothing their children.

He shifted in his seat and leaned forward, resting his forearms on the table.

"Aren't you worried your father will force Isa to take your place in the marriage agreement with this man?"

I noted that this subject caused him enough discomfort to swing the conversation back to me. I wouldn't push him on it, not when he looked ready to climb out of his skin.

"No. She isn't what he's looking for. He wants me, specifically."

He arched a beautifully groomed, crimson brow. "Why?"

I shrugged, even though I was sure I knew exactly what he wanted with me. "He sees me as a trophy. A challenge for him to conquer. He doesn't care about what I want or how I feel."

He laced his fingers together, and I could almost hear the bones groaning as his knuckles turned white.

"If that's the case, you can rest easy here. I won't let him come anywhere near you."

I looked him up and down, really looked at him. He was slender, even if I could make out every cut muscle underneath his clothes. Louis would snap him in two if he ever made it here. I shoved the thought out of my head.

"Can I expect to see anyone else at the castle?"

His eyes cut to mine, and I swallowed.

"If you see anyone else, you run. You come find me or Lucien. I don't care where we are or what we're doing."

What an odd command to make. This was a castle, it required more than just a few people to even keep it functional. Granted, from what little I had seen, it didn't seem like it was functioning at all.

"Are other people not allowed here?"

"It's not..." He sighed, a frustrated sound. "Look, Belle. There are things I just can't tell you." He kept his gaze on the table ahead of him.

"How can I be okay here? How can I survive here if you won't give me the information necessary to do so?" This was absurd.

Was it Lucien? Did he forbid him from saying anything? "Just tell me what could harm me. Please, Elie."

He scrubbed his hands over his cheeks and growled deep in his chest.

"Nothing will harm you. I've taken care of the Marid problem—"

"Marid? What is that?"

"Fuck." He raked his hand through his fiery hair and slammed it back down on the table. "I didn't mean to say it."

"What is a Marid?" I pushed as an ache formed at the center of my forehead. I ignored it and placed my hand on top of his. "Please tell me."

He removed his hand from mine and pressed his thumbs into either side of his forehead, then dropped his hands to look me in the eye.

"The Marid are a type of...people...from Ashea. They claim to be seers, but they give out false predictions and just cause general strife wherever they go. But don't worry – Belle, you're bleeding." He shot to his feet and reached for me.

Everything was a blur as my body swayed forward. I barely registered Elie's arms around me when my vision went black.

Lucien

Elie burst through my bedroom doors, panting with sweat dripping down the sides of his face and neck. I was on my feet in an instant, ready to eliminate whatever threat drove him to run down the halls of the castle.

"What's wrong?" The panic in his eyes twisted my insides in a sense of dread until I had to swallow the vomit surging up my throat.

"It's Belle..." He stopped, dragging in one long breath and forcing it out through his mouth. "She passed out."

That dread of moments before grew into full-blown terror. Was it my fault? I forced her to stay in that room. What if she was sick? The world swayed, and I didn't realize I was moving until Elie grabbed my arm.

"Where are you going?" His fingers dug into my forearm to the point of pain, holding me in place.

"Is she alright? What happened? She's not..." The words dried up on my tongue. "Is she sick?" If I'd done what my father had, I deserved my fate at the end of this curse.

Elie wouldn't let go of my arm, even when I tried to jerk it from his grasp. I needed to go to her and ensure she was alright – see it with my own eyes.

"I can see where your mind is going, Lucien. This is *not* that."

He stepped under my gaze and held it until my muscles relaxed.

"You are not your father, and she is not your mother." His grip loosened. "She's alright, just resting now."

I ripped my arm away from him and splayed it out to my side. "Then tell me what happened."

A thread of ease beckoned me to listen to him. I ignored it. His lips set in a line, and he stepped back.

"We were talking, and she suddenly got a nosebleed, and then she passed out."

"What were you talking about?"

He ran rough hands over his cheeks and dropped his gaze.

"I brought up the Marid." A vein throbbed in his neck. "I didn't mean to; it just slipped out."

"And?"

She wouldn't have known of them, not in her current state. It's not like I could blame Elie when those shits kept trespassing.

"She asked what they were, and as I was explaining it, her nose started bleeding." He hesitated again, eyebrows bunching together.

"Lucien, I don't think we can tell her about our world. Not without serious repercussions." His golden eyes shimmered with fear in a way I hadn't seen since the day I pulled him from the dungeon. "I think the *other* curse will kill her if we do."

My inhalation was sharp and painful. "How deep do you think it goes? If just mentioning Marid..."

Fuck. I raked my claws through my fur. What could we tell her? What could we say without fear of killing her out of sheer recklessness? Cold iron wrapped itself around my heart and squeezed. I would kill Aamon for this if I made it out alive.

"How can I get her to accept me if I can't even show her the truth of our world?"

"I don't know, Luce. I think it's okay to tell her about our personal histories as long as we leave out *what* we are. And nothing about the history of our people."

He stared at a spot on the wall so intently his gaze might have burned a hole in it.

"I told her about some of my past and she was okay, so just stick to yourself. Should be easy enough for you." His dry laugh lacked any humor. "Just pretend you're a human and go from there."

I snorted and rolled my eyes at that comment.

"How the hells am I supposed to know what humans do?"

As if being cursed into this body didn't make everything harder, now I was supposed to pretend I was human? How preposterous.

Elie finally broke his solemnness with a smirk.

"You have all those books in the library. Why don't you try reading one of the romances?" The look he gave me set my blood to boiling. "You might learn a thing or two."

"Do you really think that *I* need to learn a thing or two from some *romance* book?" It was an even more ridiculous suggestion than pretending I was human.

"I can give you some of Belle's favorites."

I was going to punch him. My muscles itched to do it. Between his teasing and my irritation, I barely noticed when the weight of guilt lifted off my chest and allowed me to breathe easy for the first time since he barged in here. It was his specialty.

No matter the situation, whether he was rescuing me from the cruel hands of my father or helping me escape a lover's husband, he always knew exactly what to say.

I stared at my door, every instinct screaming at me to go check on Arabelle. But what could I do for her right now? With everything that had transpired, I was probably the last person she wanted to see.

CHAPTER
TWENTY

Arabelle

Seven women gathered around a pile of burning embers, the glow a deep purple, coloring their faces in eerie shadows. Their mouths moved, but I could hear no sound save for the soft crackling of the burned-out wood pile.

As they spoke to one another, a creeping darkness prowled around the edges of their circle, whispering to them, "Kill, destroy, take what should've been yours."

Cold sweat dripped down my face, my arms, my back. The darkness had no form, no features, it was only a mass of malice and hatred seeking to rob the world of life.

It paused its circling, and even though that thing didn't have eyes, or a face, or even a head, it looked right at me.

My breath clouded in front of me, the darkness slithering around the women, rubbing up against them like a cat. It worked its way toward me.

Closer and closer it came. There was no escaping it.

Golden light wrapped around me, shielding me when the darkness lashed out. The voice shrieked at the denied kill as I was whisked away.

I doubled over, dry heaving because there was nothing in my stomach to empty.

"What was that?"

A gentle hand rubbed my back, but I could not see her through the brilliance of all the shining gold.

"They fell prey to the promises of the darkness. Don't make the same mistakes when it comes for you. Let the light of hope guide you."

And just like before, she was gone.

Searing pain blanketed my mind for a full day after I passed out, and Elie hadn't stayed to talk since. Every time he looked at me, his eyes dulled with a heavy guilt. It wasn't his fault, but for some reason, he seemed to think so. It made time pass at a torturous pace.

It had been two weeks, and Lucien still kept me locked in this god forsaken room. Elie continued to bring me meals and books, but I was bored.

I pulled everything from the wardrobe and went through the assortment of clothes. I rooted around in the drawers on the vanity and dresser. Nothing could sustain my focus for long.

Even the books Elie showed up with grew old after a few hours. Being cooped up in this room, even if it was twice the size of the cottage, left me seething and ready to tear the walls down.

"At least it's not a cell," Elie had said during one of his visits.

Maybe I went too far. Lucien did try to show me a little consideration that morning, but my anger flared at it. Not even twelve hours prior, he threatened me with violence. I groaned my frustration at the window, pressing my forehead to the glass as I stared out.

I want out of this room.

A knock rapped on the door. The regularity of Elie's visits kept me grounded; they were precisely at the same time every day. The lock clicked, and he greeted me with an apologetic smile as he opened the door and carried the tray in.

He set it on the small table by the window and turned to leave, but I reached for him, pulling my hand back at the last second. He hadn't stayed to talk to me since the night I passed out after he told me about the Marid.

"Wait." The word slipped out before I could stop it.

He heeded my request, turning those striking golden eyes on me.

"Yes?" His voice was softer than it had been that first day.

"Please stay," I blurted. God, I felt pathetic asking it of him. "I...miss having someone to talk to."

He arched one of his immaculate eyebrows at me, the corner of his mouth twitching in what could be a grin if he let it slip.

"I didn't realize you missed me so much."

I cast my gaze aside, pressing my lips in a thin line.

"I never said I missed *you*. But you are better than the alternative." Lucien was the last person I wanted to talk to right now. Not after he'd locked me in here.

"Would talking to him be so bad?"

Elie strolled to one of the chairs next to the table and sat. I joined him, the mouthwatering smell of eggs and bacon and citrusy juice making my stomach announce its hunger in a strangled gurgle.

"He's awful."

"He can be. But you haven't exactly given him a chance to be anything else."

My eyes shot to his before I picked up a piece of bacon and, with a little more aggression than needed, snapped my teeth shut on it.

"He forced me to come here because of something my father did. He's keeping me locked in my room. Why should I give him a chance?"

I didn't miss the twitch of his fingers or the narrowing of his brows. I picked up the cup of orange juice and lifted it to my nose, breathing in the sweet, tangy goodness. I took a sip, watching him just over the rim.

"You did choose to come here. And him locking you in your room...that was an overreaction on his part. He's not necessarily good at being around other people anymore."

I snorted and dug into the eggs. "You make it sound like he was at some point."

The spices made my taste buds sing their approval, and I fought back the groan that wanted to erupt from my lips.

"Oh, he was. He used to have everyone willing to fall to their knees and worship him. But things happened. And now we're here."

He watched me eat, and a kernel of self-consciousness took root. I set the fork down.

"What happened?"

I only knew of one thing that could change a person like that. Pain. Memories of my own hurt flooded back in waves – first my mother, then my siblings. Louis flashed before my eyes, that day he struck me when I fled into the forest with Isa.

"A lot of things have happened. Most of which are his story to tell you when he's ready. Just...trust me. He's worth knowing. I think you'd feel differently about him if you did."

Sadness glinted in his eyes before he masked it with that calm smugness he was so good at portraying.

I shifted in my seat, studying the contents of my plate. Elie was trying to open my mind to his friend. It bothered him, the way I spoke of Lucien.

"Tell me something about him."

"Like what?"

"I don't know, something that proves he's not just some monster locking young women in a castle."

Show me that I can survive here was what I didn't want to say.

Elie leaned his head back and scrubbed at the stubble on his cheeks. He dragged a deep breath in through his mouth and exhaled through his nose, eyes coming back to mine.

"There was a time when I did...something...that resulted in me being locked in the dungeon. Lucien argued and stood up for me, but when that didn't work, he broke me out. Said if anyone had a problem with it, they could take it up with the point of his sword."

It was my turn to lift a brow. I tucked away the tidbit of knowledge: they hadn't always been alone here.

"What did you do?" I knew the laws of the land, but this place somehow seemed outside of them. If he was locked in the dungeon, it must have been serious.

He laughed a humorless laugh and rubbed at the back of his neck, eyes falling to the table before closing. "I may have assaulted the king."

I tilted my head with an arched brow. "Why?" I was surprised he was still breathing after something like that. Who the hell was Lucien, if he could break Elie out of the dungeon with the mere threat of violence? I swallowed.

There hadn't been a king in Grienia for a long time, but exactly how long slipped from my mind like grains of salt through my fingers. Elie wasn't much older than me. If he told the truth, maybe I stepped through more than a gate. Maybe even a portal to another world.

This time it was anger flaring in his eyes, turning the gold molten. I could have sworn flames rippled off his pale skin. "He hurt someone I care a great deal for." He shoved a hand through his hair, schooling his features into calmness again.

"Anyway, Lucien saved me at the risk of his own life then." He gave me a wry grin. "So, does that change your perception of him just a little?"

Lucien was willing to sacrifice himself for his friend. Was he so different from me then? Maybe I *was* a little harsh with him. "Was he always..." I didn't know how to word the question so it didn't sound rude. I gestured to my face, hoping he understood what I meant.

"No. He was like us once." He leaned back in the chair with a sigh. "But, again, this is a discussion you should have with him. When he's ready."

If he was once human, then what had happened to turn him into a beast? Elie wouldn't answer any more questions, and I wasn't sure I wanted to ask Lucien.

"How can I have the conversation with him if he's locked me in here?" I shot back at him, a little venom in my voice.

He winced. "I'm sorry about that. I'll talk to him." Elie's head fell back against the top of the chair, the knot in his throat working as he swallowed. "He's got quite the stubborn streak. And a hell of a temper."

"I'm aware."

He leaned up and smirked at me. "You seem to bring it out of him with such ease." He leaned forward, placing his forearms on the table and lacing his fingers together. "I'll work with him on it if you'll give him the chance to make it up to you."

I leaned in and mimicked his stance. "I'll give him a chance if you tell me more about this place and your past."

We both sat, staring at each other for minutes, waiting to see who'd break first. "Deal. I'll give you one piece of history for every day you spend with him."

That wasn't much to get out of any deal. I narrowed my eyes at him as I frowned. "That's not much. I want at least three." I folded my arms across my chest, until I noticed the dip in his gaze. I dropped my hands in my lap.

"One is plenty enough."

I studied him, the sharp angle of his jaw, the way his hair framed his face, the perfectly arched eyebrows, and the golden eyes that were dancing with amusement. "Fine."

"Great. I'll start tomorrow." He stood and walked to the door. "Good talk, Belle." The lock clicked, and once again, I was trapped in this room.

TWENTY-ONE

Lucien

I didn't leave my room in the weeks that I ordered Arabelle locked in hers, be it a punishment to myself for losing my cool so easily or, as Elie liked to chide me, to sulk. I stared at the rose garden that had been there since before I was born. My mother was the one who planted it.

You have no hope of breaking the curse if you won't even let her out of her room. You don't have the luxury to be this stubborn. Elie spoke on Arabelle's behalf every day when he brought me food, begging me to let her out, reminding me this wasn't going to help anything.

I won't change my mind, Elie. Stop bringing it up. It always ended up with me snapping at him.

I was sure today would be no different.

A knock echoed in the silent room, the door creaking open seconds later as footsteps sounded from behind me. The aroma of honeyed ham overpowered the rest of the food Elie brought me for lunch. I glanced over my shoulder at the sound of wood scraping against metal to see him sliding the tray onto the table.

"Are you still intent on being an ass?" Elie asked.

"If your question is whether or not I've changed my mind about keeping her in her room, the answer is no." I turned back to the window.

"Luce, you can't keep this up. If you don't let her out, you'll ruin any chance of winning her over."

"Me? She's the one acting as if I've done some awful thing to her." When I huffed, a cloud of dust billowed up around the window.

"To her, you have. You didn't even give her time to adjust. How would you feel if someone peeled you away from your home? Your family? And demanded you live with them somewhere completely new?"

"This isn't about me." I hated when he tried to spin things like that, bring my feelings into it.

"But it is," he paused, "what is it about her that has you so on edge? I haven't seen your temper this bad since—"

"I'm not on edge." I snapped, whirling on him. "Do I look like I'm affected by her in the least?" I bristled at the implication. She was difficult and stubborn, not at all like the women I'd been with in the past. Her words, the looks she gave me, they burrowed under my skin and set my temper to flame before I could manage to drown it.

"Yes." There was no hesitation, no falter in Elie's voice when he spoke, and it pissed me off.

Red lined the edges of my vision. "Let me assure you, I am not." Every word was slow and deliberate.

"Then let her out of her room. Show her you're not her jailor." He folded his arms over his chest. "I know you still have it in you to be compassionate."

His words grated on the fraying ends of my nerves, and I wanted to throw him from this window, but I breathed instead. "Compassion has gotten me nowhere in life."

"Well, that's blatantly wrong." A smirk tugged the corner of his mouth up. "Otherwise, we wouldn't be friends."

I rolled my eyes and strode to the table, picking up the fork, and stabbing it into a slice of ham. "We're friends because your father ordered it." I stuck the whole piece in my mouth, the morsel singing to my tongue in an array of sweet and savory flavors. "Also, there was no one else for you to talk with back then."

Elie tipped his head back and laughed, the sound earning a grin from me. Things were tense between us since that first morning, more my fault than his. A weight that settled on my chest weeks ago finally eased off.

"There's some truth to that. But I made my own decision to be your friend. After seeing you stand up to your uncle for that serving girl, I knew I made the right call." His grin didn't waver.

"My uncle was as much an ass as my father. And he deserved that punch." Even if I had gotten a good tongue lashing from my mother afterward, it was worth it.

"See? You've got good in you." I didn't notice Elie move until his finger jabbed me in the chest.

"I have my days."

Elie stared up at me for an eternity of a moment before speaking. "I told her about the day you pulled me out of the dungeon."

My body went rigid. "Elie." That time wasn't something I enjoyed talking about, not even to Elie, who'd been the one I broke every rule for.

"Relax. I didn't give her a lot of details. Just enough to prove you're not some monster keeping her locked up in here. I told her how you stood up for me, broke me out, and threatened anyone who tried to put me back in there." Elie shifted, stepping back. "The rest is up to you to share with her if you want. It's not my story to tell."

My shoulders slumped in relief. "Part of it is." I forced the memories back into the deepest recesses of my mind. I didn't want to think about them, not ever.

His eyes darkened with the same memories that were clawing at the back of my mind to come out and play. "Telling her any of that is your choice, Lucien. If you do, and she decides she wants my side, I'll gladly give it to her. But not until you tell her yours." He tore his eyes from me. "I just... I can't stand seeing her think of you as a monster."

"She's not wrong though." I gestured to my face and general appearance. "I am one." My hand dropped back to my side.

"You're not. It's the curse." He gave me a contemplative smile. "And maybe that temper of yours. You should come back to training, blow off some steam."

I heaved a sigh. Not this again. "I already told you; I'm not going."

"Afraid I'm gonna hand your ass to you? What's it been, Luce? Nineteen years and then some?"

"Like hell you'll beat me." I couldn't tell him I was afraid. Right after the change, I'd attacked my father because of how he spoke to me. I cringed at the bloody memory.

I never would have raised a hand toward him under normal circumstances – it was punishable by death, even for me – but when I became a beast, my anger took on a life of its own.

And I unleashed it on the man who took everything from me. Everything I became was his fault. I would rather die than let that loose on Elie. Training with him in this form was out of the question.

"Prove it."

"I don't need to." I stepped back and ate another slice of ham. "I'll consider letting her out." That should get him to shut up for now.

He blinked wide eyes at me and, for a second, I wondered if he heard me. A smile split his face. "I'll drop the subject of training if you agree to try harder with Belle."

Belle? Did she allow him to call her that? Or was it just Elie being...well...Elie? I rolled the name around in my mind. "I don't think she wants to be around me."

"All I'm asking is that you try. Reach out to her until she reaches back."

"And what if she never does?"

"She will."

"How can you have so much confidence?" I lost all of mine the night I became a beast.

Elie just shrugged and walked toward the door. "I have faith in you. In the person you are underneath all the fur, claws, and fangs."

TWENTY-TWO

Arabelle

Warmth enveloped me from head to toe in a summer's embrace as I sat on a bench in one of the castle gardens. A wall of stone rose up on one side stretching toward the near cloudless sky. Dark pink Nerines bloomed all around me, their thin petals swaying in a gentle breeze.

I wore the same dress I did that first morning. Instead of my hair being pinned up or braided in my usual style, it hung loosely around my waist. I hated how the dress made me look like my mother. I could also do without it pushing out my chest like a display for anyone who looked my way.

My eyes dropped to my lap and the weight there. A book lay open and face down over a thigh. I scanned the silver inlaid letters on the cover. It was the same one that Elie brought me that night with dinner. He promised that Lucien was considering letting me out of my room.

I hated the wait. Waiting to see if he'd let me out, waiting for him to show any kind of compassion.

The crunch of boots on rocks snapped my gaze up to the approaching figure, a sweeping relief taking over me at the familiar golden locks and blue eyes. He still wore that mask over his features.

His throat bobbed as his gaze moved down my body and back up again, lingering in the spots where my dress fit snug against my curves.

"What are you doing here?" Gooseflesh rose on my skin at that deep timbre, my blood heating from the way his eyes devoured me.

I glanced down at my book then back up to him. He wore a black, cinched vest over a white linen shirt with the cuffs rolled up his forearms. His black pants showed off every beautifully carved muscle in his thighs and calves. His boots rose midway between his ankles and knees, the silver buckles shining in the sunlight. I clutched the book in my hands as I released a breath.

"The day was too beautiful to stay cooped up in the castle, so I wanted to come read in the garden," I said, hoping that my voice didn't betray any of the fire surging through my veins at the sight of him.

He was too damn beautiful.

His striking eyes fell to the book in my hands. "What are you reading?" He moved to take a step forward but seemed to restrain himself.

"It's a story about a fallen prince who reclaims his kingdom. Though he did have to sacrifice the one he loved. It was sad. They went through so much, yet he still couldn't have both." I ran my thumb over the spine of the book.

"Do you like those kinds of stories?" he asked with a genuine curiosity that made warmth bloom in my chest.

"I do. But I prefer the ones where the lovers end up together." I smiled to myself as I looked back over the words on the pages. "What I wouldn't give to experience a love like that."

He shifted from one foot to the other. "Have you never experienced it before?"

"Love?" My eyes met his, and he gave me a quick nod. "No, I haven't." I closed the book on my lap.

"Why not?"

It was my turn to squirm under his gaze. "It was never in the cards for me. My lot in life was to marry whoever my father chose for me." My fingers tightened around the spine of the book. "For a woman, falling in love means losing the freedom to live how they want."

"Was..." The word rolled off his tongue, and this time, he did take a step. "But not anymore. You can choose yourself." He took another. "Falling in love will not cost you that freedom."

My eyes fell from his as I stared at the rocks under his feet. "I'm not sure I have any more of a choice now than I did then. Not when I'm trapped in this castle."

"You do have a choice. You'll always have a choice under this roof." He pointed to the castle. "You will never be forced to do anything."

"Except stay here."

His lips were set in a line. "Do you...hate it here?" The question caught me off-guard, and I wasn't quite sure how to answer it. The castle was huge and the comforts grander than anything I could have dreamed of.

But I could see none of it, experience none of it from the confines of my room. If it weren't for Elie's visits, I might have succumbed to the depths of loneliness.

"I... I don't know. I haven't been given the chance to see any of it. Lucien locked me in my room." My fingers tightened on the book. "I hate being trapped." My voice was barely more than a whisper.

Rocks crunched and he claimed the space next to me on the bench. His thumb and forefinger tugged my chin up so our eyes met. My stomach did backflips off a fucking cliff at that touch.

"I'm sorry, Belle. I know how it is to be...trapped." He brushed a stray strand of hair from my face.

I studied his eyes. The blue wasn't just one color, but many shades. The gold rimmed both his pupil and the outer edge of his iris – not as brilliant as Elie's gold, but a soft, gentle gold that stood out against the all blues. "How do I find you?" I breathed the words out, still lost in his gaze.

He dropped his hands into his lap. "You have to look deeper, Belle. Don't be fooled by what you see." The breath of every word left me yearning for just another touch, but just like before, he was ripped away from me.

The shrill chirp of birds yanked me from the dream before I could taste him, and I growled my frustration into the shadowed room. The heat of his hands still warmed my cheeks as I brought my own hands up to replace his. Warmth still lingered after being so crudely ripped away with sudden consciousness.

I squeezed my eyes shut and tried to force myself back to sleep, back to the beautiful man, but it was useless. I let out an irritated sigh and rolled out of bed, my night dress falling down to my knees in a swoosh of fabric.

"Another day of sitting in here, doing absolutely nothing," I said to no one and ignored the wardrobe. There was no point in getting dressed if I was locked in here. I bathed, applied the healing salve to my scars, and pulled on a clean robe as a soft knock sounded at the door.

After the lock clicked, Elie opened the door and stepped in with the familiar tray of food, but I noticed the lack of a book. Weeks of him bringing me one or two books a day and now he didn't have one. Did I say something wrong? Do something wrong? I chewed my lip. "Are you angry with me?"

He lifted a brow at the question. "Sorry?"

It was a break in our ritual, one that left a little twinge of hope sprouting in my chest. I reined it in. I couldn't let it blossom only to have it destroyed. "You didn't bring me a book today. You can't mean to tell me I've read them all." I pointed to the empty space on the tray.

"Oh. No, I'm not angry," he said with a chuckle. "I figured you wouldn't need it. Since Lucien decided that you don't have to stay in here anymore."

"He did?" A wave of excitement crashed through me, and I fought to keep it from showing on my face.

"He did. Try not to piss him off like that again." He gave me a wry smile and set the tray on the table. "I'll leave you to your meal." He turned to the door.

"Am I...still expected to have meals with him?"

Elie glanced back at me over his shoulder and gave a simple, "Yes," before he was through the door and gone.

Without locking me inside.

This was my chance. I could finally look for the beautiful man from my dreams. I dug into my breakfast and gulped down the juice, leaving the empty dishes on the tray when I finished. When I found him, we'd both escape this place.

Lucien let me out.

I couldn't fight the smile as I dressed in a fine, navy dress, with black trim around the seams. The wide neckline scooped down low enough to show the swell of my breasts. I braided my hair and let it hang loose over my shoulder, tying the end with a piece of ribbon. I slipped on a pair of flats and breezed out of the door without so much as looking back.

The everyday, simple gowns I wore now were far more extravagant than some of my best dresses from before we lost our fortune. They were made of rare and exotic fabrics; some were even in the styles of lands I'd never visited. The elegance wasn't something I enjoyed, but the comfort – that was what I really appreciated.

Everything fit and moved with my body like it was an extension of me. Even the shoes cradled my feet just right. If I didn't think better of it, I might have wondered if everything in the wardrobe were made with me in mind.

Fire danced in a soft glow inside the crystal sconces lining the stone walls, flickering to life as I passed by and dimming when I was a good twenty paces past them.

The normal rush of panic that dragged me under when I was near fire was somehow missing with these flames. It was a mystery I didn't need solving. Or perhaps I was letting go of some of the terror that gripped me from that night. I continued to follow the path the lights led me, as if they wanted to take me somewhere specific.

I couldn't help but notice the once crumbling floors and walls were somehow repaired during my time locked in the room. Did Lucien have stonemasons come into the castle and fix it? But it was done too quick for the extensive damage. Even the dust and dirt in the corners were missing.

The next hall I turned down was laden with windows that reached for the ceiling, the sun shining through clear, clean glass and lighting up the stone hallway. The golden candelabras caught the beams blazing through the windows and reflected long arcs of gold onto the stone. Yet the little fires still blazed to life, and I followed to sate my curiosity.

I stopped in front of a door at the end of the hall and pushed it open, sliding inside a dusty storage room. "I guess they haven't gotten to all of the castle yet," I said as I waved a hand in front of my face to shoo the dust away. I squinted, trying to see through the dimness until I spotted a window on the far side.

It smelled of old stone and a tang of something metallic – iron maybe. I had to step over objects strewn about the floor, move around stacks of forgotten crates, careful with each step I took. The last thing I wanted was to break an ankle or end up trapped somewhere. I'd starve to death before they ever found me.

Metal creaked in resistance when I pushed on it, refusing to give way. Was it stuck? I moved my foot back to better leverage myself and gave the frame another hard shove, a loud groan signaling my victory.

Something jutted out from behind a chair, covered by a sheet of white cloth. My fingers danced over the top of it, and I pulled the heavy object out, the sheet falling away. Although the faces were a bit hard to make out in the limited lighting, especially with the film of residue covering it, I could recognize the similarities in them.

It was a family portrait. A blond-haired man with a ruby-encrusted crown on his head, a blonde woman with a matching tiara, and two young boys. Both blond with stunning blue eyes – the same boys from the locket.

A strange sort of familiarity draped over my mind as I studied the family. Maybe they lived here before Lucien came and took over the castle. Their names were on the tip of my tongue, but I couldn't grasp them.

I turned and fled from a memory that wouldn't form.

The sconces outside the storage room led me toward a narrower hall and staircase. This castle was enormous, and there were so many places to search for a captive. I blew out a steadying breath and took my skirt in hand before climbing the small stairs.

I used the wall to help ground myself as the stone threatened to close in around me. I wasn't trapped, there was a way out.

A rush of relief nearly took me to my knees when my feet landed on the top step, the hall beyond opening up. If I didn't master this fear soon enough, it would suffocate me in a sea of my own terror.

The first door I came to was cracked open; only a sliver and the flames seemed to beckon me inside. The hinges creaked when I pushed it open.

Shelves lined the walls, holding what looked to be leather-bound books. Hundreds of them. A desk sat in the middle of the room, parchment stacked in a neat pile on one side. An old oil lantern sat on the other.

I slipped inside and pushed the door back into its original position. Was this some kind of study? Lucien didn't seem the type to keep such records, so it must have been Elie's. I plucked one of the books off the shelf and flipped it open.

Reading over the tidy, small handwriting, I realized that it was a journal. I pulled another one down and skimmed the pages. It was a detailed account of the daily activities of the royal guard. If this was a record of castle security, then the prison records must be in here somewhere.

I turned the book over in my hand but there was no title scrawled on it, not even on the inside cover or first page. Only dates.

He had to be a recent acquirement, which meant that Elie would keep the records somewhere close, right? I had no idea when the boys could have been taken. Those paintings looked only a few years old, but that just meant that the owner of the locket took care of it.

I placed both books back onto the shelf and moved to the desk. I nodded to myself to quell the rising unease in my blood.

The parchments were all blank. The drawers were empty. I couldn't find a scrape of information about any prisoner, or even where they might keep them if they had them. Where else might they keep those kinds of records? In Lucien's room? Elie's?

This was all assuming he was even real. That any of them were real and still alive. Unease slithered through my veins like a serpent, and I shoved the thoughts out of my head.

I raked my fingers through my hair until they caught in my

braid. I wasn't mistaken. I refused to believe it; a persistent voice in the back of my head refused.

How long had they kept them locked up? Where did they keep them? The castle dungeon seemed the likeliest of places, but where was it? I had so many questions and not a single person I could ask.

Unless I could figure out a way to ask them without raising suspicion. I could ask for one of them to show me around. I stood from the worn leather chair.

It was settled.

Whoever I ran into next, I would get them to tell me.

Room after room had doors splayed, revealing empty spaces, save for the sunlight glinting off dust. Except for the last one I came to.

It was far from the elegance of the room I stayed in, and others I'd seen on that floor, with only a single bookshelf on one side, an ornate rug, and a simple wooden chair and table set.

And Lucien.

Breath froze in my lungs at the sight of him. His gilded fur and horns made him look more like a majestic protector than some wild animal. I knew from the moment I met him he wasn't the monster my father claimed, even if the last time we spoke to each other he decided to imprison me in my room.

Anger warmed my cheeks, and I moved to turn around until my eyes fell on what he had in his lap. The tome was worn, the pages cracked at the edges, and the cover half fallen off.

He glanced up, doing a double take when he saw me. Our

gazes slammed into each other in a silent collision. "What are you doing up here?"

"You like to read?" Of course he did; if not, he wouldn't be up here with a book. I could have turned and ran right then.

He didn't frown, didn't roll his eyes, didn't judge the question ridiculous at all. "Yes. It helps keep my mind off certain things."

"What are you reading?" I stayed in the doorway, making no move to enter the room or invade his space. A part of me anticipated the rage that was likely to erupt from him at any moment, but a small, tiny sliver of my mind hoped for a bridge to connect us. Even if it was fragile. He was a lifeline to freedom in this place – and from it.

He studied me, eyes moving up and down my body before locking on mine. *The Rise and Fall of a Hero: A Legacy Left behind by Apollyun.*

I moved closer, only a few steps. "Is it any good? Elie brought me several books, but they were always romance."

"Do you enjoy reading?"

"I do. It was something Isa and I did together." Memories ripped into my chest and stole my breath from me. I missed those nights.

"Have you been to the library yet?" He closed the book and placed it on the table next to him.

"You have a library?" My voice betrayed too much of my excitement and color flared on my cheeks. "I haven't seen one in a long time." Only those with high social standing were allowed in them.

The decision I made earlier left my stomach churning. All I needed to do was ask him to show me around, but my tongue might as well have been paralyzed for all the good it did me.

"I can show you where it is." He stood from the chair, the wood groaning against the stone floor.

I retreated a step.

"That's okay."

My shoulders slumped forward, and I dropped my gaze to the floor. Unease sluiced through my veins as that closed off space deep in my chest opened just a sliver.

"I don't want to take you away from your book." I forced a laugh, the sound dry of humor. I turned and fled from the swirl of confusion and pain I saw in his eyes.

CHAPTER

TWENTY-THREE

Lucien

My steps echoed in the empty hallway. Elie was wrong about this. It was a mistake to even try talking to Arabelle. I made one simple offer, and she curled in on herself, then ran away. My fingers clutched into tight fists as I fought the desire to rake my claws down the newly repaired walls.

At this time of day, Elie would be in the hot springs already. The egg-like smell of sulfur hit me before the humidity clung to my fur in sticky patches. I would never understand why my ancestors decided to build the castle walls around the spring instead of leaving it on the outside. It trapped every bit of the soupy air in here.

I rounded the corner to see Elie with his legs stretched out in front of him, his elbows perched on the rocky sides of the spring, and his head leaned back. He was relaxing while I toiled away, attempting to make this woman who hated me overlook the fact that I was a beast and fall in love with me. I ground my teeth.

"I can't do this, Elie. She doesn't want anything to do with me." My anxious energy needed an outlet, so I paced behind him.

His brows bunched together, and he cracked open one eye just

153

a sliver. "Come on, Luce. I'm sure that's not true." He closed his eye again.

I continued my pacing in widening circles. He mentioned she liked romance books, so why refuse to let me show her the library? "I offered to show her the library, and she just ran away from me." I thought it was a kind gesture, something that would open a pathway to conversation.

Elie's chest rose and fell with a sigh, and he opened both his eyes this time. "You have to give her a little time." His golden eyes locked onto my gaze. "With your massive fuck up of locking her in her room, of course she's going to be skittish around you."

I growled and ripped a hand through my fur. "How much time am I supposed to give her?" He said it himself, there wasn't much left. If I couldn't do this...I shook my head to clear the thought before it could drag me down into darkness.

"Haven't you ever had a woman angry with you?" He cocked a brow, the twitch in the corner of his mouth said he was struggling not to smile.

Yes. "No."

"Liar."

I rolled my eyes. "Fine. None that I've ever had to fix things with." At this point, my pacing encircled the entire pool of water Elie soaked in. "What am I even supposed to do in this situation?"

The amusement fell from his face before he spoke again. "Have you tried apologizing?"

I shot him a glare, but he only lifted his shoulders in a shrug.

"Didn't you ever have fights with—" but he cut himself off, knowing the wound that would open.

I growled my frustration to the world above. "I don't know how to do this. Any of it." I stopped and splayed my arms. "How can I ask her to love a monster like me?"

I didn't mean my face this time. Memories of women and homes destroyed because I didn't care enough about who I fucked flooded my mind. Memories of a boy who didn't say anything against his father when he abandoned a wife and son. It wasn't for my sake I wanted to break this curse.

Elie's eyes softened at my last words. "I do wish you'd stop calling yourself a monster." He slumped down into the water. "You've done some shitty things, but we all have. You decided to change those behaviors. Isn't spending twenty years locked in this place enough of a punishment?"

My throat constricted around a growing lump and threatened to deprive me of any air. "No. It'll never be enough. Not when I let them die."

He sat up straight, his posture going rigid, a vein protruding in his forehead. "That was not your fault. You were a *child*."

"It was." My voice came out a whisper, almost too quiet to hear. It was my fault. They went to that town for me and were exposed to the Crimson Plague because of it.

"Look, Lucien...you need to figure this out. Not just with Arabelle," he paused, giving me a once over, "but your past too. If you continue to let it eat you up, that anger is going to destroy everything."

"I'm trying."

He kicked his feet back again and leaned against the rocks. "Well, try harder. Talk to Belle like you talk to me."

I snorted. "Absolutely not. I want her to like me, not hate me even more."

Elie's laughter bounced off the walls, and it inched its way into the cracks of my being. "I don't hate you, Luce. I find you quite charming."

"Only because you like the perks of being my friend."

He snorted at me this time. "What perks? Being stuck in this big castle with only your grumpy ass to talk to?" His lips curled up into a smirk. "I'm glad Belle's here now. I've missed having a pretty young thing to look at."

I bared my teeth at him in a snarl before I had the thought to shove that surge of jealousy down.

His smirk widened into a face-splitting smile. "If you want to win her heart, I think you should open yourself up to her. Tell her something about your past. It doesn't have to be the worst of it, but women tend to be more empathetic with a good little heart-breaking story."

The thought of reopening those wounds was heavy enough to crush me under the weight. "I'll think about it." Opening myself up to someone again would only result in more pain when she rejected me.

I couldn't remember leaving the hot springs. My mind was consumed with what parts of my past I could let Arabelle see. But now I sat on the piano bench, and all that mattered was the feel of the keys under my fingertips and the music carrying me to a world far removed from this one.

TWENTY-FOUR

Arabelle

Getting lost in the castle was not how I wanted to spend the majority of my day, but here I was. Twin oak doors with deep gashes torn into their surface broke apart the dreariness of grey stone. I traced the scarred wood with my fingers. What could have made him this angry? One door slid ajar, and the soft lilt of a piano beckoned me inside.

Each of my steps reverberated back to me, sound bouncing off the ivory walls, the intricate gold trim catching the setting sun from the windows at the end of the room. Crystal chandeliers twinkled from the high, vaulted ceiling, lights flickering to life. At the far end of the room, gilded by the light, and seated on a raised platform was an alabaster piano – and playing that piano was Lucien.

His song swept me to a past I thought I had long forgotten, but my fingers twitched at my sides in time with his notes as I pictured each keystroke in my mind. I hadn't played for almost a year, and a need to do so called to me.

Outside of the gouges in the doors, this was the only other room in immaculate condition – no dust or crumbling walls. The floors glistened in their ivory and sandstone diamond patterns. I breathed in the air free of that musty scent that hung in the other rooms.

I waited until Lucien finished his song in a crescendo of vivacious notes before I approached the piano with slow, deliberate steps. "You play beautifully." The instrument was a work of art in and of itself. I traced a fingertip over the edge of the raised lid.

"For a beast?" His hands fell away from the keys, his eyes following the movement of my finger.

"For someone who lets his anger rule him." Distance needed to be kept from him. I couldn't be sure how he would react to me being in here. He told me before it was a favorite place of his, and here I was intruding on it.

His eyes became transfixed on something outside of the window when he next spoke. "My mother taught me to play. It's one of the only things that brings me peace."

A sea of trees and sky waited outside the window, on the other side of a rainbow of plant life. "Music has always been my escape too. That and the reading," I said as I let a small smile curl my lips. When I played, Isa would dance and dance. To see her that carefree again was something I longed for in the deepest part of my soul. I pulled my hand away from the piano as if it were a snake about to strike.

Our gazes locked and, for the first time, I really looked at him. My heart somersaulted in the confines of my ribs, and it left me breathless. It was as if God spent a lifetime of effort just to paint every last line of blue in his eyes.

"Have you heard many musicians play?" he asked.

Elie could be right about him. He might not be as bad as I imagined him to be.

It was a dangerous game to let him see all the little pieces of my soul that made up who I was. But those damn eyes. There was a familiarity to them that I just could not place.

"I used to sneak off to listen to them whenever I could as a child. Much to my mother's dismay."

He shifted on the bench. "Do you have a favorite?"

"I do. His name is…" I reached for the memory skimming my fingertips, but it slipped away. "I can't remember." Throbbing pain replaced the fleeting thing, and I rubbed at the center of my forehead.

Something black tugged at the corner of my eye, and I turned to see an instrument case. "What's that?" I didn't wait for his answer, desperation driving my steps to escape the unease of blurred memories.

I grabbed it and examined the fine leather with the initials LRB embossed on the top. I popped up the clasps and opened it to the most beautiful violin I'd ever lain eye on. The body was made of ebony and rosewood, resting against dark red, velvet padding.

An image of the beautiful blond sliding the bow across the strings of the instrument swirled in my mind.

The soft whine, alternating timbres, the climb and fall as the song changed tempos, I could almost hear them. Each note brought forth an array of colored, shimmering strands of light, dancing in the air, looping to and fro, twisting in on themselves, tangling and untangling. I wanted to reach out and touch them, pulsating as if it were the most natural thing for them to be alive.

But why him?

When did I close my eyes?

The snap of the case lid slamming shut ripped me from the beautiful images in my mind. Lucien stood over me, lips curled back in a snarl as rage danced in his stormy eyes. He snatched the case from my hands and put it back where I'd found it with such careful movement that I wondered if I imagined the anger.

"I didn't give you permission to touch this." He whirled back to me. "So…please…don't," he growled, though the fury leeched out of his words as if he sucked it back in.

My face heated. Was he trying to make a fool of me? I wouldn't allow it. "If you don't want someone to touch it, don't just leave it lying around," I snapped. Why was he acting this way over a damned violin? My anger rose to meet what I expected his to be beyond that mask of calm.

"This is my castle; I shouldn't have to hide what's mine." He straightened to his full height, towering so far over me I had to take a few steps back to keep glaring up at him.

"It's not like I was going to steal it from you," I spat.

"Why should I believe that? You're the child of a thief."

"I've never stolen a thing in my life." I let the rage shine in my own eyes. "And where would I take it? I can't leave the grounds, remember?"

He snorted, a rush of hot air that blew past my face and Lucien pushed past me. Though the touch of his hand on my shoulder was gentle when he moved me aside. He stomped out of the room.

I struggled to swallow for the minutes following, anger uncoiling itself from around my muscles. Once the footsteps faded into nothing, my rapid breathing slowed to its normal rhythm again. "Asshole," I muttered to the emptiness he left behind.

I left the music room and strode down another hallway, following the lights from room to room until I opened double doors and stepped into the biggest collection of books I'd ever set my eyes on. My jaw hit the floor.

The library was at least three stories tall, shelves twice my height on each of the floors with rails for sliding ladders. Windows at the top of the room let in natural light, as well as a massive skylight on the ceiling. Tables sat in rows on the bottom floor, books stacked and left open on each as if people came in to study or read all the time.

I walked by the shelves on the bottom floor and ran my finger over the spines of the books, so many books. Is this where Elie got the ones he brought me to read every day? I skimmed the titles, there were non-fiction and fiction, history books and romance books, atlases of the land and seas.

I could spend a lifetime in this library and never read all of them. I pulled one from the shelf and flipped it open, the aged aroma of old paper a haze over my senses as I sat in one of the armchairs and started reading.

CHAPTER

TWENTY-FIVE

Henri

THE MORNING AFTER ARABELLE LEFT

Horses neighed just outside, and I blinked into the bleary light leaking through the boards of the cottage. My horse returned to the cottage before I did, but the meager stables were too far away to hear inside. When I cracked the door open, two horses stamped their feet into the slush of the melted snow, a chest strapped to the back of each.

Parchment fluttered in the morning breeze, tucked into one of the leather straps. I plucked it out and flipped it open, reading aloud, "The beast allowed me to send these trunks. Give Isa the dress and use the rest to live a modest and comfortable life."

Anger roiled through my blood when I read the name at the end of the note – Arabelle. I stormed back into the cottage, ignoring the loud snap of the door as I shoved into Belle and Isa's room and, sure enough, Belle was gone.

"What's happened?" Isa asked, blinking bleary eyes up at me, but I turned around without answering.

Of all the selfish things, she was supposed to be on her way to marry Louis this morning and she just left? How was I going to explain that one? He expected her there. He would ruin me if she didn't show, more than I already was…My jaw groaned as I ground my teeth together.

I unfastened one of the straps and yanked the chest off a horse but lost my grip as it fell to the ground with a heavy thud. The second wasn't any lighter. What the hell did that girl pack into them? Stones? I sank to my knees in front of one.

I barely noticed when the horses ran off. I didn't much care about it as I released the latch on a chest and flipped back the lid.

There most certainly were stones. The morning sun gleamed off the gold, set the jewels to sparkling, and my jaw dropped at the small fortune sitting before me.

That bastard had all this wealth in the castle, and I didn't even realize it. Where was he hiding it? And if he could spare this much, he had to have a mountain of it.

My fingers roved over the contents of the chest until I spotted two pieces, and my breath caught in my throat. Statues with emerald and ruby eyes stared back at me from beneath piles of gold coins. How did they end up in the treasure Belle sent back?

"That bastard Callum must've sold them to him," I said as I rubbed a hand over my scruffy cheek. "Wait. No. Louis bought all the treasure. At least, that's what he claimed. It is possible he's the one that sold it."

I opened the second chest, snatching up the dress and tossing it aside. "That monster is rich. He has to have way more than this stashed away in that castle." A wicked grin tugged at my lips.

Two trunks full of gold weren't near enough to buy Belle from me. No, I'd make him give me everything. And if there was one person I knew I could turn to, it was *him*. I slammed both chests shut. "I think I need to have a little chat with a certain captain."

With a great heave, I dragged the chests toward the cottage

one at a time, tucking them into a hole behind a loose board of the foundation to hide them from any who might stop by. Not that I thought anyone would steal from me; they'd assume we have less than nothing and pass us by.

Never had I been so grateful for the little hovel we lived in than that moment.

I walked back into Isa's room and nudged her awake again. If I left her here alone she might follow after Belle. I needed at least one of them to give as a wife to Louis. If Belle wanted to be a slave to some beast, then Isa would do. "Wake up. We're going into town today. I have inquiries to make."

She groaned as she rubbed the sleep from her eyes and then went still as stone. "Into town? I thought I was going to that castle?" The ice in her voice sent an invisible chill over me.

I hated who she'd become after the fire, after Simon left her. Belle was the one who I had always struggled with, and now Isa had somehow transformed into a worse version of my late wife – all clever lies and sweet smiles to cover up the sharp mind she possessed.

"It would seem that Belle selfishly decided to go in your place." Her gaze shot to the empty bed behind me. "That's part of why we need to go. I can't just let that monster have her." The lie came easy, and by the frown and rigidity in her shoulders, she believed it.

"But what about the deal you made?" Her fingers tangled in the blanket over her lap, knuckles turning white from the grip.

"I'm breaking it. Get dressed." I left the room.

The weight of the gold in my pocket was a comfortable

reminder of what I once was, and what I would become again. We'd need to stay in town to meet with both Callum and Louis, especially if I was going to talk them into working with me.

The damaged ship meant that Callum and his crew were stranded for a while; they should be feeling restless any day now. All the nights of drinking and whoring around only went so far when it came to men like that.

Snow still clustered in shadowed ditches and under dense pines, but the roads were clear again. Even with Isa's slight build, with us both on the horse, it took longer to get to Starside than I wanted.

The bustle from my last trip was scarce but a fragment of activity today. The cold must've chased most people indoors. I slid off the horse and held a hand up to Isa to help her down as well.

"I have a man to see in the pub. Can you take Oscar here to the stables and have him tended to?" I took a gold piece from my pocket and pressed it into her palm. It was too much to take care of a horse, but I didn't have anything but the gold.

The pub was just as rowdy as the last time I was here, though the smell of booze and sex was heavier on the air now – another effect of the cold weather. All I needed this time was information, but Callum was a damn stickler who never parted with *anything* unless the price was right.

I spied the locks of golden hair at a far table. His chair was askew, a wench pressing her generous breasts into his chest with her legs on either side of his waist. She draped her slender arms around his neck and twined her fingers in his hair.

"Good to see you spending your fortune wisely, Captain," I said as I approached the table. The brute from before shot to his feet and reached for me. I held my hands up in surrender, taking a step back.

"I'm not here for a fight. I just have a few questions for the good captain."

Callum threw a glance over his shoulder at me and gave the woman an emphatic smack on her ass. She huffed, wrapping her arms around him tighter but he removed them and lifted her from his lap.

He turned his chair to face me fully.

"And what might those questions pertain to?" His voice was a purr as he braced his forearms on the table between us.

I pulled out one of the golden statues from my cloak and held it out to show him. "This."

"How did you—"

"The how isn't important." I put it back in my pocket. "I want to know who you sold it to." I side-stepped the mountain of a man and took a seat at the table.

"And what makes you think I'd tell you that?" A smirk edged up his mouth in a tilted curve, and Callum's eyes met mine, pure defiance dancing in them with every word he spoke.

I plucked a gold coin from my pocket and rolled it across the table. He slapped his hand down on it. Dim light reflected off the coin as he picked the piece up to examine it. Whether it was a slight or he doubted its authenticity, I didn't know or care, as long as he accepted the payment.

"I'm prepared to pay for your information."

"And just how did you get your hands on gold, Henri?" He leaned back in his seat, an arm draping over the back of the one next to him as he watched me with a lazy smile.

The atmosphere in the pub shifted to one steeped in murderous intent as the ring of blades sounded from every direction in a cacophony of noise, growls rumbling through throats, and a hushed silence falling over every person present.

I steadied my breathing. This wasn't anything I didn't expect, not when I'd been so cheap as to hire pirates. That's why I only brought the gold I knew I'd need for the stay here and a little extra for his information. I lifted my chin and schooled my features into the cool, confident mask I'd perfected over the years.

"Again, the how is unimportant. Will you answer my questions or not?"

One of the men hissed from behind me while others chuckled, but Callum held the coin between the knuckles of his middle and forefinger. "Give me four more of these and ya got yourself a deal."

The silence held for a moment longer before breaking back into the jovial sounds that greeted me when I walked in. I dropped the gold pieces on the table, and Callum was quick to snatch them up.

"I sold 'em to the same person I sold everything to: Louis."

"Louis," I spat the name like venom on my tongue. "I'll be on my way then." I didn't want to be indebted to Louis, but maybe I could twist this into a favorable outcome for myself.

Amusement danced in Callum's eyes as he slid the gold into his pocket. "What are you up to, Henri?" His voice came out as smooth as velvet.

"Something big." Like hell I'd tell him anything.

"Need some help?"

"So, you can take my treasure out from under me again?"

The tilt of his head was predatory until he leaned back and howled in laughter. He squared me up with a look so cold and calculating that ice chilled my veins. "I think I've taught you a valuable lesson in fair wages. Fifty-fifty split and we're in."

"I'll keep that in mind." I would never give him half of what was in that castle. But having the extra men could come in handy. I couldn't go head-to-head with that beast.

The chill air was a blessed relief from the muggy atmosphere of the pub. Time to find Louis, granted he would probably find me first. It didn't matter how sudden my visits were, he always found out when I was in town. The longer I knew him, the more I suspected he had everyone in town in his pocket.

I fought the beginnings of a grin as an idea took form.

Callum wanted in on my plans.

His men would need payment.

And Louis had plenty of coin to spare.

If I played this right, I could ensure that Louis was the one who took the brunt of the risk when we stormed the castle. His obsession with Belle would work in my favor. He'd go in there after her without questioning it. I wouldn't have to offer him Isa after all. A smile tugged at my lips, but I bit it back when I heard the rushed footsteps behind me.

"Henri." Louis only stopped long enough to sign a parchment handed to him before he could rush by, then he closed the distance between us in a few easy strides. "I hope you're back in town because you've brought my bride. Where's my beloved Arabelle?" He scanned the area.

"I had some questions for Callum about some statues I sent him after." I deliberately chose not to answer about Arabelle.

"Oh? What statues would those be?" His green eyes came back to rest on me with an arched brow.

I pulled out the statue and showed it to him. "These."

Louis fell silent as he studied the golden statue, a somber expression replacing the usual smug smile as a glint of recognition shone in his eyes. "Where did you get that?"

"It was sent to me. As payment. By Arabelle's captor." I made sure to choose each word with care, knowing just how foolhardy and possessive he had become over my daughter. And this fool had means he'd part with just to claim her.

Rage flickered in Louis's eyes despite the calm in his voice. "What do you mean 'captor', Henri?"

"She was stolen from me. By a foul...monster...stowed away in a castle outside of town. That's why I came to ask about the statues. I need to find out who bought them and if they're a regular in town. If they are, I can follow them back and rescue my little girl." A muscle ticked in his jaw. Perfect. He was falling for it.

"The guy I sold them to was a servant of some richy rich lord. Tall, well dressed, red hair, and most notably, golden eyes. He was looking for something unusual. I've heard he's been coming into town every few months." Each sentence was short and to the point as the edge of his voice sharpened into something more dangerous than a blade.

The beast wouldn't come himself—not looking the way he did —I knew that, but who was the red-haired man? I didn't see anyone else in the castle, but then again, it was vast in size. "What's his name?"

"Come now, Henri. Do I look like a man who gets the name of everyone I do business with?" He raised his hands in a shrug and shook his head.

I forced a look of dismay onto my features while hugging the statue to my chest. "Am I to wait months to find out? He has my daughter. There's no telling what he's putting my poor Belle through, what he's doing to *your* future wife." I glanced at him through hooded eyes. He was so bent on having her that he didn't care if she was sullied or not.

Louis's features were etched in a frown. "I can't give you what I don't know." He gripped me by the shoulder with a rough hand. "But I promise you, I'll get Arabelle back. No matter the cost."

Good. *Give everything, fool.* "Callum has offered his aide. I'm sure he would be willing to make a favorable bargain." *And leave my future fortune out of it.* I cast my eyes down to the ground.

"The beast is in a castle. Arabelle snuck a note into the straps of a trunk he sent as payment. You'll need men to breach it."

"Let us discuss how we might rescue her by ourselves first. I'd rather not resort to hiring those filthy pirates, but if that's what it takes for me to get her back, then I will hire Callum and his crew to tear the whole place apart." Louis gave my shoulder a squeeze, and I couldn't mask the wince.

"I will not rest until I have Arabelle safely in my arms. And once I save her, she'll be my wife."

"Thank you, Louis." Showing him any gratitude made me want to shove my face into a forge's fire. "If you'll excuse me, I must get back to Isa." I added with a fake quiver to my voice.

"Isabelle's here?"

The hopeful lilt to his tone surprised me. I smothered it. "Yes." I moved to step away from him, but he didn't release my shoulder.

A grin cracked his lips, and he finally let me go. "Sorry to keep you from her," he paused and looked past me as if he could see her, "don't do anything dumb, Henri. You can't handle a threat like that by yourself. Better to leave it to the real men." The slap to my shoulder almost sent me sprawling to the mud.

I damn near let the internal grimace show on my face but forced a smile in its place. "You have my word. I won't."

My skin crawled at the way his eyes glinted. "A brilliant idea just occurred to me, my good friend. Instead of you waiting at your little...home...why don't you and Isabelle stay with me?"

Suspicion knotted my gut, and I shoved it down. This was better than I could have hoped for. I'd save the coin I'd otherwise spend at the inn and get to ply Louis until he did everything I wanted him to.

"Oh no, we couldn't possibly intrude on you."

"It'll be no intrusion. You're soon to be my family, and I always take care of my own," he said and clapped me on the shoulder again. "Besides, this way you'll be in town when that crooked bastard shows up again."

"If you insist."

"I do. Go fetch Isabelle. I'll wait for you here."

I gave him a curt nod and made my way to the stables. I hadn't counted on that offer, but after seeing just how easy it was to manipulate the muscle-bound idiot, I wasn't about to pass it up. Getting Arabelle back wasn't my original plan, but I wouldn't pass up an opportunity to do so. Then the beast's riches would be mine once they killed him.

As I neared the stables, I slowed my pace, noticing a young man speaking to Isa in an animated manner, waving his hands between them. She laughed at whatever it was he said but went rigid as he tucked her bangs behind her ear, revealing that god awful scar.

"Who might your friend be, Isa?" She stiffened further as her gaze swept from his to mine, the softness hardening into steel.

The young man spun around, black curls swaying in movement as his grey eyes locked with mine. He straightened and stepped between me and my daughter. "My name is Armand de Cordevaux."

He was immaculate in his appearance: a crisp clean, white linen shirt that billowed down his arms, covered by a dark royal blue vest with a gold chain drooping from pocket to the center button. Black leather boots ended at his knees, and a cloak that matched his vest draped over his shoulders.

"That's a strong sounding name, Armand. I'm Henri, Isabelle's father." I offered my hand and reveled in the way his eyes widened a fraction, and a muscle feathered in his cheek as he took the proffered hand, giving it a solid shake.

"Apologies. I didn't know you were her father." He released my hand and let his drop back to the side.

I gave him a saccharine smile. "It's alright. I respect you for trying to keep Isa safe." I rifled through the stores of information in my head until I remembered the name Cordevaux. "The Cordevauxs are the presiding lords of this region, correct?"

He gave me a pointed nod. "Yes. My father brought me to town to collect taxes. Says I need to learn how to talk to the common folk. But it bores me. He sent me outside so I wouldn't embarrass him." Armand rolled his shoulders and glanced back to Isa. "I happened by your daughter, thought she was quite enchanting, and decided to introduce myself."

"I'm sure you're not as enchanted now that you've seen she's marred." I didn't miss the way her shoulders drew back, and I knew the words cut deep when I looked past Armand to her in time for that cold vacancy to come back to her eyes.

"On the contrary, Sir. I find her just as radiant, if not more so."

I rubbed at my chin and arched a brow at the young man before me. "If you introduce me to your father, perhaps I can arrange a marriage to her." If he wanted a scarred bride, then that was one of my problems taken care of. I had my doubts that his father would accept the match though.

Armand's eyes gleamed as a smile lit up his face. "Consider it done. Will you be in town long?"

"Yes. You can call on us at the Durand Estate. We'll be staying there for the time being." I watched him spin back to Isa and take her hands in his.

"I will definitely come find you again." He pressed a kiss to her knuckles before dropping her hands and striding back to the center of town with a final wave to her.

"We're staying with Louis?" Isa never spoke to me with the same kindness she showed others – not since before the fire, since before I forbade her and Simon to marry earlier than their arranged date.

"Yes. He offered, and I accepted. If you have a problem with him, you'll need to get over it. Now, come on."

We left the stables and headed for the estate.

CHAPTER
TWENTY-SIX

Arabelle

I sat alone at the excessively large dining table, eyeing the roast duck just waiting for me to dig into it. The lingering hunger haunting the back of my mind most days had all but vanished when I'd come to the castle.

I glanced down the row of seats. This place had such a vast space that it could house over two hundred people. Elie made it sound like no one else was allowed here. I didn't know what I'd do with myself if they were the only company I'd ever have again.

"Talk about lonely," I said, slumping a little in the chair.

The door groaned behind me, and Lucien stalked in, taking a seat across from me. I straightened my posture again.

"Where's Elie?"

"He's attending to an important matter right now."

He didn't look at me as he started serving himself.

"Oh."

I cut a small piece of the duck off and skewered it on my fork, flinching at the sound the plate made. *Oops.* Without Elie, this was going to turn into an uncomfortable dinner.

"Did you enjoy your exploration today?" He stared down at his food, refusing to meet my gaze.

Was he still angry about earlier? How petty could he be? It was just a damn violin.

"I did. I grew up in a manor, but it was a far cry from," I paused, making a semi-circle in the air with my finger, "this."

I didn't miss the raised eyebrows at my admission. Civility would go a long way in making my time here bearable. And if he was one of only two people I could talk to, it should at least be pleasant.

"How do you get the candles to light by themselves? I've never seen anything like it."

"Would you believe me if I told you it was magic?"

He pushed the food on his plate around with a fork.

I fought the urge to roll my eyes at the comment. "Magic doesn't exist save for fairy tales."

If he truly believed there was magic in this world, he was delusional. Yet, something scratched at the back of my mind, something that wanted to believe him.

Lucien half smirked, and for a long moment, the only sound in the room was the ticking of the grandfather clock tucked away in a corner.

"What rooms did you go into?"

I rested my hands in my lap, trying not to let the surprise show in my eyes at his question. Perhaps he made the same decision regarding civility. I fought back the grin trying to emerge at the corner of my mouth.

"I rummaged around a dusty room filled with all kinds of stuff." I raised my hand to where the locket nestled between my breasts, hidden beneath the bodice of my dress, the boys coming to mind as I remembered the painting. "Why throw all those paintings and the furniture in a room? I would think the family portraits—"

"It's just a bunch of junk. What do I care what happens to it?" he interrupted.

Tension thickened the air as Lucien clicked his tongue against his teeth, and the seemingly permanent scowl etched itself further into his features.

It seemed a shame for him to consider all of it junk, but I continued, leaving out my little excursion into that study. "I stumbled onto your reading spot. I kind of got lost for a while."

I never expected to have common interests. Not only did we both enjoy reading, but the way he played the piano earlier...my chest tightened.

The look he gave me had me changing the subject before he could speak the words I was sure were on the tip of his tongue: I should have let him guide me.

"I found the music room, as you know." The fork in his hand trembled, and I chose my next words with care. "Isa used to listen to me play when we were younger. I haven't played in a year. I miss it."

"You play?" His gaze caught on mine, and for a moment, a spark of excitement flashed there and died out.

"Yes." A thrill ran through me at the memory of my fingers on the keys. "One of the many things my mother insisted I learn. But..." I paused, lacing my fingers together as a memory of pure joy filled me. "From the first time I played, little else has made me *feel* as much as music."

"Maybe...one day..." he started, but the rest of the sentence was strangled in his throat. "Nevermind. What else?"

I tilted my head and watched him pick at the duck on his plate. I bit my lip to silence a question. I shouldn't push, not when we were having an actual conversation.

"I saw the library. It's magnificent. I've never seen so many books in one place." A smile played at my lips as I recalled the books Elie brought me.

"When you told me there was a library, I never imagined it would be that enormous." A small laugh bubbled up my throat. "Elie didn't seem like much of a romance reader, so I wondered where the books came from. Now I know. I feel like a lifetime wouldn't be enough to read all the books in there, though I wanted to stay and try anyway." With a long breath, I went back to that wonderful place in my head.

"You're more than welcome to try." The humor in his voice tugged at a string in my chest, prying that little opening a bit wider.

"I wish I could show it to Isa; she would love it." My eyes sank to the table, but I forced a smile back onto my face a moment later.

"You miss her." It was a statement, not a question.

"She's my sister and I love her, so yes. I'm also worried because my father has been cruel to her since the fire—" I cut myself off as memories of scorching flames and heat and screams inundated my mind. This wasn't a conversation I wanted to have with a veritable stranger.

"The fire?" he prompted, raising his gaze to meet mine, and a piece of my chest caved at the kindness I gleamed from eyes I'd thought nothing but cold.

I cursed myself for so carelessly bringing it up and chewed my bottom lip. I shouldn't have said that. I shouldn't open myself up to him more.

Against my better judgment, I continued, "The fire that took away our fortune. And the lives of our other siblings." I wanted to shrink into myself and disappear. I wasn't able to save them.

"What about your mother?"

"She died before that." The memory was covered in a fog of bleariness that I had to wade through. I was so young then. "From some illness that broke her down on the inside."

I couldn't remember the illness, just the weakness, the blood. I swallowed back the sob tearing up my throat. She wasn't a kind woman, but she was still my mother.

"I'm sorry. I shouldn't have asked." The sharp, harsh edge went out of his words and lulled me into a sense of comfort.

My eyes snapped up to his, the sting of tears at the edge of my vision.

"It's okay. I—" How much should I tell him? Was it okay? "I never get to talk about them. My father won't listen, and Isa... well...she's got enough to worry about."

"How many of you were there?"

The once tense air relaxed. Was it just me, or did his icy stare melt into something akin to a summer sky? Warmth blossomed in my chest as another set of blues came to mind, and the rigidity left my shoulders.

"Six. I had two older sisters, Ember and Garnet, and two younger brothers, Marc and Roy. Then there's Isabelle and me. We're twins." Each of their faces flashed before my eyes as I said their names.

"I had a younger brother once," he paused, and my chest tightened as I saw the pain take hold in his eyes, his mouth set in a thin line. "He died young. Not long after my mother."

My fingers twitched with the desire to reach out and touch him, offering a small comfort for what he lost, but I dragged my hand off the table and let it settle in my lap instead.

"May I ask how? Or is it something you don't want to talk about?" I wouldn't pry the information out of him, but he listened to me. This was the least I could do. He didn't pull away.

He stared at the spot my hand had been moments ago.

"It was the Crimson Plague." The muscles in Lucien's jaw ticked as his gaze went straight through me, past me, past the castle walls, maybe even to the past itself. "My mother and brother wanted to surprise me with a present for my birthday. The surprise was that I'd never see them again."

Tightness wound around my heart like a serpent, and I clutched my fingers under the table.

"I'm sorry, Lucien."

It was nothing. I knew it was nothing from the countless times it had been thrown at me from all those in the wake of my own mother's death. Of my siblings' deaths. But it was all I had to offer him.

"The violin…" I started.

Lucien stiffened. I wasn't even sure he breathed.

"That was the present, wasn't it? The reason you were so angry."

He ran his hand over the length of his face. "I shouldn't have snapped at you for touching it."

I tracked his movement, my fingers wringing in the fabric of my dress now.

"It's something special to you, I understand."

"That's no excuse."

When his hand reached the base of the horn he stopped and recoiled before he dropped it back to the table.

An idea flitted through my mind, and I couldn't contain the wide smile that curved my lips. "You can always make it up to me." I swallowed.

This could go bad, very bad. Yet, a nudging little voice urged me on.

His brows bunched as that gaze found mine again.

"How?"

"Play something for me."

It was a simple request, but if his mother bought him that violin, it must be what he enjoyed playing the most. Elie wanted me to give him a chance, but it was a two-way road; he had to give me one, too.

He twisted his mouth to the side.

"How do you expect me to play the violin with…" He held up his clawed hands. "The hands of a monster?"

"Is that not just an excuse?" The question left my mouth before I could think better of it, and I watched as part of that melting ice froze again.

"I can play something on the piano instead." He flat-out ignored my question, but the sadness in his eyes made my chest tighten.

"Let's make a deal. I'll let you play the piano for me, but only if you agree to play the violin for me later." I folded my hands on the table and tried my best to imitate the stature I witnessed my father use for all those years.

Lucien studied me with a smirk tugging on his lips. "A deal usually comes with equal terms. What am I to get from this?"

Whatever confidence this led my father to have failed me terribly. I slipped my hands from the table and tucked them under my thighs as a sudden rush of nervous energy flooded me.

"What do you want?"

He was quiet for so long that I wasn't sure if he would answer or not.

"Join me for a walk through the garden."

That was easy enough.

"When?"

"Tomorrow."

"Will you play for me tomorrow, too?" It was only fair, right?

My heart hammered in my chest. I studied him—the blond fur, the horns curling around his head, the blue eyes. That first day, he was grungy and wore rags. But now, he was clean and donned well-made clothes, even if the fit was a little off, given the shape of his body.

"Would you like for me to?"

"Fair's fair, isn't it? A walk won't take that long; you can play for me after."

"Alright. First a walk, then I'll play a song for you."

"Only one?" I bit my lip to hide the smile at my small victory.

"Is one not enough?" His brow shot up toward what would be his hairline, and the heat of a blush colored my cheeks.

I traced my fingertip along the detailed carving on the edge of the table, avoiding his eyes.

"I thought I would get more." I tried not to let the disappointment show on my face or in my voice.

"When you look like that, it's hard to argue." He huffed a sigh and tilted his head back. "I'll play for as long as you like."

I thought I banked the discontent, but maybe not. I looked him in the eye and then away again, hiding away the small grin on my lips. He wasn't as hardened as he seemed if he would bend just to prevent me from being displeased with such ease. A small flutter of excitement danced through my belly at the thought.

"You don't have to—"

"I want to."

Our eyes locked across the table.

"It's been a long time since anyone has asked me to play for them."

I had to pinch myself to make sure it was real because I saw joy lighting up his eyes.

"I can play violin for you in two months' time."

I arched a brow this time. It was an oddly specific timeline.

"What will be different two months from now?"

A feline smile to match his features crossed his face. "I'm…a bit rusty. Give me the chance to practice so you won't run screaming."

Now, it was amusement I saw. This was a different Lucien than the one of a few weeks ago.

"I'll look forward to it then."

"Is there anything else you like? Besides reading and music?" he asked, fixing me with those deep, enchanting eyes of his. The surly aura he tried so hard to put up almost fell away completely. *Almost.*

My mouth twisted to the side as I stared at the table. What else did I like? I opened my mouth to answer and closed it again. I couldn't separate what I did out of necessity and what I did for entertainment anymore.

"I like working with my hands." It was the first thing that came to mind.

"Like gardening?"

"How'd you guess that?"

"When you arrived, you were covered in dirt and had small mud stains from where I assume your knees had been dug into the ground. Gardening seemed like the obvious choice."

"I didn't realize you were paying such close attention." How embarrassing. To have him remember me being a mess the first time we met. I didn't even consider cleaning up, just that I needed to leave while I had the chance.

"My mother liked to garden. She was similarly disheveled at times. Most of the gardens on the grounds were started and tended by her."

Was that why he wanted to show them to me?

"They must mean a lot to you. I've never seen some of the flowers here. How did she get them to grow?"

My heart skipped a beat. If his mother had started the gardens, and my father had taken one of the roses...my shoulders hunched forward. His reaction to him stealing the rose made sense now.

"She had a...talent for growing things."

I could feel his eyes on me, and it made me want to slide under the table to hide.

"Are you—"

"What do you like to do? Besides music." I stopped the question before he could finish. I didn't want to talk about the rose.

"Not much brings me joy anymore."

"Why not?"

The drop in atmosphere was palpable, and my heart lurched in my chest, sensing the rest of that melted ice completely refreezing all over again. I faltered. If I kept pushing, he'd tip over into rage again. So much for having a nice conversation.

His chair squawked against the floor as Lucien pushed it back and stood.

"I'll leave you to your night." He rounded the table and headed to the door.

"Lucien, wait—"

He stopped when I called to him and asked over his shoulder, "Could you bring yourself to love me...as I am?"

The question was like a kick to the gut in how fast it robbed my lungs of the ability to hold oxygen. Heat spread across my face and danced up and down the column of my spine like it was a midsummer night's celebration. It scrambled the words in my head, and I couldn't come up with the right ones to string together.

Could I love him? An animal – a beast? And wasn't it too soon to be asking me this? Yet...my heart quickened with the possibility.

"Yes or no. I won't get mad," he promised, shoulders set in a rigid line, hands hanging by his sides in loose fists.

I pressed a hand to my chest to steady the rapid beating of my heart.

"I-I don't know. It's way too soon to be talking about love."

I forced a laugh; a dry, humorless sound. That was the answer: just laugh it off. He couldn't be serious, right? It had to be a joke. My hand dropped to where the locket sat between my breasts. But the moment my eyes fell on him again, I knew.

"Good night." And he was gone.

"Good night," I said to the empty room, my heart sinking into my stomach as emptiness spread through me.

TWENTY-SEVEN

Lucien

Blades of sunlight pierced through the gaps and holes in the curtains. My eyes followed a stray clump of dust as it flitted in the gentle light. Arabelle and I had an actual conversation. I rubbed a hand over my face. The amount of loss she'd suffer was equal to my own, more in fact.

My gut twisted. I wasn't sure if I could go through with this. I already made her a promise about today. What was I thinking? Telling her I'd play my violin for her. "Ugh." I scraped my claws down my cheeks without digging into the flesh.

The door creaked as Elie opened it and stepped inside my chambers, glancing around until he found me still in bed. He frowned.

"What's this? Don't you think you're a little old to be sulking in your room?"

"I'm not sulking. Leave me alone, Elie."

I rolled onto my side, putting my back to him and curling in on myself.

"What's the matter, baby Luce? Did things not go so well last night?" His mocking tone elicited a growl from me.

"Not that it's any of your concern, but *things* went fine."

His footsteps sounded from behind as he rounded the bed and walked into my sight.

"Then why are you in here, still in bed, instead of getting ready for breakfast?" He leaned over me and raised a brow.

"This isn't going to work." My eyes met his for a brief second before I looked straight ahead again.

"Why not?"

"She's been through too much. I can't put this on her, too. Asking her to fall in love with me, accept all of this." I gestured to my face, the horns. "I can't do it to her."

"It's her choice, Luce. You open yourself up to her, gods damn your looks, and you let her choose whether or not she wants to accept you, to love you."

"I can't—"

"You can. What you *can't* do is tell her about the curse or about what happens if it doesn't get broken in two months—" He cut himself off, baring his teeth in a flash of white, and shook his head.

"Just be you, Lucien. Don't worry about anything else."

I flopped onto my back again, arms stretched out to my sides.

"It's easy to say that, but not so much to *do* it."

"This from the man who used to have a different woman in his bed every week." I shot Elie a glare, but he just smirked at me.

"That's the reason we're in this mess in the first place, or did you forget that?"

"No, I haven't forgotten a single thing about that night. I'm just surprised you, of all people, are struggling to woo a woman," he paused, rubbing his chin between his thumb and forefinger. "Did you ask her about her likes?"

"Of course I did. I'm not a total dunce. At any rate, this is different than the other times. I was only trying to bed those women."

"Did you offer to do any of those interests of hers with her?" He leaned his shoulder against the bedpost and stared down at me, the gold in his eyes swirling like fire.

I let my silence be the answer. Getting between the legs of a woman was easy enough, especially with a handsome face and title, but sex was different than love. I breathed a sigh. There was only one who I let get that close to my heart in the past. My nose crinkled at the memory.

"Thinking about Daija again?" Elie's voice was soft and tentative, careful of the wounds that name would open up.

"What'd I tell you about saying her name in front of me?" I snapped, almost coming off the bed in a snarl.

Elie raised his hands and stepped back.

"Sorry, I forgot. We don't talk about her."

He looked me over, still half sitting on the bed.

"Get up."

I shot him another glare, but he grabbed my ankle and twisted my body so my feet were on the floor.

"I said get up. You're getting off your ass and coming to train with me."

He rummaged through my armoire and pulled something out. He threw the clothes in my face, the shirt dangling from the tip of my horn.

"I've told you before—"

"I don't give a shit what your excuses are. You've dallied long enough, and I'm tired of hearing it. It's time to put that anger to use instead of taking it out on everything else."

He braced himself by holding onto either bedpost at the end of my bed.

"You forget who you're talking to," I growled at him, yanking the shirt from where it swayed and pulling it on.

"No, I haven't forgotten a thing. A single thing, Lucien. You're not the only one going through this, and I'll be damned if I just let you sit here and wait for the clock to run out. So, get your ass up before I drag you out of that bed."

I grumbled but was already putting the restrictive pants on. If he was so damn insistent on me joining him, I'd show him why it was a bad idea. Why I'd been refusing all this time.

The practice grounds were divided up into sections depending on the type of training needed. A partition wall that reached my waist separated the areas. The first area was long, with ten targets lined up in front of the far wall. The next section had five similarly stuffed hay men scattered in the center, slash marks and deep gouges cut into them.

The one opposite the archery range looked like nothing more than a dirt pit, soil packed down into a hard surface. That was where the new recruits got their first taste of hand-to-hand. I rubbed my jaw, remembering the first time Elie slugged me and just how the dirt tasted. Next to that was an enclave with the castle forge, dark and cold for the past twenty years.

At the end was the sparring ring, a white circle of softened dirt stretched to the edges of the section, leaving only a few feet from where the ring ended to the walls surrounding it. Elie stopped at one of the benches, pulling linen wraps from his pocket and tossing them to me.

"You remember how to do this, right?"

I wanted to knock that smug smirk off his face.

I wound the linen around my knuckles, down my hand, and over my wrist, covering both hands to protect them. Elie did the same with his, and we walked to the center of the circle, the soft soil squishing between my toes. He brought his hands up in a defensive position.

"Let's start with the basics."

Elie was just as much of a hard ass as his father, Camael, and in this moment, I hated him for it. I panted, struggling to land the last of the one-two punches he had me doing for the last hour.

"You're worse than your father." I pulled in a long breath, tilting my head back.

"I'll take that as a compliment." Amusement flashed in his eyes. "Gotta get you back in shape, Luce."

"I'm not out of shape," I grumbled as I squared up with him again, raising my hands.

"If you can barely do these punch combos, you're out of shape. Enough dilly-dallying; let's go again."

"Anyone would be winded after an hour of this." But I punched at his palms anyway.

"I do this every day with no problem." The smack of my fist on his hands echoed off the walls and into the fields behind us.

"Some of us have better things to do with our time." I stumbled on my step back but managed to catch myself.

"Pouting in your room is not a better use of your time than this," Elie said. "I spotted some Marid just inside the gates a couple of days ago. Again. They've left us alone for these last twenty years, but now they're up to something."

He dropped his voice to a whisper. "You need to be at the top of your game."

He'd given me reports on their offenses before, and there was the Daeva attack – when was it? Right before Arabelle arrived.

"Why would they make a move now? It'd be easier to wait it out."

My stomach twisted into a knot. Was it just a few? Or was Ashea making a move? We didn't possess the military might to go against them as we were. We possessed *no* military might.

"I don't know. There were only five of them, no more than a scouting party. But we should be prepared in case they do attack."

"Do you think they know about Arabelle?" The thought had my heart in my stomach, but I couldn't fathom any other reason they'd risk crossing into my lands.

"Don't worry, Luce. I promise I'll keep her safe. The Marid are nothing, especially in small numbers." He caught my hand and wrapped his fingers around my fist. "I will give you as much time as I can if they try to interfere."

The sympathetic look in his eye told me he felt my trembling.

"I asked her to go on a walk with me today," I blurted. I didn't want to think about what the others were up to or if they had sent their soldiers here to stop me.

Elie blinked and released my hand. "That's a start. Did she agree?"

I resumed my punches with a small sigh of relief.

"Yes, in exchange for playing the piano for her afterward."

Elie dropped his hands, and I stumbled forward with the momentum of my swing and nothing to hit.

"You're going to play for her?"

"Why do you sound shocked? I'm a great pianist." I straightened and puffed my chest out at the incredulous look he gave me.

"I know that. That's not what I meant." He stepped back and brought his fists up this time.

"Let's change it up."

I barely had the forethought to dodge his punch when he swung.

"You've never offered to play for someone personally. Not even...*her*."

I sidestepped another swing and reached for him with his back still to me.

"What I did before isn't going to work with Belle. She's not some shallow aristocrat."

He rolled with the momentum and stayed just out of my reach.

"No, she's not. But music has always been your special place." He leaned from side to side in an evasion of my combinations. "I'm surprised you are willing to share it so easily."

"It's not easy, Elie, trust me."

He caught my arm and landed a kick to my ribs that had me stumbling back. I coughed, trying to drag breath back into my lungs.

"She told me that she used to play."

"Oh. So, you intend to make use of the skillset your mother left you."

He waited until I was back on my feet again, but only just before his fist cracked into my jaw. I leaned with the punch to take some weight out of it and responded with my own brutal jab to his left cheek as my temper flared.

"I would never sully the memory of my mother by using what she taught me to seduce a woman."

Elie wiped the blood from his mouth with the back of his wrapped hand, staining the white linen crimson, then raised his hands.

"I wasn't implying that, Luce."

He dropped to a crouch and swiped my feet out from under me, letting me crash into the ground.

"For what it's worth, I think Lady Helaine would be happy to know that what she taught you won the love of someone who truly saw you."

I didn't move to get up, letting my arms lay at my side as I watched the clouds roll by overhead.

"What am I supposed to do?" Daija was the first and last woman I let close enough to see my scars. I had locked away my heart after her – to my father's great jubilation. "What if I can't do it?"

Elie's chest heaved in a sigh, and he ran a hand through his hair.

"You've gotta let go of what your father said. He was a cruel bastard for what he did to you."

I grasped the hand he offered, and he pulled me back to my feet.

"That wasn't an answer."

I swiped my hands over my clothes, knocking the white dust off of them.

"Where do you plan to take her for your walk?" He held one wrist and rotated his hand as if it was sore.

"Through one of the gardens."

I looked anywhere but at him, grateful for the fur that covered my face. It hid the heat of a blush on my cheeks.

"You should take her to the southern garden. That was Lady Helaine's favorite." He rested his hands on his hips. "That one also has the pavilion. You can have a picnic out there together." The corner of his mouth edged up in a half grin.

My heart rate ratcheted up to a frantic pace, and I willed it back down with a deep breath. We didn't talk of my mother, and Elie was careful never to say her name around me, but this was twice in an hour.

"I'm not sure I'm ready to share that place with anyone else."

"Lucien, you don't have time to be uncomfortable. You can't hope to win the heart of someone else without putting yours on the line as well." He clapped me on the shoulder, a cloud of white dirt erupting from me.

I hung my head. "I'll trust your judgment, then."

"Good, because it's great judgment." His laugh died when I didn't even smile. "If it goes wrong, we can come back here, and I'll let you kick my ass." He gave me a half-shrug.

I snorted and rolled my eyes. "As if you need to let me."

CHAPTER

TWENTY-EIGHT

Lucien

Elie might have had a point about me being out of shape, because even after soaking in the springs for an extra-long time today, my muscles still ached. I kneaded into the underside of my arm to loosen the knots before I dressed in black trousers and a white shirt.

I found Arabelle already in the dining room, and when I laid eyes on her, nerves gripped my insides in a vice. She'd chosen a chair closer to mine. I moved a little stiffer.

"Are you ready for our walk?" I swallowed down all the queasy, anxious nerves.

"What about lunch?" she asked.

The table was empty of the usual spread of food, which should have waited us around this time.

"We'll be eating elsewhere today."

She stood and, to my surprise, took my proffered arm. The small bit of shock escaped my body through my lips as I pretended to smooth the wrinkles from my shirt. I needed to make sure my heart was in my chest and not where I could have sworn I felt my pulse pounding in my ears.

As Elie suggested, I led Belle to the southern gardens, and at her soft inhale, I knew he had the right of it. There was an old fountain in the center of the stone courtyard, leafy vines growing up around the column and over the side of the white marble. Four arches surrounded the fountain: two leading into the garden, one wound back toward the castle, and the last leading to the gates.

We walked side by side through the right gate that took us deeper into the garden. Belle's eyes darted over the vibrant life all around us. It was more a forest of flowers than anything else. Trees shaded the majority of the ground, letting in a patchwork of sunlight.

Some of the bushes were taller than me, blooming pink and red. Some were just above our ankles with yellow, orange, and maroon flowers. Others were scattered along the ground in blues and greens. Vines wrapped up trunks and hung in drapes off the branches. Ferns nestled against the trees and under bushes.

"I've never seen anything like this. It's beautiful," she said with a soft voice, raising her hand to her chest.

"It was my mother's favorite garden. We used to walk these paths, and she'd tell me the name of each flower and plant, most of which I've forgotten by now. An ancestor of mine started it centuries ago, and it was left to grow wild." The sweet mix of floral scents filled every bit of air.

"Your mother had exquisite tastes."

Warmth swelled in my chest, and I couldn't help seeing the image of my mother overlapping with her.

"Yes, she did." I didn't stifle the pride scratching at the back of my mind.

For long minutes, the only sound was birds calling to their mates in song, and the rustle of leaves as a gentle breeze played with them. Arabelle finally broke that silence.

"Can I ask what your mother was like?"

I faltered in my steps and bit back my initial instinct to say no.

Elie's words sounded in my head. *You can't hope to win the heart of someone else without putting yours on the line as well.*

"She was kind. I never heard or saw her treat the castle servants less than how she'd treat the nobility," I paused, a flash of her standing up to my father when a serving girl spilled a tray in the dining room passing through my mind.

"She loved gardening—I mentioned that before—but I think she really loved to cultivate and nurture things. We have some of the rarest plants in these gardens, thanks to her.

"When I was still young, I wandered into the music room and heard her playing piano. I thought it was the most beautiful sound I'd ever heard, and I wanted to learn it. She taught me that and the violin.

"During my father's parties and balls, we'd play for the guests." I stared up at the treetops and smiled, ignoring the feeling of my fangs showing over my lips. "Those were some of the happiest days of my life."

Darkness wrapped its cold tendrils around me. My fingers clenched into tight fists, the tips of my claws biting into flesh.

"She didn't deserve to die the way she did."

"No one deserves to die like that." Arabelle squeezed my forearm. "The Crimson Plague was a horrible illness."

"Especially when you're forced out of your home and abandoned by your husband." I didn't mean to say it; it just slipped out.

"What?"

I ground my teeth as I remembered my father ordering his men to remove my already bedridden mother and perfectly healthy brother.

"He had his men take her from her sick bed and forced her and my brother to an estate far away. I don't even know where it was." I swallowed the lump of anguish. "I never saw them again."

"I'm so sorry, Lucien." Her fingers held fast to my arm. "That's awful. Why would he do such a thing? Didn't he love your mother?" She paused in her questioning, the muscle in her jaw flexing. "And why send your brother, too?"

I exhaled. "As good as my mother was, he was her opposite. He believed falling in love only made you weaker. More vulnerable."

A dull ache spread down my throat as I drowned the sadness in fury.

"As for my brother, he was exposed to the same illness. My father wasn't going to risk any more lives, especially not his precious heir."

Pain swam behind her eyes. "I understand what it's like to have a terrible father."

The look on her face made me want to track down her father and tear him to pieces all over again.

"When your father so willingly accepted my deal to give me one of his children, it took everything I had in me not to slaughter him where he stood. I thought he didn't deserve a child if he so easily gave them away." I placed my hand over hers.

A humorless laugh bubbled out of her. "If only that were the worst of it."

She wouldn't look at me.

"He's done worse?" Rage burned under my skin like hellfire, the muscles in my jaw working as it tightened, my teeth groaning their protest.

"Before I came here, he sold me off like chattel to a horrid man. I was to be his wife." The disgust lacing her voice said it all. "I only agreed because he said he'd take in Isa, too."

"You're betrothed?"

My heart plummeted straight through the ground. I would have assumed that it has, if the beat of my pulse wasn't pounding in my ears. If she was promised to someone else, I had already lost.

"I wonder." She stared out into the expanse of trees. "I didn't call it off, but it's not like I can marry him when I'm here."

"Do you want to marry him?" I controlled my breathing. *Please, any god listening, calm this thundering thing in my chest.*

"No."

"Then don't. You're free to do as you like as long as you live in this castle." Relief flooded my system and left my knees wanting to buckle under my weight.

"Except leave."

I flinched. That wasn't a retort I wanted to hear. I thought I might stand a chance when she agreed to this walk. Maybe I was fooling myself.

"Is it so bad? To live here?"

Arabelle breathed in, held it, and exhaled so slowly I didn't know if she'd stopped breathing altogether or not.

"No," she paused and kept her eyes straight ahead. She took a couple of steps away from me, and half-turned with her arms splayed.

"If I'm honest with myself, the more time I spend here, seeing all of this, the more I'm grateful I chose to come."

A spark of hope ignited in my chest, warming me from the very core of my being.

"I'm grateful you came, too." I forced myself to steady. Should I say the rest? I had to take the risk. "I was worried you might always hate it. And me...for making you stay."

She spun back around, facing off with me, her skirts twirling around her ankles.

"You were kind of an ass those first days," she deliberated, placing a forefinger to her chin in mock thought, "and also the following weeks when you kept me locked in my room."

She dropped her hand, a ghost of a smile on her lips when she looked me in the eye.

"But Elie thought I should give you a chance to make up for it."

Her grin was a lance through my heart.

I snorted and rolled my eyes.

"Elie's a busybody." I folded my arms over my chest, puffing out a breath of air that lifted stray strands of fur hanging over my eyes.

She laughed – actually laughed – and I couldn't help but smile at one of the most beautiful sounds I'd heard in such a long time.

"That he is. But I'm glad." Her amber eyes caught mine, and damn if all the air in my lungs didn't vanish. "You aren't what I expected."

A flutter of color flitted between us, and Arabelle's eyes followed it as the source landed on the broad surface of a leaf. It was a Spirit Fly, the iridescent wings shifting from silver to blue to purple to pink and back again as they flattened and retracted.

"What kind of butterfly is that? I've never seen anything like it," she stated as she moved closer, inspecting it.

I stepped up behind her, careful not to close in on her space.

"They're called Spirit Flies." I forgot it was almost time for their migration.

"Spirit Flies?"

"Yes. Some believe that spirits of the dead are carried by these when they leave the body, taken on their journey to the next world."

I held out a finger, and the creature inched over to my claw. I brought it closer to let her see the changing colors in the limited light.

"Do you believe that?"

"I don't *not* believe it."

She snickered, and the Spirit Fly flitted away. "That's not what I asked."

I chuckled from deep in my chest.

"Are you hungry?" I offered her my arm again, and she looped hers through it as a blush tinted her cheeks in color.

"Yes, I am."

I led her to a field full of pale pink flowers surrounding a pavilion. The columns were carved in an intricate thorn and rose pattern from a pale ash wood winding down and across the rails. A spread of fluffy rolls, chicken smothered in a light gravy, cheeses, and wine covered the table that sat in the middle of the pavilion.

Arabelle sat on one side, and I settled on the bench across from her. I took the wine decanter and filled both of our glasses while she started serving herself the meat and cheeses.

"Have you read many of the books in the library?" She grabbed a bread roll, cracking it open with a tendril of steam rising from its center.

"I've read them all," I answered absently as I filled my plate.

She coughed, pounding on her chest after almost choking on her food. She grabbed for her wine and swallowed two mouthfuls.

"How is that possible? There's so many."

I tried to hide my grin by pursing my lips. "I've had a lot of time on my hands. What better way to spend it than reading?"

She huffed a sigh, placing the wine glass back on the table. "Do you have any recommendations?"

"For you to read?"

"No, for me to build a fort." She rolled her eyes, but I noted the amusement there. "Yes, to read."

I cut into the chicken, the gravy running down the sides and pooling in a puddle underneath.

"I can bring you one when we get back."

I took a bite, savoring the way the moist morsel melted on my tongue in an explosion of flavor.

"Aren't you supposed to be playing some music for me when

we get back?" She arched a brow at me while mopping up the gravy on her plate with the bread.

"Can't I do both?"

"I guess you can." Her gaze swept to the castle rising up over the garden's luscious plants. "Let's go to the library, then."

Arabelle leaned back against one of the tables in the library while I shifted around books on a shelf in search of one of my favorites. The binding was cracked and slightly falling apart from wear and tear, but the pages were still in good condition.

I handed the tome to her. "Here. It's a story about a warrior who's tired of being used to fight in battles for an ungrateful king, so she takes her people and withdraws from the world."

"Thanks." She tucked the book under her arm. "Now, let's go so I can hear you play for me." She nudged me toward the double doors, and I obliged.

"I'm a little rusty. I haven't played for someone else in a while," I said as I swung open the doors to the music room, holding one ajar as she walked by. I squashed the instinct to breathe in her deliciously sweet scent.

"If it's bad, I can always plug my ears."

Was...was she teasing me? I couldn't contain the grin nor the thrill of excitement buzzing along my skin. I followed her to the small, raised platform.

I sat down on the bench, scooting it closer as my nerves twisted my stomach and tried their best to devour me alive. I ignored the feel of her eyes on me from behind. I could do this. I had played for kings and lords, small audiences and big.

It should be no different this time. I breathed in through my mouth and out through my nose to steady my heart. This was different, felt different. I was about to slice myself open to show her my very soul.

My fingers moved over the keys in the familiar rhythms and patterns I learned as a child, the music splitting the silence in a slow melody. With each note I played, I drifted into that space in my head where no other sound could reach me.

I leaned into the movements of my hands, feet finding and pressing the damper pedal down to let the notes linger in the air a bit longer.

By the time I finished the last notes of the song, I was only vaguely aware that Arabelle had moved up to my side and watched me.

"I thought you were rusty."

"I am."

Her mouth twisted to the side. "It sounded perfect to me."

Pride swelled within me as I started another song, only faltering a fraction of a second when she sat next to me on the bench, our thighs pressing together. My heart lurched up my throat, and I fought every urge to glance down and make sure the damn thing was where it was supposed to be. It was such an unusual feeling; no other woman had ever made me this nervous or jumpy.

"Can I play with you?"

The question caught me off guard and my fingers froze, the music stopping all at once.

"You want to play together?" My voice came out soft, so soft that if it wasn't me who spoke, I wasn't sure I'd have heard it.

I gave her a sidelong glance, her eyes softening as she stared at my hands.

"I can feel the joy in the music when you play. I can feel it here," she said and placed a hand over her heart. She let it drop and looked up at me, worry lighting her eyes. "If it's not okay, something you don't want to share with me because of your mother, you don't have to."

"No." I shifted my hands back to the starting position. "I'd be happy to play with you."

I opened the music folder that sat on the stand, and we played until stars dotted a blackened sky.

Arabelle

My mind still swam in an ocean of some faraway place from my day spent with Lucien. Before, he was my jailor—some beast keeping me locked up in his castle—but now I could see through the cracks into who he was. I had suspected there was pain in his past but never that it was something so horrible.

Hinges creaked when my door opened, and my eyes snapped up to Elie. He carried a tray with alabaster ceramic mugs, swirls of vines, and leaves painted on the sides.

"How was your walk with Lucien?"

He sat the tray down on the small table by the window. I joined him as he placed one of the mugs before me.

"He told you about that?" Elie always knew what happened between us. Maybe Lucien went to him for advice on what to do. I bit my lip to stop the grin tugging at the corner of my mouth.

He took the seat across from me, propping his cheek on his fist with a smirk.

"Dear, sweet Belle. There's not a thing Lucien doesn't tell me."

I held his gaze as I took a sip from the mug, the warm steam embracing my cheeks. I savored the rich, sweet chocolate.

"You promised me information for time spent with him; one piece of information per day, if I'm not mistaken."

I had questions. Questions I didn't want to voice to Lucien, not yet. I didn't want to rip open the wounds that had never even healed properly.

He quirked a brow as he took the other cup of cocoa. "I did. Anything in particular you'd like to know?"

"You knew his family." He straightened at the statement. "What were his mother and brother like?"

I already had some idea of his father. I knew enough that I didn't care to know more.

Sadness dulled the vibrant gold of Elie's eyes.

"Helaine was the most beautiful person I've ever met. And I don't mean just on the outside. She was like a second mother to me in every sense. She praised me when I did well, scolded me when I didn't, and even took care of me when I fell sick." A slow smile stretched across his face. "She's where Lucien gets his compassion. Even if his father tried to beat it out of him."

"What?"

My grip on the cup tightened. His father had beaten him for being compassionate? Just how cruel of a man was he? I swallowed the anger that wanted to rise up from the depths of my being.

Elie ignored my question, though, and continued, "And his brother? He was a little spitfire. He always wanted to be where Lucien and I were. He tried to sneak into one of our training sessions with us once. Luce beat the kid's ass. Earned a good scolding from Helaine in the process."

"It sounds so very—"

"Violent?"

"Normal." I don't know what I expected his childhood to be like, but that was not even in the realm of what I imagined.

"What else would it be?"

I shrugged, taking another sip of the cocoa. "I don't know. I guess I thought his past would have been a bit more exciting."

"Oh, trust me, there was plenty of excitement." Mischief set the gold in his eyes ablaze as he chuckled.

"Like what?"

I wanted to hear it, about Lucien's past. The answers to all my questions lay within this man before me. He told me Lucien wasn't always a beast, but I needed to ask him about that myself. I wanted to, during our time together yesterday, but we were having such a nice time that bringing up the past like that might have wrecked everything.

He clicked his tongue at me.

"That's your little bit of information." He stood and turned toward the door. "Come find me after you see him again, and I'll tell you."

The grin on his face made me want to throw my mug at his head. He refused to divulge more than a little at a time. I huffed and crossed my arms over my chest, pushing my bottom lip out for emphasis.

"You are such a pain in my ass." Damn him and his little rule.

He faced me fully and sketched a dramatic bow, then stalked out of the room with his usual smug expression.

I turned the covers down and slid beneath them, clutching the book Lucien gave me in one hand. His mother, Helaine, sounded like such a wonderful person. Both he and Elie only ever had nice things to say about her. I wished I could have met her, seen the person Lucien was around her. I smiled to myself. I'd bet he was as gentle as a lamb.

How could her husband send her away to die alone? It was

such a cruel thing to do to someone he was supposed to love. Then again, love didn't always play a role in marriage. That was something I knew too well. I never would have loved Louis, and I didn't think he would have loved me. Falling in love wasn't an option.

I leaned back into the pillows and hugged the book to my chest. The look in Lucien's eyes when I mentioned Louis was something akin to a slow-burning ember ready to burst into flame again. It wasn't the first time I noticed it; he was trying to control that fiery temper of his. He had tried to hide the tremble of his muscles when he leashed it and held it tight.

With every new thing I learned about him, it became easier to find comfort in his presence. The thought took me by surprise, and I tugged the blankets a little tighter around me.

I studied the book Lucien had lent me on our trip to the library. Cracked leather caught on my fingertips as I ran them over the cover. The pages were worn. This book had been well-loved; he must have read it often. I read the name.

My breath froze in my lungs as recognition barreled into me like a runaway carriage. The binding was worn and tattered, but I would never forget the name of the book which kindled my love of reading. Without knowing much about me, he gave me a copy of one of my favorite books, one that I hadn't read in years because it was so rare to come by.

I opened it and began to read, letting images of magic and princes and adventure fill my mind.

Lucien

A balmy breeze blew through the castle gardens as Belle and I sat on the sun-warmed stone bench. A deep discussion about music and instruction brought us outside to enjoy a moment of quiet peace. The tangy citrus scent filled the area surrounding the orange trees that hung overhead. I breathed in that smell, a reminder of summers spent running and playing outside.

"What kind of books do you favor?" I already knew about the romances, but was that all she read? I hoped not.

"Believe it or not, I actually like romance and adventure about the same." She smiled and gazed out at the orange trees. "Though my sister and I have a soft spot for fairy tales."

"It's no fairy tale, but if you like those types of books, you'll like the book I gave you."

A petal fluttered down and landed on her shoulder. I plucked it up and held it in my palm. Her eyes were on my hand as I held it out, and the wind swept up that petal to join the rest.

"Is it an adventure book?"

I stared straight ahead, contented just to sit here and talk with her.

"It's a little bit of both."

"I find it surprising you'd read something with any romance at all."

I glanced at her from my peripheral and noticed the smile she fought to contain. I fought my own grin when I spoke.

"Why? Because I'm a—"

"Because I've never met a man..."

She crinkled her brows. I knew the thought in her head that instant; I didn't need my magic to read it.

"A male...who reads it."

I scoffed and rolled my eyes. What fools. Truly. If women enjoyed those types of books, the best way to pull them into bed was to read them as well.

"It's their loss, then. You can learn a lot about winning over a woman from them."

I realized I'd said the thought out loud too late. I raised my brows and turned back to her, the wind blowing through my fur.

"If you were into that sort of thing."

"Lucien."

She was silent for seconds, and my insides twisted into knots as I dreaded the next words. She'd resent me, hate me as I hated myself.

"Are you a lady's man?"

I huffed and turned away again. Lady's man? Absolutely not. I was selective in who I chose. "Lady's man" made me sound like some creep.

"Let's talk about something else."

Silence filled the space between us again. It was times such as these that I wished I still had ahold of that power, the one I inherited from my mother – the ability to mind walk, to see and hear what was in another's head. I could only use it in my sleep now.

"Lucien, about last night, I really—"

"Ah, look at this. Did the lord of the castle finally deign to come outside?" A voice purred from behind us.

I went still as death. How could I let someone sneak up behind me? Now, of all times? I was distracted. I should have paid closer attention to our surroundings.

In seconds, I had both of us on our feet, putting myself between Arabelle and the men.

"Marid scum." I bared my fangs at the two of them.

"What a pretty little woman you have here, *Beasty*. Does Lord Aamon know about her yet?" one of them asked in a silky voice that made my skin prickle.

If they told him about her, then he would come to kill her just to make sure I couldn't be saved. Were Ashea and Hesnen working together then? Were all the Lunar Courts involved in this curse? The tips of my claws dug into my palms.

It didn't matter.

I had to kill them.

I needed to draw them away from Arabelle. I forced a confidence I didn't feel into my voice and posture. "No, he doesn't. And he never will."

The second Marid laughed, a sound that raked my spine with chills. "What makes you think we're not going to tell him?"

The laugh in my throat was a foreign sound to me. "Because I'm not going to give you the chance to. Or have you forgotten how we deal with your kind?"

"Lucien, what are these two?" Arabelle's voice pulled me back from the ledge of savagery I wanted to unleash on the men in front of me.

"They're Marid. Elie told you about them, remember?" I held onto the hope that because she had already learned of them, she wouldn't suffer consequences from the curse.

Both men hissed at the sound of Elie's name.

"That dog of yours has killed a lot of our friends," the first said with a nasty sneer.

"Maybe we'll have some fun with your woman once we've dealt with you." The first stepped closer.

I swallowed against the panic rising faster than my temper. What was the best way to get her away from them? I could take on two by myself, but not if I had to protect her at the same time. An idea struck.

"How about a deal instead?"

The first raised a brow. "A deal for what?"

"For her safety. What will it take for you to leave her alone? To forget you ever saw her?" Please, to whatever god listened to my prayers, let this work.

The two looked at each other, then back at me. "Your head."

"Deal."

"Lucien, no." Her hands grasped the ends of my shirt. "I'm not going to let you die for me."

But I grabbed her wrists and twisted to meet her gaze.

"Run. Go find Elie." I kept my voice low enough for only her to hear.

She stared up at me, tears lining her eyes.

I read the hesitation there and let her go, gathering up the anger boiling just under my skin, and roared, "Go. Now."

She ran.

One of the Marid clicked his tongue.

"Such brutality. It's no wonder you were cursed." Their blue eyes tracked her as she disappeared into the darkness of the castle. "Come with us, Ruby Prince."

They didn't fear me. They would soon learn that was a mistake. Even without the use of my magic, I could shred them to pieces with these claws and teeth.

We left the castle, the Marid leading while I followed, heading into the forest. Deeper and deeper until it surrounded us on all sides.

A desire to rip them apart flooded through my veins; they would have done the same to her. They would have taken her away from me, and they would have delighted in killing her slowly, leaving her body for me to find.

At least they weren't Daeva. Fear sluiced through me in a shudder that had my knees wanting to collapse. I wouldn't have even found a body if *they* were the ones after her. I wanted to hurl when they mentioned Aamon's name – at the thought of Daeva being involved.

The Marid stopped amid a small clearing in the forest. I steadied myself, extending my claws and dropping into a fighting stance. They may want my life, but despite that deal, I wouldn't just *give* it to them.

At least, that was my thought. Until three more of those pale blue bastards stepped from the shadows of the trees and surrounded me.

They set a trap for me—an ambush. My snarl rose to a roar that boomed in the eerily silent forest.

I swiped my claws at the one to my left, but he jumped back, and I only cut a line through his shirt. I let my old training guide my instincts, where to strike, where to dodge, where to block, but the flurry of their movement was hard to follow.

Their cackle ignited a spark of fury in me, and I launched myself into them. A fist snapped my head sideways, and tangy blood coated my tongue. Another landed a kick to the back of my knee that brought me down.

I spit a mouthful of blood on the forest floor and curled my lips back as I grabbed for the closest one. Another slammed a foot into my ribs so hard I thought I heard one crack, and I doubled over.

"What's wrong, Little Ruby Prince?" one of the preening

assholes said to me through a row of teeth with a similar blue tint as his skin.

"We knew you wouldn't come quietly, even with the threat on the woman." One of the original two laughed.

Another squatted down next to me and leaned in, grabbing my horn and yanking my head closer to him.

"Can't you take on a few of us Lows?" He let go, and I whipped my head back with a growl.

"I thought all you Solar Court goodlings were supposed to be strong and gallant. But here you are...weak as a mewling Piskie babe," another one of them said from somewhere behind me.

To lose to these men left a bitter taste in my mouth. If it weren't for this damned curse, I would have no problem taking every one of them out without breaking a sweat. Well. I might have broken a sweat given the gap in my training for nigh on twenty years. I gritted my teeth as the one in front of me drew his fist back.

I waited, but the impact never came. Instead, there was a rush of movement and metal on bone. The point of a sword protruded through the mouth of the one who'd kicked me in the ribs. The blade ripped from the dead man's corpse. It was all a blur of red and silver as one after another fell under his blade.

When the last one fell, Elie hooked an arm under my shoulder and heaved me back to my feet. I leaned my weight into him, and, to his credit, he didn't buckle under it.

"Jeez, Luce. I really thought you could hold them off until I got here."

His hand held firm to my waist as he led me to the forest's edge.

"I thought so, too."

It wasn't just my magic that had been weakened. The longer I was like this, the more my strength was sapped from me.

"You were right, Elie."

Warmth from the sun's rays welcomed us back from the shadowed forest. Elie pointed toward the Life Spring.

"Usually. But you'll have to be more specific, Luce."

I heaved a long sigh and rolled my eyes at the snark. "I shouldn't have skipped out on training."

"Well, that's an easy fix. Let's get you to the Spring and get those wounds healed up."

The strength in him amplified the weakness clinging to every fragment of my being, and while I didn't fault him that, a part of me hated it. He wouldn't let me hear the end of it for some years. I frowned at the phantom aches and pains of days past. If I wanted to protect Belle, I had to go back to training.

THIRTY-ONE

Arabelle

You're to have every meal together. That's what Elie had said that first morning. I glared at the empty seats down the table, the tap of my fingernails on the wood echoing off the stone walls in the dining hall.

"Where are they?" Neither one of them had shown their faces since those creepy blue men approached us in the garden.

Their eyes still haunted me. The way the pale blue irises almost glowed against the inky black. Unlike the horned men from before, who were brutal, beautiful, and cruel, these men were enchanting and terrifying all at once. A shudder raked through my body at the memory of them.

When Lucien made that deal with them, my heart wanted to burst from my chest. Even if it was a ruse, how could he say it? It was to protect me, to get me away from them, but the pain was all the same.

He may not have seen me as the daughter of a thief anymore, but he offered his *life* in my place. It was all he had in this crumbling castle, outside of Elie. I would never allow him to give it up for my sake, not when we hadn't tried every other avenue.

I had no idea where to even start searching for Elie when I ran. It was pure luck that he'd been walking by a window and seen the Marid approaching us. When I burst through the doors, he had already been halfway down the stairs, yelling at me to run to my room and not come out until he gave the all-clear.

After all that happened, Elie had only slipped me a note explaining what happened and that the castle was safe again. I chewed my lip until I tasted blood. Where was Lucien? Was he okay after that?

I shoved the concern down. I had to stay focused on finding the others. Even if every day spent with him left me doubting my initial conclusion about them. The beast gentle enough to hold something as delicate as a Spirit Fly was at odds with one who could imprison innocent people – children.

A chime from the clock vibrated against my bones. I was tired of waiting, and my stomach had been grumbling louder than my thoughts. *Where are they?* I showed up to these damned meals like they wanted me to, they could at least have the decency to eat with me. I tore a chunk of bread off with my teeth.

When Lucien started opening up to me, playing the piano with me, I really thought he had moved past whatever resentment he had because of my father's actions. I jabbed at the sausage link on my plate.

Maybe I was wrong. I let out a frustrated sigh and slammed my utensils back on the table, rattling the ceramic dishware. I needed some fresh air.

As I passed through the door, I ran right into Elie's broad chest, his hands gripping my upper arms in reflex.

"Elie, where have you been?" I didn't bother to hide the annoyed tone as I took two steps back to put some space between us.

The smile he gave me was more of a grimace with the way he knitted his eyebrows together. "I was having a talk with Lucien."

"About?" Thank God he was alive and well enough that Elie was here with me.

"You."

"What about me?" They'd been talking about me? Unease settled at the bottom of my stomach. Just what I needed. More men making decisions for me without consulting me.

"Lucien asked me to keep you company on your walks through the castle for a while." He must have seen the argument in my eyes because he added, "Just until we know that no more intruders will show up. To make sure it's safe for you to be alone again."

"I don't need to be looked after like some child." I lifted my chin to him. I wasn't so weak as to need an escort everywhere.

"That's not what he thinks. He's just worried about you." He rubbed his temples with his thumb and forefinger. "When the Marid attack, they attack in groups. Even if we taught you self-defense tactics, you're more like to piss them off."

"Would you?"

Learning how to defend myself would be beneficial to me when dealing with more than just these Marid. I wouldn't have to wait for help. I could save myself.

"Would I what?" He dropped his hand.

"Teach me self-defense. I should be able to defend myself."

The gold in his eyes glittered with delight. I might have made a mistake. His slow smile had my stomach leaping to my throat. I *definitely* made a mistake.

"Walk with me," I said before he could speak again and confirm exactly what I thought.

I needed to move. To provide some distraction from whatever was now stirring in that head of his.

Sunlight kissed my skin, warming the exposed parts of my arms in the simple, chocolate-colored dress. The skirt swayed with every step as Elie and I walked side by side.

"I want to see something new today." My gaze fell in the direction I came to the castle from. I knew what was over there, though I *would* like to revisit during the day. But today, I had an escort who could answer questions I had about prisoners.

"Have you seen this side of the castle?" Elie directed me to the south.

A cobblestone path, bordered by lush hedges, led me and Elie alongside the castle and toward the back. The gentle slosh of water came from opposite the evergreen shrubs that bordered the walkway. As we followed the path, it opened up to a large pond, the sunlight glittering off the surface like it was filled with diamonds instead of water.

Pebbles crunched under our boots as we walked the winding path around the curved bank. The waves lapped lazily over the stonewall that separated land from water. A bridge arched over to the other side of the pond, and we took the stairs two at a time. I stopped in the middle and let the peace of the moment wash over me with the breeze.

Elie stopped behind me, remaining quiet the whole time. It wasn't an uncomfortable sort of silence, but I had grown accustomed to his sly remarks and teasing.

"It's not like you to be so quiet. What's on your mind, Elie?" It was disconcerting that he was this somber, that he wasn't acting like the Elie I'd come to be fond of.

He leaned back on the bridge railing, slipping his hands into his pockets.

"I almost didn't make it to Lucien in time. With the Marid." He gazed out over the water.

"I'm supposed to protect him. But I can't guard this entire place on my own. Those bastards got in without me noticing. They got close enough to kill him without me even knowing they were here."

"How very uncharacteristic of you to feel sorry for yourself." I hated seeing him dejected. He should be smiling and laughing, not beating himself up for something that was out of his control. His gaze was fixed on the castle, and I turned to follow his line of sight.

It took a minute to realize this was the pond I could see from my window, with the sculpture in the middle. I thought it was a fish, but it wasn't.

The top half was carved into the shape of a lithe, beautiful woman, hair flowing behind her as if she were a living creature climbing from the water up onto that rock. The bottom half was a fishtail, the scales incandescent and shimmering dark green in the sunlight.

He scoffed. "I am *not* feeling sorry for myself."

"Whatever you say."

I snuck a glance at him, but he remained silent. Well, damn. Cheering him up would be harder than I realized.

The waves of the pond lulled my mind back to Lucien. My earlier admission to him on our walk had taken me by surprise. It wasn't a lie or even a half-truth. I really was grateful I chose to come here. It saved me from a marriage that could have ended in my death if I went through with it.

Elie had been a gift from above. I clasped my fingers together as I stepped to the side of the bridge. It was hard to stay angry and hate this place with all his snide remarks and humor. Even Lucien, despite all the anger and temperament, was turning into someone I looked forward to talking with.

Their presence offered me comfort like Isa's did. Guilt settled in me like a stone tossed in a lake. What happened to her after I left? I had written my father that note in hopes he would understand, that he would see the wealth in those chests and be content. But a lurking, nagging thought pressed in the back of my mind. What if he didn't?

Would Lucien allow me to see her? I just wanted to make sure she was safe and not being used as a pawn in another of my father's schemes. I would ask. It wouldn't hurt to ask.

The serenity of this place was like something out of the books I read with Isa. Our cottage was quiet enough, but there was always something that needed to be done: wood to chop, food to cook, weeds to pluck, gardens to tend.

Here, I wasn't obligated to do a single thing. A small part of me longed for the days when I had things to keep my mind and hands busy. *Maybe I'll start my own garden here.* Or I could tend the gardens his mother planted.

Would Lucien even allow that? The thought sent a mixture of unease and excitement rippling through me. Better that than let the thoughts run rampant through my head. There were flowers and plants everywhere I looked, but I'd yet to spot a vegetable garden.

I leaned over the side of the railing and breathed in the damp scent of wet stone and mud. A glimmer below the surface of the water caught the sunlight just before the fish leapt, snapping up a dragonfly that skittered across the pond. *Or I could take up fishing.* I wrinkled my nose at that.

A soft breeze wafted through the loose braid that hung over my shoulder, and my eyelids drooped as I leaned into it. A distancing thought surged forward, along with the face of a handsome man who haunted my dreams.

My jaw tightened. He was trapped somewhere in these walls, and maybe not just him. Could they be in the dungeon? If I asked Elie, he might be willing to show me. I didn't want to ask Lucien about it, not if he was the one who imprisoned them. Even if it was at odds with the Lucien I was getting to know.

Look deeper, Belle. The words echoed in my mind again as if a church bell were beckoning parishioners to the pews on the day of worship. Deeper had to mean underground; nothing ran deeper than that.

I would convince Elie. I had to. A month had already passed since I came to the castle, and I still hadn't found hide nor hair of him, of any of them. I inhaled deep, that earthy scent awash in my nostrils. My stomach did somersaults at the idea of asking. What if they *were* locked in the dungeon? I could be next for figuring it out.

A squawk from a bird flying overhead snapped my attention back to reality and put a stop to my impending question. I gazed up in time to catch the black and white feathers of a duck as it flew through an open door on the side of the castle.

"What's that?"

There was movement just beyond the opening – no way it was just the one animal. My feet were moving before my mind, and I crossed the cobblestone path toward that open door. As I approached, the excited chirping of birds filled the warm air.

Hurried footsteps crunched behind me, but he was too late to stop me from going inside. I poked my head into the door to be greeted by a furious flap of wings from another black and white blur, only this one was much larger and had a crown of crimson feathers.

My weight shifted to my back leg, and I rocked into Elie as it honked an obnoxious sound at me, spreading its wings. A droplet of sweat ran down the length of my cheek and neck.

"It's the Aviary." Elie's voice came from behind.

My eyes shot from the animal to him as he slid by me and grabbed a dark green apron hanging from a hook on the wall.

He rolled his sleeves up, showing off his toned forearms. The squawk of the birds quickened as he tied his hair back at the nape. He picked up a rusted pail filled with seed in one hand and a trowel in the other. "It's about time to feed them anyway."

The Elie of minutes ago melted away and back into his usual self. Was it the normalcy of his chore? Whenever that deep well of hopelessness threatened to swallow me, routine always grounded me.

"Do you do this every day?" I paused as I watched the duck from earlier waddle its way across the aviary floor to a bowl underneath a perch.

"Yes. One of the many things I do around here." Elie dipped the trowel into the pail and deposited seed into several dishes as birds of all kinds swooped down and swarmed him. "I think you should get Lucien to escort you instead of me."

He gave me a sidelong stare. I thought Elie enjoyed my presence as much as I enjoyed his, but I could be wrong. He might well resent having to escort me around like this. If he was as affected by the attack as he said, perhaps he wanted to be alone.

"Are you tired of me already?" I tried to keep my voice light as I scanned the area.

There was a table with various tools spread over it: pails, gloves, bags of seed to the side. When my eyes came to Elie again, it was then that I took note of the green edges of a bruise on his cheek.

"No, I just...Do you not want to be around him?" He pressed his lips in a line as he sprinkled some seed over the floor for birds who couldn't get to the bowls.

I didn't want to answer that.

"What happened to your face? Did Lucien hit you?"

In all his anger, Lucien never lifted a hand to strike me, but maybe it was different with Elie. A knot tightened in my stomach.

"Ah, this?" He lifted a hand to his cheek, careful not to touch it. He chuckled as if it didn't bother him at all. "I finally got him to work off some of that anger. It happened during training."

"So, he didn't hit you because he was angry?"

"Oh, he was angry, alright. But I can take it. I'm built sturdy." He slammed a fist into his chest and dropped it.

"And I got more than my share of licks in," he said with a smug smirk. "Is that why you don't ask him to show you around?"

"It's not that. You are already with me." I dropped my gaze to the floor and watched the birds peck at the ground. "He can be a bit unpleasant at times, though."

He laughed as if I told some joke. "You're not wrong."

The metal of the pail rattled against the table as he sat it down with the trowel inside.

"I need some time to myself and to put together a training regimen for you. But where Lucien is concerned..." He leaned back on the table, gripping it with his hands on either side. "He's been through a lot."

"You said you've known him since you were children, right?" I studied his posture, the slump of his shoulders. He was remembering something.

"Yes. My father was his father's High General. Led his armies." Elie fixed me with his golden eyes.

"Armies? Lucien's father had armies?"

Only high-ranking lords commanded armies. Was Lucien really a lord? I should have at least known *of* him. My brows crinkled as I scoured my memory for anything I could remember about lords in this area, and the only ones I could come up with were the Cordevauxs.

"Yes. He was the king, so naturally, he had armies." Elie let go of the table and folded his arms over his chest, crease lines between his eyebrows.

Lucien's father was a king? Pain thrummed behind my eyes. Not this again. How did I not remember? What happened here that they weren't known by anyone – everyone – in Starside? Especially the nobility.

"Does that make Lucien a prince?"

Elie gave me a smile that didn't quite reach his eyes. In fact, those beautifully unique, golden eyes darkened when he spoke.

"Right now, Lucien is no more than what you've seen."

"Tell me about how you two met."

I wanted to know more—more about this castle, about Elie, about Lucien. He promised me details, but I didn't think I would be okay with only one at a time. I would need to go back to the library and find everything about their history that I could.

"When I was old enough to start training, at seven, my father brought me to the castle so he could teach me the ways of a warrior. He also trained me to lead so I could take his place some-day. The king decided Lucien should also be trained to protect his people, his crown. Lucien joined the training under my father with me.

"We fought at first. I thought he was nothing but a snobby prince who would never be able to hold a sword right, but we became friends—after I put him on his ass a few times—and got into all kinds of trouble."

The corner of my lips curled in a grin as I pictured a younger version of Elie and Lucien, causing havoc on the unsuspecting folks of the castle. I had no clue as to what he looked like then, but my mind took the liberty of filling in the details—blond-haired, blue-eyed, too much like another I kept seeing.

"I wish I could've seen that. Sounds like you had a lot of fun."

But good God, Elie was a *warrior*. No wonder his eyes sparkled like a child's when I asked him to teach me self-defense.

"We did. At least until his mother died." A muscle in his neck pulsated just under his skin, and fire danced in his golden eyes.

"Is that when he changed?" Lucien told me about his mother and brother dying, but he didn't give me a lot of details about either.

"Yes. His father saw to it."

Pain and fury etched into his features. His fingers tightened around his biceps, crinkling his sleeves.

The air around both Elie and Lucien changed every time either one brought up Lucien's father. They never delved into detail about what he had done to make them hate him so, but I could almost see that hatred radiating off them.

"Why?"

It twisted my stomach in knots, and I wasn't entirely sure I *wanted* to know what horrid thing was done to elicit such a reaction.

"He was a cruel man, Belle. The things he did to Lucien..." he paused and turned his back toward me. He braced his hands on the worktable, the muscles in his arms and back rippling under the tight shirt. "It was bad."

A lump crawled its way into my throat and lodged itself there. I tried to swallow around it.

"What did he do?"

I held my palm to my chest. Elie had said he assaulted the king, and the queasiness in my stomach told me this was the reason.

Elie glanced over his shoulder. "That's not my story to tell. You should just..." He raked his hands through his red curls, pulling them free of the leather band. "You should wait until Lucien opens up about it. I know he can be a stubborn ass, but that kind and compassionate boy I used to know is still buried in there."

There was no way I could say no to that, not when Elie looked as if he might fall apart at the seams right in front of me if he let go of that table. A flash of blond filtered through my mind's eye. I needed to ask about the dungeon now while he was off kilter.

"Where's the dungeon?"

His body went rigid, and he tossed me another glance over his shoulder before turning to face me again.

"Why? Do you want me to lock you in a cell?" A wicked grin played at his lips as his gaze raked up and down my body despite the color leeching from his skin.

"Where is it?" A bit of relief swept through me as the Elie I knew came back.

The playfulness faltered, and the grin fell away. "Why do you want to know?"

"I've never seen one before. I'm curious what they're actually like," I lied and prayed that he was far enough away not to pick up on my fingers fidgeting in my skirts.

The amusement winked out of his eyes altogether as he pinned me with a golden stare. "Be glad you don't. They're dark and dreary and smelly. Not a place for a beautiful thing such as yourself."

"Come on, Elie, please show me?"

He frowned at me this time. "Lucien wouldn't be happy with me if I took you down there."

Down. It was a confirmation that my gut feeling was right.

"He doesn't have to know about it. I can keep a secret," I pushed. Elie would bend easier than Lucien. It was clear every time he brought me a book to read, in every appeal he made on his friend's behalf.

"I don't keep things from Lucien, Arabelle."

My back straightened at the sound of my full name on his lips. His tone said it was the end of this discussion. Or maybe he wouldn't bend that easily. I huffed a resigned sigh.

"Fine. Guess I'll find something else to pique my interest."

It didn't matter that he wouldn't show me. It was enough to know it was below us.

With Death the Bird-monster busy scarfing down food alongside the other birds, I stepped further into the aviary, moving through an archway. Sunlight poured into the room in an array of different colors from the stained-glass windows. The outside wall was made up of colored glass, depicting an elderly woman with an outstretched hand.

Trees of various sizes lined the walls, with ferns, heart-shaped

Colocasia, and cordyline plants underneath. A two-foot-wide stream snaked its way around the room, small wooden bridges crossing over it at opposite ends. The door was removed from the frame to allow the birds the freedom to come and go as they pleased. A dull ache bloomed in my chest; I wished I had that kind of freedom.

I turned back to Elie. He'd gone back to feeding the birds. I needed to know who it was coming to me in these dreams – who the boys in the locket were.

"Elie?" In this light, he looked truly young.

"Yes?" He lifted his gaze to meet mine.

"Lucien is the Master of the castle now, and before him, it was his father." It wasn't a question but a statement of fact.

"Yes."

"And his brother is dead?"

Elie stiffened a bit at that. "Yes."

"Did he have any other brothers?"

"No. Just the one."

"Where is he? His father, I mean."

A vein popped in Elie's neck, no doubt pulsing in time with his heartbeat. "Dead."

"Does Lucien have any cousins?" I needed to find out if there was a connection between *him* and Lucien. It couldn't be some random coincidence. My mind flashed back to the Marid with their beautiful faces, and for a moment, I considered the possibility that this dream man wasn't an alley here to help me.

No.

That wasn't the case. It couldn't be. His eyes were kind, and he was always wrapped in that golden light. He was my way to freedom.

His eyes narrowed on mine. "Why are you asking these questions, Belle?"

I chewed my bottom lip. I needed to find out if he was alive or dead, like the others. My heart cracked open at the thought. My fingers tangled in the skirts of my dress.

"Just trying to get an idea of who he is."

"Then you should talk to him."

My hand reflexively went to my chest, where the locket hid. I could trust Elie; he might be in Lucien's corner, but he was a good man. I tugged on the chain, pulling it from under the bodice.

"Who are these boys?" I asked as I clicked it open before taking the few steps toward him.

Sweat gleamed on Elie's forehead and neck as his eyes locked on the paintings. His jaw tightened.

"Where did you get that?" His voice was low and laced with sorrow.

I closed the locket and tucked it safely away again, then met his golden stare.

"All you have to do is tell me where they are. I'll take care of the rest."

Elie's eyes burned with rage as he held my gaze, making me take a step back in retreat. I'd never seen him with such anger on his face.

"I can't tell you about them. Not yet."

A chime sounded somewhere in the castle, and Elie cursed under his breath.

"I have to go."

He pulled the apron off and tossed it onto the table before walking out the door I came in.

THIRTY-TWO

Arabelle

When I left the aviary, I didn't recognize the hallway at all. The castle was so much bigger than I imagined. Fires from sconces glistened off the marble floor as I made my way through, the soft click of my heels echoing in the silence. I went through the first door I came across.

Beams of colored light shone through the stained-glass window in the middle of the opposite stone wall. The panels were arranged to depict a man standing before a hunched woman and a hooded figure. I stepped closer to the window, my hand reaching for the man as my chest tightened. That yellow hair was familiar.

I turned my back to the scene, and my eyes caught the glint of light against marble. A chess set sat on a table next to a fireplace. I strode across the space and picked up one of the pawns. The piece was cool in my hand as I rolled it back and forth.

"Do you know how to play?" His gruff voice gave me a start, and my heart jumped into my throat.

I dropped the pawn as I spun to the door where Lucien now stood.

"W-what?"

"Can you play?" He leaned down and snatched the chess piece before it rolled under a chest at his feet.

"I-uh, yeah. I can. But I haven't played in a really long time. I was never really any good at it. My mother always beat me." My fingers curled into loose fists at my side, and I avoided his gaze.

"Would you like to play?"

My eyes snapped up to his, and I swallowed, trying to calm the rush of my heart. How long had it been? Mother taught me how to play, but I stopped after she died. Seeing the chess set brought an array of memories, being told I wasn't good enough, forced to sit and learn strategies, to play for hours, and go without food if I didn't win at least once. My eyes dipped again.

"You don't have to if you don't want to."

He set the pawn back on the board and turned to walk away.

"Wait," I said as my hand snapped up and clutched the loose sleeve hanging from his arm.

If I could get closer to him, he might tell me where the dungeon was or take me there himself.

"I want to play. Just...take pity on me." I forced a smile I knew didn't meet my eyes.

I sat in the chair furthest away from the fireplace and ignored the quizzical look he gave me as he took a seat across from me. The pieces were already set up as if they'd been waiting for the moment someone might come play again.

A soft click sounded when Lucien made his first move. I studied the board before moving my own pawn up a square. The steady *click, click, click* of chess pieces connecting with the board was the only sound for several minutes as we played in silence.

I could ease into a conversation with him, ask something that only required a simple answer.

"What happened to those men from before?"

"Elie and I dealt with them. They won't cause you any more trouble."

His eyes never left the board, and I couldn't tell if it was because he was focused on the game or avoiding eye contact.

My brow furrowed in frustration as each turn became more complex than the last, my strategies being shattered one after another by Lucien. He moved each piece as if he saw into my mind and knew every play I would make. I didn't know for how long I could keep up with his brutal play style.

A piece clicked on the board.

"I want to learn to fight, to protect myself."

His brows shot up. "Are you afraid we can't keep you safe?"

"It's not that. You and Elie can't always be with me. I might actually try to stab you again if you tried." I kept my eyes on the chess board. "I want to have the skills and strength to protect myself."

"Alright." Another click echoed off the walls. "If that's what you want."

I narrowed my eyes on him. He was giving into this demand easier than I expected him to.

"You're not going to tell me it's not lady-like? Or that women shouldn't be on a battlefield?"

"No. It's your choice, Arabelle. Do I want you to fight? No. Do I want to see you on a battlefield, bleeding and risking your life? No. But you've made a valid point. If it gives you a better chance of survival, then we'll teach you."

I stared at him, awed by his words. Never in my life had anyone allowed me to make such a decision for myself. Maybe getting to see Isa would be as simple as asking him.

"Lucien..." I worried my lip between my teeth. "Would it be possible for me to see Isa? Just to visit – just to make sure she's doing okay."

His hand froze over the board, eyes still set on it. "With the Marid in the area, it's too big a risk to let you go."

"But you could go with me, stay outside while I just—"

"I won't leave this castle." He snapped the piece down.

I swallowed. If I kept pushing, he might unleash that quick temper of his. I needed a subject change, something completely different than this topic. I ransacked my mind for anything when my earlier conversation with Elie came back to me.

"Elie said your father was a king," I said with a tentative glance up at him. I was met with an icy stare before his gaze fell back to the board. Not the best of subjects, then.

"Elie needs to learn to keep his mouth shut." He moved a pawn.

"Is it true?" I moved my rook to take one of his pawns.

"Yes." If the short answers and the way he snapped the pieces down on the board were any indication, he didn't want to talk about this.

"Why is it only you and Elie now?" I moved another piece.

"There used to be courtiers buzzing around everywhere you looked. We staffed and housed many servants. There was scarce a place to get a moment's peace." He overtook my bishop in a clever move.

"You sent them away for being too noisy?"

Why was I surprised? That seemed exactly like something he would do. I slid another of my pawns forward a square.

"They went away on holiday." His mouth was drawn taut. "They have yet to return."

He knocked my pawn over and replaced it with his own, picking up the piece and moving it off the board.

An ache spread through my chest at the pain he tried to hide.

"Do you think they will?" I moved my knight and captured one of his rooks.

"I have hope they will. Even if I'm not around to see it." He replaced my knight with his queen and set it with the rapidly growing pile of my pieces off the board.

"What do you mean even if you're not around? Are you planning on going somewhere?"

The statement settled me with unease, and I squirmed in my chair. It shouldn't matter to me if he left, but some inner part of me didn't want him to. A part I crushed down. I moved my queen to take his knight.

He claimed my queen with a rook, and I cursed under my breath for not seeing that move.

"You weren't kidding about not being good at this game. I thought you said you've played before?"

My chest swelled. The amusement in his voice was a balm to the uneasy anxiety that gripped my insides, even if he'd changed the subject. The man from my dream could wait for just a little while.

"I did ask you to go easy on me."

I straightened in the chair as the log in the fire split, and embers fluttered behind him. It was Lucien's turn to be inquisitive.

"You don't like fire, do you?" His eyes softened.

"Fire, small spaces, being trapped..." I gave a half-hearted chuckle, trying to make light of it. "Being stuck in a burning building does that to you."

I returned to my quiet somberness when he didn't smile. He raked his clawed hand through what would have been his hair, swerving around the horn.

"I'm sorry I locked you in your room. It must have brought back some memories of that night."

I blinked at him. He was not only apologizing, but sincere about it.

"It's fine. Actually, the room is so big and spacious that I didn't have the usual flashbacks at all." I couldn't bring myself to worsen the look of regret on his face.

"Even still, it has never been my intention to make you suffer while you're here."

He stared at the game board for a quiet moment, then his eyes met mine. A wry smile curved my lips.

"If you want to make it up to me, you could tell me more about yourself."

I might be able to learn more about that man and the boys if I learned more about Lucien, but I found myself full of genuine curiosity. Elie knew something; it was clear as day when he saw the portraits. And if Elie knew, Lucien had to.

"What do you want to know?"

"Do you have any other family?"

If there were a beast equivalent for a scowl, it would be the look he gave me. I shrunk in my seat, wanting to disappear into the shadows.

"Everyone in my family is dead," he said as he captured another of my game pieces with his queen.

That ache in my chest spread and gripped my insides for what he lost. My family was taken from me, but I still had Isa and, despite his faults, my father. I didn't know what I'd do if I were left all alone.

"Did you…"

"Kill them? You assume because I look like this," he gestured to his beastly face, "that I would butcher my family?" Familiar anger dripped off every word.

My shoulders slouched as heat spread over my body. I knew better than anyone that looks didn't equate to a person's nature. Louis was beautiful but a horrid man.

I looked at him and saw an animal, something – someone –

that could slaughter his family. He deserved better than that. Especially after the kindness he'd shown me. I dragged my lip between my teeth. Could he really have people locked up in this castle? I was beginning to doubt that possibility more and more.

Elie had even said as much, that Lucien had never intentionally hurt someone innocent. I thought I'd made it a point in my life to never judge someone by anything but the merit they showed, yet here I was, judging Lucien a killer because he was a beast. My face blazed, and I couldn't look him in the eye.

"To be frank, that's exactly what I thought," I whispered.

Shame was a solid weight in my chest. I studied the board to mask the embarrassment gripping me by the throat.

Hot breath kissed my skin as Lucien huffed out a ragged sigh. "Why did you stop playing chess?"

I had no idea if he changed the subject because he could sense my feelings or if he was uncomfortable. Either way, I could have sung praises to God for it.

At least until I had to answer the question. My breath hitched as a sob tried to claw its way up my throat. He knew my mother had died, but was it okay to open up about this part of my past? I didn't even talk to Isa about why I stopped playing. It was something I kept close to my heart.

I opened my mouth and closed it again as my eyebrows drew together. This was a vulnerability I didn't trust anyone with. I bit my bottom lip, dragging it between my teeth.

I glanced up at him, his hands folded as he waited with more patience than I'd yet to see of him. He let some of his own vulnerability show when he told me of his mother. I could do the same.

"My mother was a harsh woman, but I loved her. And when she died, every time I looked at a chess set, it brought an overwhelming amount of sadness with it. I couldn't bear it, so I never played again. Until today." I pushed my rook across the side of the board.

"Check," Lucien said as he moved his queen. "You didn't have to play on my account. If it brings you nothing but heartache."

I slid my king a space to my left.

"I don't feel that right now," I admitted, surprising myself.

It wasn't a lie. Somehow, playing with him brought back the joy I once found in the game before my mother tried to turn it into a political weapon they could use for a better marriage match. The strategical mindset would provide me with the know-how to navigate the cutthroat court politics. I stared down at the board as my lips curved upward.

"I never thought I'd feel like this when playing again."

"After my mother died, I didn't touch an instrument for eight years. It was too painful. But there was a night after..." He trailed off as he flexed his fingers. "Playing the violin, while still weighing heavy on my heart, brought me a sense of comfort. Like she was there with me in a time when I needed her."

I lowered my eyes, watching his fingers as I thought about his promise. "You really won't play for me sooner?"

"Impatient, are we?"

His mouth quirked up. If I didn't know better, I'd swear he was grinning at me.

"I just don't understand why I have to wait."

I crossed my arms over my chest and pushed my bottom lip out in a mock pout.

He chuckled, a deep, rumbling sound. My own smile responded without my permission.

"All in due time, Belle."

A rush of heat electrified my spine at the sound of my name on his lips, and I pressed my own in a thin line to fight my smile back into neutrality.

"Do you ever leave the castle?" The change of subject was clumsy. "I mean, you know, with the way you look. I'm sure people would be scared."

He said he wouldn't leave when I asked to visit Isa, but he had to leave at some point. My heart stuttered, and I cursed myself for saying it when I saw the darkness veil his eyes once again.

"No, I don't leave. I send Elie whenever I need something." He moved again. "Check."

"That makes sense."

I claimed the piece, threatening my king, masking the stab of pity crawling up my throat.

"If you grew up here, I'll bet you know this place like the back of your hand."

I glanced up through my lashes, wishing that darkness away. He was different when he laughed and teased. I much preferred that version of him.

"I'll bet you could show me all kinds of fun places. Like secret passageways, secret rooms, the dungeon. I've always wanted to see what a castle dungeon looked like in person. I've only ever heard stories." I tried to keep my voice steady and casual as I spoke.

"No one's been down there in a very long time. It's probably a decrepit death trap by now." His eyes moved over the remaining pieces on the chessboard.

"But if you're with me, everything will be okay. I know you won't let me get hurt down there." I shifted in my chair, trying to use the same seductive tone I'd heard my older sisters use to get their way.

"It's not a place you should go. Unless you want me to chain you up down there?" He lifted a furred brow and stared at me with those intense blue eyes that had my insides twisting in knots.

"It sounds like *you're* the one who wants to chain *me* up."

God, what was I saying? Why did I say that?

Heat exploded on my skin, and I'd put gold on the fact that my face was as red as the roses in the garden.

His eyes widened in what I assumed was shock at my statement before he blinked it away.

"Only if you enjoy that sort of thing."

Liquid fire burned in my belly and thrummed in my veins to the beat of my heart, pooling between my legs as the image of being chained up in a damp dungeon cell shoved any other thought out of my head. Stripped bare before him, his claws scraping just light enough over my skin so they didn't draw blood.

"I shouldn't have said that." My voice was almost a whimper.

"I'd be happy to oblige. I'm sure we could find a suitable cell and some chains."

He dragged the tip of his claw across the top of the table in a long scrape as if he knew exactly what image flashed in my mind.

A shiver danced up my spine as I imagined what he could do with it. I struggled to swallow with a dry throat. Was he...teasing me? It had to be a wild act of my imagination. I clamped my thighs together, the wetness at my core already building to a point where I'd need to go straight to my room after this.

"No, no. It's quite alright."

"Are you sure?"

He inhaled deeply as if he could smell my arousal. Could he? God, he was practically an animal, and they had a stronger sense of smell. I tugged my lip between my teeth.

"See? You don't actually want to go down there," he said with another chuckle that set my skin on fire.

"It's not nice to tease me like that."

"Oh, I never claimed to be nice." He paused, studying my face with a new kind of amusement. "And it's damn good fun. You turned such a lovely shade of red."

My jaw clenched tight enough to hurt. Trying to keep the smile off my face was an effort. I liked this side of Lucien.

"All of that aside, will you show me around the castle? It's so much bigger than I thought." I held my breath for his answer.

"Yes. Checkmate."

He had my king pinned.

Damn.

"I really do suck at this game."

I hung my head, and we both laughed. That was a sound I could grow fond of.

THIRTY-THREE

Arabelle

When Elie had asked me to follow him after breakfast this morning to start our training, I expected an odd room in the castle, not a fully equipped barracks and training ground. Unlike much of the castle, the upkeep had been maintained.

My eyes fell on the red-haired warrior in front of me. He took care of so many things here, including both me and Lucien, yet I had never heard him ask for a thing. Not even a favor, outside of his request for me to give Lucien a chance.

We passed by bundles of hay with red circles painted on them, ones shaped like men, rings of dirt, and a cold forge. How many men had been here before everyone left? He stopped next to a building tucked into the wall of the castle and turned to face me. He scanned me head to foot and back up again.

"First thing: you need to change into something more suitable to train in."

"What's wrong with what I'm wearing?"

I had nothing else to wear; this was one of the simpler dresses I found in the wardrobe.

"You can't properly train in a dress, Belle."

He ducked into the building, and I followed.

"Then what am I supposed to wear?"

This was all new to me; we didn't have soldiers or even guards training at our manor before the fire. How was I to know what was appropriate or not? I'd certainly never seen a woman training before.

Elie rummaged through an old trunk, metal clanging against stone as he tossed old swords and daggers to the side. He spun back to me, holding a bundle of clothing.

"You wear these."

I took the bundle and held up each piece. A black shirt and a pair of pants. They would be fitted to my body. I couldn't recall ever wearing pants, even to garden, or cut wood.

"I can't wear these."

"Why not?" He tilted his head as a bit of amusement shined in his eyes.

He was enjoying this. I glanced down at the clothes again, trying to think of one good reason to give him that he couldn't rebuff. I came up empty. I bit my lip.

"A dress will prevent you from moving freely. You could get hurt. Wearing tight-fitting clothes will help prevent that."

This was the man who'd been training since seven, speaking a truth I knew to be fact but wanted to be wrong.

"You can change in here, I'll wait outside."

He did just that, stepping to the side of the building and out of my sight. I sighed and stripped my clothes off, changing into the ones he gave me.

Elie had not been wrong when he said the outfit he gave me would be tight-fitting. It clung to every curve of my body. A blush crept up on my cheeks as I stared down at my breasts, stomach, and legs, all on full display through the clothing. Even the chain of the locket stood out.

He whistled low when I stepped out into the bright sun, his eyes going right to where the locket sat against my skin.

"You'll need to take that off."

"Why?" My hand shot to that golden trinket, fingers wrapping around it.

"Because anything around your neck can be used as a weapon against you. Plus, you don't want to risk damaging it during training. You can leave it with the rest of your stuff in the barracks." He waved a lazy hand at the building behind me.

The locket had somehow become a crutch in my time here, something I clung to in order to keep me focused on the task I needed to accomplish – find the captives within the castle. I slipped it off and placed it with the dress I left folded in a chair.

He waited in a ring at the end of the training grounds, watching the sky as the clouds rolled by. The sun reflected in his eyes in an array of gold, it set his hair ablaze in fiery reds and oranges. He looked as if he was built for fire – to burn wild and fierce and free.

At the sound of my steps, he turned his head to me with a grin on his face that made my stomach dip.

Lucien was nowhere to be seen.

"Where's Lucien?" I asked, a flutter in my chest at the thought of him being here.

A sly smirk crept across Elie's face. "Probably pouting in his room. I told him not to come today."

I could have kissed the man for that. I couldn't help but wonder why though. Not that I'd complain; letting him see me in these clothes did things to my stomach that I didn't even want to consider.

"Why?"

Elie's eyes softened just a bit as he watched me. "Learning something like this requires all of your focus. I don't need him distracting you or making you feel too self-conscious to properly do the exercises."

Fair enough.

"I'm going to start with the basics. Just a few techniques that don't really require strength but can get you out of a bad bind."

He shook his hands out and waited until I stepped into the circled area.

"Don't go easy on me just because I'm a woman." I shut down the need to bristle at the implication that I didn't possess enough strength.

"Oh, trust me, I wouldn't dream of it." That grin widened into a dazzling smile. "Now, come here, and I'll teach you the first move."

I narrowed my eyes on him as I approached. Did the warrior in him sing in delight at the opportunity to dance again? I stopped only a step away.

"Grab my wrist," he said and held his arm out.

I hesitated, then did what he said. In a flash of movement, he had my arm twisted and me on my knees. A yelp slipped from me, not from pain but surprise at his quickness.

"When someone tries to grab you like this, put your free hand over their fingers, then swing your arm to grab their wrist. Once you do that, push down until they hit their knees." He let go and backed away.

I straightened; my face flushed with heat as I faced him again.

"That seems easy enough."

"It is. But we're going to practice until it's muscle memory for you." He flexed his fingers at his side.

"Alright, what else do you have."

He curled his finger in a come-hither motion and pointed to his hair. "Grab it."

I pressed my lips in a line. Hair pulling? This was one of his techniques? I sighed with a shake of my head and reached up, grabbing a handful of that red hair.

I marveled at the soft texture for all of a few seconds before he swung his arm around mine and, again, had me on my knees.

"Never let someone get control of you in a dangerous situation. Bad men will use shitty methods like this." He offered me a hand up with a warm smile. "It'd be a shame for someone to use that beautiful hair against you."

With my hand still in his, he tugged me closer and leaned in.

"Lucien likes women with long hair; he would be sad if you had to cut it." His whisper left my face scorching with heat.

A question burned in my mind, one that had taunted me from the darkest corners for weeks now.

"How did Lucien become...what he is?"

Elie had told me that he'd once been like us but wouldn't go into more detail. Humans didn't just become beasts. Something else was at play, and I wanted to know what it was. Whatever force changed him might be responsible for taking that man from my dream as well.

The joy that sparkled in Elie's eyes moments ago guttered out.

"Lucien is...complicated. He's asked me not to speak on certain things, and I will honor his wishes."

He tilted his head back, the muscles in his throat working as he swallowed. His gaze caught mine again.

"But you'll know the answer when you're ready, Belle."

"But—"

"Enough about that. Time to learn another move; this time, how to get someone off of you if you're pinned down."

He proceeded with the rest of the lesson without bringing Lucien up again. I had no idea that there were so many ways I could defend myself from attackers, or that there were that many possibilities of being attacked. He walked me through every one, carefully instructing each step until I could do them myself.

Whenever there was a free moment between maneuvers or a break for water, I pondered what he meant when he said I'd know the answer to my question. It could be a game or just a way for him to dodge my question.

The more I thought about it, the more I realized that something horrible had happened to him to make him this way. And that was a thought that stole my breath from me.

THIRTY-FOUR

Lucien

Warmth leaked in through the windows atop the highest reaches of the library, filling it with a gentle glow and highlighting the hundreds of books nestled on the shelves. I turned the page of the one in my lap. Elie would never let me live it down if he saw me reading one of these, but Arabelle enjoyed reading them, and he was the one insisting I try harder.

Her name was a balm to the occasional burning in my lungs, the sharp aches in my bones, the throb in my skull. Days were fading faster and faster. I found myself begging the gods for a few extra days. Not to break the curse but just to bask in the calm of her presence a little while longer. With the deadline a little more than a month away, my doubt grew heavy – far too heavy.

The large double doors creaked as she slipped through them. Our eyes met across the room before hers darted elsewhere.

"This place is so big that I keep getting turned around," she said with a sigh, rubbing a hand over her jaw and back through the underside of her hair.

She approached me, no longer displaying even an ounce of

hesitation after our walk through the garden. Elie's suggestion to open up to her was working. The corner of her mouth tugged up in a grin as her eyes scanned the title of the book in my hands.

"My, Lucien, are you reading a romance book?"

My skin prickled and heated at her words. For once, I was grateful for the fur hiding my face.

"And if I am?"

"You struck me as more of an adventure kind of guy." She leaned over the side of the chair, bracing her hands on the arm as she careened to see the words on the page. "Especially after the one you gave me to read."

I tilted the book away from her. "Don't you know it's rude to read over someone's shoulder like that?"

She let out a small huff, rolling back on her heels and lacing her fingers together behind her back.

"I just want to see if it's one I've read or not."

She was pouting. Actual lip puffed out, sulky shoulders, full-on pouting. And it was adorable. I couldn't stop the smile from pulling at the corner of my mouth.

"Do you want me to read you a passage?"

Arabelle's eyes glistened with excitement, and she straightened her posture again. Her parents must have taught her it was inappropriate to show it. I tightened my jaw and then forced myself to relax it. My own father was strict when it came to emotions; it shouldn't surprise me that others were the same.

"Would you?" she asked in a soft voice.

"Of course."

I shifted in my seat, opening the book fully in front of me again. I scanned the paragraphs; I already knew what I wanted her to hear. I swallowed my anxious energy and cleared my throat, glancing at her before I read:

"And if you told me you wanted to dance among the stars, I would gather those brilliant, shining little lights and drop them at your feet. I would spend an eternity dancing among them with you. And if I can have nothing else in this life, choose to give me a piece of your heart, because you have all of mine."

Arabelle's breath trembled, and her fingers tangled together in front of her.

"How beautiful it would be to dance among the stars." Her voice was light, almost dreamy.

"It would pale in comparison to the radiance of your own beauty."

I swallowed around the knot taking form in my throat, fear preventing me from looking her in the eye. I couldn't bear to see the repulsion there, the rejection of all I was. Belle was a beauty amid my fallen world, bringing life and joy with her, but I was just a beast who deserved her loathing.

The silence stretched, growing ever more uncomfortable until I couldn't stand it anymore. When I looked, when I finally met her gaze, it wasn't disgust there, not even hatred. It was a tenderness I never allowed myself to hope for. My heart exploded in a flurry of a thousand fluttering wings.

"Fetch me some stars to dance in, and we'll compare," she said at last, her cheeks blooming with color.

My eyes shifted between hers, a rush of gooseflesh running down my arms and legs as I imagined her in a glittering gown, twirling through the beautiful glow of the night sky.

"Consider it done." The words came out of my dried throat in a rasp.

"Do you have time to show me around the castle today? Maybe some shortcuts to keep me from getting so lost." The smile she gave me sent those butterflies skittering through my chest again.

"There aren't really any shortcuts," I paused as I snapped the book shut and sat it on the table next to my chair. "If you get lost, if you need my help, just call for me, and I'll come save you."

I let a little bit of my old arrogance seep through. She perched her hands on her hips and puffed out her chest.

"When you put it like that, it makes me less inclined to do so. I can save myself, thank you very much." Her lips twitched as she fought and failed to keep the smile from them.

I stood from the chair and bowed at the waist in front of her, sweeping my arms out.

"I have every bit of confidence that you can. I just pray you'll let me be the gentleman and save you at least once. Even if it's just from the numerous halls of my castle." I glanced up, fighting my own smile now.

She let her arms fall to her side. "If you're going to be that insistent about it, I guess I could let you save me *once*."

I straightened to my full height again.

"I'm ever grateful to you, my lady," I said as I offered my arm to Arabelle. She wrapped hers through it.

It still managed to surprise me that she didn't twist away in repulsion. I never thought I'd feel these nerves swimming through my stomach again, yet here they were, resurfacing at her simple touch.

"There's a lot to the castle. From the hot springs that we told you about before to training grounds and even an artisan quarter. And that's saying nothing about the wonders outside these walls. It's too much to see in a single day. But I'd like to show it all to you."

I led us from the library, holding the door for her. Her grip held firm even when I expected her to let go.

"I want to see it all, Lucien. This place is enchanting."

"Where to first?" Our steps echoed in the large stone hall.

A grin spread over her face.

"The hot springs. I want to see what all the fuss is about."

"The hot springs it is, then."

THIRTY-FIVE

Arabelle

Humidity slammed into me as we passed through the cavernous archway into an area of the castle that looked to be carved out from the side of a mountain. Puffs of steam rose from cracks in the floor as we wound around a slanted wall, and the room opened up into a huge pool of water.

Leafy ferns lined the outer edges of the room with the large, veined leaves of alocasia plants mixed in. Ivy climbed up the stone walls, as if reaching for the windows to escape into the sun. Clusters of deep purple orchids grew proud at the front of the small garden, their stocks sinking beneath a layer of small black, grey, and white pebbles.

On the opposite side, large flat rocks were laid out to form wide steps into the deeper recesses of the spring. My hand slipped from Lucien's arm as I left his side and took a few steps into the sweltering room. Tiny wisps of steam rose off the crystal blue waters.

"Wow. You really do have one in here. How is this even possible?"

"It's a secret only lords of the castle may know," he leaned down and whispered into my ear. I could have sworn he purred at the shiver dragged out of me by his hot breath.

My eyes caught on a wooden structure built into the castle's wall.

"What's that?" I asked, pointing to it while trying to hide the way his closeness snatched my breath away.

"It's a stone sauna." If it weren't for the sweltering heat of the room, a chill might have cooled me from the empty space he left.

"I can see why this is one of Elie's favorite places. It's gorgeous and relaxing."

I could see it, the two of them here. Lucien's fur soaking up the hot water while Elie kicked his feet back and pointed out every wrong thing Lucien had done that day. It brought a grin to my face, and I bit my bottom lip to force it back.

"Would you like to take a dip in the hot springs?" His voice held a teasing lilt that heated my blood in a strange, new way. "Or shall we continue with the tour?"

I avoided his eyes as I turned away from the room and prayed he assumed my pinkened cheeks were from the balmy air and not his doing.

"Let's continue the tour."

What was my heart doing? Not just pounding for the man in my dreams, but now Lucien? I chewed my lip. Lucien had done so much for me, though, giving me freedom and bringing back my love of music. He'd shared parts of his past and experiences he treasured with me. And the man from my dream was just that – a dream.

There was no actual confirmation he was real. I couldn't find anything about him. Elie's recognition of the locket and the paintings within gave me hope that I was onto something. But what if whatever was bringing him to my dreams was bringing him to both Lucien's and Elie's?

I tracked Lucien as he brushed past me and turned back when I didn't move to leave.

"Coming?" His velvet voice thrummed against my spine like the plucked string of a harp.

It was okay to let my heart flutter for someone who'd offered their life in my place. It didn't have to mean more than simple infatuation.

I gave him a sharp nod, and he led me through the hallways with all the confidence of a king. His father *was* a king. A thought tugged at the back of my mind: an image of a beauty so painful that it robbed me of breath, but I mentally batted it away; it wasn't possible.

Without ever seeing Lucien as a human, the chances of dreaming of him and knowing what he looked like weren't possible. But if there was magic in this place…I squashed the blooming hope until it guttered out.

The next room Lucien showed me to was alight with the sun beaming through wide windows that stretched over two walls and half the ceiling. Dusty tools and old canvases were scattered on a worn, peeling worktable nestled against the wall just inside. The wood was stained in various colors from spilled pigments and water. Splotches of dried paint dotted one corner as if the painter had simply gotten up and walked away in the middle of their work.

An easel stood next to the table with a stool in front of it. The charcoal lines on the canvas were barely visible through a thick layer of dust and grime.

Where the windowpanes met in a corner, a half-carved statue stood, waiting. I stepped toward the sculpture, running my fingers along the smooth stone, admiring how the woman looked as if she were climbing out of the marble to stand next to me. If I hadn't touched it, I wouldn't believe she wasn't a living, breathing person.

I turned and took in the beauty of what was before me: the paintings, the sculpture, the works of art that littered every inch of the room. They were magnificent, unfinished as they were.

"Did you make these?"

Lucien let out a shallow breath as his eyes swept over the room like mine had.

"No. My father employed a portrait painter during my childhood. This was his studio." He stepped up to a half-finished sketch, the lines barely more than a blur now. "My brother studied under him. Art was his escape, much like music is ours."

"Did he paint portraits of you?"

I swallowed and dragged my bottom lip between my teeth. It was risky to ask if he wasn't willing to open up and share that part of his past with me. If there were portraits of him as a human, I could have an answer to a question that had quietly blossomed in the back of my head.

"Yes. But you won't find any on the castle walls."

He wouldn't meet my gaze. Instead, he opted to stare out of the window into the vast distance. I followed his eyes, and it hit me that I had never realized how much land belonged to the castle. The green hills of grass stretched as far as I could see, yet it was winter outside the gates.

So much for finding out that way.

Elie's words about his father clanged through me, and an ache bloomed in my chest. He was the king's son, his heir. He should have been lauded over.

"Why not? Did your father hate you so much that he refused to hang them?"

A flash of anger died on his face as his eyes locked with mine. "I took them down."

That ache grew as I stepped toward him.

"Why, Lucien?" I placed my hand on his arm. It was warm and so soft, so inviting I wanted to nuzzle into it.

I choked out the desire. There was a man being held captive somewhere in this castle, possibly more than just him. I had to remember that. I should just ask Lucien about him. *That* thought chewed a hole through my stomach. I wasn't sure I wanted to hear his answers regarding it. Asking him meant I'd risk giving up whatever this growing seed between us was.

"I couldn't stand to look at them." His gaze fell to where we touched, then to the floor.

I chewed my lip, but he reached up and tugged it from my teeth with his thumb. His fingers moved with a gentle grace as he brushed the tips over my cheek. I caught his wrist before he dropped it, holding it there as I stared into the once cold eyes, eyes that grew warmer and kinder by the day.

"If you're ashamed of how you look, you shouldn't be," I paused and placed my free hand against his cheek, mirroring the way I held his palm to mine. "It's beyond your control."

My eyes bounced between his, and a part of me wanted to give in to the possibility that it was him. That he somehow came into my dreams as his true self.

Lucien's breath skittered over my skin, sending a wave of warmth down my arm. He leaned into the touch like it was his sole lifeline, keeping him on this side of the gates of hell. I stroked my thumb over the soft fur underneath it.

"If only that were true, Arabelle."

All at once, he pulled away, leaving me longing for the closeness of him in a small way. I wasn't ready to risk this, not yet.

He cleared his throat and said, "if you enjoy this room, let me show you the gallery."

A thrill burned through my blood. I hadn't walked through an art gallery since before Mother died. It wasn't a far walk from the atelier, in fact, it was just on the other side of the hall.

Words died on my tongue as I stared in stunned awe. The marble statues stood out against the dark stone walls, and the floor-to-ceiling arched windows gave the room an abundance of natural lighting to bring them to life.

I moved closer to the first one, unable to stop myself from touching the white veined stone that looked so much like a piece of silken fabric wrapped around the figure of a woman. Her feathered wings stretched out behind her. Surely, she would take flight right here.

The next was a male, donning intricate armor; even the scars from battle were carved into it. He held a shield in one hand and a sword in the other. The frozen war cry and swinging sword gave me pause as if the statue might just come to life at any moment and take off my head.

Further in was a bust, the same fabric design covering the face of a woman bearing an iron circlet with a flat medallion dangling at the center of her forehead. When I looked closer, the strange symbol was familiar to me, a word on the tip of my tongue that slipped away when I grasped for it.

Behind the bust statue was an opening that led to another part of the gallery, fires flickering to life in the crystal sconces and candelabras to reveal walls lined with paintings.

I stopped in front of a painting of a woman on a throne made of gold and pearl, her long, blonde hair cascading in waves to the floor. Even in a painting, her eyes were full of a vast ocean of wisdom, yet they remained kind. I swallowed the shock. This was the woman from my dreams, the one who kept trying to show me something, but the darkness swallowed it up.

"Who is this?"

"She's called The Architect. A...woman of great power."

Lucien stood close enough that his body heat warmed my back, yet he never came any closer. With a nudge, we moved to the next portrait.

"These are the previous kings of this land," Lucien's voice came from behind me as I walked by each portrait.

There were big portraits and small ones. Some were full-body paintings, while others only showed the shoulders and up. But the last one was thrice my size.

As I approached the last painting and stopped, I glanced back at Lucien.

"Your father?"

I turned back to the man in the portrait. This was the answer I needed, and he'd brought me right to it.

There was a cruel, vicious beauty about him. His blond hair was short and slicked back from the sharp features of his face. His blue eyes were absent of any warmth. He pressed his lips in a straight line with a slight downward tilt to them. The collar of his shirt showed off the angles of his jawline. Even the colors he wore screamed the brutality he was likely to inflict—black and a crimson that looked the same shade as blood.

"Yes," Lucien's response was short and clipped.

The angle of his jaw was familiar, but my breath evaporated from my lungs when I stared into the eyes. The blues, rimmed with gold. My mind spiraled. Was the king the man in my dream? The hair was wrong, but it could have grown if he'd been imprisoned for years.

But Elie told me he had died, Lucien said as much too.

They could be lying.

My mouth ran dry. He could be trying to use me to free him so he could take revenge on Lucien for locking him up.

I refocused on the painting in front of us. Both of them had said that the king was a cruel man, that he had done something to Lucien in the past. He deserved to be locked up deep underground. But what if I was wrong? The ground swayed under my feet. *What should I do?* I did all I could think to.

I shut him out of my mind and turned back to Lucien.

"There is no kindness emanating from him at all."

The similarity had to be a coincidence because he looked like a much colder, hateful version of him. My eyes cut to Lucien, then back to the portrait. I folded an arm over my stomach and stared at that portrait. But what if...I didn't even finish the thought.

"No. He wasn't a very kind person."

A shudder ran down my spine.

"Let's go. I can feel the sneer behind those eyes. Even through the paint."

And I did. It unsettled me in a way I couldn't explain. I just wanted to be away from that painting. I took Lucien by the hand and walked out of the gallery, walked away from the line of dangerous thought.

I held fast to the heat of his palm as we walked through the darkening hallways, the sun setting over the horizon. The one place I wanted him to show me was the dungeon. I needed to know, without a doubt, if anyone was down there. Yet the words died in my throat every time I tried to ask.

Every day I spent with Lucien, learning about him and of his past, the more I wanted to know. He never asked anything of me, never expected me to act a certain way or do anything specific. I touched the bodice of my dress over where the locket nuzzled next to my heart, the rapid thud like the flutter of a million butterfly wings. I could trust him.

"You said no one has been in the dungeon in a long time."

"Yes, I did."

"There's no one locked up down there?"

"No, there's no one locked up down there," he repeated my words as if to reassure me of what he said.

My thumb rubbed circles over the back of his hand. If he said no one was in the dungeons, I'd believe him. I would have to work harder to find those records – if they existed.

I calmed my rapidly climbing pulse with a deep breath. Lucien wouldn't keep an innocent locked up for no reason; that wasn't who he was.

It hit me like a stone wall, so hard that it left me stunned.

Was it possible that I *wasn't* just dreaming of a random man, but of Lucien? If his father caused him to look like this, he *was* a captive in a twisted sort of way. It also explained the similarities between the king and the man in my dream.

He *did* lock me up when *I* had done nothing. I glanced up at his profile and quickly looked away again. But he had never lied to me.

"It's almost time for dinner. Elie will get in one of his moods if we're late," he said with a teasing glint in his eye, pulling me from the depths of the hole I'd fallen into.

"Oh? Is he the kind that gets cranky when he doesn't eat on time?" My lips curve in an unbidden grin.

"Don't let him hear you say that. He'll deny it fiercely. But yes. He can get a bit cranky."

For the first time since we met, the laughter reached his eyes, and my heart cracked open a little more.

THIRTY-SIX

Henri

After a month of back and forth, Louis and I were still no closer to figuring out a way to find the castle to get Arabelle back. We looked for the man the statues were sold to, but he hadn't shown his face since. Louis insisted that it was still another month before he would turn up again if patterns held true.

The teapot clanked against the edge of the cup as Isa poured tea for us while we sat at the large table. Chains rattled around her ankles as she walked. The girl had been foolish enough to attempt to run away. I was sure it was to find Belle. Louis insisted on the chains, and I obliged.

Louis could hire servants to take care of his home but got some thrill out of making Isa do it instead. *It's a woman's job to serve a man, and if she's going to live here, that's what she's going to do,* he'd said when we arrived weeks ago.

His demands and hovering made it difficult to secure her a match with the Cordevaux boy. None of that would matter if I could get back to that damn castle; I couldn't even remember the way.

I chewed my thumbnail at the quick while watching Isa set out small plates and delve portions of biscuits onto each. Louis leaned onto one fist while drumming the fingers of his other hand on the table as he, too, watched her with all the patience of a rabid dog in front of a trapped rabbit.

"I think, since you haven't come up with a viable way to bring Arabelle back to me, I'll take Isa as my wife instead." The tapping stopped. "At least she's obedient. Outside of that one incident."

Her entire body stiffened as her gaze settled on Louis, ire burning beyond the amber. Her mouth opened, but she snapped her jaw shut again, cutting off whatever was on her mind to say.

I bit a chunk of my nail off as I dropped my hand. If Louis backed out of this arrangement, I'd miss out on the gold in that castle. I couldn't let him do that, not when the only thing I lacked was a way back in.

"But, Louis, surely you'd prefer someone whose face isn't scarred so horrendously."

"I would. But in the absence of one who fits that criterion, Isa will do. She'll still give me beautiful children; I'll just have to hide her from the guests."

The teapot rattled in her hands, and her body trembled, but it wasn't from fear or disgust; it was pure rage.

"Isa, why don't you go back to the kitchen and put away the tea."

If she stayed in here much longer, she might shatter the pot over his head. Apparently, she had already done something similar. Talking him out of the beating for that was hard enough.

"There is a way to save her if you'd only agree to meet with Callum. I know you don't trust him, but he's already offered to help me. He and his men are just what we need." I flattened my hand on the table as he pinned me with a furious gaze.

"I told you before." His eyebrows lowered over his eyes. "I'm not keen on accepting help from that pirate. He may pretend he's gone straight, but we all know the truth of it."

I shifted my weight from one side to another. Isa finally left, and I could breathe easy. My eyes met his again.

"Given what we face, it might do us good to hire someone like him. He won't care who gets hurt so long as he gets paid."

Louis ground his teeth, the muscles in his neck bulging in his frustration. "You have a point. I don't like it, but you have a point. Tell me though, how do we trust him not to harm Arabelle? He could just as well kill her as anyone else in the castle. Or claim her for himself."

"We'll just have to go with him then."

And while he would be busy taking on the beast and any other creatures lurking in the castle, I'd be free to find the coffers and take the gold for myself.

"He'll want a substantial amount of gold for this." Louis rubbed his broad hand down the stubbled side of his face.

"Is Arabelle not worth it to you?"

She was. Louis had set his eyes on her long ago and would do anything to make her his.

"What kind of question is that? Of course, she is."

"Then it's settled. We can find Callum and his men at the pub, I'm sure. We can ask him for his help." I placed both hands on the table and pushed myself up.

"In the case of failure, I will take Isa. Know that, Henri. I won't be denied what your daughters can give me." He stood as well.

"When this is all over, you can have whichever one you want. Take them both if it pleases you."

I didn't care anymore. I'd have enough riches to start over.

"Isabelle, fetch our cloaks. We're going to the pub, all of us," Louis shouted to her in the kitchen.

When she brought our cloaks, we left for the pub that Callum and his crew had resided in these last two months.

The place was the same as when I had visited before, but the smell was exponentially worse – the musky scent of unwashed bodies lingering in the air. I had to breathe through my mouth. That was worse. I could *taste* it. Isa walked close behind me, but she didn't flinch away from anything as we moved deeper into the debauched chaos.

Callum was seated at his usual table, though he lacked any of the wenches he'd usually have perched on his lap. A handful of his men sat around him, the conversation dying on their tongues when we approached.

"Henri. How nice of you to join us again." The cadence of his voice sent a chill spider walking down my spine.

"Does your offer of help still stand?" I positioned myself between two of his men's shoulders, each placing hands on their weapons.

"That entirely depends on the ask. What do you need my help with?" The captain leaned back in his chair and folded his arms over his chest, his shirt unbuttoned enough to see the hard muscles and black lines of tattoos underneath.

"There's a monster—"

Louis pushed past me, placing his palm on the sticky table.

"We need the help of you and your men to save my bride."

Isa squared her shoulders and lifted her chin when Callum's eyes slid from mine to hers and then finally to Louis, a glimmer of animosity flaring to life. It was better to let Louis do the talking, lest I invoke his wrath and ruin my chances of him taking care of whatever payment the pirates would demand. Callum's gaze shifted back to me as if he could see straight through the façade and knew the real reason behind our visit.

"What's in it for me?"

He tilted his head like a predator assessing its prey. Were we worth the effort? Would the ends please him? That's what the look said.

"Is the knowledge of saving a damsel not enough for you?" Louis all but spat at him, and even though I knew that anger wasn't aimed at me, my body still tensed for the briefest of moments.

Callum scanned over Louis in a manner that suggested he was searching for the perfect spot to shove one of the daggers sheathed at his waist.

"Do I look like one of those bleeding sanctimonious halfwits, mate? The only damsels I care about are the ones I can fuck. So, unless you're planning to hand the lass over, I'll be expecting payment of a sort."

Louis bristled at the words, fingernails leaving gouges in the years of caked-on grime covering the wood as he scraped them over it.

"I'd never hand Arabelle over to scum like you, pirate. If it's coin you're after, name your price."

Callum's lips turned up in a smirk. "That's what I like to hear. Tell me more about this little endeavor of yours. You say there's a monster?"

I cleared my throat and stepped forward again, Louis backing off. "He's a vile animal. I've never seen a creature so big. Looks like hell spat him out. He's got horns on his head like some kind of devil, and fur matted with blood, no doubt. He threatened my life, Captain."

The smirk turned into a face-splitting, wicked smile. "Sounds like a right fun bastard to play with."

"We're not hiring you to play with the beast. You're to kill it," Louis said.

Callum hefted a sigh. "Just because I mean to kill it doesn't mean I can't have some fun first."

"Fine. Do what you will. Just make sure none of your ilk touches my woman."

"Pray tell, if we can't touch the lass, how are we to get her back to you?" Callum arched an unusually immaculate brow.

"I'll be coming along on this little excursion with you."

"She must be quite the woman to draw out a little lordling such as yourself."

"I'm more than just some lord; I'm the greatest warrior in the land." Louis clenched his fist in front of his face as if that would show any form of intimidation.

I held my tongue at that admission. From what I knew of Louis, he was no more than a bully to the meek and powerless. I had my doubts that he could stand up to a real warrior, but given his build and cruelty, I wouldn't speak a word against his perceived assets.

"Oh? Then why do you need my help?" Callum scoffed and leaned his forearm on the table, waiting for an answer with amusement written in every line of his face.

Louis opened and closed his mouth like a fish out of water, crimson staining his cheeks as his fist dropped back to his side, limp.

"That's what I thought." The captain laughed with his men, chiding Louis for his bluster.

I watched the rage blotch his face and neck before speaking up to prevent the explosion that I knew was coming.

"We need some kind of plan to find the castle and get inside."

Callum's cool gaze settled on me with raised brows. "You don't know how to get there?"

It was my turn to bristle under the scrutiny.

"No. I don't." It wasn't a lie. I'd tried several times to find my way back, but all attempts proved unsuccessful.

"Then I suggest you figure that out first. Once you do, come back and ask for my help again. Preferably on your knees." He looked through me, eyes running up and down Isa's slight frame before finding mine again. "And without the poor girl. This is no place for creatures such as she."

"First, you don't get to give us demands. I'll bring the girl if I damn well please. Second, we have a lead." Venom coated Louis's tongue. "There's a man that comes into town every so often that we think lives at the castle. He's due for another trip here soon. We could use your help to catch him."

Callum leaned forward on both arms, the whites of his teeth showing in a twisted sort of grin.

"Well, why didn't you say so? I can work with that. Tell me more about this man."

"He's a large sort of fellow. His clothes hide it, but he's built like a warrior. He's got hair the color of fire, the reddest I've ever seen. And golden eyes."

It was as if Louis memorized every facet of this man.

Something flashed in Callum's eyes and vanished an instant later. I couldn't even guess what it might have been. A muscle ticked with his pulse along the line of his jaw, and the humor faded from his face.

"I'll have my men on the lookout for him. When he steps into the town again, I'll know. And we'll have our way into that castle."

"Good. As soon as Arabelle is back safe in my arms, you'll receive your payment." Louis stretched out a hand to him.

"Not a chance, mate. We'll be taking our payment up front."

Callum's gaze sharpened on Louis, and for a moment, I thought he might skewer him with the sword hanging off the back of his chair.

"You look the sort to weasel out of it."

Red splotched Louis's face. "And you lot are pirates. Not to be trusted at all. I won't have you run off with my coin." He dropped his hand.

"And where would we run to? Our ship is still being repaired. And it's too damned cold to be trekking across the countryside," Callum said with an exaggerated roll of the eyes.

Louis set his mouth in a line. "I'll give you a quarter of the payment now. Rest when the job is done." He might drown if he walked outside in the rain with as high as he held his nose up at them.

"All or nothing, little lordling. My men don't work for free."

Much to my chagrin, Callum didn't rise to the belittlement Louis threw his way with every word exchanged.

"Fine, half."

"All. Or. Nothing." He wouldn't budge.

"*Fine*. I'll see to it my men bring it within the hour. Now we leave."

Louis snatched up Isa's small wrist and dragged her behind him. She stumbled over toppled chairs and sprawled pub patrons, that chain around her ankles raking across everything.

One second, Callum was grinning to his men; the next, he was across the room, dagger in hand with the blade pressed into Louis's throat. It happened too fast for me to follow, before I even knew something had happened. Isa stood behind him, startled but untouched. The captain was lean, but I'd never seen anything move that fast.

"Women are not animals to be chained, nor are they things to be dragged around and treated so roughly, mate. For a man who's so desperate to get his bride back, you're awfully handsy with this one." His words came out in a vicious growl.

Louis struggled against Callum's grip, but he held firm, allowing no give.

"What do you care? She's nothing to you."

Callum's eyes darkened. Fuck. He was going to kill Louis.

Right here and now. I needed to stop him. But what hope did I have when he made Louis look like a helpless lamb?

The blade drew blood as Callum pressed it harder into his flesh.

"I won't allow any man to mistreat someone so vulnerable." He leaned in closer, his voice barely more than a whisper. "If you put your hands on her again, I'll remove them myself. And then I'll remove your balls and force-feed them to you. Do we have an understanding?"

"You can't talk to me like that. I'm giving you gold. You do as I say, not the other way around."

Louis tried his best to straighten his stature, to bow up his chest and make a play for the threatening man most saw him as, but Callum still stood taller, and the blade drew a steady trickle of blood down the line of his throat.

"I said, *do we have an understanding?*"

Louis sneered up at him but relented. "Yes. We do."

Callum backed off, letting Louis fall to the sick-covered pub floor, grasping for his neck. He pulled his hands back, bloodied, and glared up at the pirate captain but held his tongue. Better to remain silent than risk having his head removed. Holy hell. And I screwed him out of his pay how many times? I'm lucky to still have *my head.*

He met my eyes, and my blood ran cold when his lips curled up.

"You served a purpose, so I let you keep your head," he said.

I didn't say that aloud.

Callum brushed by me, sword still drawn, and stopped in front of Isa. With two slashes of that blade, the chains clunked to the floor. He moved closer, taking her chin between his thumb and forefinger as he lifted her face to his.

"You'd be so much more interesting if you said all those delightful things in that little head of yours."

Cold fire burned in her eyes, and her lips set in a smile so wicked that I realized I didn't know her at all.

"Get your hands off me, pirate." She bared her teeth at him. "And stay the fuck out of my head."

Callum's answering smile told me two things: one, that he was ready to play this game with her, and two, I'd been underestimating these two this entire time. My gaze shifted to Isa. What else had my own daughter been hiding from me? A veil of unease fell over me. The two of them together were dangerous.

THIRTY-SEVEN

Arabelle

The scent of pine wrapped itself around me like a blanket filled with memories of home. The evergreen logs crackled in the hearth as the fire devoured them. The curtains were thrown back in a spectacular display of the night sky with stars speckling in a dark blue, almost black, canopy above. Candles cast the room in a gentle, flickering light.

I stepped closer to the fireplace, as close as the dread prickling my skin would allow. Its warmth chased away the chill settling in with the absence of the sun.

"You haunt me in both my dreams and waking hours." The deep voice came from behind.

He walked just out of my reach as he passed in front of me and circled around until I could no longer see him. He leaned in close enough that his body warmed my back. Strands of my hair tickled the back of my neck when his breath breezed through them.

When I caught his gaze as he passed, I searched for the beast I knew in those eyes. The lack of gold in Lucien's eyes gave me pause, but maybe it was caused by whatever magic changed him into a beast. It could have dulled the beauty of him.

Heat rushed to my face and dipped down through my chest, settling in my lower belly.

"I could say the same of you." I tried to steady my voice.

He moved, bringing his face around to my other side, fingers caressing up the bare skin of my arms. The nightgown I put on before bed did little to hide my body, but I didn't care as long as he kept touching me like that.

"And yet, you still haven't come to me." My ear burned with the heat of his breath.

"I'm trying," I said, leaning into him as the soft touch sent a delightful shiver deep enough to reach my bones. Maybe not as hard as I could be, not when Lucien had begun to take up so many of my thoughts.

One of his hands slid under my hair and traced the curve of my neck along the edge of my jaw. He dragged the pad of his thumb agonizingly slow across my lower lip.

"Do you want me to touch you?"

My lungs held my breath prisoner inside my chest. I could let myself believe it for now, couldn't I? That they were one and the same. It would save me the pain of being torn in two – of having to choose. I wanted them both; I didn't care if it made me selfish.

Pure liquid fire pooled between my thighs, and I squeezed my legs together as if it might pour out of me.

"Yes." My response was a demand and plea wrapped in a single need to feel his hands on me.

His broad hands roved down my sides and wrapped around my front. His touch was softer than I expected, fingers moving in thoughtful and precise strokes. My nipples peaked against the fabric as he dragged the tip of his index finger along the side of my breast and over the top. His hand engulfed it in a gentle squeeze, the other holding my hip as he pressed into my backside.

I arched into him, and his hold on me tightened. His lips grazed along the side of my neck, leaving a trail of kisses before dragging my earlobe between his teeth and squeezing it. His ragged breath tickled my ear.

Every inch of his body was hard with muscle, but the firmness that captivated me most of all was below the waistband of his pants, straining within the confines of that tight fabric. My core throbbed with the possibilities of feeling that inside of me. It begged to be free. I reached behind me for his belt buckle, only to have him snatch my hand.

"I didn't give you permission to do that." The command in his tone was a familiar one, one that reminded me of a certain blue-eyed beast. I threw myself into the possibility, if only for now.

"But—"

"No buts, Arabelle. Be good, so I don't have to punish you."

The way he said those words had me wanting to do everything to both earn and avoid his punishment.

He slid his hand inside the collar of my gown and cupped my other breast, the warmth of his skin on mine causing a cascade of blistering flames straight to my center. I squeezed my eyes shut, biting my bottom lip to stifle the gasp wanting to escape me.

The sound of his groan was almost enough to undo me on the spot, the rumble in his chest vibrating against my back as he raised his hand to tug my lip from between my teeth.

"You have no idea what that does to me."

His hips undulated against my ass. The only thing between us was my nightgown and his pants. His fingers dug into my flesh almost to the point of pain—but the hurt was too delicious to make him stop.

"I've wanted to get my hands on you for a while now. To feel you, know every sound you make when pleasure addles your brain."

He dragged his fingertips down my neck, collarbone, and chest, letting his nails scrape over the skin and silk until he reached the hem of my short gown.

"What's stopped you?"

My breath was heavy with need. My skin burned wherever our bodies met, the desire for his touch emptying my head of rational thought.

"If it wasn't for this cage of mine, nothing would."

His fingers slipped under the edge of my gown, and he splayed his palm over my thigh, his large hand covering half of it. My head fell back on his shoulder as that hand inched upward, moving toward the wetness waiting for him, a wetness so easily brought about by his mere touch and words.

He wrapped his other arm around my waist, locking me in place as his fingers slid closer and closer.

"Are you sure this is what you want, Belle?"

God, the sound of my name on his tongue sparked madness in me, and I writhed against him, trying to urge his hand higher.

"Yes, yes, yes." I would get on my knees and beg him if it meant feeling those rough, calloused fingers plunge into me.

A sound rumbled up from his chest, and his fingers tangled in the fabric of my gown as he traced up along the front of my hip and down again through the course curls. He stroked down my center, and he hissed through his teeth.

"Gods damn, you're so wet."

I latched onto the rolled sleeves of his shirt and drew a broken breath in, arching my body into his touch. If I didn't have a hold of him, I might very well evaporate into the night sky. His deft fingers circled ever closer to my entrance without pushing into me. I bucked my hips, wanting him inside me—needing it.

"Please." I didn't care how it sounded, how the desperation seeped into my voice at the merest tease of him in my most sensitive of places.

"Can you beg for it like a good girl?" His words shot straight through me, and my muscles clenched.

Damn him. Damn him and his teasing. I squirmed and writhed in his grasp, doing my damnedest to impale myself on those fingers of his, but he was too good at keeping them from me.

"Please. I want to feel you inside me," I whimpered when he pulled away again.

He slid his finger down my slit.

"How bad do you want it?"

He brought that same finger to his lips, flicking his tongue out and licking up the wetness with a rumble of approval from his chest.

"I'll burn alive if you don't."

Fire seared through my veins, hotter than the one I'd been trapped in months before.

"We can't have that now, can we?" He slipped the tip of his finger inside me, and my knees went weak.

My grip on his shirt tightened as I sucked a breath in through my teeth, a moan vibrating at the bottom of my throat as he worked that finger deeper and deeper. He pumped slowly at first, then faster until he found a steady rhythm that started a slow build of tension at the core of me.

He dragged a low moan from the bowels of my being when he pushed a second finger in. The stretch burned so damn good. He curled his fingers inside me, finding a spot that triggered tiny bursts of pleasure. Each one fed off another.

My moans grew louder with each stroke, my hips moving in time with him, riding his hand as he worked this strange spell on me. His thumb found the bundle of nerves at the apex of my thighs and rubbed against it.

It was all too much. Ecstasy blanketed my mind in a hazy fog. My knuckles turned white from my grip, the muscles in my center clenching tight around him. I was going to explode. I couldn't stop it.

"Come for me, Belle."

His teeth clamped down on the crook of my neck, the pain mixing with the pleasure he was wrenching from my body in a singular explosive crescendo.

His command was enough to push me over the ledge, sending me into a freefall of pure bliss as wave after wave shuddered through my body, from my center all the way to the tips of my fingers and toes and back again.

A scream tore from my throat and shattered the warm, silent air of my room. My eyes snapped open, my body coming down from the throes of my orgasm. Blood rushed to my face, and I covered it with my hands, rolling over onto my side and burying my face in a pillow.

"I can't believe I had a dream like that."

It hadn't just been an erotic dream, but a wish—that the beautiful man I dreamed of was Lucien. That it had been him who dragged such an earth-shattering orgasm from me. Because I couldn't reconcile having Lucien's face flooding my mind at the apex of my pleasure while someone else gave it to me.

I rolled onto my stomach, kicking my feet under the covers and letting loose a frustrated cry into the pillow.

How could I face him after that? I rolled onto my back again and stared up at the soft folds of fabric hanging over my bed. Sunlight streamed in through the cracks in the curtains.

"Maybe a cold bath will help."

I yelped when I slid my body into the icy water in the tub, shivers wracking my body in waves. I hugged my knees to my chest as the heat leeched out of my skin and disappeared. I forced myself to stay in as long as my body could stand, which wasn't very long, and jumped out again. I wrapped myself in a thick bathrobe and huddled into a ball in one of the chairs next to my window as I waited for the shaking to subside.

Once my muscles released their tight grip and I could relax again, I slumped over my knees and buried my face in my hands.

Nope. I couldn't do it. I couldn't face Lucien after such a dream. They'd read it all over my face anytime I looked at him. Why did I have to have a dream such as that? I let out a frustrated groan. It would be better to hide somewhere for the day and just let it pass.

I waited until after breakfast had come and gone, hiding in my room like some kind of recluse. By the time I worked up the nerve to leave, however, a soft knock sounded on the door, and my stomach lurched into my chest.

Elie cracked the door open and peeked inside, catching sight of me before slipping into the room.

"You missed breakfast and this morning's training session, so I came to check on you. Is everything alright?"

My cheeks blazed with heat. I refused to look him in the eye. No. Everything was not alright. But he wouldn't understand that, understand what it meant to have *that* kind of dream about someone you were still getting to know.

"Perhaps if you tell me about it, I can help."

The door snicked shut, and I looked at him through my fingers. He leaned against the door with hands in his pockets.

My shoulders slumped with the sigh I exhaled, and I dropped my hands to my sides.

"I've been having dreams...about a man."

He arched a brow at me and pressed his lips in a thin line.

"And just who is this man?" His weight shifted from one foot to the other.

"I don't know," I started, and it was like a vault opened, and the words just spewed from me. "He asked me to help free him. I can't do that unless I find him. I thought Lucien had to have him locked in the dungeon, but he says no one has been in them for a long time, so he can't be down there. I don't know where else to look. And then last night's dream was of him..." I buried my face in my hands again. I couldn't believe I told him all of that.

I left out the part where I'd wanted it to be Lucien in my dream. Even now, I wanted to let myself believe it was him.

Amusement lit up the gold in his eyes.

"Did something different happen in last night's dream?" He found humor in this.

I glared up at him, and he had a damn smile on his face—he didn't even try to hide it.

I chewed my lip, the tang of blood on my tongue before I spoke.

"Yes." Fire scorched through my veins at the memory. "It was erotic."

"Erotic?" He choked on the word, sputtering to regain composure.

"Yes. Only..." I clamped my teeth down on the meat of my lip until a droplet of blood bubbled up. "He wasn't the one on my mind when I woke."

He straightened at my comment, removing his hands from his pockets and letting them hang loose at his sides.

"Who was?"

My cheeks had to match his hair by now. I couldn't hold his gaze any longer and dropped mine to the door behind him.

"Lucien."

He pushed off the door and circled around me.

"My, oh my, Belle." He stopped in front of me and crossed his arms. "Do you have feelings for our dear Lucien?"

I quickly shook my head, taking a step back.

"No." Maybe. "We've only just started tolerating each other."

There was no plausible way that I could have *feelings* for him.

CHAPTER

THIRTY-EIGHT

Arabelle

Hours flew by while I spent my time in the library, only leaving to sneak some food when my stomach grumbled louder than the fire burning in the hearth. I set down another book on my growing stack. It was the third one I finished today.

The book Lucien had read to me still sat on the table next to his chair. Didn't anyone clean up in here? I picked it up and flipped it open. Once I finished, I stared at the last page.

Nowhere in the book was the passage he read to me. My heart launched into a gallop, and I snapped the book shut, putting it back on the table. He couldn't have meant those words.

I pushed the thought out of my head and went to one of the bookshelves. My fingers skimmed over dust and cracked spines as I searched for another book to read, studying the gold and silver trimmed lettering indented into them. I reached the end of one row and circled around to the backside when I noticed a large table through an open door I hadn't come across before.

Curiosity drove my feet, and I found myself inside the room—a cartography room that smelled of stale ink, old books, and the musky rot of paper. Dozens of scrolls were stacked in cubicles lining the far wall.

It was a long shot, but maybe there were records in here. Somewhere else I could look to ensure the man from my dreams was just that – a dream. I searched through shelves and drawers and once again came up empty. The library, as far as I could tell, only contained fiction books, and this room only held maps. I thought there had been nonfiction, but when I scoured through them, it was all about faeries.

I sighed and let my head fall back. How could there be no indication of someone else in this castle? No sign, no record, not even a sound that might suggest it – not that I'd hear it if there was. I couldn't even find a scrap of the castle's history, nothing on Lucien or Elie, nothing on their parents. It was like someone combed through the library and removed everything. I glanced around the space.

On another wall, two maps stretched almost from floor to ceiling of the small room.

I ran my fingertips over the words of one as I read aloud, "Grienia."

A red ruby was painted in the southeastern region over a drawing of a castle. That's where I was. I'm not sure how I knew that, but I did.

I moved over to the larger map. Bold, curling letters spelled out "Asteria" along the bottom left corner. Each region was labeled in the same script within the confines of its borders; other illustrations of castles and various gemstones were painted within them as well.

Grienia was along the western coast. I touched my fingers to the castle in the southern part of it. This was home. I studied the map, counting in a silent whisper. There were seven kingdoms, each marked by a different gemstone, whose names I could read: Grienia, Ashary, Dothya, Ofril, Eskea, Croa Flary, and

Drieca – that land had a splotch of dark purple covering much of it.

I squinted at the lettering for the far eastern regions, but it was illegible, smeared as if someone tried to wipe them off the map. I rubbed at my temples as a dull ache spread through between them.

These kingdoms – they scratched at an itch somewhere in my head, but I couldn't drag out any memory I might have had of them. Even the name of our own kingdom pulled at strands in my mind like it wanted to unravel.

I didn't recognize any of this. How was it I didn't even remember the basics of my own home? I knew the name but had somehow forgotten there'd been a king.

The pain grew to a pulsing throb that had me wincing. It wasn't uncommon for folks in a kingdom to know little about the rest of the world, but given my education, I *should* have the knowledge. My parents wasted no efforts in making sure I'd be the perfect wife of some rich noble.

I rubbed at the grooves forming between my eyebrows. This wasn't the whole world though. The eastern lands stretched into something bigger. Why were only these regions mapped out? The thought nagged at me as I picked up a dust covered tome that left a clean spot where it sat. It was the only book in here.

I wiped the front of it with the edge of my dress and turned it over in my hands. There was no title on this one. I flipped it open and scanned the messy, handwritten words scrawled on the pages.

"When The Nullifier granted dark magic to the humans it triggered a war that divided the world. The loss of life was so catastrophic that ten of the strongest leaders brought their warriors together for the first time in history to fight against these malevolent forces that threatened our very existence. They sat their own blood feuds aside to work as a single entity to put a stop to the slaughter of our people."

It read like a journal of sorts, but this wasn't a history I was familiar with. There was no such thing as magic. Maybe it was a work of fiction that someone left behind.

But those words…Dark magic. Another set of images raced back to my mind, of women dressed in black, shrouded in a darkness so malevolent that it threatened to consume everything. It *wanted* to consume everything.

I blinked. That same darkness stalked through my dreams, chasing after the golden light that urged me on. They both had a presence, a sense of self, and at times, I could *feel* them both tugging me in opposite directions, like I was being torn apart from the inside.

I kept reading.

"After The Architect cleaved our peoples apart, those same ten leaders called a meeting to divide up the land given to us. It was this day that the Jewels of Asteria were born."

I paced around the table as I continued reading, doing my best to ignore the aching throb spreading from my temples to my forehead.

"The Jewels are as follows: The Ruby Court of Grienia, The Emerald Court of Dothya, The Sapphire Court of Eskea, The Diamond Court of Ofril, The Sunstone Court of Ashary, The Amethyst Court of Croa Flary, The Opal Court of Drieca, the Onyx court of Hesnen, The Bloodstone Court of Lasmil, and The Moonstone Court of Ashea."

I hissed through my teeth and pressed my thumb into my temple as the pain sharpened. It felt like the edges of my mind were beginning to fray, but I couldn't bring myself to put the book down and stop.

Who were these courts? Why were they important? Why were

those other territories wiped off the map? The answers were all at the tip of my mind, just beyond the pain. I pushed further.

"Peace between the courts lasted only a few centuries before petty squabbles broke out, and larger conflicts eventually led them to divide further. The Onyx, Bloodstone, and Moonstone Courts broke off into what is now called the Lunar Courts, where the others are known as The Solar Courts."

"Belle? What are you doing in here?"

Lucien's voice was drowned out by pain exploding in my skull. It would have taken my legs out from under me, but he caught me in his arms, the soft fur tickling my nose. I dropped the book and clamped my hands over the sides of my head as I bit back a sob. Daggers sliced through my brain for no reason.

What was this? Why did reading this book cause this pain? And it wasn't the first time. The same thing happened every time I learned a little bit more about this place, the past, the people. Warmth trickled down my lip as I looked up at Lucien.

"Are you okay? Your nose is bleeding."

The concern in his voice would have been endearing if the pain in my head left room for anything else. But it drowned everything else out. I didn't care how. I just needed it to stop.

I swiped at my lip with my thumb; it came back bloody. I leaned away from him, leaving the book on the floor as I found the cloudy mirror sitting on the corner of a desk.

Blood oozed from my nose. I searched for something to wipe it with and finally had to settle on an old, dirty rag.

"What are you doing here?" I asked while still dabbing the cloth to my nose.

His ear fluttered at my words. "I haven't seen you all day."

I swallowed the lump of iron that lodged itself in my throat. I just had to face him. It's not like it was really him in the dream anyway, even if I let myself believe it was. That was it. Not a big deal at all.

Lucien tilted his head as he gave me a once-over. "Have you been in here the whole time?"

"Pretty much. I did sneak some food from the kitchen a few times."

I glanced at the windows through the door; the sky was awash with orange and pink. I didn't realize it was already dusk.

"Did I do something to upset you?" His words were an arrow straight through my chest and I looked anywhere but at him, not able to stand the guilt I glimpsed there.

I dragged my lip between my teeth and wrung my fingers in my hand.

"No. It has nothing to do with you."

I couldn't tell him I came here because of a dream or that I was avoiding him because I woke up to an orgasm ripping through my body, and I'd wanted it to be him who caused it.

"Then what happened? Did Elie say something to you?" His posture told me he wanted to come to me but fought off the desire to do just that.

"It's...I just...I wanted to spend the day alone. That's all."

It was my turn to have the guilt gnawing at my insides as I watched his countenance change.

"What about tonight?"

My brow arched at that. He was nervous. He shifted from side to side, albeit so slightly I could barely tell. He wrung his fingers in front of him, eyes searching for something to focus on instead of me. A small grin curved the corner of my lips.

"Is there something happening tonight?"

"There is a gown waiting for you in your room. I'd like you to wear it and meet me in the foyer after sundown." His gaze finally caught mine, and my stomach erupted into a flurry of flutters.

"Why?" I tried too hard to stop my voice from trembling, and I winced at how aggressively the word came out.

"It's a special night, and I want to share it with you." He nodded his head in a slight bow and left.

I couldn't fight the smile that spread from cheek to cheek as my eyes fell to the dinner waiting for me on a table.

THIRTY-NINE

Arabelle

I stared at the over the top, lavish gown waiting for me on a wire mannequin in my room. How was I supposed to even put it on? There was no way I could do it by myself. I ran the soft black chiffon through my fingers. Even before we fell into poverty, I never saw anything of such exquisite workmanship.

The skirt flowed in layers to the floor, opening at one hip to reveal a delicate crepe in dark red. The fitted bodice was made of charmeuse of the same dark red chiffon pulled taut over it. A tangle of black thorns overshadowed the dip of the sweetheart neckline as they reached their fingers out over the bust and wrapped down around to the back of the waist.

A light knock shattered the silence, and the door creaked open. Elie poked his head into the room.

"Normally we would have a lady in waiting for you. But since it's just us, you're stuck with me."

Apprehension clenched in my gut, and I glanced from him back to the gown.

"I don't know how I feel about a man helping me dress."

A playful smirk graced his lips. "It usually goes against my nature to get someone so beautiful *into* a dress. But I'll make an exception this time."

He stepped through the door and leaned against it until it clicked shut.

"Unless you refuse the idea altogether, but I do hope you'll consider dear Lucien's feelings if I have to go tell him you won't join him tonight."

He lifted his hands in an off-kilter shrug.

Guilt and unease prickled my skin. Lucien went out of his way to invite me to whatever this was, and he was nervous about it. I couldn't bring myself to not show up.

"That still leaves the problem of you seeing me naked."

I rubbed a hand up my forearm, guarding myself from his gaze that, much to my surprise, didn't move from mine. His eyes softened from playful to something a bit more sympathetic, the candlelight causing the gold in them to glitter.

"You can put the underlayers on first, without me. I can help with the rest."

Blood rushed to my face and set it ablaze. "That's still the most indecent anyone has seen me in a long time."

I didn't know why I argued with him. I needed his help, I knew that. Maybe I just wanted to prolong whatever it was that happened next. I wasn't sure my heart could handle what Lucien had in store for the night.

"If you can't look indecent in front of a friend, then are you really friends? Don't worry, Belle. I've seen Lucien look far worse."

Mischief danced in those enchanting eyes, and a sense of ease filled me. This was Elie, the same Elie that had been not-so-subtly pushing me toward his friend this entire time.

"Alright, Elie. But if you try anything." I straightened to make myself seem just a little more intimidating. "I'll tell Lucien you broke his piano."

His lips curled upward in an amused smile, and he folded his arms over his chest, still leaning against the door. "That'll be awkward, considering his piano isn't broken."

"It will be when I'm done with it." I placed my hands on my hips, shifting my weight to one side and raising my brows at him. "No funny business, Elie."

Elie lifted his hands in surrender. "Okay, okay. You have my word. I will absolutely behave myself."

Satisfied with his promise and the dissipated tension, I dug through the wardrobe until I found a black linen underskirt and matching corset. I passed Elie, who now looked over the gown Lucien chose for me to wear, circling around to study the back as he wedged his chin between his thumb and forefinger with a lifted brow.

"I didn't expect him to let you wear *this*."

The bathroom door snicked shut by the time he got the last word out. The dress must have been special. I shimmied out of the clothes I wore that day and pulled on the skirt first, then fastened the corset over it.

When I walked out, Elie turned toward me and gave a curt nod.

"Let's get you ready."

Propriety still had me curling in on myself as I crossed my arms to hide my breasts, the nip of the air reminding me just how much skin was exposed.

"Hang on," Elie tugged at the hem of the corset with a frown. "This is too loose. Turn around so I can fix it."

I put my back to him, pulling my hair over my shoulder to get it out of his way. The corset slackened before being tugged in at the waist as he tightened the strings until it held fast to every curve of my body.

I stared at the ceiling; he was too damn good at lacing up a corset. Those deft fingers reminded me of another set of hands exploring my body. My dream came back in an instant, and heat pulsated through me. I pushed it out of my head, forcing other images into my mind. Images of feet, leaking pustules, ruptured boils, disease-addled rats, giant spiders, anything that disgusted or terrified me.

"How's that feel?"

His voice tore me from the slideshow of horrors flashing through my mind to prevent me from thinking about his hands or the others that I craved to feel on me again.

I twisted my hips and bent side to side, testing my range of movement.

"It's great. And I don't feel like I'm about to fall out of it anymore."

"Good."

Elie rummaged through the wardrobe until he found black stockings and red silk ribbon garters. He tossed them on the bed, then walked to the dress, kneeling and reaching under the voluminous skirts of the gown, and pulled out a pair of black heels with a golden buckle over the top. He set them at my feet.

"I'm sure you can manage these by yourself."

"I'm not totally helpless." I rolled my eyes and snatched up the garters first. I sat on the bed, lifting my skirt enough to slide the band up to my thigh, repeating with my other leg. Once they were in place, I pulled on the stockings and latched them to the garters.

I reached for the shoes, but Elie grabbed them up before I could.

"Allow me," he said and knelt in front of me.

He took one of my ankles in hand. His touch was a warm caress. He slid a shoe onto one foot, then the other, tying the red ribbons up around my ankles.

"Perfect."

"You seem to be enjoying dressing me up; I never would've

guessed that was your thing, Elie." I grinned down at him, still kneeling in front of me.

"Oh, I have many *things*, Belle. One of which is turning beautiful people into shining gems."

He stood until my neck craned back to hold his gaze. He stepped back and went to a wall, pulling what I thought was a normal wall sconce, triggering a panel to pop open.

"I didn't know that was there." I leaned, trying to see inside, but the angle was wrong, and I didn't want to plant my face on the floor.

"That's the point of secret rooms," he said over his shoulder as he walked in. "It wouldn't do to have people know where the jewels are kept."

I thought back to that first night, the room full of gold, jewels, and all things finery that Lucien instructed me to choose from to send home. I hoped the chests made it. What I wouldn't give to see Isa's face when she had opened the trunk to see that dress. I sighed at the thought of her. I missed her, missed our daily chores and the bedtime stories we read together.

I blinked away the tears threatening to fall and glanced back at the opening. I assumed that one room was the extent of Lucien's wealth, but the more I learned about him, the more he gave me such extravagant things, and the more I doubted what I thought I knew.

"Jewels?"

"Yes. They belonged to Lucien's mother."

Metal clicked against metal, and drawers opened and closed from beyond my sight.

A knot tied my stomach as I thought about wearing his mother's jewelry and everything it implied. Was it his idea? Or Elie's? There was no telling with those two. I swallowed the growing lump in my throat. I just hoped that if it were Elie's choice, Lucien wouldn't be angry about it.

I pressed my palm to my chest as if I could grab my heart and slow the rapid beat. Lucien's mother meant a great deal to him and was taken much too soon. I didn't want to see him hurt because I showed up wearing her jewels.

Elie came back out of the secret room, his arms laden with glittering things in silvery white gold and glistening red.

"No, he doesn't know," he said as if he read every thought in my head just now. "He hasn't seen these pieces since she died."

He laid them out on the bed.

The grandest was a filigree white gold collar with a palm-sized ruby in the center. There were two cuffs and a pair of earrings that matched, as well as a hairpin and clip, the end of the pin set with a jewel in the shape of a blooming rose.

I traced my fingertips over the detailed craftsmanship of the collar, and my eyes burned. The last person to wear these was Lucien's mother.

"Elie, I don't know if I can wear these. They're so beautiful, and I'm sure they're special to him in a way I'll never understand."

"They are." Elie picked up a cuff and took my hand in his, slipping it onto my slender wrist. "But I think you might be, too."

Instant heat scorched my cheeks and ears, even spreading down my neck.

"Do you really think he'll be okay with me wearing these?"

"I think he will be elated to see them again, especially on you." His eyes fell to the golden chain at my chest. "You'll have to take that off, though."

My hand shot to the locket, and my heart stuttered.

"I guess it wouldn't look as elegant with everything else."

"Here." Elie reached under my hair and undid the clasp, lifting the locket from between my breasts and placing it on the table next to my bed. "This way, you'll know where it is."

"Thanks, Elie."

"Of course," he said and twirled his finger. I turned my back to him.

He placed each piece of jewelry on me with such gentle care that one might assume he valued it more than life. The clasps and chains sat flush against my skin to ensure they looked immaculate. He gestured to the vanity across the room, and I crossed the space in a rustle of tulle.

Elie brushed my hair and swept it up into a loose bun, curling a lock of my bangs around his finger and letting them hang in front of my face as he pinned the rest in place with the clip set. I never imagined my hair could look this beautiful. I reached up to touch it, but he smacked my hand away.

"You'll mess it up."

Only the dress remained. He took it off the mannequin and held it low enough for me to step into it.

"Time to get this on."

I used him to brace myself as I stepped into the gown, cursing my off-balanced center when my fingers dug into the hard muscle of his shoulder. I let go when I had both feet under me again, and he raised the gown up over my body. He tightened the laces on the back, careful to leave room for me to move and breathe.

The dress rustled with each and every movement, but it wasn't as heavy as I expected it to be. I ran my palms down the bodice and top of the skirts as I stared at my reflection in the mirror. I turned to one side, then the other.

"I don't think I've ever worn anything so..." I trailed off as words escaped me.

Elie stepped up behind me, staring over my shoulder.

"It suits you."

He was silent for a moment that stretched on and on.

"You should get going. He's waiting for you."

I huffed out a small sigh. "He hasn't explained what the occasion is."

I caught Elie's eye in the mirror.

"You'll find out as soon as you get down there," he said with a smirk, stepping back away from me.

I spun to face him and stuck out my tongue before making for the door.

"You don't have to be so secretive about everything."

He folded his arms over his chest and raised a brow at me. "But it's so much fun."

Despite the smile on his lips and amusement in his tone, his eyes told a different story, one of sorrow and pain. I pushed that to the back of my mind for now and rolled my eyes, giving him my best smile.

CHAPTER

FORTY

Arabelle

Walking to the foyer took longer than normal. Every step I took had to be calculated and measured so I didn't step on the gown and trip or risk getting caught on any one of the numerous items that I failed to notice having such jagged edges before. Or maybe they just appeared to have them now because I worried about tearing a hole in the damn dress. I forgot how troublesome it was to wear clothes like this.

A glow of moonlight was cast over the sweeping steps leading down to the foyer as I came to the top edge. Sure enough, Lucien waited at the bottom, donning a suit that could be a damned matching set with the dress I wore. His attention snapped up to me when my heels clacked on the first step as I made my descent.

"You must have stepped down from the heavens because my heart refuses to believe you were born of this place." He gripped the banister, claws scraping against the wood as his eyes bore into me, devouring every inch.

I couldn't fight the smile, so I let it play off as a cool and unfazed one instead.

"Is the big, bad beast resorting to flattery now?"

His own smile answered mine. "The big, bad beast will use every tool in his arsenal if it means catching a glimpse of that smile."

The words sent my heart aflutter and a blush darkening my cheeks.

"I bet you say that to all the women you capture in your castle."

"Only the ones who insist on challenging me at every turn."

He kept his eyes locked on mine as I descended the stairs, meeting him at the bottom.

"It must be hard for you to not have control."

"If it's control you want," he paused and extended his arm out to me, "you need only ask."

His eyes dipped to the collar as he looked down at me but met mine again.

I threaded my arm through his, and he led me out of the castle. "If I told you to bow to me, would you?"

His pace was slow, much like it was when we walked through the gardens, and he showed me around the castle. He could have walked much faster, but he made the concession for me.

"If you told me to get on my knees and worship you like a goddess, I'd fall to the ground and offer my soul in sacrifice."

I might've enjoyed seeing him on his knees in a different kind of worship. Images of just that filtered through my mind, bringing my blood to a boil before I shoved them away.

I tried to hide the small discomfort his words brought me when the image of him giving up his life for me sprang into my mind.

"Maybe not quite that far."

He quirked a brow at me, glancing sideways as we walked along a cobblestone path leading away from the castle. "You don't like the thought of me on my knees?"

"I don't like the thought of you giving up a single thing for me," I said the words before I had a thought to stop them. They were true, and that realization tied my stomach in knots. I didn't know when I went from wanting to escape him to savoring his presence, and the thought stole my breath away.

"You wouldn't change anything about me?" He raised both eyebrows this time, his voice barely holding steady.

"Maybe those lopsided horns of yours." I pointed to the left one. "I think one is lower than the other."

"They aren't lopsided." His free hand shot up and touched one horn, then the other, something I had yet to see him do in the months I'd been here.

As he dropped his hand, I snickered.

"I was just kidding."

He snorted out a breath, the fur on his chin and chest parting at the force of it. He puffed out his chest and threw back his shoulders as if he wanted to appear dignified.

"Lopsided or no, I am a dashing beast."

There was no anger, no temper, not even annoyance on his face. Where was this Lucien when I showed up? He didn't come off arrogant like Louis, but rather, he radiated confidence with no need to flaunt it. I held fast to his arm, pulling myself a fraction closer.

"You are."

I paid no mind to where he took me while we talked, not until we crested a hill and on the other side was a field. The sight robbed me of words, or maybe my breath entirely. The field was speckled with countless glowing white, silver, and pale blue lights that mirrored the night sky. They stretched as far as I could see. Some hovered close to the ground while others drifted up toward the stars. I couldn't tell where the field ended and the sky began.

"What *is* this? It looks as if the sky couldn't contain all the stars, and they fell down here." I touched the ruby sitting against my heart as my eyes beheld the sight.

Lucien leaned down and whispered in my ear, "The Field of Stars."

He led us into the grassy planes.

"Every year, on this night, spirits gather in this field. Once they've let go of their worldly tethers, they float into the sky to join with the stars."

I released him and stepped toward one of the lights, reaching my hand out to touch it. My fingers slipped through what I imagined clouds felt like, leaving a trail of dusky light in their wake.

He placed his palms under one that hovered just below his line of sight. "We call this night Nocturnum Lucir.

"When I was a child, my parents threw magnificent celebrations in honor of the spirits passing on. They brought people from all over the realm, and those past our borders too, just to join in and celebrate life." The orb of light cast his face in an array of sad shadows.

"There would be music, and food, and drink. Elie and I watched from the castle every year, wanting nothing more than to join in on the fun. We weren't allowed to because we were too young," he paused, and I watched as the memories drew a smile from him.

"We snuck into the party one year and got drunk off our asses on some imported wine. We danced with the rest of the crowd and were complete menaces. At least, that's what my mother said when she caught and lectured us." The smile on his lips warmed my heart.

"She was *not* happy about it. She told Elie's folks and left the punishment up to his father."

He laughed this time, an actual, true laugh that drew a smile to my own face. He raked his palm through the fur over his face.

"I thought my arms and legs would fall off. That man was such a sadist, I swear."

Lucien tilted his head back and stared up at the night sky, and then his eyes fell to me again, holding out his hand.

"It might not be an eternity, but I can give you this night."

The warmth in my chest blossomed and spread up to my cheeks and ears and down through my stomach and toes until every inch of my skin was ablaze with a fire bursting to life within me.

I took his hand.

Lucien pulled me to him and swept us into a dance into the spirit laden field, leaving a glittering trail of light everywhere we went as we passed through them.

Joy bubbled up from within me, and I let my laughter ring out in the night as we spun and twirled. How long had it been since I last danced so freely? And Lucien, who looked no more than some ferocious animal, was the best partner I could remember having.

With the finishing steps of the dance, he stepped away from me. "I haven't been able to enjoy this night in such a long time."

"I'm glad you wanted to share it with me."

I took a step toward him, but he held up a hand for me to stop. My brows bunched together until I heard it—the soft notes of a piano. I turned and searched the field, but we were the only ones here. Where was it coming from? My eyes met his again, and he wasn't surprised by it in the least.

Lucien stepped toward me and raised his hand to the back of my neck, pulling me into a slow turn. I mirrored his moves in time with the music; I knew the dance and recognized the song. His hand slid from my neck and took mine in his, spinning me with enough vigor that my skirts flared out.

In the dim candlelight, I didn't realize, but now, with the light of the spirits and stars, the gown I wore glittered as if it, too, wanted to be one of them.

The waltz continued, and we moved in such a comfortable tandem that every step flowed through us like flowers dancing with the wind. Every turn, every spin, was executed with flawless precision; Lucien knew how I wanted to move before I had a mind to do it.

If Mother were still alive to see it, I'd never have to take another lesson accompanied by the verbal tongue-lashing again.

I was falling into the ocean that was him, and in this moment, I had no intention of coming up for air. In his arms was the safety, the security that I always longed for, and more. He never stifled me, never asked me to change. In fact, all he ever wanted from me was my time—was me.

With an upward crescendo in the music, he wrapped an arm around the small of my back and lifted me in a spin, holding the crook of my knee to keep me in place. Our bodies pressed together, sending a rush of scorching hot blood pulsing through my veins. He smelled of soap and a hint of birch trees.

Lucien dipped me low enough that had my hair not been pinned up, it would have touched the blades of soft grass underfoot. He lifted me back up, holding me close to him, eyes dropped to the collar around my neck, then locked with mine.

"My mother's jewels suit you."

I stroked my fingertips over the ruby. "I wasn't sure about wearing them. Elie talked me into it. I hope it's okay with you."

"I'm okay with it," he said, then huffed a hot breath that tickled my neck. "Elie likes to meddle too much."

"He does." My fingers clutched his arms as he still held me off balance. "But it comes from a good place. He cares a great deal about you."

"I know." His eyes darkened a bit with wherever his mind dragged him down to. "There is nothing he wouldn't do for me."

"Except go easy on you," I said, desperate to pull him back to me and away from the shadows of a past I knew so little about, a past that wanted to consume him.

He snorted and rolled his eyes. "Except that."

The light returned to his eyes, and I breathed a small sigh of relief. It was absent when I first came to the castle, but now it burned bright in him. It matched the one that blazed in me.

We danced and danced until the black sky gave way to purple and then orange as the sun rose just beyond the horizon. My cheeks hurt from how much I laughed and smiled. The joy I thought died such a long time ago reignited, brought back to life by him.

As the sun broke over the skyline, Lucien let me go and clutched his side, doubling over as a coughing fit shuddered through his massive body, taking him to his knees in a matter of seconds. Concern tangled in my gut and held me prisoner as the coughing worsened.

"Are you okay?"

I braced him with my smaller frame, letting him lean into me for support as his muscles seized and trembled.

"I'm fine," he said in a rasp. He offered me a weak smile that failed to hide the pain in his eyes. "I just lost myself in our evening and forgot to drink anything for a few hours. We should go back to the castle so you can get some rest."

"Are you sure you're okay?"

His swallow was almost audible. "Are you worried about me?"

He kept that same weak smile on his face. I rolled my eyes at the tease in his voice.

"If you can make light of it, then clearly you are." If I wasn't afraid he'd collapse without my help, I'd step away.

"What a shame. And here I thought you'd grown fond of me." He straightened, taking the extra weight off me, and smoothed out his vest and shirt.

"Of course, I've grown fond of you." I reached up and scratched under his chin. "I've always wanted a pet."

His growl vibrated along my fingers, and it sent a shudder through me.

"I am no pet." Despite that, he still fought against the smile.

"But you're so fluffy. And follow me around everywhere just like one."

He bristled in a way that puffed up all the exposed fur on his body, and I laughed, hooking my arm around his.

"Let's go get some sleep."

I tried to swallow the anxiety crawling up the back of my throat, if for no other reason than to keep his mind at peace.

FORTY-ONE

Arabelle

The soft singsong chirp of birds and the gentle scent of flowers offered a calming ambiance for my racing mind after the excitement of the night before. The way Lucien looked at me sent my heart catapulting into a freefall that left my stomach in my throat and my cheeks awash with heat.

He was so much more than I first thought. I found myself wanting to search him down just to be near him, craving his presence like nothing I'd ever felt before.

The coughing, though. It nagged at me for the rest of the morning. He said he was fine, but he was lying. The way he clung to me, I thought he'd fall if I pulled away from him for even a second. I chewed my thumbnail, staring at the letters on the page, but none of them broke through the fog of my thoughts.

A chilled breeze blew through me, sending a bone-rattling cold down to my soul and carrying a hint of fresh snow and pine with it. The comfort from moments before vanished as everything fell into a disquieting silence. Something about it *felt* wrong, but I couldn't put my finger on what exactly it was.

I closed the book and set it on the bench next to me. The cold in my veins drove me to investigate the cause of such an absence of life. I passed through a brick and iron gate left ajar, vines climbing up over the arch and almost covering the whole of the bricks.

I stilled, holding my breath as a tall, raven-haired man stood on the other side of it, his hands in his pockets. A small gasp escaped me when he looked up with the blackest eyes.

Every instinct screamed at me to turn around and run as I watched the edge of his mouth tilt up into a smirk that dripped smugness. I bit back a whimper. He was waiting for me. Some deep instinct buried in my gut screamed it.

"It's been a while since I was last here. You must be Lucien's new pet." His brow arched, and his smirk widened into a smile when I bristled at his words.

"Who are you?" I forced as much venom and disdain into my voice as I could. His preternatural stillness disconcerted me more than I would let him see.

"I'm an old friend."

"You don't strike me as an old friend, skulking about in the outer gardens," I spat at him, taking a wary step back toward the gate. "Why didn't you come to the door?"

His hair hung in loose, wavy strands that framed a beautiful, angular face.

"Because Lucien and I didn't part on such great terms the last time we saw each other," he said with a nonchalant shrug.

"Is sneaking onto the grounds your way of making it up to him?"

Run away, run away, run away, my mind screamed at me, but I kept my feet planted firmly in place.

He took a step toward me, and my whole body tensed.

"Who said I was the one needing to make anything up?" He tilted his head to the side but didn't move any closer. "I'm sure you've seen his temper."

Did he notice the inclination to flee? See the tensing of my muscles? I held my chin up, refusing to show this man any more of the fear digging deep into my bones.

"Then what are you doing here?"

I looked him over. The black tunic cinched over a matching shirt, sleeves rolled halfway up his forearms, where dark geometric tattoos covered his pale skin. Tight leather pants showed off every hardened muscle in his legs, and black boots reached just below his mid-calf.

"If you know his temper, you know he's not keen on apologizing."

Amusement flared in those onyx eyes as a smirk quirked the corner of his lips.

"Oh, I like you."

Faster than my eyes could track, he was in front of me, brushing the backs of his knuckles down my cheek.

"How about you ditch the beast and come home with me to be my pet, instead?"

I recoiled from his touch and question all at once.

"I'm not in the habit of going anywhere with pretentious assholes. And I'm damn sure not anyone's pet," I snarled at him through bared teeth and backed out of his reach.

His eyebrows shot to his hairline.

"Pretentious?" He raised a hand to his chest and had the audacity to feign hurt at my jab. "And yet you're here with little Lucien." He closed the distance I'd been trying to put between us until my back met with the sun-warmed stone of the gate. "He hasn't told you about his past at all, has he?"

The grin he gave me was void of any warmth. I shrank in on myself, pressing my back into the bricks behind me and wanting nothing more than to disappear into them.

"Yes, he has." My tone wasn't as sure as I wanted it to be, and I cursed myself for it.

"Has he?" The bastard caged me in with his arms. "Has he told you why he looks the way he does?" He leaned down, the ends of his hair grazing my cheek. "Did he tell you about his curse?" His hot breath caressed my ear, and a tremor raked down my spine.

My throat was dry as a desert, making it difficult to swallow—to speak.

"W-what curse?" My heart pounded a hellish beat against my ribs.

His chuckle damn near took me out at the knees. "The one that forced him into the body of a monster instead of that of a man. The one the witch cast. The one that will kill him if he doesn't break it." He pulled back, taking my chin in between his fingers and tilting my head up to look at him. "It will kill him very soon."

Panic seized my heart, and my eyes burned with tears I refused to shed in front of this man. I wouldn't give him the satisfaction he wanted in that.

"Lucien is going to die?" My traitor of a voice trembled when I whispered the words.

He tucked a lock of my hair behind my ear, moving his fingers feather-light over my skin. "In a matter of weeks."

Fear squeezed the breath from my lungs. It came out in ragged bursts. A dull ache speared through my chest, and my throat constricted around the sobs, wanting to rip their way through me.

"But breaking the curse will save him?"

"Yes." His black eyes burrowed into my soul, and I wanted nothing more than to collapse into a sobbing mess right there. "It's something only you can do, Little Dove."

"How?"

I didn't care if I had to beg and plead with this beautiful stranger, give him anything he desired; I would go with him to the depths of hell itself if it meant I could save Lucien.

He stepped back, slid his hands back into his pockets, and

lifted his eyes up to the castle. I didn't notice them before, but lines of tattoos poked out from the collar of his shirt.

"That...you'll have to figure out on your own." His gaze fell on me again, that damned smirk back on his lips. "It wouldn't be as fun if I gave you *all* the answers."

No. I couldn't let him leave it at that.

"Please," I started, reaching for him. I needed to know how to save him. I couldn't let Lucien die.

The smirk melted away into a frown. "I just came to check on an old friend. The breeze from the East has shifted, and we need all the pieces back on the board."

My brows furrowed at that. "What are you talking about? What breeze from the East? That makes no sense."

He huffed out a breath and raked a hand through his silken hair.

"He'll know."

He turned to walk away, but I jolted forward and grabbed his arm.

"Wait. What's your name?" He couldn't just come in here and drop all this on me, not without telling me who he was.

He tilted his head back to look at me over his shoulder, and I could see a gleam of the amusement from before shining in his eyes.

"Do you intend to moan it as you pleasure yourself to my beautiful face?"

My cheeks flushed white hot at his comment, and I immediately released his arm, taking several steps back.

"Absolutely not. I would never—"

"It's Aamon." His dark chuckle lingered as the very air in front of him ripped open to a black void. He stepped through, and that rift disappeared into wisps of black smoke that drifted away with the wind.

Of all the arrogant bastards I had dealt with, he was the worst.

I blinked at the spot where he stood moments ago. That name...I'd heard it before.

Does Lord Aamon know about her yet? A chill ran its icy fingers through my veins. He was working with the Marid. But he didn't do anything. Didn't try to harm me. My brows furrowed. Was I wrong in my assumption, then?

I glared at that spot. How did he just disappear like that? Plenty of strange things happened in the castle, but I could usually reason them out. But this? This was different. How did a person simply vanish in a puff of smoke? Lucien asked me once if I believed in magic. I was starting to.

My heart cried out in a pain I'd never known before. Lucien. Was he really cursed? And if so... "He said Lucien only had weeks left to live..." Fear collided with the realization that I might lose him; it coiled in my gut, and the breakfast I'd eaten threatened to make a reappearance. I needed to see him—I needed to ask Lucien about it myself.

FORTY-TWO

Lucien

Streams of sunlight poured in through the tears on my curtains, searing into the backs of my eyelids. I turned my back to them, exhaustion soaked into every cell in my body. It was well into the day, and I still lacked the energy to even sit up.

That's what I thought, at least until a rasping cough exploded out of my throat, and I lurched up and over the side. I held a hand over my mouth as it persisted, my lungs on fire with the exertion both at dawn and right now.

Blood coated my palm, clots of it sliding down the curves. I wiped it on the already filthy sheet of my bedding. There wasn't much time left. I could feel the curse growing stronger in my blood and bones. It would rip me from this world before too much longer. I sprawled on my back and stared up through the tattered canopy.

Arabelle's face came to the forefront of my mind, radiating with that beautiful smile and joyous laughter from last night. I rubbed the spot over my heart. I couldn't remember the last time I enjoyed the company of another, nor the last time I craved it even before the witch showed up at my doorstep. It had been years since I felt such immeasurable happiness.

I just needed to hold on until the Blue Moon, still a month away. Then I would be back in the form of a man and could go to her. I cursed the changes for many years, but now it was my one chance. "If I don't win her heart, I die." It was the last opportunity I'd have to break this gods damned curse. If I failed in this, everything would be lost.

Another coughing fit wracked my body. I rolled to the side of the bed and grabbed a handkerchief. Weakness overtook me. I couldn't even hold myself up and fell to the floor, my shoulders heaving with violent coughs. When they finally subsided, I curled into a ball, letting the cold stone suck out the feverish heat from my flesh.

A soft knock sounded through my room, and all at once, my body went rigid. What was she doing here? I gave her specific orders to stay out of this wing, yet it was unmistakably her scent on the other side of the door. I pushed myself up, stomped to it, and ripped it open with such ferocity that, if not for my claws, it would have slipped from my hand.

"What are you doing here? I *told* you never to come to this side of the castle," I snarled, not giving her the chance to speak.

"I need to talk to you, Lucien," she said through heavy pants, wiping the back of her hand over her forehead to catch a drop of sweat sliding down her brow.

"It can wait until breakfast," I growled but looked her over.

Her hair clung to her face and neck in patches, soaked by her sweat. Color stained her cheeks pink in a flush that traveled below the neckline of her collar. Something was wrong. I clenched my jaw; it didn't matter.

She straightened herself, closed her eyes, took a deep breath through her mouth, and held it before letting it out in a slow exhale.

"You *missed* breakfast," she said.

Her gaze snapped to mine, and something inside my chest cracked at what I saw there.

"What is it?" I softened my features and released the anger boiling up from the pit of my stomach.

My anger always simmered just below the surface of my skin. It raged in her presence as if it somehow knew she would be the one to extinguish it. And she did.

She took another deep breath to steady herself and looked me straight in the eye.

"The reason you look the way you do...is it because you're cursed?"

The blood drained from my face in a rush of panic, leaving my ears ringing with her question. How did she find out? Was it Elie? We agreed not to tell her about it, to let her make her own choices. Damn him. With the deadline approaching, he must have gone to her behind my back.

"I—"

What was I supposed to say? Lie? I couldn't tell her what I was, the reason that witch cursed me.

"Lucien, tell me the truth." She stepped toward me, reaching out a hand, but I stepped back.

"Yes."

How much did she know? How much did he tell her? I ground my teeth, the coppery taste of blood filling my mouth, my throat as raw as my heart now was. How could Elie betray me like this?

"How did you find out?" I needed to know.

"How I found out isn't important. Why didn't you tell me yourself?" Unshed tears lined her eyes, and her chin quivered. "Don't you trust me?"

I wanted to reach out and stroke her cheek, hold her, beg her to forgive me, give her any comfort I could, but I stayed my hand.

"It's not that." Damn my pride for locking my muscles in

place. "It's my problem." Damn it for not letting me ask for help. "I didn't want to burden you with it." I wanted to rip it to shreds for the pain I saw in her eyes.

She curled her fingers into fists and trembled with an invisible strength she tried to force into place. "He was right; are you going to die if it's not broken?"

He. There was complete silence in my head. He really did tell her everything. And she came here, worried for my life. "I'm going to be fine, Arabelle. I won't die." I needed the lie to ease the anguish on her face, in her heart.

She dragged a long breath in and met my eyes. "Don't lie to me, Lucien." Her voice shook with accusation.

My own breath threatened to abandon me, but I didn't waver and held her gaze. "I'm not lying to you." I wouldn't let her face this burden with me. I did this to myself.

She grabbed my wrist and turned it over to reveal the bloodied handkerchief still clutched in my hand.

"Then explain this." She raised the scrap of fabric between us.

"It's nothi—"

"I'm not a fool, Lucien. People who are healthy don't cough up blood." Her fingers trembled as they latched onto me.

I opened my mouth and closed it again, guilt twisting my insides into knots as I met her watery eyes, willing my own to plead with her to let it go.

"How do I break it? I'm the only one who can, so how do I do it?" Her voice broke on the words, and pain lanced through the core of my being.

My throat constricted around the words I needed to say. It was as if my entire body rejected me voicing them to her, but I forced them out anyway.

"I can't ask that of you."

She gripped my hand tighter, pulling it toward her.

"Just tell me how." Her eyes burned through me.

I couldn't take it anymore. Anger clawed its way up from the deep pit in which I buried it over these past months.

"Tell me how you found out about the curse. Who told you all this?" I would rip him apart for putting me in this situation.

"Your well-being is more important than who told me, so it doesn't matt—"

"It *does* matter." My voice trembled with the barely contained rage wanting to burst from my veins and devour everything in its path. I fought to shove it back down before it destroyed everything I'd been working toward with her. I didn't want to let her be a casualty of my temper any longer.

"It doesn't."

She didn't back down, standing firm against me with her shoulders back and chin held high, and damn if I wasn't already lost in her, this moment would steal my heart from my chest.

"Who told you, Arabelle?" The fire rose in my blood to meet her defiance as my words echoed down the hallway.

"How do I break it?" She raised her volume to match mine.

"Answer my question."

"Tell me how to break it—"

"No!" I roared at her, fangs bared and mere inches away from her face. Instant regret coiled around my insides the moment the word left my lips, and I watched her recoil, dropping my hand and cowering from me.

"Belle, I..." I reached for her, but she turned her back to me and sprinted down the hallway.

Arabelle's swift steps still sounded in the hall when I clutched my chest and doubled over, my insides shredding apart from the center. Blood spilled over my lips and splattered onto the floor before I collapsed.

CHAPTER

FORTY-THREE

Arabelle

I didn't pay attention to where my feet carried me as I raced down the corridors. The thud of my boots rang loud in my ears. Realization hit me when leaves crunched underfoot. I left the castle. And trees surrounded me on all sides.

I bit into my lip, using the pain to ground myself. Lucien hadn't let his temper off the leash like that since I first came here. I knew my questions were broaching on a sensitive topic; the fear and panic in his eyes grew with each exchange.

Less and less light filtered through the trees as I followed the barely-there path. Twisted limbs and gnarled roots turned my world upside down. Or maybe it was the rock that took my feet out from under me.

Pale blue flashed in front of my eyes on the forest floor. Was it a firefly? I sat up to get a better look when more blinked into existence and glowed along the trail. A breeze carried a whisper through the damp air—a command. One I couldn't refuse as I stared, transfixed by the gentle glow.

"Follow," it said. And I did, heading deeper into the misty woods.

The lights led me to a half-collapsed archway, stones over-turned on the ground and eaten away by moss and vines. They clung to all the plant life here. The blue lights stretched beyond the arch, and I stepped through.

As I passed through the stones, the air shifted, becoming thicker, buzzing with energy, like static clinging to my skin. The entirety of the trail lit up in the same pale blue that led me here, but not just that. Incandescent pink roses grew out of dead plants as if the life force was sucked out to give them the magnificent glow they radiated.

The tree canopy choked off the sunlight from high above, leaving the forest in a haze of darkness aside from the pink flowers and blue path that I noticed was no longer a dirt trail but made of stone. Even the pollen at the base of the roses glowed, mixing the pale blue and pink together in swirls of purple.

I ducked under low-hanging branches and pushed dead vines aside. The trees fell away, and an old iron fence greeted me through the ever-thickening fog. The gate squawked an awful sound when I pushed it open, the entire length of the fence shuddering when it slammed shut.

I counted twenty-three headstones on the other side. I tried to read the names on them as I passed, but they were so old and weathered that I couldn't make out a single letter or number. Unease prickled my scalp if I stood still too long.

An old, rickety shrine waited just beyond the cemetery. The stairs groaned and bowed under my weight as I climbed them, hoping they didn't buckle and send me sprawling. I circled the outer edge of the shrine, because in the middle of it was a black pedestal carved in the form of a fanged, scaly beast, and on top of it sat a ruby twice as big as my fist.

The draw to it was a living thing, tugging at my center until I reached my hand down to touch it. Dullness vanished from the gemstone as a speck of light flickered inside, growing from its core until the entire thing shone as bright as a crimson star, and yet I still couldn't take my eyes off it.

My body moved on its own as I watched from a cage deep within. At the graze of my fingertips, the light of the gem speared for my chest.

I recoiled, but there was no pain. I pressed a hand to my chest, but there was no wound, and when I looked back, there was no ruby. Where did it go? That light went inside me. The buzz of its energy pulsed through my veins like lightning.

Twigs snapped under heavy feet and when I spun around. There were several men with coiled horns stepping through the dense veil of fog. My heart lurched into a frantic beat as I watched their eyes settle on me and grins crack on each of their faces.

They were the same as the ones before, the ones Elie saved me from. Fear locked my joints and my muscles, and all I wanted to do was fall to my knees and plead for my life.

"Lookie what we have here, boys," one of the middle ones sneered at me, jabbing an elbow into the one to his right.

"It's not very often we come across such a beauty." The one on the far left practically drooled, licking his lips as his eyes swept over my body.

"Too bad we're under orders. We could have some fun," the one to his right said in a voice that grated against my nerve endings.

The one on the far right let loose a snarl that raked iced claws down my locked spinal column.

I swallowed around the mass of iron lodged in my throat as I cursed myself for wandering so far from the castle. But this was the first time I'd seen anyone else besides Lucien and Elie since the Marid. Neither of them mentioned that it might be dangerous if I ventured out. I should be safe. My mind flashed back to a tall, raven-haired somebody who started all this.

"Who are you?"

"She doesn't know who we are," one cackled in a sound that set my hair on end.

"Where is it, girl?"

"Where's what?" I tried and failed to steady my thunderous heart as they came closer and closer. I tracked each of their movements. If even one got out of my sight, I was dead; that's what my gut told me.

"Don't play dumb—the Ruby. Our Master said it's been found. Sent us here to retrieve it and kill whoever found it," the middle one spoke again, his black armor swallowing all but a few dulled glints of light.

I stepped back, bumping into the serpentine pedestal, trying to put as much space between me and these men.

"I didn't find any ruby."

"We know you have it. But please, do continue to deny it. Makes our job that much more fun."

The vulpine look he gave me sent a chill racing up my spine and gripped my muscles in an ancient fear.

"Let's carve her up," the one to the far right all but squealed, his eyes sparkling in delight, saliva glistening on his lips.

I steeled myself. I'd be damned if I let my fear get me killed.

"You're trespassing on this land." I just needed to get back to Lucien or Elie. "If you know what's good for you, you'll leave."

Deep down, I knew they wouldn't buy the bluff, but I had to try.

All four men let out bellowing laughter that had me trembling down to my bones. They weren't going to leave. I had to run before it was too late. They continued their advance on me, spreading out when they were only feet away from the bottom step. I backed into the far railing of the shrine.

"Oh, the Ruby Prince won't be saving you, girl. He's far too weak in his current state," the first one snickered.

They reached the platform edge, moving to circle around me. I lunged and shoved the pedestal forward, and they hissed, but I bolted.

I spun and leapt over the back railing, my arms flailing out to the side for the few feet I dropped. I didn't wait for my balance to right itself before sprinting into the forest again, thorns and branches tearing at my skin and clothes as I dashed through them.

Their steps were a stampede behind me as they barreled through trees and brush, screeching curses at me. Another glittering path took me to an archway—a different one—a shimmering distortion in the space inside.

I ran as fast as my legs would carry me. I prayed to whatever god would heed me. I didn't care at this point.

Please let me make it back to the castle, back to Lucien.

Sweat beaded on my forehead and dripped down my neck. A thistle jutted out and snagged my dress, shredding it down one side, but I didn't dare slow.

Thick arms wrapped around my middle, yanking me off my feet and slamming me into the ground. The wind rushed from my lungs at the impact as one pinned my wrists above my head. Another of the horned men straddled my waist, trailing a clawed fingertip along the curve of my jaw. A whimper slithered up my throat. His black eyes held a cruel grace when they met mine.

"What a wasted effort. A little, weak thing like you can't possibly get away from us."

He gripped my jaw and leaned in close, the smell of rot on his breath. I twisted and kicked, trying to pull free from him.

"Give us the Ruby, and we'll make your death far less painful."

The tips of his claws dug into my flesh, warm blood bubbling out and trickling to the back of my hair.

"I don't have any ruby." I yanked and yanked at my hands, but the one who had ahold of me held firm.

"I know you have it." Heat seared my skin from his touch, and a scream ripped from my throat, leaving it raw.

"I don't," I whimpered, willing the sobs back down. "But I'll tell you where I hid it," I added in a desperate attempt to get them away from me.

He leaned even closer. "Tell me, girl." I tried not to gag on the scent of death wafting from his revolting mouth.

I dragged a deep breath in and held it, slamming my forehead into his nose as hard as I could. He jerked back with a curse, clapping both hands over his face as blood poured between his fingers. I twisted my hands, grabbed the one holding my wrists, and wrenched my body under his. I smashed my foot into his gut. His grip loosened, and I was up and moving again.

Breath burned in my lungs as I sprinted through the fields. They cut off my route to the castle; I had no idea where to go. Where was safe? I couldn't make it to Lucien. I was going to die at the hands of these monsters. Tears burned my eyes, blurring my vision as I swept them over the area.

My knees almost buckled in relief when I spotted a shack just over a hill. I ran for it, letting the momentum carry me, air a precious, fleeting commodity. I slammed my body into the heavy door and shut it behind me, yanking down barrels full of seed in front of it, barricading myself inside.

"You're not any safer in there, girlie!" the man whose nose I broke bellowed from outside the door.

I flattened my hand on my chest. I needed to calm down. But panic continued to ratchet up my heart rate as the walls closed in on me. I was trapped.

My breath came in heavy pants. No one knew I was out here except the men trying to kill me. There was no way out. I shoved the thoughts away, breathing in through my nose and out my mouth in an attempt to quell the anxiety.

I just had to wait them out. Elie or Lucien would notice I was missing before too long. This shack was within sight of the castle and once they saw these bastards, they'd come running.

Every thought, every hope I clung to eddied out of my head, and a cold sweat broke out all over. I sniffed the air, my mouth going dry.

"No..." My stomach vaulted into my throat because of that smell, that acrid scent billowing up from the crack at the bottom of the door—that was smoke.

"Looks like we're having barbeque tonight, boys," one of the damned bastards laughed just outside the door as tendrils of black smoke snaked up the door.

Even if I cried out, there was no way he could hear me. I didn't even have the confidence he would come. But what if he did? I cut off my hyperventilating with a deep breath.

"Lucien!"

FORTY-FOUR

Lucien

My heavy footfalls cracked the remnants of marble flooring as I paced back and forth, ripping my hands through the fur on my head. Chunks of stone littered the ground where I tore them from the walls. My gaze snapped up when the door creaked, and Elie entered my room.

"What's wrong?" he asked, eyeing the new bits of destruction as if he had no idea why the rage burned through my veins.

"You damn well know!" I stormed towards him and snatched him by the collar, lifting him from the floor. I slammed his back into the wall with such force that a sconce fell and shattered on the ground.

"Lucien, get ahold of yourself." He gripped my wrists, fingers digging in and meeting my fury-fueled glare with confusion.

"How could you tell her?" My voice quietened to a low growl rumbling through my body as I held him there.

Pain thrummed in every cell, but I ignored it. I needed to know why Elie would betray my trust like this. Arabelle no longer looked at me like the monster I was. At least, she hadn't until today.

"Tell her about what?" Elie's red brows bunched together, creasing his forehead.

He made no move to fight back, even though I knew he could get out of my grip in seconds if he wanted.

"About the curse." My claws dug into the soft leather of his tunic, tearing through the cured hide. "I told you not to tell her."

She knew. She knew about this wretched curse of mine, knew that I was a beast of a man who deserved this. Elie must have told her everything.

"I didn't say a word about it. I swear to the Embers, Luce, I didn't tell Belle about the curse." His golden eyes bore into mine.

I clenched my jaw, searching for the lie, but I couldn't find it. My grip loosened.

"If you didn't say anything to her…" Elie's toes touched the ground, and I released him fully, stepping back and dragging my fingers over my furred scalp. "Who told her?"

Who knew about my predicament? Who could have said something? There were only two people who knew of the curse outside of me and Elie, and I hadn't seen them since it was enacted.

"Who else even knows about it?" He asked the question burning through my mind, and I had no answer for it.

"As much as I enjoy watching you scramble like newborn babes, I was the one to tell your little pet about the curse."

Both Elie and I whipped our heads to the darkest corner of the room, a familiar dark-haired nuisance stepping out of the shadows. I loosed a growl that shook the dust from the wall crevices.

"Aamon, what are you doing here?" Elie stepped to my side and spat on the ground at the bastard's feet. I seconded the sentiment.

He lifted a brow at the disrespect. "Still as pleasant as ever, E."

Aamon raked his hand through his hair, gold glinting in the

light from five hoops pierced between the lobes of his ear and the point.

"You don't get to call me by that after you lot decided to curse us," Elie growled his displeasure at Aamon.

A sly smirk played at the edges of his lips, and he tilted his head in a serpentine way.

"Is that what you think?"

"Who else would do it?"

They were the ones with the grudge and access to old magic. I stalked toward him. Once we were the same height, but now I towered over him in this beast form they cursed me in.

"What do you want? Answer before I tear out your throat."

"In your cursed state? Not likely."

In an instant, Aamon was behind me, hand on my shoulder, just to prove he could.

"I've told the girl what *I* want." His fingers clamped down on me, and I ground my teeth to chase away the pain. "That is inconsequential right now. You *should* be asking what it is my travel companions are after."

"Travel companions?"

"Oh, yes. They were given orders to retrieve something."

I caught Elie's eyes as they widened to show the whole of his pupils.

"There have been Daeva on the grounds lately. No matter how fast I put them down, there's always more." His throat bobbed. "They answer to you, Aamon. What did you tell them to find?"

Aamon stepped around me and faced Elie, the usual cunning smirk nowhere to be found, and that alone set every hair on my body on edge. In all the years I'd known him, he never took anything seriously. For him to now, what the hells was going on? I opened my mouth just as he started to speak.

"There are things in motion you have no idea about. Just know that the Daeva are no longer under my control." He slid his hands in his pockets, slinking back to the dark corner he'd emerged from.

Fear ratcheted up my throat, and I turned to Elie.

"Why didn't you tell me they were on the grounds?"

Cold fingers of panic stretched over the back of my mind. Did she go outside after our fight? If she did and the Daeva found her... I struggled to swallow.

"You know exactly what they'll do if they find her first, Lucien." A wicked smile split Aamon's face, delight sparkling in his onyx eyes.

I charged through the door, damn near taking the thing off the hinges, Elie only mere steps behind as we tore through the halls and burst through the front doors. I didn't care that I left Aamon unattended in my home. I didn't care what he was here for anymore. Only one thing mattered – I had to find Arabelle.

I sniffed at the air and winced at the burn of ash in my nostrils. Gravel tore at my feet as I spun and barreled toward the back of the castle on all fours. Smoke billowed up in a column of grey that darkened the sky over an old farming storehouse. Something like a thread tugged at my chest in that direction, and I took off toward it. That's where she was.

Flames engulfed the storehouse as I skidded to a stop, the roar of the fire filling my ears. I searched, but I didn't see her.

Was she inside?

Elie ran around to the front and shouted, but I couldn't hear him over the screaming of my own mind.

"Lucien!" he bellowed, and I snapped my attention to him, the silver gleam of metal in his hand from the small sword he had drawn.

Four Daeva were on the other side of the shack. My roar shuddered the ground below our feet, and I launched myself at the closest one, clamping my jaw down on the man's throat. The tang of blood coated my tongue as flesh gave way and ripped free from the body. The only sounds that came from him were strangled gurgles as blood poured from his wound and pooled under him.

The others moved to grab their weapons, one wielding a long sword, the other two holding battle axes in each hand. I lunged for the latter, and the dark metal breastplate he wore screeched with the sound of my claws raking down his front.

In a few carefully placed movements, Elie had one of the remaining Daeva disarmed, and the other ran through with his sword.

"Where is she?" he shouted at the remaining one.

Rage addled my vision as I moved no different than the animal I was on the outside.

"Tell me where the woman is," I snarled, my bloodied muzzle only inches away from his face, all of my teeth bared.

The Daeva's eyes darted to the shack, then back to mine, and that was all I needed. I grabbed the bastard by the front of his armor, lifted him above my head, and slammed him back down into the ground with so much force that cracks spider-webbed out. Blood sprayed in an arc as I slashed my claws across the man's jugular.

"Lucien, the fire—"

I rammed my shoulder into the door, but it didn't budge. I cursed and backed up, taking a running start before slamming into it again. The door splintered apart, and I climbed over the barrels barricading it shut. *Smart.* I shielded my face as I searched through the smoke.

My knees wanted to buckle at the sight of her crumpled on the far side of the shack. I moved to her side. She was covered in soot and dirt. I picked her up and held her to my chest, shielding her face as I carried her out of the fire.

Elie sheathed his sword, having killed the last of them, and was at my side.

"Is she alright?" He was as frantic as I was.

I fell to my knees and placed her on the ground, keeping my hand under her head while holding the other over her mouth. My heart stopped.

"She's not breathing."

"You have to save her." His words didn't help.

I *knew* that. This was my fault. I shouldn't have dragged her into my problems, shouldn't have tried one last time to break this gods forsaken curse of mine. My eyes burned from smoke or the tears threatening to spill.

I held my hands over her chest. This was the last of it, the last dregs of magic remaining in my veins. I closed my eyes, reaching deep for those scraps left behind. For her, I'd give it all up. I tugged at it, ripping it from the seams of my being and forcing it to the surface.

Red light glowed around my palm as I placed it on her chest, willing that magic to weave into her being and heal what the smoke had taken from me—from her. Pain sluiced through my skull, and I swore, but I didn't stop. I couldn't stop.

The red glow guttered, and I sent up a prayer to the gods that my magic held. Just long enough to save her. That's all I needed. "Please..." Please let me save her. My body was tearing asunder. Sharp pain tore through every cell as the last of my magic drained.

Arabelle gasped in a deep breath, and I felt the rise and fall of her chest under my hand. My own chest caved. Thank the gods. Her hand clasped mine, and I fought to keep my sobs down, fought the tears, fought against the sheer terror of losing her.

Her eyes cracked open for only a second, and she squeezed my hand with her small fingers.

"You found me," her voice croaked. "You saved me."

"Of course, I did." I pressed my brow to hers. "I always will."

She was unconscious again. Unconscious, but breathing

I took Arabelle back to the castle and tucked her into my bed.

Aamon was nowhere to be found, and Elie stayed behind to deal with the bodies of the Daeva.

I sat beside her, counting every breath she took, watching the flutter of her eyelids and sending prayer after prayer of thanks to the Architect that she wasn't taken from me right when I'd finally opened my heart again.

"Please wake up, Belle. Wake up so I can apologize." I held her hand in both of mine.

Exhaustion overtook me, and I laid my head down on the feathered mattress. I just needed a few moments of rest. Then I could continue my vigil until she woke.

FORTY-FIVE

Arabelle

The last thing I remembered was the heat of fire and smoke filling my lungs. Those horned men who chased me set the shack on fire. Lucien was also there. He found me and pulled me out. I tried to raise my hand to rub at the throbbing ache in my head, but something heavy weighed it down.

I blinked my eyes open to an unfamiliar room, the tattered fabric of a canopy hanging overhead. I glanced down to see why I couldn't lift my hand, and my heart stuttered.

Lucien's head leaned against my side, trapping my arm underneath him. His breath was soft and steady, nothing like it had been when I came to find him about the curse. I ran the fingers of my free hand through the silky fur along the top of his head.

"You're awake." His voice rumbled through my body when he spoke, pulling me from my thoughts. He lifted his head to look me in the eye.

The differing shades of blue pulled me into the depths of him. Each of the varying darks and lights reminded me of the ripples on a crystal-clear lake. The shades of blue tugged at a thread of memory, and another set of blues came to mind. If only Lucien's had the golden rim around them, I swallowed against the thought.

"Did you stay here all night?"

He cupped my cheek in his hand, caressing the pad of his thumb over it.

"I couldn't leave you." He stared at me as if I might vanish before his eyes. The anger from before was no longer there.

I swallowed, throat so raw I thought I might've eaten glass and shredded it. "Those men..."

He stiffened.

"They've been taken care of; you don't have to worry about them."

There was a flash of something feral in him, and it wasn't until then I noticed the dark stains in the fur surrounding his mouth, down his neck, and his hands.

"You killed them." It wasn't a question. They were on his land. They attacked me. I would have been more surprised if he hadn't.

"Yes."

"What *were* they?"

They looked like something let loose from the deepest bowels of hell with their sharp teeth and black eyes. And then there were those horns. They were the same as the men who attacked me and Isa before I came here. Just remembering how they looked at me, the feel of their hands on me twisted my stomach in a way that had me grateful I hadn't eaten anything.

Lucien pressed his lips in a thin line, and the relief broke apart for the stormy rage in the blues of his eyes. "They're called Daeva. Horrible creatures that have a taste for flesh."

"Are they devils? From Hell?"

"They might as well be." His voice was just this side of audible.

"What were they doing here?"

I already knew the answer to that question and pressed my

palm to my chest. They wanted the ruby I found. But why? Would he know about the ruby or their goals once they had it? I clutched the blanket hard enough that my knuckles turned white.

"They've been showing up for the past month," Elie said, leaning against the doorframe, arms folded over his broad chest. "It wasn't until today that I learned they were looking for something specific."

Lucien stared down at the bed, opening and closing his mouth. He was struggling to say whatever was on his mind. I squeezed his fingers in mine. It was all I could do to ease the trepidation he must be feeling after everything.

His body heaved and shuddered as he looked up again. "Why didn't you tell me about Aamon when you came to me earlier?"

I bit my lip as I thought back to that fight.

"You were so angry and kept refusing to answer my questions. At first, I didn't think it mattered who told me about it." His hand tightened on mine. "But when you snapped, I just wanted to be anywhere but here."

"You have to tell me about these things. He could have killed you or taken you and done far worse things." There wasn't a hint of temperament in his eyes, just fear—fear for my sake. I sank deeper into the bed.

"What did he tell you, exactly?"

I dropped my eyes from him, unable to look at him as I recalled the handsome raven-haired stranger who told me the devastating secret.

"He said you were cursed. And that you'll die soon unless it's broken."

"What else?" he urged without the ferocity that was in his voice when we talked of it last. His thumb rubbed circles over my palm.

"He said I was the only one who could break it." I released the blanket and pressed the heel of my hand to my brow. "He told me that 'the breeze from the East shifted' and that 'we need all the players on the board.'"

"The East?" Elie asked from behind, pushing away from the door and dropping his arms to his sides as he strode to the bed. "You're sure that's what he said?"

I looked from Lucien to Elie and back again.

"Yes. What does that mean?"

Their faces told me it was far more serious than I thought when he first said it. It reminded me of something. Something I'd been told by that blonde haired woman—the Architect—in a dream. A warning of something dark that wanted to consume me.

Elie dragged both hands through his hair, pacing in a wide circle and mumbling something I couldn't hear. I almost asked again when Lucien spoke.

"Nothing good."

He shifted his weight and made to stand, but I grabbed his hand. I didn't want to be left alone, not after that attack. These two wouldn't let anyone in the castle, I knew that, but I wanted him to stay by my side, just a little while longer.

"You should get some more rest." He placed his other hand over mine and gave me a look of understanding.

"Stay, please."

I didn't want his understanding; I just wanted him to stay. I hated how it made me feel, how weak I was, that I couldn't do anything to save myself back there. It was all I could do to just barely escape, and I still got myself trapped. So much for all that training.

"Lucien, if there's movement in the East, things are about to get really bad," Elie said, dropping his hands again. "If they attack, we're fucked. It's almost time. If you don't—"

"I know," he said over his shoulder, his whole body slumping in an all too familiar move I'd not only seen but done myself, one I used when my mind slid into hopeless despair.

"It's almost time for what?" My eyes moved back to Elie. "What's going on? Who is this...Aamon...that told me about the curse? What's this breeze in the East?" The questions poured out of me.

They looked at each other and then Lucien moved to sit on the bed, careful of where my legs were so he didn't crush them.

"It's..." he started but shook his head. "You'll know soon."

"I want to know *now*."

"We can't tell you *now*," Elie spoke when Lucien remained silent for too long.

"Why not? If the castle isn't safe anymore—"

"This castle will always be safe for you," Lucien said, squeezing my hand. "I won't let anything happen to you. Never again."

But it wasn't.

"It wasn't safe yesterday." They nearly killed me. If Lucien and Elie hadn't shown up, they would have. "Those...Daeva were on the grounds. Elie says they've been here for a while now. And this time they attacked me. You weren't there."

His lips curled back in a snarl.

"Do you think I don't know that?" There was the temper I'd grown accustomed to. "Do you think I haven't been sitting here, damning myself because I wasn't there?"

I pressed my lips in a line. That anger wasn't directed at me but at himself. Was all his anger the same? Was he so full of rage at himself that it leaked out onto everyone else around him? Had he let it consume him this whole time?

"It wasn't your fault, Lucien."

"How was it not?" His voice cracked. "I snapped at you, and you ran away."

"I made my own choice. I was being just as stubborn as you." I gave his hand a squeeze back. "But you came for me. Even though you lost your temper with me, even though you were sick, you still came to find me."

"I always will." He brushed a knuckle over my cheek. I had to resist the urge to nuzzle into that soft fur.

If the Daeva and Marid were a problem for us, they might be attacking people outside the castle as well. Isa and my father were unprotected, and even if they used the gold to move back into Starside, there were no warriors to protect them.

"Lucien, I want to see Isa. I need to know she's okay and to explain everything to her." I held his gaze, hoping that he understood my intention: my worry over a sister I had left behind.

"I told you, it's too dangerous." His voice strained around the words, unlike the last time I asked.

"That's exactly why I need to see her. Please, Lucien." I hated to beg, but for her, I would.

"I'll think about it."

It wasn't a no.

"Let's get you some breakfast."

I couldn't help the huff that escaped me. "You don't have to coddle me."

My bottom lip trembled with the effort of holding in my laugh when he frowned at me.

"You've been hovering over me since yesterday, by your own admission. I'm fine. I can go back to training and convincing you to let me see my sister."

"We'll see how you are after you eat first."

"But—"

It was Elie who spoke up this time. "No buts. We need to make sure you're okay after yesterday, physically. You'll be out there kicking his ass in no time."

He bared all his too-white teeth in a smile and clapped a hand on Lucien's shoulder.

"Don't promise her that. I'm at least as good as you," Lucien shot back with a glare that held no animosity in it.

"In your dreams, Luce. Even before you let yourself go."

"Luce?" I cocked an eyebrow at the two.

He rolled his eyes and shoved Elie back, who just laughed, never being forced off balance.

"It's his nickname for me."

"It's cute that he has a nickname for you." If I could see his face, I was sure I would see him blushing a delicious shade of red.

I paused and stared at him, at the animal features; I wondered what he looked like as a man. I reached a hand up, running my fingers over the curve of his cheek. Did his fur match the color of his hair? Was he tall? Elie had said he'd been training to fight since childhood.

An image wrapped in gold pushed its way to the forefront of my mind, one of a beautiful blond who also had blue eyes. Eyes that I couldn't help but notice the similarities in when I looked into Lucien's. I wanted it to be true; I wanted it to be him.

I blinked and jerked my hand back at the realization of what I was doing, heat blazing in my own face.

He puffed a hot breath of air out as he stared at the hand I withdrew. "He likes using nicknames for everyone."

"Using nicknames just means you're close with someone. You can call me Belle if you want. That's what my sister and father call me."

I twined my fingers together as the blush spread across the bridge of my nose. I couldn't believe I had just touched him like that without a thought of how he might feel about it.

"Alright, Belle." An explosion of butterflies flitted in my stomach at his use of that name. "Let's go downstairs and get some food in you."

CHAPTER

FORTY-SIX

Lucien

Elie forced Belle and myself to go through a grueling regime of abdominal exercises every day, which left me so sore I could barely stand. It was all I could do to make it to the hot springs for a good, long soak after he was through with us.

He wasn't a High General's son for nothing, the bastard. I had half a mind to hang him by the ankles from one of the tallest towers.

Days like this, with his intensive training, made me glad for the relief of the coughing that began to plague me on the night of Nocturnum Lucir. There was a shift after the Daeva attack, and I didn't particularly care if it was due to my near-empty reservoir of magic or because the curse was weakening.

He watched Belle and I with the smuggest gods damn smile on his face. We were both on our knees, panting, covered in sweat, and he just grinned. I wanted so badly to wipe the look off his face, but I couldn't even keep up with his moves.

I hated admitting he was right. I was out of shape because of the years I spent neglecting my training. Elie constantly nagged at me about it, and I ignored him because I was ashamed of this body of mine. I just relied on my natural animal instincts and claws.

Belle leaned on the heels of her hands and tilted her head back, exposing the long column of her neck. My eyes tracked the beads of sweat as they dripped underneath the tight training clothes she wore that hugged every curve. I fought, and failed, the urge to stare, imagining myself peeling her out of those clothes and licking every part of her. I shook my head.

"You were right, Elie," Belle started, "I think I might hate you."

She managed to steady her breathing again and wiped the back of her hand across her brow, leaving a track of dirt from the training pit on her face.

Elie grabbed a canteen and shook it, the water inside sloshing against the sides.

"Don't forget to stay hydrated, otherwise you'll start getting cramps." He tossed it to her.

I waited for him to hand me one, but the bastard just gave me a shit-eating grin and tossed a nod over his shoulder to the table behind him.

"You can get your own. You know where it is."

"You run me ragged and then make me get my own water. I thought we were friends."

My body roared in protest when I stood and stalked past Elie, ramming my shoulder into his. Despite my much larger frame, he remained planted where he stood and simply laughed.

"You're a grown-ass man capable of fetching your own water," Elie said, taking a swig of his own canteen. He hadn't even broken a sweat yet.

I pointed to Belle, still squatting on the ground and gulping down water. "She's as grown as I am, and you gave her some."

I turned the last canteen of water up over my mouth and

guzzled it down, some spilling down the sides of my face and neck.

"*She* hasn't been dragging her feet and complaining all morning." He mimicked my pointing. "Plus, you know I've always had a weakness for beautiful people."

With a wink and a grin, he took another drink before replacing the lid and setting it back on the table.

"Are you saying I'm not beautiful?" I couldn't help myself as I arched a brow at him and pressed my lips together to keep from smiling when Belle choked on her water.

Elie gave me a devious smirk that I knew meant trouble.

"Why, my dear Lucien, are you jealous of sweet Arabelle?" He placed a hand over his heart. "You know you'll always have a special place in here."

I rolled my eyes at him and shoved by again. He stumbled a few steps back and laughed before taking the canister from Belle and putting it with the others. I didn't realize how much I missed this – the laughing, joking, and ease of what once was. When we were cursed, I gave into the despair of it all and shut everyone out, including the man who was more of a brother to me than anything.

"Alright, we've still got half an hour left. Belle, you continue to work on your core exercises." The gleam in his golden eyes when he found mine was predatory, and a shiver of excitement ran through my bones. "Lucien, I think you and I are overdue for some hand-to-hand combat training."

Belle grumbled something under her breath and started the routine Elie laid out for her at the beginning of their session this morning. Even I cringed a bit at the rigid training schedule he kept her on, but I wasn't the one in charge here; Elie was. Her balance wasn't bad, but her core muscles needed work before she could start any kind of combat training.

"She's doing great." I wrapped linen around my knuckles, watching as she counted her exercises out loud.

"She is." Elie was much more proficient in wrapping than I was and had already finished one hand and started the other. "Her self-defense lessons paid off with the Daeva."

"But her hand-to-hand needs work." He flexed his fingers, testing the integrity of his quick work. "I'll make sure no one can ever take her from us again."

"No. *She* will make sure of that; you'll just give her the tools to do it," I said as I secured the linen on my other hand. "And since when is it *us* and not me?" I added.

I flexed my fingers in a move to match his. I didn't begrudge them their budding friendship, in fact, I was glad they both had someone else to talk to and confide in.

"She'll be mine the way you are," Elie said.

We circled each other, raising our hands, ready to defend or punch. I watched his micro-movements, the twitch of a muscle, the slight angle of a step, and the way his eyes tracked mine.

"You're sure confident in that," I said. The toes of his left foot angled toward me, and I lifted my arm to block his attack.

"I'm confident in *you*, Luce." He struck again with a methodical combo of punches until he broke past my guard and cracked me in the jaw. "I've seen the way you look at her."

My head whipped to the side, and I let a curse slip past my lips. I slid my foot between his and knocked him off balance, twisting and ramming my elbow into his gut, but he shoved my arm off course and sidestepped me.

He shook his hand out with a small wince, a smear of blood darkening the linen wrap. "And the way she looks at you," he said with a grin.

I wiped at my mouth. He didn't hold back.

"You're seeing what you want to," I said.

"Am I?" We locked together in a grapple, our fingers digging into the other's skin. "Did I not watch you damn near kill yourself to save her life?" Elie asked.

He broke free and followed it up with quick and precise one-two punches, giving me no quarter to strike back.

"You tore those Daeva apart, or do I have it wrong?" He wouldn't let up with his questions.

I blocked him as best I could, but he was quick and accustomed to using his slenderer form to knock bulky opponents off kilter; a technique I missed myself.

"You think I'll marry her? Just because I saved her and killed some Daeva?" I asked.

Truth be told, it wasn't something that had crossed my mind. All I wanted was to spend my last days with her.

Elie knocked my own punches aside like they were nothing, and honestly, they were compared to what they used to be. He kicked my foot out from under me and rammed his shoulder into my middle, taking us both down.

"I think you'll marry her because she's managed to melt that icy heart of yours and steal it right out of your chest," he said, twisting around until he managed a headlock.

I grabbed at his arms, but his hold was like an iron vice. I didn't need Elie to tell me how I felt about Belle. I already knew that. From the first night I saw her, the ice I'd packed around my heart began to crack. She was brave, and her damn stubbornness drove me to furious heights. She drew me to her in a way that no other woman ever had, and she wasn't even trying.

"I yield."

Elie and I untangled ourselves from each other and got to our feet. The dirt from the ring clung to our bodies and clothes in a coating of mud when it mixed with our sweat. My eyes tracked to the last place I saw Belle, and she was sprawled out on the ground.

"Is now when you'd go to the hot springs?" she asked, tilting her head to look at the two of us, moving as little as possible.

"Yes. It relaxes the overworked muscles and helps speed along recovery, rebuilding those same muscles to make them stronger," Elie answered, brushing his hair out of his face.

I walked over to where she lay on the ground and bent over her.

"Would you like me to take you there since you seem unable to even stand?" I couldn't help the grin.

She glared up at me. "I can *so* stand."

"Then prove it."

She groaned and rolled over, getting her hands up underneath herself. Her arms trembled under her weight, and I chuckled; at least she made an effort. I grabbed her under the arms and lifted her.

"Sure you don't want me to carry you? It's no trouble for me," I offered again, holding out my hand.

She stared at it for a long minute, then took it. "God, yes. I'll take any bit of relief I can get."

She couldn't even take a step toward me.

I bent and scooped her up, placing an arm under her knees and behind the middle of her back. I'd do it again just for the little noise she made when I swept her up.

"It never hurts to ask for help when you need it."

"And when do you ever ask for help?" She jabbed a finger into my chest bone, and I laughed, even if she had a point.

"Shall we all go, then?" Elie grinned at the death glare I shot him and raised his hands in defeat, backing up toward the table with the water on it. "Fine, fine."

He picked up the canteens.

"Don't forget to do your stretches before bed. It'll prevent you from getting too sore." He waved a hand over his shoulder as he left the training grounds.

Steamy air stuck to my fur as I carried Belle into the hot springs and sat her down. She turned toward me; her chin pulled up. I braced myself for her to kick me out.

"Here's how this is going to work: you stay on your side, and I stay on mine." She pointed across the area to the opposite side of the springs.

I arched a brow. "How are we supposed to talk if we're that far apart?" I pressed my lips in a line to hide the amusement trying to peek out.

"We are here to *bathe* and nothing more." She retreated a step. "I can't just let you see me like that."

I couldn't stop the eye roll and scoffed. "*You* can cover yourself with a towel." My lips curled. "I'm the one on full display here."

"*You're* covered in fur." She let out a sigh and rubbed at her temples. "You can't even see anything through it."

Heat surged in my blood, and I dared a step closer to her.

"Have you tried?" The thought rang out in my head. She might want me, as I am now.

"I—" she stammered, and her cheeks filled with color. "No, I absolutely have not tried."

I was not inclined to believe her.

I chuckled at the dismay in her voice. A loose strand of hair clung to her sweat-covered face. I brushed it away, letting the tip of my claw graze her skin.

"You're awfully adamant for someone claiming innocence, *Belle.*"

Her jaw slackened as a flash of feigned hurt crossed her face —feigned because I could see the beginnings of a smile on her lips.

"I think you just like the idea of me trying to picture you naked," she shot back at me and crossed her arms.

A dangerous game, this was. But it sent a thrill through my blood I hadn't felt in years.

"Oh, I do." I tilted my head. "You're rather adorable when you're flustered like this."

"*I am so glad* you find amusement in tormenting me." She huffed another breath out through her nose.

I just laughed. "Forgive me; it's been quite a while since I last had such a delightful conversation with a beautiful woman." I dipped my head in a small bow.

Since she found out about the curse, a weight had been lifted off my shoulders. She knew and didn't turn away, didn't ask questions. She treated me the same as she always had.

I watched as the pink in her face spread over her cheeks, down her neck. She looked anywhere but at me.

"Just—just go get out of those clothes and get into the water already."

"I'm usually the one making that demand, but I'll make an exception this time."

If we were anywhere else, I would smell arousal on her. I didn't need to smell it to know; her skin was flushed, her hands fidgeted, and she couldn't look me in the eye. I knew just what to follow that up with.

I leaned closer, taking up much of her personal space, and whispered, "I'll make sure I remember this for later."

She spun and all but ran for the alcove sectioned off for undressing. Her face had turned the color of Elie's hair, and I delighted in the fact that I caused it.

There were no other changing areas, but I found a spot on the opposite side to strip the sweaty clothes off and stepped into the steaming waters. Their heat sank into my muscles, easing the aches and pains of the day's training.

A small splash of water drew my attention as Belle sank into the spring with a groan I could barely hear from this far away. I should move closer; it wouldn't hurt so long as I kept enough distance between us. But I stayed. She asked me to give her space. I couldn't just go to her because I wanted to.

She spoke, but over the lapping of the water, I only caught a word or two.

"What?" I shouted over the sounds drowning everything out.

"I said... Does the... go away?"

I still couldn't make it out.

"I can barely hear you. You'll have to speak louder." I sank deeper into the water, closing my eyes and letting that glorious heat work itself deep into my body.

"You weren't lying when you said we wouldn't be able to talk." My eyes snapped open to meet hers.

She waded into the deeper part of the spring, hiding her body under the water. I did my best not to let my gaze drift below her collarbone.

"I asked if the exercise ever stops causing all these muscle pains." She massaged a thumb into her bicep.

"No. You just get used to it."

It was hard to keep my eyes from dipping lower. She sighed, her breath rippling in the water.

"I don't think I can ever get used to this," she said with a bit of a whine in her voice.

"The hot springs help, but if you're okay with it..." I swallowed, my throat drying out despite the moist air. "I can help you work some of the knots out."

I gestured to where she rubbed her arm. I told myself I had no ulterior motives when I made the offer.

"If you don't mind, I'd be happy for any relief." Her shoulders slumped forward, and she moved a step closer.

I sucked in a breath and steadied the raging monster in my chest.

"I don't mind a bit. If you want me to stop at any time, just say the word." I moved behind her. My blood sang in my head.

"Just be careful of those claws." The teasing in her voice lifted my lips in a smile.

Her skin was soft and warm under my touch as I placed my hands on her shoulders, working my fingers in circles, pressing into the tight muscles. Just as she'd instructed me, I was careful to keep my claws from biting into her beautiful skin.

Belle sagged into me as I moved my hands down her back. The sounds she made had me battling my own self-control from the first utterance. I worked my way back up, savoring every inch of her that she let me touch.

"Lucien..."

The moan of my name from her lips damn near snapped my restraint. I wanted to touch every part of her, to taste her, to make her keep moaning my name like that. Instincts roared in my head to claim her and make her mine now. To hell with waiting. I shoved them down and stomped on them.

At least, I did until she leaned back into me.

Gods. The smell of her filled my nose and enveloped me. I couldn't stop it. I sank down behind her and wrapped my arms around her waist, pulling her tighter into me as I buried my face in the crook of her neck.

My hands inched up her stomach, but I stopped at the graze of her breasts; that touch required her invitation even if she arched her body into mine, even if the breathy sounds she made urged me to keep going.

Her fingers wrapped around the back of my hand and guided it up, up until her peaked nipple dragged across my palm. I had to stop this. I couldn't touch her this way, not looking the way I did.

I peeled myself away from Belle.

"I'm sorry."

I leashed all the raging desire screaming inside me to drag her out of this hot spring and take her on the floor, to make her scream my name loud enough to reach the stars.

"I can't...I need to...do..." I scrambled for something, any excuse she would buy. "Food."

I backed out of the spring, unable to look at her when she turned to ask a question I didn't want to answer.

CHAPTER
FORTY-SEVEN

Arabelle

A tangle of sheets caught my hands when I stretched them above my head. I savored the way the soft silk glided across the bare bits of skin. Crickets and tree frogs chirped their songs of longing and love outside the window in a melody that said spring was in full bloom.

I cracked my eyes open, and the beautiful blond man sat at the edge of my bed. He wore nothing but his bejeweled mask and tight black pants. His magnificent long hair cascaded down his back in waves.

His eyes drank me in and lit a fire in me that only he could quench. Longing drove me to reach out for him and drag my fingertips down his firm muscles. His gaze followed wherever my hands traveled, his skin hot under my touch. I wanted his body pressed against mine, like the last time I saw him. I wanted to taste his kiss, the fire that burned within him that I could see just beyond the borders of his eyes.

He twisted his body to face me fully and lifted his hand to cup my cheek. The light grazes of his thumb sent a flare of heat through my blood. I held his gaze for long moments. The blue in his eyes was so much like Lucien's.

"You scared me." His breath was a warm breeze against my skin as he pressed his brow to mine. "I thought I was going to lose you."

He placed his other palm flat against the small of my back, pulling me closer to him.

"You won't lose me," I said as I twisted my fingers in the ends of his hair, delighting in the feel of his skin on mine. I wanted more. "I have a promise to keep after all."

"Belle."

The way he said my name could have melted my insides. His thumb rubbed lazy circles on my back, and his eyes fluttered shut.

"I should go now."

I hooked an arm around his neck and held firm to him. If this was my mind letting me be with Lucien in a way I couldn't be in reality, then I didn't want to relinquish a moment of it.

"I don't want you to go." I craved his touch, the feel of his lips and hands on me.

"If I don't go, I'm not sure I'll be able to control myself." His hand slipped to the nape of my neck, fingertips pressing into my flesh. "I want to devour you."

He threaded his fingers through the hair at the base of my skull and clenched a fistful of it. I held in my groan at the gentle tug, wetness growing between my legs as I recalled just what his fingers could do to me. The thought of his mouth on my body was almost too much for me to bear.

"Then devour me," I dared, watching as the desire-addled expression flashed to something a bit more feral.

He jerked my head back with that handful of hair. I watched as his eyes swept down my body and then back up.

"You have no idea what you're agreeing to."

He leaned forward and trailed the tip of his nose down the center of my throat, and then replaced it with his tongue and licked back up. I gasped and gripped his hair as instinct took over my logical self.

"I don't care. I just want to feel you."

I tilted my head back more when he pressed a kiss to the top of my neck, his fingers still clutching my hair. He moved, and my back pressed into the down mattress with him straddling my hips, the look in his eye nothing short of ravenous. I dragged my lower lip between my teeth, and he let loose a growl that sounded more beast than man—that sounded like my beast. He bent down, hovering inches over me, his hair falling all around us.

"I told you before." His breath ghosted over my skin when he spoke. He bit my lip.

I let out a sound somewhere between a groan and a gasp, but he let me go. His hair tickled my skin as he moved lower. His hands slid up and down my sides, hiking my nightgown up with each circuit. I writhed underneath him, trying to position myself so his hands found their way under the slip of fabric between us.

As if reading my mind, he grabbed the hem of my gown, hoisted it up over my head and tossed it aside. My body flushed at the hunger in his eyes as they drank in my naked body.

"You are exquisite."

When he lowered his mouth to my skin, the heat of his kiss drew a new kind of burn to my veins. He trailed the tip of his tongue over my collarbone, down the center of my chest, and over to one nipple. He circled it, pressing into the soft tissue until he reached my peaked nipple. He closed his lips around the nub and sucked.

I arched into him, moving to drag my fingers through his hair, but he grabbed my wrists and pinned them above my head with one of his large hands. He squeezed my nipple between his teeth and then repeated every single thing to the other.

My arousal pulsed through me, drove me to writhe and squirm, wanting any bit of friction I could get from him.

While busy with his ministrations and not willing to move on just quite yet, he shifted and pressed his knee between my thighs. I ground against him, the fabric of his pants creating such blessed friction that I could cry. He kissed his way back up my chest and neck and finally claimed my mouth. I moaned into that kiss as my hips moved on his knee, my need lifting my body off the bed.

He groaned against my lips, pulling back enough to speak. "Such a needy little thing, aren't you?"

He pressed his lips to mine again, parting them with his tongue. I rubbed my tongue against his, the taste of him sweet and tangy like the cherry frozen cream I tried when I was young. He laced his fingers with mine, his grip firm as he held me in place.

He broke from the kiss all at once, letting go of my hands and pulling his knee away from me. I let out a startled whimper at the sudden absence of warmth and pressure. He slid down my body, pressing kisses here and there as he went until he situated himself between my legs.

He found my eyes again in a silent question, and I gave him a slow nod. The feel of his hot mouth on me was almost enough to send me over the edge on its own, but when he slid his tongue up my center, I fought to hold myself together.

He dug his fingers into my thighs and lifted them onto his shoulders before feasting on me. He swirled his tongue against the bundle of nerves at my center and sucked on it, leaving my vision fracturing with intense pleasure.

His mouth worked wonders, and when he slid his finger inside me, I could have sworn I saw starlight bursting in my eyes. He curled it into the same spot he had before. I tangled my hands in his hair, afraid that if I didn't hold onto him, my body would just float away like those spirits the other night.

"I want to hear my name on your lips at the pinnacle of your plea-sure, Arabelle."

God. His mouth, his hands, I would swear it on an altar of worship that he was some deity given human form for the sole purpose of pleasing a woman.

"Tell me your name, and I'll scream it."

But it was too late.

My world splintered in an explosion of ecstasy.

The name on my lips, when my scream split the early morning silence, was a plea for the person I *wanted*, a plea for him to be the one who gave me such heights of ecstasy—Lucien.

Heat scorched my cheeks, and I clamped a pillow over my face to hide from the embarrassment of yet another erotic dream where I woke to my beast in my mind and heart instead of the beautiful face that had been there in my dreams.

Yet, in my mind, they were becoming one and the same. Lucien was my blond stranger, and my blond stranger was Lucien. My heart beat the same for both of them; my blood burned the same for them.

Lucien. My cheeks remained flushed as I lowered the pillow from my face but hugged it to my chest instead. Much about this situation didn't make sense to me. He was cursed by a witch. My entire life, I believed there was no magic in this world, but here was proof that it existed in some form.

That pale man from the other day said only I could break the curse, but what could I do that others couldn't? Had they tried? I leaned back and shoved a hand through my hair, yelping when my fingers snagged on a tangle.

Lucien and Elie wouldn't or couldn't tell me. They had, in fact, been rather remiss about the whole ordeal. I needed to figure this out on my own. Unease crawled up my spine.

He was running out of time, but I had no idea how much he had left. My mouth soured at the thought. There was so much I didn't know that, even with an endless supply of time, I wasn't sure I could ever break the curse.

I huffed out a breath, the tassels hanging from my canopy swaying in the slight breeze. I just had to try. If I listened to my gut, the stranger in my dream was Lucien. If I freed him, I freed them both. I pressed the heels of my hands into my eyes and let out a sound of frustration. But *how?*

Weeks passed by in a flash, filled with Elie barking orders at Lucien and me during our training sessions. Elie drilled me every morning in hand-to-hand combat. After every session, my muscles ached, and I sought blessed relief in the springs — without Lucien. I didn't need more chances to make a fool of myself.

Nights were almost as draining, my dreams haunted by a man making me come over and over with his hands and his mouth.

I held my ankle to the back of my thigh to stretch out the muscle before Elie finally deigned to grace us with his presence. Lucien, it seemed, had been getting the worst part of this deal. Granted, I wasn't sure Elie actually knew what it meant to take it easy on someone.

Rock crunched underfoot, and my head snapped to where Elie strode onto the grounds, tossing an animal skin in one hand, holding another at his side. I arched a brow at him and glanced back to Lucien, who watched with a grimace on his face as if he knew what was coming.

"I think we should test your agility, Luce. I've noticed you're moving sluggish these days."

The sides of the skin bulged and swayed, and I realized they were filled with some kind of liquid.

"Of course I am, you dolt. I'm twice the size I used to be." Lucien splayed his arms out to the sides and gave a roll of his eyes.

"All I hear are excuses. It's time to work on that." He tossed the skin again and snatched it out of the air to add emphasis to his words. "These are filled with goat's blood. Would be a real pain in the ass to wash out of your fur if you got hit with one," he said and held it in his palm, fingers curling around it.

Lucien bared all his white teeth in a snarl that rumbled the ground beneath our feet.

"You wouldn't dare," he hissed through those bared teeth.

"Oh, I most certainly would." Elie stretched out the first word in a taunt.

"Belle, you run through the combos I taught you because, when I'm done with this one," he paused and pointed to Lucien, the skin still gripped in his lithe fingers, "you're going to show me just how much you've locked down."

I didn't even get the chance to nod before Lucien tore off with Elie hot on his tail. I watched in a bit of awe at how fast and agile they both moved. Despite the threats and taunting, I noted the way Lucien's lips curled and Elie's shoulders relaxed.

"I don't see you moving, Arabelle," Elie said.

My spine stiffened with the use of my whole name, and I snapped into the motions that came to me like a dance, counting out loud to keep track of each maneuver as I ran through them over and over.

Whatever those skins were made of, they didn't bust open whenever Elie lobbed one at Lucien with all his strength and they hit the ground. They zinged past, mere inches from my face, and he snatched them up when they were dodged. It took Elie less than half a clock toll to smash one of the skins into Lucien.

Lucien yelped a "Fuck", but his friend didn't let up. In fact, he pelted him with another one right after for slowing down.

By the end of our session, Lucien's fur was a matted mess of sticky, reddish-brown blood that dripped off his body in globs. I wrinkled my nose at the overwhelming tang of iron wafting off him and was grateful for the lack of food in my stomach, elsewise I might have emptied the contents on the ground. I breathed through my mouth.

"I think you're going to need some help washing that all out."

There was a shortcut that led straight there from the grounds. He had showed it to me after a week. I pitied whoever would have had to clean up all the blood he traipsed through the castle otherwise.

"So, you're saying you want to bathe with me again?" He arched a brow at me, taking a towel Elie offered him and wiping his face.

"I—" My jaw hung open as I grappled for words to throw back at him. "I never said I wanted to bathe with you."

"That sounded like an invitation to me," Elie said with a smugness that made me want to punch him in the gut, but I refrained. Knowing him, he'd put me on my back just because he could.

I huffed out a breath through my nose and turned on my heels to leave.

"I thought I'd be nice and offer to help you wash but forget it." I tossed a glare over my shoulder as I stomped toward the door that led to the springs.

"Belle, wait," Lucien shouted after me, the amusement still in his voice as his heavy steps came up behind me. "That would actually be a great help." His tone shifted to sincere as he slowed to match my pace beside me.

FORTY-EIGHT

Arabelle

Balmy air greeted us as we strode into the hot springs. I made for the small changing area while Lucien went... wherever he did to get ready for the bath.

There was no sign of the anger or temper he clung so tight to at first. This Lucien was stealing my mind away from the one that haunted my dreams, and the guilt that once plagued me the first time it happened ebbed away into nothingness. The acceptance that they could be the same person helped.

I peeled my sweat-soaked clothes off and wrapped a towel around my middle. After the initial day of training, I never wore the locket when we trained again. Elie warned me that jewelry, especially necklaces, could turn into a skilled enemy's weapon.

The last time we were here together, he'd offered me a back rub. Be it because of all the flirting, or the longing buried deep within me, but when his hands were on my skin, I couldn't shove my desire down any longer. He'd run off, leaving me to stew in my own lust.

Since that day, the erotic dreams bombarded me. I may have

well summoned them myself in my desire for Lucien to touch me again. Maybe I *had*.

When I emerged, Lucien was already soaking in the water, a pale ring of red surrounding him on the surface as he rubbed at the splotches on his fur.

The water was a pleasant warmth when I stepped in, quashing the groan rising in me. Lucien's gaze snapped to me, dipping down to my bare thighs, then rising back up to where the towel hugged the tops of my breasts.

"It seems a bit," he dragged his eyes back up to mine, "unfair, for you to help me bathe and get nothing in return."

The low rumble of his voice and the way his eyes devoured every exposed inch of my body made my stomach tighten with nerves.

"Unfair to whom?" It was a dare, a challenge to see if he'd rise to meet it.

"To whom, indeed."

He was too good at the word games. I waded closer to him, watching as his eyes tracked my every movement like a mountain cat ready to pounce.

"I guess I could let you wash my back." This was a dangerous dance that had my blood singing in my ears.

His silence stretched the seconds into minutes and to eternity, eyes never leaving me – not even to blink. I wanted to squirm out of his locked gaze, but I had nowhere to go, nowhere to hide. I was trapped here.

"Alright."

He grabbed one of the sponges on a wooden table that bobbed on the small, gentle waves. His every step toward me had my heart shuddering with nervous energy.

"Turn around." His command stirred my insides into a pool of molten lava.

I turned my back to him and leaned forward, tugging the

towel loose and hanging it low on my hips. I almost choked on my own breath when the wet sponge glided from one shoulder to the other in a surprising, gentle caress.

His knuckles grazed the back of my neck as he lifted my hair and washed underneath it. Each swipe of his hands sent a wave of shivers down my spine, his touch leaving me craving more and more.

"Are you sure you don't want me to wash anywhere else?" he asked, not because of the flirtation I realized, but because I had leaned back into him, a soft hum buzzing in my throat.

I straightened, digging my nails into the flesh at my knees to bring myself back to some semblance of sanity.

"Yes, I'm sure." I pulled the towel back up around my body. "You're turn."

He turned in the water, sinking deeper into it. I reached out and pulled back my hand. I had touched him before; this shouldn't have caused such a knot in my gut.

I breathed in deep and ran my fingers through his soft fur, the blood washing out into the water as I savored the silky smoothness of it, until my fingers grazed over a bit of raised skin buried underneath it. Lucien's body tensed beneath my touch.

The sound of his hiss through gritted teeth broke the silence when I ran a fingertip along the bumpy ridge of skin. I pulled my hands away so fast I nearly toppled backward; what I felt under that fur was a thick scar.

"What happened?" The words were out of my mouth before I could stop them or even have a thought to.

"I don't want to talk about it." His muscles were locked in rigidity, and even his words came out forced.

I placed my palm over one of the raised scars underneath his fur.

"You can't heal if you keep it locked inside, Lucien. It'll become a rotting infection that will destroy you from within."

Water splashed from the small fountain on the other side of the room as Lucien refused to speak—or maybe he lacked the words. His voice startled me when he finally did.

"My father really *was* a cruel bastard."

Anger bunched my brows over my eyes. "He did this to you?"

My own parents were callous, but they would never have done something this vile. How could anyone hurt another like this? It left my stomach unsettled enough that bile threatened to bubble up into my throat.

"Yes." Lucien's answer was short and curt. I was teetering a fine line with him in this moment, a line that would tell me if he'd really let go of that anger or not.

I dared to lean into it, dared to take that step and risk falling to that horrid temper of his once again, prepared for the shouting, for him to lash out.

"Why?"

Again, he fell silent, and I thought he wouldn't answer me. It wasn't anger that I sensed in him, but such astounding sorrow that had my knees wanting to buckle. "You don't have to—"

"My father saw any show of emotion as a weakness," he started but stopped, the water at his waist rippling from his tremors. "When I cried at my mother and brother's funeral pyres, he was furious, told me I embarrassed him."

He took a shuddering breath in.

"When we returned to the castle, he had his guards drag me out to the stables, and I was chained to the rafters."

I pressed my palm to my chest and fought the burn in my eyes as I stared at the slump of his shoulders, the tremble I saw there breaking my heart to pieces.

He leaned forward, propping his elbows on his knees and cupping his face in his hand. I wanted nothing more than to throw my arms around him in a hug, to hold him, but my fear stopped me—fear of what that might mean.

"He would show up periodically, take a lash to my back for what seemed like hours." A growl rumbled through him. "After a few days, he brought an iron poker with him. I thought it was to beat me with."

He shuddered.

"I still remember the smell of my flesh being seared with it. I was thirteen."

I winced at the sharp pain in my palms, not realizing that my nails bit into the flesh from how tight I clenched my fists.

"No one stopped him?" I blinked the tears back, tilting my head to look at the far-away ceiling.

"He was the King; they feared his wrath should they interfere." He raked his hands through the fur on his head. "I thought I might actually die out there."

"But you didn't."

"Elie found me, took me to the healers. They did the best they could to prevent scarring, but he made sure I'd have reminders."

"I am so sorry, Lucien. Parents are supposed to protect us." I clasped my hands together to stop myself from reaching out.

He hung his head low. "It's been decades, and I still can't go into the stables."

His shoulders shook, and it was then that I understood. He was holding it all in—the emotions that his father tried to quite literally beat out of him. I couldn't stand it anymore. I draped my arms over him and leaned against him, hugging him to me, stroking my hand down his chest in a soothing motion.

"Belle—" his voice choked off.

"You don't have to hide it from me, Lucien. To be alive is to feel these things." Tears gathered on my lashes. I swallowed around the rising lump. "And the deeper that you let yourself feel them, the better you are because of it."

He moved so fast that I had no time to react. He wrapped his arms around my middle and buried his face in my chest, holding me in place with a firm grip. His body shook.

I wrapped my arms around the back of his neck and pressed my cheek to the top of his head, careful not to bump the horns I'd seen him avoid touching time and again. I wasn't sure how long we stayed like that.

When Lucien finally leaned back, tears lined his eyes as he looked up at me.

"Thank you." His voice was thick with emotion but steadier now.

"You don't have to thank me. You've given me so much since I've come here." I traced my fingertips along the edge of his jaw, and he nuzzled into my hand. "This is the least I can do for you."

His eyes found mine, and he wrapped his fingers around my wrist, holding my hand in place.

"You don't owe me a thing." I felt the rumble of his voice through my body as he spoke. "But I will take anything you're willing to give me."

Somewhere in the recesses of my mind, a voice whispered in response. *And what if it's everything?* I tightened my jaw. Giving into what grew in my heart meant letting go of all I had in my life, all that I longed for. Pain coiled itself like a serpent in my chest in a dull, thudding ache because, in this moment, I wanted to.

CHAPTER
FORTY-NINE

Arabelle

After Lucien confided in me about his father, something nagged at the back of my mind, something Elie said to me months ago. I needed to talk to him, to ask him about it. He was a creature of habit, I'd learned, who always followed a specific routine in the mornings. It was easy to find him.

The sound of the stone on steel rang out through the silent yard as I approached the armory. These last weeks he'd taught me how to walk with a lighter gait to my step – to better sneak up on enemies, he'd claimed.

His muscles rippled under his shirt with every swipe of that stone against the sword he held across his lap, and I couldn't stop myself from admiring it. It was times like this I could see the warrior behind the man, behind the jokes and laughter.

Without even turning around, he spoke, "Did I not work you hard enough this morning, or do you just enjoy gawking at me?"

He tossed a glance over his shoulder, lips curled in a smirk.

I moved closer to him, wringing my fingers in my hands as I reeled for the right words to voice my question.

"Lucien told me what his father did to him after the deaths of his mother and brother."

Tension thickened the air, and I fought to keep the words down as his body stiffened, his hand freezing mid-way down the sword's edge. The groan of his jaw sent my stomach into a frenzy of somersaults, and I bumped into the table when I stepped back. I'd seen this fury in him before, months ago.

His body trembled, not from fear but rage—it wafted off him in waves of heat.

"When I found him...when he told me who did it," he said through his teeth, "I wanted to kill that fucking bastard." He dragged a hissing breath in and relaxed his jaw. "And I was going to. After I left Lucien with the healers, I went to find the King."

Ice water thrummed in my veins. Here was the warrior—the killer—I had grown to know and learn from.

"Did you?" He told me before that the king was dead, but he never said how.

"No." A muscle in his jaw ticked in time with his heartbeat. "My old man stepped in and stopped me. But not before I landed a *really* great punch."

His hand moved with the stone on the sword again.

"He's the only reason I'm alive today. If I'd been anyone else, I'd have been executed." He dropped the whetstone on a table next to him and grabbed a bottle and musky rag from it. "Instead, I was thrown in the dungeon and left to rot for a month."

Elie uncorked the bottle with his teeth and tipped it over the rag, a yellowish, oily substance pouring out. He popped the cork back into the bottle and set it on the table again.

"Lucien got me out, all recovered and pissed that I got myself in trouble."

The rag left a glistening sheen on the metal as he wiped it up and down the blade. "He told me that my father took responsibility for my actions, and should anything happen again, it wouldn't just be my head on a pike. Because of that, I was too afraid to cross the King again."

The gentle glow of the fire highlighted the fiery red color of his hair, making it truly look like flames. He shook his head and tossed the rag on the table next to the oil and sheathed his sword.

"Gods," he dragged his hands through his hair, holding them there as he tilted his head back. "The things I had to endure him doing to Lucien..."

His hands dropped to his sides again, and he turned his beautiful, golden gaze on me.

"He broke him. And I had to watch." His voice cracked.

"I wish you did kill him." The bloodthirsty thought surprised me at first, but seeing Lucien break apart last night and Elie now, I didn't, for one minute, regret that his father was dead.

"That makes two of us."

"Was he always that bad?" I just couldn't wrap my head around it to have so much disdain and hatred for his own child. To want to harm him in such a way.

Elie released a tension-soaked breath. "No. He wasn't the best kind of man, but he didn't turn into the cruel, evil bastard until Helaine got sick." He slumped down onto the stool he sat on when I arrived, facing me this time.

"I don't know if she kept it at bay or he just changed. But after she died, everything was different. He took his beliefs to the extreme. He sent one of his concubines to Lucien on his fifteenth birthday to seduce him and break his heart because he didn't want him to become, in his words, a love-addled fool."

Elie folded his arms over his chest, the shirt going taut with the bulge of his muscles. He stretched his long legs out in front of him, flexing his calves like he'd just finished an intense workout.

"At first, my own father defended his behavior, claiming it was to strengthen and protect Lucien and, in turn, protect the realm. He believed that because the king lost one of his heirs, he was doing everything to protect the other one."

He closed his eyes, took a slow, deep breath in, and then released it.

"I saw it for what it was. A man with power toying with the lives under his control."

I covered my mouth with my fingers, my stomach bottoming out, and my eyes burning. This was why Lucien had been so standoffish. He was protecting himself because everyone else in his life had failed him.

I dropped my hand to my chest.

"Thank you for telling me, Elie."

I wanted to see him, to ask him about the moment he decided to lock everyone out. I stopped at the doorway, turning back to look at him, the fire gilding his features and making him look nothing short of a god of war on the eve of battle.

"And thank you for insisting I give him a chance."

I left to find my beast.

I searched and searched but couldn't find Lucien anywhere. I somehow wound up on one of the upper levels of the castle, where an open door led me to a secluded room with a second door thrown open.

As I approached it, I recognized that balcony, only the last time I saw it, there was a particular blond man. Now, Lucien stood on the other side of the door, gazing out over the vast land that made up the grounds where we lived.

His fur parted in the high winds, the ends of his clothes flapping with every gust. I admired the strength in his back and shoulders, how he now held himself with a bit more confidence than before, and a small part of me hoped I helped him find that.

When I stepped into the fresh air, my plaited hair whipped in a frenzy, lashing about like a wild animal.

"I didn't know you came up here," I said to his back.

He didn't move to look at me, but his deep voice carried over the sounds of the wind tearing through the sky.

"It seems you found my favorite hiding place." His arms were crossed on the rail, hands draped over the side.

Another thing they had in common. It was too much to be a coincidence. I wanted to ask, but a part of me was too afraid to. That fear paralyzed my tongue. Because what if they weren't the same? That kernel of doubt stayed my question.

I half turned back but didn't take the steps to the door. "I can leave if you want to be alone up here."

He tilted his head and glanced at me from the corner of his eye. "No, stay."

I joined him at the balcony edge, resting my hands on the cold, biting stone, and stood next to him. It was much more terrifying to look down from up here, outside of the dream world.

There wasn't an easy way to bring it up, so I just did. "Tell me about the concubine."

Lucien's jaw worked, muscles tightening and relaxing in a methodical rhythm, his throat bobbing with the words he might say before he cut them off.

"Elie always was a bit of a gossip."

I arched a brow at the dodge and decided to play. "So, what you did to the cook wasn't true, then?"

He turned to me, finally, eyes flickering with that long-lost light. "His eyebrows grew back just fine."

I forced my lips into a thin line, fighting against the smile that tried to take form there. He heaved a sigh, his breath tickling my cheeks, and rolled his eyes.

"He never told you about that, did he?" He stared down at me with a bit of mischief in his eyes.

I stopped trying to hold in my laughter.

"No, he didn't. But now I want to know what you did to that poor man." I wiped tears from my eyes.

Lucien ran a hand through his would-be hair. "We were young and stupid. There was blasting powder involved." He shook his head. "The point is, he was fine."

The deep timbre of his laugh was a sound I'd grown fond of and found comfort in. I would do anything to hear more of it. The echoes of our laughter died out over the towers of the castle, and we fell into a comfortable silence as he turned back to the beautiful lands, he was lord of—king of.

"I want to show you something: a place I used to go to escape my father." He pointed to a dense forest shrouded in a pale pink mist.

"Another one? How many secrets does this castle have left?" I laughed, but unease pricked at the back of my skull.

He chuckled and turned back toward the door. "More than you could possibly guess." He held out his hand and I took it, relishing the warmth of it in the crisp air this high up.

If not for the incessant ache in my thighs from the morning's training and then the hike over here, I might have thought I'd died and crossed into the next plane of life. The river wasn't visible from the castle; I wasn't sure how, but despite the wide-open sky, it was hidden. The sky was bedecked with billions of shimmering stars and rivers of color that stretched from one side to the other.

Trees with plumes of pink leaves lined the riverbank, their

limbs twisting and jutting out in all directions. The lazy flow of the water carried leaves and petals of pink downstream until they disappeared into the distance.

"This place is beautiful." I crouched next to the water and dipped my fingers, warmth washing over my skin. "I can see why you wanted to escape here."

I straightened and turned back to him. His eyes tracked my every move, the light guttering in them. I swallowed. It wasn't easy for him to open up like this. Not to anyone.

He was silent a long moment, then said, "Daija was the first woman I loved." His voice cracked on the last word. "She was kind to me when few others were. She never seemed to care about my father's crown. My heart was utterly open for her to walk into."

My chest started to cave in on itself. I already knew where this was going, but to hear him tell it broke my heart so profoundly that I wasn't sure I'd ever be able to piece it back together.

"I chased her around like a feckless child." He stared up at the stars, their silver light gilding him in a majestic glow.

"You *were* a child."

I took his hand in mine, and he looked down at it, then at me. There was pain in his eyes, and I wanted to reach inside him and tear it all out.

"I was a prince; it was unbecoming to traipse after a woman like a love-addled fool. But I didn't care." His index finger glided up the inside of my palm, the smooth claw cool against my skin.

"I showered her with gifts and affection."

"You're too hard on yourself." I laced my fingers with his larger ones. "You were in love, you were happy."

He stared at our joined hands for a moment. Two.

"I thought I was." His fingers closed over mine, the claws reaching past my wrists. "I now know it was a fleeting infatuation." He reached up and tucked a windblown strand of my hair behind my ear.

"After months of courting, I finally took her to bed."

Bile rose at the back of my throat, imagining him with her. I didn't want to hear it. I blinked. It was jealousy, barreling over me like a herd of oxen on a rampage. I hated the idea of him with her – with anyone. Never in my life had I felt something so raw, so hateful, so maddening. It was like someone pumped liquid fire into my veins, and I would burn.

"After we...finished," he continued, "my father came into my room, looked at her and then to me, and asked how I liked his gift."

My heart splintered. I covered my mouth, and tears burned in the corner of my eyes. I squeezed his hand in mine. I wanted to stop him. I didn't want to hear any more of it, but he needed to say it. It might be the only time he'd said it to anyone, or even aloud to himself.

He closed his eyes, his breathing ragged, his entire body shaking.

"She went to him, said she was tired of being pawed at by a boy, dropped to her knees, and serviced him right in front of me." He rubbed a hand down his face.

"I decided then and there to lock my heart in a cage of ice and never let anyone near it again." His breathing hitched. "I never wanted to feel that kind of pain or betrayal again." He turned to me, bringing our joined hands between us.

This close, I could smell the musk of him, heavy with the scent of dirt and leaves and rotting wood.

"I made a vow, a rule, to never fuck the same woman twice." I winced at the coarse language he used. "In order to protect myself. I was damn near close to becoming the same man as my father when I was cursed."

His head sagged, and he wasn't able to hold my gaze any longer.

"Part of me is actually grateful for it."

My heart sank into my stomach. That was when he broke. When he gave up the parts of himself that were good and light and kind. I reached my hand out and cupped his cheek, bringing his gaze back to me.

"You deserve to be loved, Lucien." I untangled our fingers and held his face between my palms. "You deserve to have someone to give love to."

"I don't." He grasped my wrists but didn't move my hands, lowering his brow to mine. "I did terrible things, Belle." His voice broke. "I hurt so many people, not just with my actions, but my arrogance as well."

"But you feel regret about it all, so you can fix it. Do whatever it takes to make things right." I leaned into him, willing my own strength into him.

"And if it takes everything I have?" His voice was low, a whisper only for me, and my heart split open for all that he offered me of himself.

"Then I'll give you all that I am, because I don't want to think about a world without you in it."

There, I said it. Without realizing it, and with enough force to take the breath from my lungs, the understanding swept over me. I cared about him, about Elie, more than anyone else in my life except Isa.

"You'd do that for me?" He lifted his head to stare at me, his blue eyes clear of the burden that once shadowed them.

"You've become a friend to me. One that I care about as much as my own family, maybe more. So, yes, I would gladly do it."

I held his unwavering gaze despite the guilt creeping in at the thought of a family I hadn't seen in months, one I had all but abandoned. Pain lanced through me in a wave that was unexpected at the thought of the sister I'd left behind. I longed to see her again, to let her know I was safe, but I couldn't. I couldn't leave. Lucien still hadn't given me his blessing to visit her.

Lucien

Belle and I ate breakfast in silence, the only sound the clink of our silverware against the dishes. Telling her about my past last night left me more exhausted and drained than I thought possible, but I was glad I did. Not even Elie knew the whole truth behind everything that happened.

I chanced a glance her way, but she stared down at her plate, moving the eggs and sausage around in a circle. Maybe it made her uncomfortable to know the truth—to know the details of my past. Perhaps it was too much for her.

Elie left a note on my bedside table before I woke. He was heading into town and wanted me to oversee her training today. Apparently, we ran out of some supplies, and he was going to get more. The bastard always knew what he was doing, leaving the two of us alone together.

Belle's words from last night still clanged through me like a church bell tolling. She'd offered me everything. Then she called me a friend. A mere friend wouldn't break this curse, but that she thought of me as more than just her captor, as someone so important to her, left a warmth spreading through my chest.

I couldn't stand the silence anymore.

"Elie put me in charge of your training today." Surely, that would garner some reaction from her. A way into some conversation. I didn't think it would be this hard to talk to her after everything I said.

"Mm." It was barely a sound, not even an acknowledgment of my presence or that I spoke.

I inhaled a deep, sharp breath and exhaled through my mouth, shoving the anger back down into the pocket I tried to keep it in. She hadn't looked at me once. The curve of her shoulders and silence told me enough. Something was wrong. I just didn't know what it was.

"Is everything okay, Belle?" I dared to ask, the expression on her face hollowing out my heart that had only started beating again for her.

Her glazed stare cleared, and she dropped her hand to the table, hitting the fork on the side of the plate and catapulting egg across the surface.

"Of course. Why wouldn't it be?"

I stared at the egg, impressed she was able to launch it that far, then back at her.

"You won't look at me and have pushed the food around on your plate throughout our meal. Something's clearly bothering you." I flicked a piece of egg that landed too close to my own plate. "You can tell me what it is."

Her eyes fell along with the fake smile she was trying so hard to maintain. "I just miss Isa. That's all."

Right. Her sister. I wasn't a stranger to the heartbreak one experienced where siblings were concerned, but what she felt for Isa made me question my own love for my brother. *That's all.* That was a pretty big thing. I had promised her I'd think about letting her visit, but the danger she'd be in just making that trip was enough to freeze my blood.

Especially now that Aamon knew about her.

A dull ache inched its way into my heart. She hadn't seen her family in months because she'd been here. It was on me. I was doing this to her, causing this pain in her. This was something I could fix.

"Do you want to leave?" The question left a bitter taste in my mouth and a hole opening up in my chest.

If she wanted to go, to be with her family, I'd find some way to accept that. I wouldn't force her to stay with me, to be separated from the people she loved.

She blinked her shock at my words, mouth opening and closing again.

"I..." Her words trailed off as her eyes fell back to the plate before her. "I don't...I don't want to leave." She cupped her forehead in her hand. "I love it here. I love waking up to a symphony of birds singing every day. I love getting to see a world I knew nothing of. To train with you and Elie."

She leaned back in her chair.

"All my life, I just wanted to be free—free from my parents, from society's expectations of what I should be." She held my gaze as she clutched her fork in her hand. "You gave me that freedom, Lucien. And you haven't asked me for *anything*."

She dropped her eyes from mine and stared at the table again. It was guilt. She felt guilty about it all. I hadn't given her freedom, not really. She could go anywhere she wanted—within the castle grounds. True freedom, the kind she wanted, would come with a cost. My life for her freedom—my realm for it.

Tears gleamed in the corner of her eyes.

"I miss my sister." She sniffed, gaze shifting upwards to fight against them. "I know it's unfair of me to say after everything you've done. But I didn't even get to say goodbye."

"It's not unfair." If the cost of her happiness was everything I had to give, I'd shred every last atom to give it to her. "My keeping you here, that's what's unfair."

This pain in my chest was nothing like before. It filled me so completely, tearing into every cell, and I fought against slamming the door to my heart shut again. I fought it because, if there was even the slimmest chance she might stay, I wanted it open for her.

"Lucien—"

"You can go home, Belle." I closed my eyes and forced my breath to be steady. "I won't be the source of your sadness."

My chair skidded on the floor as I stood.

"You have your freedom. Go and be happy." Even if it cost me my life, my kingdom.

"Lucien—"

"It's okay, Belle."

I turned from the table, the butterflies I once felt in her presence turning to bile in my stomach. I couldn't bear to look at her, to see the light come back in her eyes, knowing it was because she was leaving me, that I was the one who dimmed it.

I left her sitting at the table, not saying another word. I needed to get out of there before my temper took over. I wanted to rage. I wanted to tear the walls down, to shred everything in my path. I wanted to burn the world to the ground.

My eyes burned with tears my pride wouldn't let me shed. My bones groaned under the weight of my anger and pain. One more night. That's all that stood between me and breaking this damn curse.

If she had just given me one more night, I could have righted everything. Because tonight was the night of the Blue Moon, my last opportunity to show her who I really was. The man inside the beast. It was my last chance to save myself and my kingdom, and instead, I chose to let her go.

FIFTY-ONE

Henri

It didn't matter how often we frequented the pub to meet with Callum; every single time, my skin crawled like millions of insects were just beneath it. Between the way his crew looked at us and the filth covering every surface, it all made me want to dash out the minute we stepped through that door.

When we arrived, I half expected a wench to be perched on Callum's lap. He always had the same one, whispering and laughing with her. Such foolishness. I had to fight to keep my face passive whenever I saw it.

Today was different. It was just him and a few of his men sitting at their usual table. One of them snatched up the parchment laid out and rolled it up, stuffing it in a satchel at his waist.

Despite how much Louis claimed to hate this place and hated dealing with the Captain, he had a smile on his face and looked as if he might break into song and dance.

"We need to discuss the final details of our plan, my good man."

"We already know it." Callum arched a lazy brow at Louis and leaned back in his chair. "We're just waiting on word from you."

"Do you care to enlighten us?" The smile faltered a fraction, and I thought Louis might leap over the table to attack to Callum.

He rolled his eyes in exasperated boredom before the icy chillness burrowed into us again.

"We get the manservant, find the castle, and rescue your girl."

"What of us?" I didn't want anything to do with going into that castle until the beast was dead, but with this man, I needed to be sure he understood that.

He tilted his head the same way a large cat would right before toying with its prey. "You stay out of our way."

Louis splayed his hand out to the side. "I paid for this. I'm the one who is going to rescue Belle."

Callum clicked his tongue, annoyance lighting in those cold eyes of his. "Fine. But if you get yourself killed, that's on you."

"Good. Because I've had news that the red-haired servant will be coming into town soon. I'm told he has a shipment waiting for him."

Callum's gaze settled wholly on Louis, leaning his cheek on his fist, elbow propped on the table. The candlelight caught in the gold and silver rings he wore on his fingers.

"Which shop?"

"The general goods store."

Since taking up residence with Louis, the sheer number of people in his pocket astounded me. Once the same who were in mine, but he didn't control them with coin alone. No, he used violence and fear to keep people's tongues speaking true and free. If I wasn't so disgusted by his methods, I might be awed by them.

The captain's eyes shifted to the two men seated across from him, and he gave them a nod. They vacated their seats, gathered their coats and weapons, and left the pub. His eyes fixed on us again. "At least two of my men will be on watch until he shows up."

"And what's to happen once he does?"

Callum was a hard man to gauge. I could never tell if he was scheming or being genuine. There was a voice in the back of my head that whispered he wasn't in this just for the coin, not with that feral look I sometimes caught in his eyes when we discussed what to do about the beast.

His calculating eyes shifted to me, and he yawned as if to show me just how bored he was of these conversations. "Then we make him show us where the castle is. You get the girl back. And we take whatever we want."

"It's abandoned. I doubt there's any treasure worth taking from it." I didn't want them snooping around and taking all the gold; it'd make this whole endeavor pointless.

"I never said I was after silver and gold, mate. What I want has no price tag." His eyes darkened as shadows claimed his face.

"Take whatever you want, so long as you kill the beast, and I get Belle." Louis sat in one of the abandoned chairs.

"How will we get into the castle? I want to make sure my daughter doesn't come to harm because we're caught." I took the other chair.

Callum tapped his fingers on the table in a rhythmic beat and hummed. "It would be best to go in at dusk. With a small group. Maybe just two."

Louis leaned into the table, his forearm braced against it, fingers curled in a tight fist. "Send whoever else you want with me. I don't care."

The captain gave the large man next to him a glance, and he nodded in return. "Gabin will go with you. When you enter the castle, you move as silently as possible and avoid the creature in there. Once you get her out, we go in."

The muscles in Louis's arm relaxed. "Sounds perfectly reasonable to me, if you're sure of your man."

"I'm more sure of him than I am of someone like you, who's

untried and a bit too pompous for my taste." Callum looked him over with a bit of distaste written on his features.

"And what if the worst should happen?" I shoved into the conversation before Louis could say whatever it was that simmered with rage on his lips. We needed a plan, but more than that, I needed to keep these two from tearing each other apart until I got what I wanted.

"What if they encounter the beast? What if they cannot find Belle? What if they do not come back out of the castle?"

Louis turned to me and clapped a hand on my shoulder. "Rest assured, Henri. I will not fail to retrieve your daughter. And should the beast show his face, I'll have my pistol on me."

"Henri does have a point," Callum inspected the dirt caked under his nails. "We need to plan for everything. In the event that the plan goes array, we storm the castle and kill the beast, keeping in mind that the girl is still in there." The chair creaked when he leaned back. He crossed his arms over his chest.

"How will we know to do that? It's not like they'll know where to find her, and the castle is huge."

That was one thing I'd discovered in my short time there. No doubt there were hundreds of places she could be hidden, and I wanted to keep them from looking in too many of them.

A grin curved the captain's lips upward in an unsettling tilt.

"People are predictable, my dear Henri. Your daughter is no exception." He stretched his legs out under the table, kicking one of mine out of his way. "We ask the servant when we have him in our grasp. He'll know where she is."

With the way he spoke about the servant, I'd swear that he knew him. But that wasn't possible. No one in this town knew anything about the castle or its beast. I couldn't believe anyone would know the servants.

"It's settled then. As soon as we catch him, we force him to take us to the castle." Louis stood from the table, the ambiance of the pub finally taking its toll on him. "Send one of your men to fetch us the minute he's in your custody."

He turned to me. "Henri, let's go."

I gave Callum another look, but his grin just widened, showing his teeth in a vicious sneer. I rose and followed Louis out.

It wasn't even half a day before there was a heavy knock on the door, and one of Callum's men stood outside. He shook off the snow that gathered on his shoulders when the door opened.

"Cap'n sent me to let ya know that the manservant has been caught. Bastard put up a damn good fight. Took out two of our men, but we got 'im."

Louis snatched his cloak off the coat rack by the door.

"Isa, make sure you have dinner ready by the time we get back. My bride deserves a nice welcome home and a celebration of her freedom." He grabbed my cloak and thrust it at me. "We've got a damsel to rescue."

True to his word, when we arrived, Callum had a red-haired man tied up and on his knees, a fiery hatred in his golden eyes that he glared all of right at the captain.

"That was quicker than expected," Louis said as he paced in front of the captive, examining him as if he were some foreign entity. "Where is the castle?"

"I'll never tell you bastards anything," he spat on the ground at our feet.

"I just want my daughter back. Please tell us where it is." I tried to offer him a line of sympathy to grasp onto.

He laughed, a cruel, wicked sound. "You? You who traded her life for your own? Belle's told me all about you. I wouldn't help you find her if she were knocking on death's door and you were her sole lifeline to this plane."

"It was never supposed to be Belle," I hissed through my teeth as anger flooded into my veins. "It was supposed to be Isa. God knows I can't seem to get rid of that one."

His face contorted in rage. "You don't deserve either of them. You'd sell your children to the highest bidder. Or just to save your own skin. I've known men like you. Cruel and hateful and cowardly wretches. You'll never see her again if I have anything to say about it."

His head snapped to the side when Louis's punch connected with his jaw. He spit out a mouthful of blood and turned those hate-filled eyes on him.

"You *will* tell us. It's none of your business what Henri chooses to do with his property." Louis shook out his hand at his side.

Fire burned in the gold irises as he glared up at us, heat radiating off him in a shimmering coat of clear air. I took a step back, a preternatural fear of him bursting into flame rising up my spine – it was a ridiculous fear with no basis. Humans didn't spontaneously combust, but my instincts couldn't be silenced.

Callum strolled over and dropped into a squat, draping his arms over his knees. He was eye to eye with the servant. He tilted his head to one side, both of them locked in a silent stare as if they were communicating inside their minds.

I glanced between them until the captive paled, his features going slack. He swallowed hard, his throat bobbing.

"I don't need you to tell us where the castle is because I already know how to find it, don't I?" The captain sneered at him, and the servant dropped his head.

"You've known how to get to the castle all along?" Louis all but growled at Callum, stomping toward him and reaching, but Gabin shoved a palm into his chest to halt him.

Callum adjusted the leather cuff on his wrist, unruffled by

Louis's attempt to assault him. Whether it was arrogance or confidence in his own men, I didn't know. By any stretch of the imagination, Louis would take Callum in a fair fight; he was larger and more volatile. Yet, the captain had a dangerous air about him that left me wondering how I was still alive after all I did when I employed him and his men.

"I needed to be sure which castle you were looking for. When you told me the description of my old friend here, I had a suspicion I knew, but I don't like making plans on gut feelings and a few scraps of knowledge."

One of his men stepped forward with a black coat, and Callum slipped it on.

"If you know, then stop wasting our time and take us there. Belle is waiting."

Hatred lined Louis's face, and he may very well decide to kill the captain out of spite before we were done.

"Follow me, fellas. Time to get your lass back." He nodded to his men, and they yanked the red-haired man off his knees and shoved him toward the town line.

Excitement sang in my blood. Soon I would have all the wealth of that monster, have that veritable fortress, and no one could stop me. We were going to the castle, and everything in it would be mine.

CHAPTER

FIFTY-TWO

Lucien

Light glared off the pale, sandy dirt in the training pit, seeping between my fingers as I held my head in my hands and leaned against a crumbling wall. There wasn't a thought in my head when I came out here. It was just a habit at this point.

Belle wouldn't show up. She was sure to be long gone now that I gave her my blessing to leave. Why did I come all this way? I raked my hands through my hair and curled my fingers around the back of my neck as I let my head rest on the hard stone.

Elie would be furious when he got back. I threw away my chance at fixing everything with only days left because I couldn't stand to see that look of sadness on Belle's face, knowing I was the cause and that I could erase it.

I got up and paced circles in the yard, my claws swiping the air beside me with each cycle as I grew more and more restless. I kept going until my knees refused to hold my weight any longer, and I plopped to the ground, a cloud of dust billowing up around me and settling into my clothes and my fur.

Trying to convince myself she was gone was pointless. I knew she was still in the castle; I could sense it everywhere I went. Her sweet, honeyed scent haunted me like the ghost of a jilted lover. I propped my elbows on my knees and hung my head low between them.

Steps crunched on the hardened dirt, and I flinched, clutching my forearms, afraid to raise my head and look at her.

"You haven't left yet?" I hated the rasp that clung to my voice when I spoke. It mocked me with the emotion I tried so hard to keep locked away, one that was now roaming free through my being.

She stopped close enough that I could see the toes of her boots at the edge of my vision. She clicked her tongue at me.

"You seem to be under the impression that I'm leaving for good."

My head snapped up, and our eyes met. She couldn't say that. Not when I clung to the last shreds of hope that she might feel the same way I do, that she was the one that would *free me*.

"Besides, did you really think I'd leave without saying goodbye?"

I wasn't sure I was breathing.

"I'm nothing but your captor. I didn't expect anything from you." It was a lie I kept trying to convince myself of all day.

"I haven't thought of you as my 'captor' in a long time now." Her words shattered through my thin veil of self-deceit. She crouched down in front of me, my eyes tracking her every movement. "I meant what I said about you and Elie being my friends. And I meant what I said at breakfast. I don't want to leave you."

She reached out and took my cheek in the palm of her hand. "I just want to go check on my sister. I promise I'll come back to you."

I stayed silent, the only thing I could do against the raging storm in my chest and fighting that little kernel of hope trying to take root in my heart. She wanted to stay. She wasn't going to abandon me.

"You thought I was already gone," she said it as if she were convinced it was true. "Why did you still come here?"

I hefted a heavy sigh. My shoulders slumped a little deeper, my head hung a little lower.

"I don't know." It was a lie. To her. To myself.

Belle sank onto her knees.

"Look at me, Lucien."

My gaze had drifted from her. It was the same demand I wanted to scream at her this morning but held my tongue.

My eyes burned against the unshed tears that wanted to form on my lashes, but I wouldn't allow it. I didn't want her to see the weakness, the amount of pain that just *thinking* she was leaving for good had caused me.

She gave me only seconds before she grabbed my face and lifted my gaze to hers.

My throat ached with every swallow, but here she was, everything I had hoped for, longed for, and she wanted to stay.

"Did you hear what I said?" Her eyes bounced between mine as her words dug somewhere deep inside me.

Because I hadn't acknowledged it yet that she'd said she was coming back.

"You're going to return." My heart fluttered with that damned hope I tried to keep on a leash.

"I'm coming back. This is my home now, where I want to be."

She dropped her hands to mine. Her fingers squeezed my much larger ones, offering warmth and comfort I never thought I'd see again. I never noticed how the sun lit up streaks of red in the amber of her eyes when it hit them just right.

She wanted to stay. It was a thought I had to keep reassuring myself of. It wasn't a dream, wasn't an illusion, but real. She chose me. I wanted to roar it from the peak of Lucir Solaris, scream it into the Void despite the hell Aamon would rain down on my head for it.

She dropped both hands into her lap with a sigh. She sat back on her heels.

"When does Elie get back? I want to talk to him before I go, discuss what to do if the Daeva or Marid show up again."

"He went to town. It'll be nightfall before he returns."

That seed of hope grew and opened into a bright and blossoming thing inside me. Maybe the curse would be broken after all. Just a little longer, then everything would be righted.

"Guess I'll wait until tomorrow, then."

I couldn't help the smile spreading across my face; I only needed her to stay until the moon rose into the night sky. I could go to her, a man again, and explain everything. Tomorrow, I could go with her, never having to wear this beastly form again.

"Since you're sticking around until Elie gets back, we should get on with your training, or else he'll kick my ass." He'd do it anyway once he found out that I had agreed to let her leave thinking she wouldn't come back.

I soaked my aching muscles in the warm, sudsy water, the subtle smell of the cinder wood soap hanging in the air. I hid myself away in my chamber for most of the day after parting with Belle.

She said she wanted some time to herself to prepare for the trip, but I watched her steal away in the direction of the library after her usual hot springs visit.

I both hated and loved that I knew her routine. I knew where to always find her; it quietened a part of my heart that had burned with anxious energy since the day the Daeva almost took her from me.

I sunk lower into the inviting water. Whether Elie was a damn good teacher, or she just picked up on it fast, I was impressed by her rapid improvement these last weeks. She almost had Elie on his back several times in the last session and stood her own against me when running through the maneuvers, even as a creature more than twice her size.

Water dripped off my fur as I stood up and stepped out of the tub, shaking the excess from me before grabbing a towel. I prayed that Elie took his time coming home, prayed that he would be delayed and give me just a little more of it with her. I knew it wasn't fair to him, and I'd have to apologize for it later, but I didn't want to part with her just yet.

I strode to the window, the golden disk of the sun touching the line of the horizon and setting the sky ablaze with orange and purple and blue. Only a little longer.

If my plan didn't work, then I would die in two days. The sickness subsided after Belle's brush with death, whether because I used the last of my magic or something shifted between us that day. I didn't know, but I was grateful to be rid of the coughing fits that sometimes kept me awake.

The sun's bright rays sang their last song of light for the day and sank into the dark and welcoming embrace of night. Movement from the corner of my window caught my eye—a bird or some other animal, perhaps.

It didn't matter.

Or at least I thought it didn't, until a memory snagged on the edges of my mind, and something Elie said flitted back. *I've been seeing Daeva on the grounds.* And there had, indeed, been Daeva.

Ice ran through my veins as if I were born in the frigid peaks of Eskea. Aamon claimed they were looking for something when he was here. I shoved the windowpane open and walked onto the balcony in time to catch the heels of a man running behind the outer wall of the castle.

Fear raked its claws up my locked spine. Elie wasn't here, and Belle was alone in the library. I didn't waste the time wondering if they were here for me or her as bile burned at the back of my throat, and my head hollowed out of every other thought but to get to her.

I shoved my still-wet legs into too-tight pants, the seams groaned their protest. I yanked a shirt over my head. I ripped the door open and hurried down the hall. My footsteps were chased by anxiety until I was almost at a sprint.

Once I knew she was safe, I'd deal with the intruders. They were lower on my list than her safety. I had to get her to her chambers; it would be safe there, but I wouldn't let her make that trek alone, not with enemies in the castle. And if they were Daeva... My heartrate ratcheted up to a thunderous roar in my ears.

The library was too gods damned far away. All was silent aside from the slap of my feet on the floor until I heard it, a scream—*her* scream.

I barreled forward into an all-out sprint on all fours, claws ripping up the marble below my hands and feet as panic seized my heart in an iron grip and refused to let go. The bastards were here for *her*. I'd kill them. I'd rip them apart slowly and savor their screams before I killed them. Fury burned through my body until a rumbling roar tore from my throat and reverberated off the stone walls in a symphony of rage.

CHAPTER

FIFTY-THREE

Arabelle

My muscles locked up as fear carved itself deep into my bones at the sight of the man holding open the two oak doors leading into the library. Blood drained from my face.

"Louis?" I tucked my arms into me, balling the fingers of one hand into a fist and clutching my book with the other. My heart pounded against my ribs hard enough that it might snap one and leave me gasping for air. He couldn't be here. This was a safe place.

The double doors swung shut as he stepped through them, every footstep cinching a cord around my frantic pulse.

"I've come to rescue you, Arabelle." He held a hand out to me, slowing his approach. "Come."

"How...how did you find this place?"

Tendrils of fear tightened around my limbs, locking me in place. I wanted to turn and run in the opposite direction. The book slid from my grasp and landed on the floor with a thud.

"We caught the manservant." A vein in his forehead popped

with impatience. "Now come, Arabelle. We don't have time for this."

Elie.

They had Elie.

Louis took another calculated step forward, placing himself between two tables and cutting off my direct route to the exit. I backed a step. *We.* The word clanged through me a second later. He wasn't alone.

"Who is *we?*"

The smile on his face faltered, revealing a fraction of the monster lurking beneath his skin that I saw the day he chased us into the forest.

"Me, your father, and a crew I hired. Isa is waiting for you at my estate."

The lamb I'd eaten for dinner turned laden in my stomach. "I don't need to be rescued, Louis. I agreed to come here on my own. You can leave." Something wasn't right. My father wouldn't risk coming back here for me.

"That monster has you under some kind of spell." His lip curled back. "You need to snap out of it and come with me. Now." His hand was inches away.

Fear cowed my vision to him alone and blinded me to much of my surroundings, so much so I didn't notice the table until I backed into it. I stumbled against it, and he lunged.

"No!" The training Elie drilled into me took over in a rush of instinct as I twisted and slipped from his unsure grip.

"Don't make this harder than it needs to be." He growled and grabbed for me again, his fingertips grazing my arm.

This time, *I* struck *him*, putting all my weight behind the punch as cartilage crunched under my fist. He staggered back and covered his nose with his hand as a roar of pain shot past his lips.

"Fuck!"

He pulled his hand back, and blood poured down his mouth

and jaw from the broken nose I gave him. A hint of pride bloomed in my belly. I managed to defend myself.

His eyes darkened, and unlike the last time, it wasn't an open-handed strike he leveled at me. My vision flashed white when his fist connected with my cheekbone, sending me sprawling to the floor.

Stars spotted everywhere I looked, and my face sang with the sting of his punch, pain lashing out in waves against my skull when I tried to get my hands under me to stand.

That was when I heard it and as my eyes met with Louis's, I knew he heard it too, saw it in the ragged breath he took. That sound was unmistakable, the rage in it a balm to the panic rising in tidal waves through my body. *That* was the sound of my beast coming for me.

"Get her up. I'll deal with the beast." I didn't see who he was talking to until broad hands scooped me up under the shoulders, turning me to face him.

He frowned at the bruise that no doubt already bloomed on my cheek, a darkness taking root in his eyes that I couldn't understand. He didn't say a word before he threw me over his shoulder, and my world turned upside down. My hair hung in loose waves down his back, blocking my vision; the hem of my dress rose up, and the bodice twisted to an uncomfortable angle.

"No!" I screamed at him, pounding my fists into his wide shoulders. "Put me down!" I kicked at his front until he hooked an arm over my knees.

I didn't see him; I didn't hear his approach, and I didn't need to when my captor went rigid beneath me, the hold he had on my legs weakening as his head tilted up.

"I'll give you one chance to put her down and walk out of this castle." His growl was the sweetest melody that my soul would ever hear.

"I'm taking my fiancé back, beast," Louis's words came from

the same direction as Lucien's, and my heart leaped into my throat.

There was a ring of metal on metal, a sword being drawn. Lucien snarled a ferocious response, heavy footsteps drawing closer.

"You're not taking her anywhere."

"Perhaps you don't understand how this is going to go down." Louis's voice was like broken glass shredding apart my skin. "Her father gave her to me. She is *mine*. And I am going to take her with me when I leave this castle."

"Like Hell she is." Marble and stone crunched under heavy feet. "Belle is her own person and free to choose who she loves— who she wants to be with." A low rumble. "And it doesn't seem she wants you if you have to drag her out."

Lucien's words pierced through the last dregs of terror, holding tight to my insides, and I stopped the random thrashing as a new kind of strength flickered to life within me. I twisted my body and slammed the back of my elbow into the base of my captor's skull.

"Gods damn it, girl," he shouted and dropped to a knee, gripping the back of his head with a free hand.

When my feet hit the floor, I drove my knee into the bastard's face and shoved off him, keeping my balance as Elie had taught me. He fell onto his back, both hands shooting to his face, blood oozing between his fingers. I spun to Lucien and ran for him, but Louis grabbed my wrist and yanked me back so hard I thought my shoulder would dislocate.

"Let go!" I gritted and pulled against him, but his grip was iron around me, unyielding no matter how hard I clawed and scratched at his skin.

"I see you've been filling her head with this nonsense." He pulled me to him and wrapped an arm around my waist, still clutching that wrist. "No wonder she doesn't want to leave." He shoved his nose into my hair and inhaled. "Unfortunately for you both, that's not how the world works."

"Let her go." The calmness of his voice, the sheer demand in it, was far and wide more terrifying than any amount of raging I'd seen Lucien do.

"No, I don't think I will." Louis stroked a finger down the cheek he struck, and I flinched away at the sharp burn of his touch over my swollen skin.

I forced back a whimper at the pain searing down to my bone. My eyes met with Lucien's; a cold fire burned within them when they traveled down to the bruise marring my face. At a speed I had no chance of following, he moved, slammed a palm into Louis's chest, and threw him into the tables behind us.

He took my chin between his thumb and fingers and tilted my face until the light illuminated it for him to inspect.

"Which one?" The demand in his voice sang to my bones in a way that threatened to crumple me to the ground at his feet. "Who did this?"

"I did," Louis said as the tip of his blade shoved through Lucien's shoulder. "Someone has to put her in her place."

Louis twisted the sword, and blood sprayed my face from the wound. There was no pain etched on Lucien's face, only the hardened scowl of a predator as his head turned to look over his shoulder – a slow, agonizing movement.

The roar he unleashed locked up every muscle in my body as if it had the power to cause paralysis all on its own. He jerked forward, sword still piercing through his flesh as he turned to face Louis.

Lucien's roar *did* cause paralysis. It wasn't just me that couldn't move; my eyes fell on the man frozen in the exact spot he tried to ambush my beast from. Lucien reached over his shoulder and pulled the sword free, tossing it aside in a clatter of metal on marble.

He grabbed Louis by the throat, lifting him up and up and up until his toes dangled feet from the ground.

"Belle's place is here. By my side. And far away from you."

Louis reached for the fur-laden arm with jerky movements, kicking his feet and digging his fingers in as blood trickled down his neck from Lucien's grip.

"I...won't let...you have her...you *beast*." His hand dropped from my sight before reappearing with a pistol.

Not pointed at Lucien, but at me.

The gunshot rang out in the silence of the library, and I snapped my eyes shut, dropping to the ground so fast that my head smacked into the floor hard enough it bounced. Pain exploded behind my eyes.

He shot me.

I was going to die.

"Belle," Lucien's voice was soft. A warm hand cupped my cheek, thumb caressing the ridge of my jaw. "Did you get hit?"

The gentle concern was such a contrast to the brutality of moments before.

I blinked my eyes open. Lucien sat on his knees, hovering over me. I scanned him for more injuries, but outside of his shoulder, there were none. Blood still pooled at his knees, dripped from the claws of his left hand and, oh god, soaked the fur up to his elbow.

I looked past him to Louis, who was prone on the floor, the front of his body ripped open, his insides on the outside.

Sick burned the back of my throat as I scurried back on my elbows until I rolled over and emptied the contents of my stomach on the floor.

I wiped the back of my hand across my mouth and dared to glance back over my shoulder, the firelight gilding his shredded body in a horrid display of violence.

"Are you alright?" Lucien's tone was stern now, but it still held onto the tenderness underneath. He placed a bloodied hand on the skirts of my dress.

I kicked his hand away and hauled my legs up to my chest, curling into a tight ball. I couldn't look at him, see the blood drenching him, the gore on his hands. Sobs racked my body with violent shudders.

"Arabelle, please." There was pleading there.

He told me about killing the Daeva. I knew he was a warrior, but seeing him kill someone with my own eyes, seeing the blood, it was too much. Fear coiled around me so tight I thought I might suffocate, thought my heart would stop.

Lucien made no move to come closer. He didn't try to touch me again. He just stared at me with pleading eyes.

Silvery light breached the large windows on the second level of the library and bathed his pale fur in a gentle glow. Fur that started to fall away.

"Fuck. Not now." Panic sounded in his voice. A voice that was deep but didn't rumble with the primal ferocity of a beast.

The claws shrank back into the fingers of a man, the horns withdrew into his skull, his muzzle shortened until all that was left in front of me was the familiar, beautiful man that haunted my dreams in the months since I'd come here. I'd been right. The two were the same.

His once ill-fitting clothes hung loose on his smaller frame. The waist of his pants sat low on his hips, and the open collar of his shirt gave a spectacular view of his broad, muscular chest.

"Lucien...?" I hated how my voice cracked. Betrayal was a bitter taste on my tongue as moments of passion and pleading flashed through my mind. He never told me. All this time and *he never told me.*

"Belle, I—" He cut himself off, sliding onto his knees. "This isn't how I wanted you to find out."

"You were the one in my dreams."

Pain from every broken piece of my heart cut through me like the steel of a blade. Even if I had accepted it on my own, how could he have kept this from me? Was it no more than a ruse?

"Yes." His voice trembled. His head hung, that beautiful blond hair draping over his shoulders in a soft curtain gilded in shades of orange and red.

"How?"

I touched my chest, my throat. The things he had said to me, had done to me in those dreams... Was he just looking for a way to get off? Was it all a trick to fool me? Louis was right. My eyes slid to his body. He put me under a spell, and I'd been compliant enough to let it happen. Tears burned in my eyes.

"It's...complicated. If you'll just—"

"Why? Why would you invade something so personal? Something private?"

The bite in my tone was full of accusation. I intended it to be. I wanted to lash out, to hurt him in the same way I hurt.

"You would barely speak to me, barely look at me as a beast. I didn't see another option at the time." He splayed his hands, eyebrows knitting together.

"So, what? Your plan was to seduce me in my dreams? Trick me into your bed? Is that how to break the curse?" I scrambled to get my feet under me.

"No, no, not any of that." He reached a hand out to me, but I recoiled, disgust on my face at the thought of his hands on me. "Belle, please. Just let me explain."

"I don't want to hear your excuses. You're no better than Louis. Or my father." My vision blurred until hot tears poured down my cheeks. "You're just like *your* father." I knew the words hit home the way I wanted them to when devastation flashed in his eyes.

He looked up at me, tears at the edge of his own eyes as pain and despair shone there. In that moment, I knew the heart he kept surrounded in ice was free of its confinement. That cage had melted in my time with him. I saw it in the way he spoke to me and Elie, the way he laughed, and the way he carried himself.

I took in the beauty of him, and it robbed me of breath, of ration, every thought of anything else. My mind and heart were at war with one another. I wanted to throw my arms around him and thank my lucky stars that the man I'd so desperately wanted to free was right here in front of me, that I finally found him.

But on the other hand, he'd lied to me.

Kept things from me.

Tricked me.

I was stuck in the middle of a chasm that kept widening, and I'd plummet if I didn't decide.

"Belle—"

I ran.

A cry tore from him as my body smashed into the doors, and I shoved through them. I raced down the hallway, sliding into the stone walls when I took a turn too fast. I needed to get back to my room.

I couldn't hear my name on his lips one more time. I couldn't keep staring at that enchanting face without throwing myself over the edge and praying he'd catch me.

Hands snatched my wrist, my momentum nearly taking my feet from under me as I was slammed into a broad chest. An arm wrapped around my neck, and the air in my lungs became a fleeting thing as the edges of my vision blurred.

"Make sure you don't snap her neck. Cap'n says we need her alive."

It was the last thing I heard before the world went black.

CHAPTER

FIFTY-FOUR

Lucien

My hand dropped to the floor when the doors closed behind Belle. She ran. How could the gods be so cruel to allow her to see me transform right this minute? With blood on my hands and the man she was betrothed to dead at my feet.

It was their fault. I forced myself onto unsteady legs. They cost me everything. I picked up the sword and walked to the burly man who had his hands all over Belle when I got here.

"I knew he was a bastard, but I didn't think he was such a wretch to hit a woman." The man didn't plead for his life. Instead, he cast a look of pure hatred at the dead body behind me. "Got what he deserved."

"Are you not employed by him?" The leather of the hilt groaned in my hand when I squeezed it.

"No. I serve one man, and that sure ain't him." He faced me, holding his chin high and meeting my eyes with no fear in his.

"No pleading for your life?"

"Never. I'll take my punishment for failing with dignity."

Sweat coated my palms, and I swiped one down the side of my pants. There were so many questions to ask.

"How many of you are there?"

"Two dozen or so."

"How did you find my castle?"

"We grabbed the redhead servant in town. Cap'n took him prisoner. Said he knew him and led us here himself."

"Where is Elie now?" I dragged the tip of the blade down the man's chest and stomach, stopping just over a soft, vital spot.

Still, his countenance never changed, never gave away a hint of what he feared or any other emotion.

"He's with my Cap'n." His gaze dropped to the sword in my hand and then moved back to mine. "If you kill me, he might not be so benevolent with your man."

"You hurt her."

"Alls I did was pick the lass up and stop her from hittin' or kickin' me. She did a whole lot more of the hurtin' than I did."

I leaned on the sword, the tip piercing flesh. Blood bubbled around the metal, soaking into the white shirt he wore.

It was my turn to be on the other end of his hate. "They're planning another attack, ya know. We were supposed to get the girl out, and once we gave the signal, they'd charge in to kill you."

"Who came up with this plan?"

"Henri, the girl's father. He roped Louis into it, and he hired me and my crew. They paid us a generous amount of coin to do it. Cap'n's not the kind to turn down that kind of loot."

"Go back to your captain, to...Henri... and tell them if they come here, they will die." I leaned closer and pointed to Louis's corpse. "Just like that bastard."

I straightened and tossed the sword.

"Get out." I took a step and glanced over my shoulder. "I expect Elie to be returned to me unharmed since I'm letting you go."

The man stood and gods. I knew he was huge, but in this form, he was a mountain compared to me. He lumbered to the doors and shoved through them, just like she had.

I gripped my chest to stop the rending of my heart. The fear in her eyes when she saw what I'd done, the betrayal when she saw my real face – I'd give anything to take this night back. I could have snapped his neck, but my anger seized control of every thought, and I let my claws reap the punishment instead. All because he aimed his gods damned gun at her.

I slumped to the floor and dropped my head into my hands. Tonight was meant to be the night I'd play the violin for her. I had it all planned out. I thought my chance was gone at breakfast, but she stayed. I was going to explain everything—the curse, the dreams, how I felt about her. I was prepared for disappointment and anger, but not this.

Instead, I still had Louis's blood on my hands when my body shifted back into the form of a man, and the moment she saw me, my face, her scent soaked in terror and pain.

"I'm as much a fool today as I was back then."

I failed.

I failed in such a horrid and devastating way. I didn't care about my own life, but my people, the realm, Elie...they deserved better than this. I was a worse king than any other before me. And I welcomed what was to come because of it.

FIFTY-FIVE

Henri

The moon hung high in the sky with a backdrop of a million stars as I drummed my fingers on my thighs in an impatient rhythm. It was taking too long. They should have been out by now. As if summoned by the thought in my head, Gabin, Callum's second, rounded the corner of the castle wall. Alone.

"Where's Louis and the girl?" Callum was quick to ask, straightening to his full height yet still a full head shorter than Gabin.

"Louis is dead. The beast found us before we could get the girl out." He glanced over his shoulder. "He let me go, said to release his servant and leave. But I figure we still got a job to do."

Gabin gave me a pointed look with a grin, lifting the corners of his mouth.

"I came here for my daughter," I nodded my agreement. "You have your coin; Louis's death matters little here."

Callum tossed a knowing smirk my way.

"Aye. That we have. Sneaking in didn't work out so well for us. Let's do this the pirate way and bust down the front door, shall we?" He leapt up onto the stone partition separating us from the front gardens, smooth as a cat on his feet.

"Let's take the castle, boys!"

He thrust his sword into the air, and his crew answered in a battle cry. Then they parted and rushed through the giant wooden doors with weapons in hand, stamping out flowers and knocking over statues in their frenzy.

The thud of Callum's boots on the ground stirred the excitement in my blood. He held some kind of power in his words. His knuckles were white around the hilt of his blade as he followed after his men, Gabin and me, on his heels, trying to keep stride with him. The man had such long and fast legs.

"Where was the beast last you saw him?" Callum took the sweeping stairs just past the door two at a time, heading I wasn't sure where—I wasn't even sure he, himself, knew at this point.

"The library. But there's no telling if he's still there," Gabin hissed out a heavy breath through his teeth. "There's something else, Cap'n. He turned into a man right before my eyes."

Callum never broke stride, but I stumbled over the corner of an ornate rug.

"What?" The word slipped from my lips in a daze. "He's a man?"

"Aye. That he is. Is the curse broken, then?" He slowed his walk until Gabin caught up with him.

"I don't think so. The girl ran from the room once she found out." The poor man's chest heaved, and I couldn't say that I was surprised if he had taken this route thrice now.

"Smart lass, that one. I won't have to worry about her getting in my way." He took off in a damn near run, leaving Gabin and me panting after him.

My chest cinched. "You still mean to kill him? Even though he's a man and not a beast?" Killing a beast was one thing, but now that I knew the truth, doubt snapped at the back of my heels.

Callum cut a look at me like he'd crush me underfoot if I spoke again, and I swallowed the knot forming in my throat.

"Oh, yes. I do." He turned his back to me and continued down the halls. "If you've turned coward, run on home. He and I have business to attend to."

I blew out a breath. Whatever this business was, it didn't concern me, and I was content to keep it that way. If he was going to slaughter him anyway, I might as well reap the benefits left behind.

The shouts of the crew faded into murmurs as we rounded corner after corner, being led, not by Gabin like I expected, but by Callum. He knew where he was going in this maze of a castle. I bit down on the tip of my tongue to stop myself from asking the questions that burned on it.

Two dark, wooden doors stood in front of us. One was left ajar. Callum slid the tang of his blade through the opening first, then pushed against the door with all of his weight.

A man sat in a chair, his body hunched over, his head in his hands, and his long, golden hair soaked in crimson patches. A shirt hung off his body, half soaked in blood, and his feet were bare; I couldn't tell if the trousers were black or caked in the same bloody mess as his shirt.

His head jerked up at the sound of our footsteps, and he jolted to his feet with teeth bared at us.

"You." His growl wasn't close to the intimidating thing it was three months ago. "What are you doing here?"

His blue eyes burned with animosity.

"We've come for the girl." Callum lifted his hands in an exaggerated shrug. "And your life." The grin he gave him sent a chill rocketing up my spine.

His eyes snapped to the captain's, a muscle pulsing in his jaw. "I'll slaughter every last one of you before I let you put hands on her."

"Ah, what a gallant hero you are. But from what my first mate tells me, she didn't think the same when you shredded through that bastard Louis. Said she ran away in tears when she saw that face of yours." His cold laugh left my bones rattling like I'd never find warmth again. "Must be quite the blow to your confidence. You always had an abundance of it."

The man's eyebrows drew together as he narrowed his eyes on the captain. "Do you know me?" His fingers flexed at his sides as if he were assessing the best way to kill us.

"Better than most, Lucy." The smile on Callum's face lacked warmth or kindness. Even his usual humor was absent. Instead, it was something closer to feral. His eyes bled with murderous intent, hiding within the gentle blue.

"You will not speak to me so casually." He gave him a once over, and his lip curled. "*Pirate.*"

Despite his grandstanding, the man took a step back from us.

"I know it's been thirty years," Callum pressed the fingertips of his free hand into his chest and feigned a hurt expression; a wicked sneer curved his lips, "but you wound me, *brother.*"

Color drained from the man's face before it turned a mottled shade of red.

"Don't you dare claim my brother's name for yourself. He is long dead." The muscles in his arms and chest twitched.

"I'm sure that's what you've told yourself all these years, to make it okay what you and father did to us."

My head swiveled between the two; there were definite similarities. Blond hair, blue eyes, the same face shape, and almost identical builds.

"Are you truly brothers? Is this why you still mean to kill him? For something he did to you in the past?"

Without taking his eyes off the man in front of us, Callum answered, "Aye. He's committed a great many atrocities since I was forced out. It's why he was cursed. Isn't that right, Lucy?"

"You know nothing of what you speak." His voice trembled now and became quieter, almost withdrawn, as the anger leeched out of it.

Callum's laugh was the cruelest sound I'd ever heard. "The girl couldn't bring herself to love you. Could she, Lucien?"

Despair flashed across Lucien's face one second and was gone the next. "How do you know of it? The only way you'd know of it is if you were involved."

This time, he didn't back down but took several steps forward until Callum leveled the tip of his blade at Lucien's throat. His lip twitched upward in half a snarl.

"Or I was told about it by someone who had knowledge of your curse." The sword held steady enough that he could shear the stubble of Lucien's cheek if he chose to.

"Who told you? I want names so I can rip their spines out for what they've done to me and my people." His eyes held Callum's.

The captain clicked his tongue and let the blade slip enough to knick his flesh. A small trickle of blood dripped down the curve of it.

It all happened so fast. I never saw Gabin move, but he was somehow behind Lucien and grabbed him around his shoulders. Callum drew back and shoved the full length of his blade through his brother's middle, just barely missing his first mate by a hair.

Blood darkened Lucien's lips and spilled down the sides of his chin until it dripped on the floor.

"This is for abandoning me and Mother to that plague."

He twisted the hilt back and forth in a slow, tortuous move that drew more blood. He then yanked the sword free with a cry from Lucien, and more blood poured from the wound, soaking even more of his shirt. He stepped back and tilted his head to me.

"The killing blow is yours, Henri. Since he stole your daughter away from you." He held the gore-covered cutlass to me.

I stared at the sword, then back to Lucien, who hung limp in

Gabin's arms as his side and leg soaked in the blood spilling out of him. Sick burned in my stomach, and I shook my head. I didn't come here to kill the man myself.

"No." I backed away when I heard the creak of leather as he tightened his grip. "I don't want anything to do with this."

The doors to the library burst open, and we all spun to them. The red-headed man servant stood in a fiery glow, covered in blood, and looked a lot like something from my nightmares. His eyes found his master's.

"Lucien!" His shout was a near roar.

He moved, and metal on metal rang out in the silent room, a chair toppling over in the aftermath of his charge. He pressed Callum back with animalistic strength, shoving the captain off his feet in a single movement. He spun on his toes and sliced his blade at Gabin's throat, but he lurched back to avoid a death blow, the tip skimming his flesh and leaving a trail of red behind it.

"Get out of here, Lucien! Get to the cave!" he commanded.

"He's damn near dead, Elie. He's not going anywhere." Callum got to his feet, rubbing the back of his hand across his mouth.

He was wrong. Lucien, somehow, ran from the room, pressing a palm over the front of his wound and leaving a trail behind him.

"Go after him!" Callum roared at me, and my feet moved of their own volition at his command as if there were some power in his voice. I didn't go after Lucien, though. Instead, I ran to the front doors and bolted from the castle as fast as I could. This was not the plan, it wasn't what I wanted, and I wouldn't be part of killing a person for Callum's damn revenge.

CHAPTER
FIFTY-SIX

Arabelle

rimson coated the sky, no cloud or sun in sight. I walked the cobblestone path cutting through the side gardens on the castle grounds, the jagged pieces of my heart beating in a dull thud as I climbed the sloping hill.

On the other side, Lucien was on the ground, arms and legs splayed. I approached him with all the caution of a doe seeking water in mid-winter, the ache growing as I looked at his face, no longer hindered by the mask he always donned.

His eyes didn't meet mine when he spoke. "You're going to abandon me, aren't you?" His voice was so quiet and laced with an emotion that ran deep in my own veins.

The hue of this dreamscape gilded him in shades of red, just like everything else within the dream. Even my own skin was saturated with the color.

A pit opened up in my stomach and swallowed every ounce of happiness and joy I'd experienced over the past few months. My heart would have bottomed out at the expression on his face if it weren't shattered itself. His eyebrows were slanted down, eyes gleaming with tears his pride refused to shed.

My jaw tightened as I forced myself to swallow in a desert of a throat before gathering my courage to speak to him.

"I'm not going to abandon you." I meant it, and I only realized that when I said it aloud. "I just... I need time."

I stared down at the handsome features of his face, the sharp angles of his jaw, the delicate curve of his lips, the way his eyebrows arched over his eyes.

Lucien's gaze left the cloudless sky and rested on mine. "But you ran. What else would you call it?"

I took a half step back, hand coming up in front of me as if someone were to strike a blow. It wasn't a physical assault that caused this agony radiating from behind my ribs. It was the piercing coldness of his tone, of his eyes.

It caught me unguarded and worked its way into the cracks of my armor before I had any chance of stopping it.

"I-I just..." I stumbled for words, grasping at the recesses of my mind for something to bring back the Lucien that not only haunted my dreams but my waking world, too.

The pounding in my skull reminded me of the anger and hurt from when I found out he was, without a doubt, the beast. It clawed and burrowed deep into my mind. I didn't give him the chance to explain anything before running, and a part of me regretted it. The other part of me hoped he'd explain it now.

The grass rustled as he pushed himself up from the ground and held a hand out to me. A nervous sweat clung to my palms, but I took it, allowing myself to be led away from the clearing.

Dead leaves crunched underfoot as we followed a path of decay into a wooded area hidden away from the castle. I chewed the inside of my cheek, warmth leeching out of me in his cold hand.

"Do you really believe I'd abandon you? After everything?" I pressed the palm of my other hand to my chest as if doing so would stop the crack in my heart from tearing me open.

"Do you care what I think?" The coldness drained from his voice, replaced by something that threatened to split me in two.

The question gripped me by the stomach, and I fought the welling tears from slipping down my cheeks. I ran from him. I saw him for what he truly was, and I ran. I hurt him. I didn't accept him. There was no way he would believe I didn't mean to abandon him. My fingers tightened around his.

"I care," I croaked out. "I've cared for a long while now,"

My voice was small and quiet in my own ears, and I wasn't sure he even heard me.

He dropped my hand and tilted his head back, closing his eyes.

"I thought you would be my salvation, but it turns out monsters can't be saved."

Tears burned in my eyes, and my cheeks flared with an all-consuming type of fire. My heart, my very soul cleaved apart.

"I want to save you. Tell me how, Lucien." I flung my hand to the side as frustration crawled up my throat in an agonizing throb. "How can I help you if I don't know how?" The vein in my neck pulsed as I tried to force the ache in my chest to just let go already.

"It doesn't matter."

My world shattered. Tears spilled over my eyelashes and dripped down my cheeks.

"Please, Lucien. Give me another chance to save you," my voice cracked, and I couldn't bring myself to care that it did this time.

Lucien bent down over a small patch of yellow flowers—primroses. He plucked one from it and stood to his full height, turning back to me. His eyes held a deep sorrow that threatened to pull me under to drown in.

"I won't leave you, not like this." My fingers found his shirt and tangled in the fabric.

"You're already gone." He made no move to touch me, no move to comfort me.

"I'll come back." Please. Please believe me.

"You'll be too late." He tucked the flower into my hair, just above my ear, and leaned in so close that his breath warmed the side of my neck. "I'm sorry, Belle."

The whispered words drifted away like the dying leaves in the wind.

A creak of wood woke me from sleep, dragging me away from Lucien, and when my eyes blinked open, the room was dark. I closed my eyes again only to jolt up in the bed with a cacophony of squeaking springs.

The sudden movement sent a throb through the back of my skull. I was struck when fleeing the library – fleeing Lucien. I glanced around the dark room, but I didn't recognize it, even after my eyes adjusted.

"Where am I?" I swung my legs off the bed. "And how did I get here?"

My shin met with something hard, and I cursed under my breath as I stumbled. I found the door in the darkness and wrenched it open, squinting into the light of the hall. I followed the scent of ginger and rosemary until I reached the kitchen, where Isa stood at a cooking pot and started at the sudden intrusion.

"I see you've finally woken up," she said as she wiped her hands on the apron around her waist. "I assume this means Louis and father were successful in freeing you from the castle since Callum's men brought you here."

"What do you mean?" I pressed my palms to the table, the ground threatening to buckle under my feet. "Where am I?"

Every emotion welled up inside me all at once until I thought I would boil over.

"Louis's estate." Her eyebrows furrowed as she narrowed her eyes at me. "Belle, they went to rescue you from the castle. Did they not say anything to you?"

"No...Yes...I saw Louis. He said he was going to bring me back, but he's dead." I needed to get back, needed to right things with Lucien.

"Dead? What happened?" Isa took a step toward me.

"I don't have time to tell you right now. I need to go back to the castle." I scanned the room. "How do I get out of here?"

I wasn't even sure *how* to get back to the castle.

Her lips were set in a line, and I could see the battle in her eyes whether to tell me or not.

"Isa, *please*," I let the desperation seep into my voice. "I need to get back to him."

His words kept clanging through my mind like a death knell. *You'll be too late.* I couldn't let that happen.

She remained silent.

I moved around the table and clutched her shoulders, fighting the urge to shake her. "I'll explain everything; just tell me how to get out of here and where I can find a horse."

"It's impossible. There are guards – the men who brought you back."

"How many?" It didn't matter. I would fight my way out of here.

"Just two."

"Two?" Easy enough. Elie taught me what I needed to do. "You find somewhere safe to hide yourself for now."

"No."

I didn't have time for this.

"I'm coming with you."

"Isa—"

"You left me." Her eyes seared through me; I couldn't recall her ever using that tone with me – with anyone. "That castle was my chance to get away from father, and you took it."

Oh.

"Isa, I'm sorry. But we can talk about this later. I'll make it up to you however you want, just please show me where to go."

For minutes, we stared at each other. I had never known her to be this stubborn, to be so hard-edged that she wouldn't even bend for me. Fear slipped beneath my skin, fear that she would refuse, fear that she would make me too late to save Lucien.

"There's a back way. The pirates don't know about it." She finally relented and untied the apron, tossing it to the floor. "Follow me."

Isa led me through a small door and tight hallway that curved away from the kitchen. We went down a narrow staircase, passed through a passage so small that the walls scraped against my arms, and then we were outside.

"The horses are this way. Do you know the way back?"

"Yes," I lied.

I could only follow the relentless tug in my chest that pulled me forward and led my steps—a tug veiled in golden strands and a warm voice that whispered *this way*.

CHAPTER
FIFTY-SEVEN

Lucien

The ground weaved to and fro underfoot as I fled the walls of my castle, a lingering coldness holding me in its icy grasp. My limbs were numb. Darkness edged in on my vision. The cave – I needed to get to the cave.

My legs carried me by memory or maybe by instinct. I didn't know or much care because, to my eyes, everything was a blur of black and purple and green until I pressed a palm to solid stone.

This wasn't how it was supposed to end. The curse was to claim me, the witch. I stumbled step over step, and my knees cracked against the ground hard enough that my teeth sang in my skull.

How did everything go so wrong? I spent these last months doing all I could to convince Belle to fall in love with me. I clenched my teeth, the iron tang of blood filling my mouth.

At first, I thought I could do this, win her heart, without throwing myself over that ledge with her. But with every passing day, I couldn't stop the fondness that bloomed in my heart, shedding layers of stone as it grew and grew.

She was an answer to a prayer I never dared speak aloud, and no amount of will could have stopped me from falling for her. I would have given anything for just a little longer with her, a few more days, a few more hours.

I doubled over, panting, hands slamming into the floor to keep myself from face-planting as my blood poured from the wound when I no longer held pressure there. It pooled in a crimson puddle underneath me. I lifted my head but could see nothing. I knew it was in the back of this cave. I just had to get to it before I bled out.

My head spun, and the world shifted around me. A soft melody played in the recesses of my mind, the first song I learned to play on the piano.

"Good job, Lucien," Mother said as she cupped my cheek in her hand, and a sense of pride washed over me at her compliment. Her eyes were like the inviting waters of a lake, warmed by the sun on a summer day, never the glacial ice of my father's.

"You'll be the best musician in the kingdom if you keep practicing." Her words stirred a warm throb against the inside of my ribs as she wrapped her arms around my middle and pulled me into a hug.

"No," I shook my head to clear the memory, and my hair spilled over my shoulders. "No, I will not succumb to this. I need to see her again."

The stone floor bit into my palms and knees as I forced myself to crawl deeper into the cave. Sharp agony ripped through my insides after only a few feet, and I ground my teeth to silence a scream.

"Come on, Lucy," Callum's young, whiny voice tugged at the threads of my heart as he clutched my hand. "Let me come with you guys."

I laughed and ruffled the mop of blond hair atop his head. "Sorry, Cal, this is for adults only. Mom would kill me if I let you come."

He huffed a breath through his nose and folded his arms over his chest. "You're not adults either. Why do you get to go?"

Elie draped an arm over Callum's lanky shoulders and leaned his weight into him. "We're more adult than you, kiddo. I've wanted to check out this party for years, and now we finally get to."

Callum rolled his eyes and shoved Elie away. "E, you two aren't even teenagers yet." He huffed again, tears glistening in his eyes, no doubt from the frustration of us refusing his request.

"You're too noisy, Cal. We can't sneak in if you get us all caught. Just wait your turn." Elie and I left him there.

I gasped and coughed blood onto the cavern's floor, my lungs filling with less and less oxygen with every breath. I pushed forward on shaky arms, strength abandoning me. I passed through an opening, and the waft of clean spring water urged me on and pulled me further and further in.

"Lucien, your mother and brother were exposed to the Crimson Plague when they went to town. There was nothing we could do for them. They've gone to the otherworld." My father's voice was an unwavering, cold sound in my ears despite the words ripping a hole through my heart.

"Their funeral pyres are being built as we speak. The rites will be performed tomorrow evening. I expect you to act with a sense of decorum and not embarrass me."

I swallowed and steadied the tremble of my chin before I responded, "Yes, Father. I understand." It was a lie. I didn't understand. I blinked and was back in my room, numbness taking me in its embrace and flooding every cell of my body.

I lifted my eyes, and there was a black leather case sitting on my bed with a piece of parchment on top. I picked it up and immediately recognized the swirls of letters as my mother's handwriting. I read it.

Happy birthday, Lucien. Cal and I had this made for you as a present. We can't wait to hear you play for us.

The note crumpled in my grip. I flipped the clasps on the case and opened it to the most beautiful violin I'd ever seen. Hot tears streaked down my cheeks and fell onto the red velvet padding.

I blinked away the sting in my eyes and inched forward until the drip drop of water grew louder. Almost there. I was almost there.

My vision went black, and when it righted again, stone walls were replaced with wooden rafters, hay, and bloodied mud that caked between my toes. I hung by my wrists, my fingers tingling from the lack of proper blood flow for days.

I didn't know how long I'd been here.

Fire seared my back from the hundreds of lash marks torn into my flesh, from the burns left by a scalding iron poker, from a serrated knife.

A familiar cry came from behind me, but I couldn't even muster the strength or energy to turn my head.

"L-Lucien?" Golden eyes were in front of me, fear and then rage burning to a depth that I knew he would never fully heal from. "Who did this to you?"

"F-Father." My throat was raw from screaming.

He gripped the chains above my wrists, and drops of melted steel fell to the ground and sizzled in my congealed blood at our feet.

When my arms dropped, my legs refused to support me, but Elie didn't. He caught me and lifted my mangled body into his arms, trying to avoid my savaged back as best as he could.

"I'm taking you to the healers."

"Stop," I pleaded with the gods, to whoever listened. "Please," My voice broke against the quiet of the cave. I didn't want to relive these things.

"I love you, Lucien." Daija's touch was warm and tender as she traced the lines of my jaw with her fingertips.

"Stop," I said with more desperation as I crawled, the edge of the spring finally coming into my view.

A withered crone stood at the doors of the castle, her wrinkled hand outstretched to me, finger pointed at my heart.

"You will know what it means to live a wretched life, Ruby Prince. And should you fail to lift this curse before the bell strikes twelve in the hour of the owl within twenty years' time, your life will be mine." Light shone from her hand as she spoke.

That light grew brighter until it enveloped me, and pain shot through my entire body, causing me to double over and clutch my middle. My ears rang with the magic entering me, and I dared look at my hand, the bones and skin shifting until fur covered it, until claws poked out of my nail beds.

I buried the memory in a sea of pain as I dragged myself across the floor, my legs losing all their strength and lying limp behind me.

A flash of a chestnut braid had my heart thundering a wild beat. My heart warmed at the face of the woman who found the bruised and battered thing in a tangle of poisoned briars.

"Belle."

This cavern was too damn big, I wouldn't make it in time. My vision was dark. My body was like ice. I was going to die. Alone.

Her laugh was a song I wanted to dance to for the rest of my life. Her smile, the pure joy on her face that night we melded with the spirits until the sun peaked over the horizon was a balm to my shriveled heart.

She didn't look at me like a beast or a monster. Having her in my arms at last righted my entire world in every single way.

She accepted me as I was.

And with that acceptance, I could finally forgive myself.

My heaving chest collapsed on the cool stone. My cheek slammed against it, the last of my strength fleeing from me, only mere feet away. I stretched my arm out and tried to pull myself toward it, but I couldn't.

"I'm sorry, Arabelle."

Tears rolled down her flushed cheeks in the last memory I had of her, eyebrows pulled together, her face crumpling, terror and betrayal flashing in her amber eyes.

"I wish I could have had more time with you. I wish I could have made everything right."

My eyes closed and did not open again.

FIFTY-EIGHT

Arabelle

Darkness closed in around us as Isa and I raced for the castle. I guided my horse to follow that tug in my chest, the path almost lighting up with that warm, glowing presence that was always in my dreams of Lucien. Isa kept her horse just behind mine.

The leather strap of the reins groaned in my hands, my fingers gripping them so hard that my joints screamed in pain. Lucien's face kept flashing back to my mind when I found out that he was the man from my dreams. And the devastation on it as I fled.

I'd spent weeks letting myself think that, but the actuality of it was different. Or maybe it was just too much for my heart to take.

I might have felt betrayed in that moment, but I let my fear control me and take me away from him. I dragged my bottom lip between my teeth and chewed on it. The memory of him calling out to me plagued my mind. My eyes could have burned from the sorrow or the cold wind, tears slipping from the corners.

"Belle." Isa's shout crashed through my train of thought like a rabid and starving wolf after a squirrel. "If we keep pushing the horses like this, we won't make it." It was a shout, because over the clap of hooves and rush of wind, I could barely hear her.

"We can't slow down, he could die."

I wouldn't let it happen. I would make it back in time and save him. He never told me how to save him, but I would make him tell me. After I apologized for running.

"Who could die? You said you'd explain, but it'd be nice to know who we're risking our lives for." Because if one of the horses slipped on a patch of ice, if one of us fell, we might very well die ourselves.

"Lucien. The 'monster' father told us about." The word left a rotten taste in my mouth. "He's not a monster. Not even close."

"What is he?"

"He's a man who was cursed." A sob lodged in my throat when I tried to say the rest, but I swallowed it down. "And he will die if I don't get back in time to save him."

She was silent for seconds.

"You're just a woman." It wasn't an insult, not a denigration, but the truth. "How are you going to save him?"

Women in our world were powerless. But I was the only one who could save him. "I don't know. But I have to."

"What happened to you at that castle? You've changed."

I told Isa everything. From my initial plans to kill Lucien to finding the man from my dreams to help me escape, all the way through the events of tonight.

She listened to me speak and let me tell my story until the end.

"That explains it."

The snapping wind ripped my hair from its braid, and it billowed behind me. "Explains what?"

I barely heard her voice. "There's been a radiant glow about you, one that must come from happiness."

My cheeks heated despite the cold. An aching crack split me

open at the realization. I was happy. I had been for a while. I spent my days with Lucien and Elie, getting to find the person I truly was under all the rules and expectations.

A nagging question burned at the back of my mind, one that had been since I woke in Louis's manor. "Why were you at Louis's estate?"

"When Father struck a deal with Louis to get you back, Louis insisted we live with him. I think it was more a contingency than anything else. He kept saying that if he didn't get you back, he'd take me as a wife instead."

My stomach turned sour. I didn't lament Louis's death at all. "He deserved worse." I wish I could have killed him with my own hands. But Lucien's claws were satisfying enough.

"Father was furious after you left. Said you were selfish for going in my stead when you were to marry Louis," she paused for moments before continuing, "I ran away. I tried to find the castle, but they hunted me down first. Louis put me in chains after that."

"I just wanted to protect you. It wasn't right for him to send you to that castle in his place." I bit into the soft flesh of my cheek, teeth puncturing the skin and drawing blood. "He's the selfish one."

"It would have been better if you had let me," I couldn't see her, but that tone in her voice left no questions about the anger that burned inside her.

My heart squeezed in my chest. "Did something happen while you were there?"

"He put his hands on me. Told me that if he didn't get you back soon, he'd take me as his wife and force you to be his mistress." Isa went quiet again. "If Callum hadn't been there..."

That's why she said what she had at the manor. If I had let her go, she wouldn't have been put in that situation. For the first time, guilt slithered through my insides about my choice to leave. I robbed her of a chance at happiness. But I couldn't ignore the feeling in my gut that told me to go.

"Callum?"

Rage boiled my blood in my veins. I wished I could bring Louis back just to kill him myself for ever thinking he could touch my sister. He deserved to suffer more than he did.

"Yes, he's the captain of the ship that came back into port with father's treasure. He saw Louis corner me, touch me, and told him that if he didn't keep his hands to himself, he'd see to it that Louis ended up in the bellies of monsters more horrifying than what even his twisted mind could come up with."

The wave of relief was short-lived when thoughts of my father came back to me. He may have claimed to work with Louis for my sake, but it wasn't to get me back.

No, he didn't care about that. He wanted the wealth in the castle. God, the wealth I'd been such a fool to show him existed when I sent those chests.

"You need to stay away from Father too, Isa. If he can't get me back or claim the riches in the castle, he'll resort to using you to get his hands on more. He's only interested in the power that he can get his hands on."

"Where am I to go, Belle? Unlike you, I have nowhere else."

The words slammed into me like an anvil, and my heart shattered for her. "Stay with me at the castle." She would be taken care of there. I could protect her there. And so would Elie and Lucien. "There's plenty of room, and Lucien and Elie won't bother you."

"And what am I to do at this castle? Be your servant? A servant to your beast?" The words were sharp and hit deep.

"Of course not, Isa. You'll be free to do whatever you want."

Pain roiled through my chest, the pieces of my heart aching. Did she really think that I'd do something like that?

That pain was eclipsed by wanting to see Lucien again, to

apologize for running and not giving him the chance to speak. For knowing that his time was short, and I'd wasted precious minutes—hours, just trying to get back to him.

"Is he worth all this? He's just a man." Was she really asking me this? Simon had meant the world to her, and she said *this* to me?

"Yes." He was worth everything. Everything I had to give and all that I didn't.

"Why? He killed Louis. He lied to you. He's just as much a monster as father said—"

"He's not! He killed Louis to protect me. As for the rest...he has his reasons. He tried to tell me, but I wouldn't listen. I want to hear them, Isa. I..." My voice cracked, and my eyes burned, an ache growing in the depths of my throat, and I choked off my words.

"I'm glad you finally found someone to love, Belle." Her words hit me like a boulder, so hard that my grip on the horse slipped.

I fumbled the reins, my heart in my throat, but I didn't fall. "I never said I loved him, Isa."

My pulse was a battle drum in the heat of war.

I could hear the smile in her words. "You don't have to. It's in the way you speak of him, defend him, and are willing to drive yourself into the ground just to get back to him." The hoofbeats shattered the silence of the night. "I'm happy for you."

"I—" A whimper escaped my lips, and I focused on the trail ahead of us, the light of the full moon gilding it silver.

Did I? This feeling of emptiness without him, the way my heart fluttered when he said my name, the warmth that soothed my anxieties when he was simply near, was that love? I clamped my mouth shut and set my lips in a thin line.

"I think *he* loves *you*, even if you haven't decided yet." Her voice yanked me back into my body.

"Why do you think that?"

"Because he's changed. If what you say is accurate, he went

from a violent, threatening presence to someone who was willing to rip open his chest and bleed everything he was out for you so that you'd understand. He saved you and sat by your side until you woke. He gave you the option to protect yourself, to choose your own future, even if it didn't include him."

She breathed a sigh, carried into the wind. "He's just like those princes in the fairy tale books we read together."

"He's a beast...I can't..."

The thought shredded to bits before it could even fully form in my mind and hollowed out my chest as if the lie scooped out everything else to make room for itself. He *wasn't* a beast. He was a man.

"Just tell him how you feel, Belle. Nothing else matters."

What did I have to lose? He would die soon if I didn't find a way to save him. The thought sent a shuddering tremor through my body. It could be my last chance, my only chance to let him know. To give him those words.

Tears welled up and streamed from my eyes, only to be stolen away by the wind, like everything else. I squeezed myself closer to the horse, urging it to go faster.

Darkness edged my vision. Not now, I couldn't pass out now. But my stubbornness didn't push it away as the veil of black fell around me.

The heels of my boots clicked against the floor in the dark halls of the castle, the rot of plant life and stone stuffing themselves up my nose. The candles that once flickered and burned with fervor when I approached remained cold and unlit. The winter air bit into my bare

skin, raising gooseflesh over my entire body, and a shiver ran through me.

My pace quickened as I took the stairs leading to the upper level two at a time and shoved through the door that led to the balcony where he told me he liked to hide.

Wilted flower petals scraped over the ground in a breeze. He wasn't there. I searched everywhere I had met him: the dining hall, the small sitting room where I first saw him, the library. I even dared venture into his chambers, but I couldn't find him.

I pushed through the front doors leading from the castle, an icy wind snapping at the hem of my skirts and ripping through the long, unbound tresses of my hair. A dark grey haze hung over the grounds, not quite a mist or fog, but a film that someone pulled over everything. I followed the garden path, a tug low in my gut pulling me along like it knew where I needed to go.

The vibrant flowers and plant life that I'd spent these months admiring had all shriveled into husks of themselves, crumpling into heaps of brown decay. There was no sign of Lucien anywhere. I kept going, eyes glued to the ground as I walked and wishing I'd brought a cloak with me. I wrapped my arms around my middle, huddling into myself as much as I could and still move, guarding against the bitter cold.

I came to a fork in the path with white cyclamens on either side. I couldn't remember seeing this before, but there was so much of the castle I was sure I hadn't seen. I turned toward the floral-laden trail and followed it. Unease worked its way into my pores. As I passed, the flowers faded from white to black and drooped toward the ground.

Each step I took on this cobblestone trail lightened the haze hanging over the area as the colors bled back into existence. A gentle glow shone from the entrance of a cave at the end of the stone path, and I hurried my steps along.

The inside of the cave was so dark I could just barely make out the cavern walls and distinct splotches of black staining the floor, leading deeper in. I drew in a breath and pressed my palm to my chest to steady my heart as if I could, and I followed.

A low burning fire illuminated part of the cave. A log snapped and split in the small firepit, and I flinched, my eyes shooting to the source and letting out a rush of air when it wasn't some monster in the dark. That little bit of relief melted into a twist of knots in my stomach, and I swear my heart cracked the stone floor when it smashed into it.

Blood pooled under a bundle of crimson-soaked blond fur. The clothes clung to him in tattered pieces. My throat ached around an ever-growing lump as my mouth ran dry like I'd never tasted a drop of water in my life.

No.

My foot shifted forward.

I won't be the source of your sadness.

That's what he told me. But then why was he lying there, unmoving? He was alive. He had to be. I stumbled over a rock and slammed onto my hands and knees, a sharp stab biting through my palms.

"Why are you covered in blood?"

I crawled to him, tears burning in my eyes and blurring my vision to the point I almost couldn't find him. I reached out a hand. My fingers refused to steady. I hesitated.

His arm was cold under my touch, but I grabbed him and shook.

"Lucien." *My voice broke on his name.*

"Lucien, wake up." *The cry bounced off the walls.*

"Please!" *Tears streaked a hot path down my cheeks.*

"Please...don't leave me...not when I've finally found you."

I tugged on his shoulder, rolling him toward me and leaning over him. His beautiful blue eyes, which I found myself drowning in more often than not, were a dull, clouded grey and glazed over. His jaw hung slack. I clutched the greasy, matted fur lining his chest, buried my face in it, and screamed my pain and rage into him, sobs ripping from deep within me one after another until my throat was raw and my lips bled from the cracks.

FIFTY-NINE

Arabelle

The horses neighed and skidded to a stop at the bottom of the castle steps. Morning light already poured over the horizon when I shoved off the back of the horse. I had no clue how I didn't fall off the horse. Maybe I wasn't fully unconscious. I glanced around, looking for any sign of him, of Elie, of anyone. But there was none.

Ice chilled my blood to the core of my being as I gripped the reins tighter and tighter. If all the dreams I had until now were his doing, then the one from last night had to be more than just a dream.

Panic gripped my lungs and squeezed the air from them. I clutched my chest and tried to breathe.

"What if he's..." the rest of the words choked off in my throat. I knew where to go but feared what I would find.

I glanced up to Isa, still in the saddle. "I should get you inside and somewhere safe."

"No." She slid off the horse. "You go find him. I'll wait here."

When did she become the strong one?

"Isa, there were pirates here last night. They kidnapped me

and brought me back to Louis's manor. What if they're still here? I can't just leave you."

"And what if your beast dies while you are trying to tuck me away?" She lifted her chin. "Go, Arabelle. Find him. Save him. I will be fine."

I only hesitated for a moment longer before I turned and ran down the cobblestone path that I followed in my dream.

Dark clouds gathered in the sky, and a bolt of lightning zigzagged through them in a flash of white. A low rumble of thunder murmured in the distance. I didn't stop, my stomach churning in a storm mimicking the heavens. My steps were swallowed by the thickening atmosphere and the crack and boom in the sky.

A drop of water fell on my cheek and slid down the curve of my face. I swiped it away with my thumb as I followed the path. Dark stains led me to a destination I knew waited at the end, my stomach sinking with each step toward that cave. Even the sky wept for what awaited me.

Whatever magic in this place was only held together by a loose thread now, and I could sense the fragile ends fraying.

White cyclamens caught my eye, and I froze, terror scraping its claws down my sensitive nerves. My gaze traced the same stone path as an icy grip wrapped itself around my insides and held them in an ever-tightening vice.

The ground weaved underneath my feet as I took one agonizing step after another. Air seemed a precious commodity that I was running out of as each breath came in a rapid, shallow spurt. I had to still be dreaming.

There was no way this was real.

The cave was there, at the end of the path.

It looked exactly the same as it did in my dream, save for the smear of blood on the stone. I hurried to it and touched my fingers to the cold rock, but the blood had long dried. I was grateful that I skipped my meals, otherwise they'd be making a reappearance right about now.

Every fiber in my body screamed to turn back, run away, to not go in there, but I pressed on, shoving it all down.

"Lucien?" I braced myself for what I knew I was going to find. Him in a bloody heap.

The lighting was no better now than it had been in the dream when I stepped down onto the cavern floor. The metallic tang of blood filled the cave, and even though I tried to prepare myself, tried to steady myself, when my eyes fell on the shape collapsed on the ground, it still robbed me of every breath.

It was the exact same—the blood, the stillness, the cold bite of air against my skin. My knees threatened to buckle. My lungs burned. My head spun. But still, I managed to find myself at his side, crouching next to him.

Blood pooled underneath his enormous body and soaked into the skirt of my dress. I ran my fingers through the coarse hair on his head, but he remained still as death. I stroked his head again.

"I should have stayed..." Guilt slammed into me so hard it nearly took me off my feet. "If I stayed, this wouldn't have happened."

When the tears stung my eyes, I tilted my head back and stared at the cave ceiling, fighting against them. I squeezed my eyelids shut until the burn went away. I opened them again and looked down at Lucien, my beast, rubbing my other hand over the sticky fur on his chest. The tears came unbidden, leaving a hot trail down my face and dripping onto him.

A sob lodged in my throat, an ache clawing its way up my jaw from where I clenched my teeth hard enough they groaned.

My hand clung to his chest.

And the faint thud against my palm.

I gasped a broken sound and leaned further over him, pressing my fingers to his snout, and hot breath caressed them. White-hot relief crashed into me like a tidal wave, and I scrambled to my feet.

"Hang on, Lucien."

I searched the cavern, looking for anything useful to me in this moment, until I spotted a ground spring just feet away, the water almost invisible in the dim light. I thrust my hands into it, cupping them, and staggered to my feet so I could hurry back to him, trying not to spill a single drop.

I bent over him, tilted my fingertips over his mouth and let some of the water drain into it.

"Come on...come on...wake up." It was a command, a plea, a prayer.

A low sound rumbled from his chest as he began to stir. Droplets of water splashed the stone floor as I threw my arms around him, letting my tears flow free. I didn't care anymore. I was done fighting it.

"I thought you were dead," I sobbed and buried my face into the soft, warm fur. "I thought...I thought I was too late. I'm sorry, Lucien. I'm sorry I ran. I'm sorry I wasn't here," I cried and pressed myself further into him.

"Belle..." His voice was barely a rasp. "The spring, help me to it."

He pushed himself up, trying and failing to stand until I let him brace his weight on me. Together, we moved toward the spring. He all but collapsed at the edge of it and dunked his hand in, slurping up the water in greedy guzzles.

When he'd had enough to drink, he lifted his eyes to mine. "What are you doing here?"

"Because... I—" The words stuck in my throat when I tried to say them, and the fear he might not feel the same way overshadowed my earlier determination. "I care about you."

A truth I wasn't afraid to speak.

"Someone—something as hideous as I am does not deserve such kindness."

His gaze fell from mine, eyes closing as he tried to rebuild that wall inside himself that I took painstaking efforts to climb over.

I cupped his face and turned it back to mine, waiting for him to open his eyes again so I could search the deep oceans inside him.

"Everyone—everything deserves such kindness."

I pressed my lips together in a thin line.

Tension uncoiled in my chest. I'd saved him. I made it back in time and he still lived.

Arabelle

When had it happened? That I craved his presence more than the heat of a fire, more than food for sustenance, than the air I breathed? I stared at Lucien, watching him sit on his haunches and lean back against the wall of the cave.

My heart swelled with a new kind of fondness, one that I would cherish for as long as I was allowed. My gaze met his, and I braced myself when he opened his mouth to speak.

"How did your visit go?" he asked, propping his forearms on his knees.

Did he seriously ask about something menial when I found him on the precipice to the otherworld? It wasn't even an actual visit but an abduction. Fine.

"It was informative. But that's not what I want to talk about right now. What happened to you?" I leaned forward, trying to see through the dimness.

"It doesn't matter," he paused and shifted, uncomfortable. "Was your sister happy to see you?"

"Lucien," I didn't miss how his body went rigid from the use of such a sharp tone. I tucked that away for later. "Stop changing the subject."

His focus shifted away from me, and I could see the scowl on his face, even with such bad lighting. The silence stretched on between us to the point that I almost spoke up again.

"Tell me about your visit."

His tone caused me to falter, even though every molecule in me wanted to know what happened after I left. Whatever it was—whoever attacked him—brought great pain to Lucien.

A dark part of me wanted to find them and cut them from stem to stern because he wasn't just suffering from the physical assault. No, there was something much deeper working into the crevices.

"I told Isa about everything that has happened here. About you." That warranted a look, and I finally caught a glimpse of those blue eyes capable of stealing the very air from my lungs if he only asked.

"What about me?"

"Oh, you know..." I started, rolling my shoulders in a nonchalant shrug, "just that you're a big, scary beast. At first." I studied the swirl of emotion in his eyes with every word.

"You don't think so anymore?"

A smile curled my lips as the things he'd done, things he'd said, replayed in my mind. I shook my head, droplets of water flying from my hair to scatter on the floor of the cave.

"No, I don't. The way you look doesn't matter. And I have long since stopped being afraid of you." I pressed my hand to my chest. "It's about what's in here, in your heart."

He snorted, tearing his gaze away from mine with a grimace. "What nonsense. I don't have a heart."

Just like I thought, he was trying to shut me out again. I wouldn't let him, not when he's shown me that fragile heart of his.

"If you don't have a heart, why did you agree to let me visit my family? Why did you share your love of music with me? Why did you take me to that star-speckled field and dance until the sun came up? Why did you save me from the Daeva? If you didn't have a heart, you would have left me to rot in a cell. You have a heart. You care about me."

"Arabelle."

My spine straightened at the use of my full name, even on a raspy voice. He glanced at me sidelong then shifted his gaze to the spring.

"Do you love me?"

The question was a spear through my chest and pierced right into my heart, spreading warmth in its wake. Color heated my cheeks. My mouth ran dry with nerves.

I swallowed my unease and responded, "Yes, Lucien. I do." I paused to find his eyes. "I love you."

A blaze of light shuddered through the cave, shining so bright I shielded my eyes from the brilliance of it, but when my gaze fell on Lucien again, the beast was no longer there.

It was the body of a man slumped in the floor, dressed in the same dirty and shredded clothes. His long blond hair falling over his shoulders.

He raised his hands, staring at them as he turned them over and again, trembling. I stood and approached him. I'd seen it once before, the night I left: his real face. The face of the man I'd chased, spending so much effort trying to find, when he was right in front of me the whole time.

I stopped in front of him and sank to my knees between his legs, steadying his swaying body by taking his head in my hands.

His shaky hands tangled in my dress, fingers digging into the fabric and holding tight, as if I was his anchor to the world.

I cupped his cheek in a hand, his stubble scratching against my palm, and lifted his face to mine.

"Lucien, what was that light?"

"You broke it."

His voice rumbled all the way to my core. I had run from him before, not giving him a moment to explain anything. I turned back to Lucien and was met with eyes the color of a clear morning sky, so blue I could spend an eternity lost in them—the same ones I so often dreamed of.

His skin was soft—warm under my touch as I brought my other hand up to trace the lines of his face.

"How?" I knew the answer, but I wanted to hear the truth of it from his lips.

"You saved me." It was like he had to reassure himself of it. His eyes locked on mine. "I'm free of that damnable enchantment because you had the courage to love me as I was."

I blinked, and my brows bunched.

"Why didn't you tell me that was how to save you?" It would have been so much simpler.

"I couldn't. You had to decide to love me on your own."

"The dreams, Nocturnum Lucir and the dancing, playing music with me, all of that was you trying to win my heart?"

"Yes."

"How did you slip into my dreams?"

"Magic. I told you once before, didn't I?" He grinned, gazing up at me. "My mother was a mind-walker. I inherited a drop of her power that allows me to slip into another's mind. Only when they're asleep, though."

He leaned into my hand, his own holding onto my waist. "It's all around us—the magic—can't you feel it?"

My eyes bounced between his as I held his gaze, searching—searching for some hint of lie or deception on his part. Magic. He did mention it before. It was real. I'd seen it—felt it—it crackled through the very air from the moment I stepped through the portcullis onto the grounds.

I etched each line of his face into my memory before my eyes fell to his lips. Since that first dream, the longing to kiss these lips, kiss the real him, haunted my every waking moment. I leaned in until his body tensed under my touch. His breath ghosted my lips. His muscles relaxed, and he slid a hand behind my neck, urging me forward.

Just a small taste.

When our lips touched, a torrent ripped through my nervous system, burning through me, and I was content to let it sweep me away as long as I was lost within him.

"Soft…" the word was a whisper against my skin.

Lucien wrapped his fingers around my wrists and lowered my hands from his face, pressing his brow to mine, not letting go of me.

"Thank you."

"For what?"

"For keeping your promise."

Heat flushed across my cheeks as I breathed him in. The tang of blood and musk mixed with an underlying scent of sweet apples and campfires and early summer mornings.

"I told you I would."

I pulled back to look at his face again, I didn't think I could ever tire of seeing this man. I took in all of him, but the angry, splotch of red flesh caused my muscles to go rigid.

"Tell me who attacked you." I made sure the tone in my voice left no room for excuses or subject changes this time.

"That would be *me*."

CHAPTER
SIXTY-ONE

Lucien

Every muscle throughout my body locked up at that voice —Callum. My eyes shifted from Arabelle to the cave opening, where Cal now stood, leaning one shoulder against the stone wall with his arms folded over the chest that had grown so broad since he was a boy. I was on my feet and pushing her behind me, a feeble attempt at protection because, without my power, I couldn't stop him.

"I would say me and your dear ole dad, but the coward ran off somewhere. I don't believe we've had the pleasure of meeting yet." His silky voice flowed with a smooth charm through every word; it made me ground my teeth. "I'm Callum Beaumont."

I'd known. The minute he told me who he was, I caught a glimpse of our mother in his eyes as he stabbed me. This was the brother I thought dead. I had no idea how he survived or what purpose my father had for lying to me about it.

"Beaumont..." Belle repeated the name, her eyebrows lowering as if she grasped for a memory just out of reach.

"Yes, I'm Lucien's younger brother. Did he not tell you our family name?"

She stiffened behind me, fingers grasping at my arm.

"That's a lie," her voice trembled, with anguish or rage. I couldn't tell. "His brother died. How dare you be so cruel."

Callum loosed a laugh that ran chills all the way to my bones before speaking.

"It's no lie, darling. It's the gods' honest truth." His eyes fell back to me, the amusement drying up in an instant. "I've come to finish the job that Elie interrupted before. I'll slaughter you before you have time to drink from the Spring again."

"What did you do with Elie?" Was he dead? Did Cal kill him? Or did he leave him injured somewhere? I kept my grip on Belle, not just to protect her, but so I didn't tumble down into despair.

"I don't think you have the time to be worrying about him right now." He stalked into the cave.

"Isa..." Belle muttered, her fingers digging into my skin. "What did you do with my sister? I swear if you hurt her..."

His eyes glittered at the threat lingering in the air. "Relax, kitten, I don't hurt the vulnerable." He took a step toward us.

"Stay away!" Belle screamed at him, her nails tearing into my flesh as she clawed and struggled to get between us, but I held her back, not about to let her put herself in danger.

"My mistake." Delight flashed in those damn eyes. "Vicious little thing, aren't you?"

He eyed the bloody scrapes on my arms and my sides.

"Don't worry, little *wild cat*. If you're that hung up on being the playing of a Beaumont, I'll take you back to my ship," Callum said with a grin that curdled my blood, taking a step toward us.

"Like hell, you will!" I roared, baring my teeth as I shoved her further back. I wouldn't let him get his hands on her; I didn't care who he was to me.

"What do you think you can do, Lucy? With your magic still spirited away to...only the witches know where."

"Your magic is gone?" Belle whispered behind me, her breath a soft caress against the back of my bicep.

"Oh? He hasn't even told you that yet? That it wasn't just one curse?" The tilt of his mouth set my blood to boiling in seconds.

"Shut your damn mouth, Callum." I couldn't let him say any more, not with the threat it posed to her life. It wasn't something I wanted her to hear either: that my foolish arrogance robbed not only me but her, her family, and every other person within my realm.

"Such a harsh way to speak to your little brother," Callum crooned, stalking further into the cave. "You sound just like him, you know?"

"Stop..." The word came out drained of the fury I'd had only moments ago. That statement hit right where it was aimed. That cruel man was someone I never wanted to be compared to.

He edged closer. The dark glimmer in his eyes told me the exact plan in his mind, and my knees threatened to buckle under my weight at the thought of reliving those memories.

"Don't do this, please." I would plead with him on this, I didn't care how it made me look. I blocked Belle from my brother as tendrils of magic swept over my mind.

Without my power, I didn't have the ability to use those mental shields I'd spent so long perfecting with my mother. My mind was completely open and vulnerable to him.

"I'm going to make you suffer the way she suffered—the way I suffered. I'll put you through every agonizing thing I can come up with. And oh, can I get imaginative," he all but purred as he dragged a fingertip under my chin.

My body went rigid as the memories I'd shoved down for so long were hauled back to the surface, memories of pain, lashes upon my back, red-hot iron melting my skin, fists cracking bone and splitting flesh. Memories of Daija.

Sorrow burned my eyes with the memory of the day I was told

of my mother and brother's deaths. The sting of my cheek when my father backhanded me hard enough to see stars before telling me tears were for little girls. The overwhelming ache ebbed from my chest, and Callum's golden tan face drained of its color.

"Lucien?" Belle's hand touched the back of my arm. "Lucien, are you okay?"

I took her hand in mine and squeezed it; the past was just that – the past. This woman was my future and healed all those old wounds one by one. "I'm okay," I said and tossed a half-smile over my shoulder at her.

Callum's lip curled into a snarl. "What did you do? What kind of trick are you pulling?" A swirl of emotions mixed together in his eyes in a loop of anger and despair.

"It's no trick, brother. Every single memory you so giddily trudged through was the reality of my life." He would have to accept it, I had no magic, no way of combatting his mind-walking skill.

"Liar!" He splayed his hands to the sides, seething. "He wouldn't treat his precious heir like that!"

"You have no idea what cruelty that bastard was capable of. Be glad of whatever got you away from him."

Rage darkened his eyes. "*Be glad of it?* Be glad that he sent Mother and me away? That he let us rot, let her die? I know damn well the cruelty of that man.

"He was a vain asshole, and you were just like him. He'd never treat you like he did us." He grew louder with every word until his voice echoed throughout the cave beyond.

"He would and did," it was Elie who spoke.

Relief took me out at the knees, and Belle went down with me. He was alive. Cal didn't kill him. My whole world spun.

Elie always came to my rescue.

"I had to melt the chains off him myself. I would've killed the bastard then and there."

Callum spun to Elie.

"Why should I believe you? He didn't come after us." He pointed at me. "None of you did."

He flung his hand out, a dagger flying from it and nicking the edge of Elie's ear. Elie didn't even flinch.

"You know he can't lie to you. He has no magic to mislead yours."

"I didn't know." I couldn't look him in the eye. "He told me you were dead."

I failed him, failed our mother. How could I not have known?

"If I'd thought for a moment that you were alive, that he'd lied to me, I would have tried to find you."

A deep, rumbling growl sounded from Callum's chest. A rage I'd only felt in my darkest moments smoldered in my brother's voice.

"Where is he?"

He didn't need to see what became of him; this I could grant him.

"A place he'll never hurt anyone from again."

"Where?"

Gods damn him and his persistence. I stared at the tensed limbs, the rigid outline of his jaw, and the muscle pulsing there.

"The dungeon." So much for protecting him.

"Then let's go pay him a visit, shall we?" The grin on his lips did little to hide the murderous fury bubbling beneath the surface of his skin.

"You know the way."

"Yeah, I do." The black tails of Callum's vest flipped out as he spun and headed for the exit, sidestepping Elie and pausing at the threshold.

"I'm sorry. I assumed the worst when you never came for us—for me," he said over his shoulder before he was gone.

I loosed a ragged breath and stood again, offering Belle a hand up and freeing her from the confined space I pushed her into.

"You don't need to see this. Go with Elie; he'll keep you safe." I ran my knuckles down her cheek.

"Absolutely not. No way am I leaving you alone with that man." Despite the effort of feigned courage, the tremble in her voice gave away her true feelings.

I could kiss her alone for that, but she took my hand nonetheless.

"If you're sure, then let's go." I knew when to pick my fights and I wouldn't win this one. I glanced at Elie. "Are you coming or staying?"

"You know my answer. I won't go down there again."

I knew. I remembered what it'd been like for Elie the last time he was down there, and I hadn't asked him to go down there again until the night Belle arrived. It was a stupid mistake that my anger led me to make. I would never ask him to go down there again.

"Elie, my sister is at the steps of the castle. Will you go find her and stay with her until we get back?" Belle asked.

"Yes, of course. I won't let any harm come to her." He handed me a shirt he'd been holding, and I pulled the blood-soaked one off and replaced it before taking Belle's hand again. We followed after my brother.

Callum leaned against a moss-covered pillar with his arms crossed and an impatient tap to his foot as he waited for us. He opened his turquoise eyes, a few shades darker than my own, as we approached.

"So. Which one is he in? Hard to believe the bastard would be quiet down here. Unless you cut his tongue out for good measure, I sure would have," he said as a wicked smirk flashed on his face.

"The one at the end." I gave the small hand in mine a squeeze and leaned down to whisper to her, "Don't look."

As we moved down the row of cells to the last one, I did everything I could to block her from seeing what waited for us in that cage.

"Seven hells, Luce." Callum stopped at the bars, gripping a black bar in each hand as he stared into the cell, not even looking back. "You killed him."

I stopped just behind him, peering over his shoulder into a prison I hadn't looked into for nearly twenty years now. The dried-up, brittle skeletal remains of our father lay crumpled against the far wall, the jawbone hanging slack, cave moss growing over the soiled clothes and bone.

"He thought it wise to attack me when I still had claws, and his were stolen away."

"He didn't suffer enough." Callum spat on the bones.

"No, he did not." Nothing would have sufficed. "Are you satisfied?"

"Never. But now I don't have to bother myself with the son of a bitch. Let's get out of here before this stench makes like a fledgling wench and gets too clingy."

I made sure to keep Belle's view blocked as I turned around; it wasn't a thing I wanted her to see, not when she ran away from me with Louis. I couldn't bear it a second time.

Arabelle

I sat at the large, ornate table with room for at least twenty. Lucien sat at the head to my left, Isa to my right, Callum across from me, and Elie to his left. An uncomfortable silence permeated the dining hall for several minutes.

Lucien kept opening and closing his mouth, words failing to come to him, and Elie simply stared at the table like it might get up and walk away.

"There's still one more curse to break," Callum finally said with a tentative glance to me, then back to Lucien.

"What curse?" I asked, my fingers interlaced and sitting on top of my lap as I held Callum's cold gaze.

"The one that was cast over the entire kingdom."

"There's a curse on the kingdom?" Isa asked with furrowed brows, taking in Callum and pinning him with a gaze just as cold as his own.

He just grinned and snapped his teeth at her.

"Callum," it was a warning from Lucien; their truce was still fragile—for both of them. They'd have to rebuild the trust that had been severed between them.

I glanced at Lucien again, his gaze fixed on his brother, and for a moment, I thought he might come out of the chair and attack him. My hand found his, and I gave it a gentle squeeze. "It's alright. I broke the other one. Let's find a way to break this one, too."

"You don't understand, Belle." The muscles in his jaw tightened. "The other curse is different. It's already brought harm to you from the mere mention of things outside the parameters of what humans should know. I won't risk your life."

"It's my choice." I saw it in his eyes then; he'd let me choose before, and he couldn't take that freedom away, even if it meant losing me.

Callum slammed his fist on the table with a loud thud. "If you had his magic, *your* magic, now by right of birth, you could easily break it."

"The magic was stolen a long time ago. Elie and I have both torn the grounds apart looking for it. We've listened for any rumor of it these past twenty years. It's useless." His gaze fell to the table, fingers tightening around mine.

Callum tilted his head with a sly grin that I could already tell was one that spelled trouble. "Come now, Luce, maybe your beloved has seen it?" His eyes shifted to me, and I couldn't help but squirm. "It's a large ruby; looks like it has a thousand stars trapped inside."

I blinked. "A ruby..." I muttered as a memory came back to me, one laced with pain, terror, and hopeless despair.

I had seen it. "Do you mean this?"

Four sets of eyes snapped to me as I held out my hands and called to that entity that had hidden itself inside me that day. A glowing, red stone materialized, magic burning bright inside it—Lucien's stolen magic.

"Where did you...?" He lifted his eyes to meet mine.

"The day when I found out about your curse, right before the

Daeva attacked me, I found this on a pedestal out in the woods. It just...went inside me. They wanted it. I had no idea what it was—or how to get it out of me—but I did know I couldn't let them have it."

Callum hummed in a wicked bit of delight. "Well now, this is an interesting turn of events. Only our family and their mates can draw on the magic of that Ruby. And if it found itself in your possession..." His words trailed off as he studied me again, those eyes peeling back the layers of who I was.

"Enough, Cal," Lucien snapped.

The implication hit me so hard it robbed the air from my lungs. "Are you saying...that I'm his..." I could barely hear my own words over the thundering of my pulse.

I shook my head, the mess of curls falling over my shoulders as I sat the Ruby on the table.

"Here." I slid it toward Lucien without making eye contact.

Mates were a made-up thing in fairy tales. Why on earth would Callum suggest something so childish? With a man like that, I had no doubt it was to play with other people's emotions.

Lucien's fingers trembled as he reached for the stone, power spilling out from its core in waves. The power was familiar, like going back to a childhood home.

When he took hold of the Ruby, the world splintered. Cracks spiderwebbed across my vision as magic shattered the illusion I'd lived under for twenty years. Memories rushed back in a tidal wave that left me panting.

Isa gripped the side of the table tight enough that wood crumbled under her fingertips. Her eyes shifted so rapidly that I knew she experienced the same thing, a flood of knowledge and memories coming back, released from the confines of their magical tethers.

My eyes drifted up to the tips of her pointed ears now protruding from her hair – the ears that marked us as Fae.

It all made sense: the fear, the instincts that had guided me for the last three months. "Lucien," my voice wobbled more than I'd liked.

Whatever curse kept us in those human bodies had broken, and his beauty before held no candle to his beauty now. His hair was like woven gold, and his eyes swirled with such devastating blue, that little ring of gold in them again. His features were smoother and sleeker, and his ears curved into delicate, arched points.

"What's going on?" Isa's voice snapped my attention to her as she stared at her hands, turning them over. "Was that the curse you spoke of?"

"Yes," Lucien answered. "It was a curse cast over the entirety of Grienia by a witch."

"Finally, I can drop this," Callum groaned. A shimmer of light shrouded him and sputtered out to reveal his real form.

"We're fae, darling. The ones from folk tales that humans share to scare their young into behaving."

My gaze traveled to Lucien's left wrist, covered by the shirt he wore—where the mating mark would be on anyone lucky enough to meet theirs. What if Callum's word had merit? My fingers clasped my own wrist, where mine had been since I was a child.

It showed up after a ball I attended with my parents when I was seven. I didn't know if he had one, but if he did, the chances of it being the same were so low I didn't even want to think about it.

Callum snatched Lucien's wrist, lithe fingers wrapping around it with that feline smile of his plastered to his face. "Do you want to know, darling?"

Lucien jerked his arm away with a growl.

"Now isn't the time to worry about that." He was right. We'd face it together, alone.

Isa's gasp drew my attention to her, but hers was straight ahead. I followed the line of sight to Elie.

"Elie, you-re—" I cut myself off, the words dying in my throat.

His appearance had changed entirely, reverting to its original state. His skin was a dark grey with orange-red veins standing out against it. The grey on his arms faded out to yellow, starting at his forearms. His hair now truly looked like fire, blazing against the dark skin. The rich gold of his eyes stood stark against it. His teeth were almost blinding when he smiled; canines elongated into the fangs the Afarit were known for.

"Ah, yeah. I'm an Afarit," he finished for me, all his features painted in the pride of a people I had only heard stories about.

"Aren't your people warriors? The grunts that filled the King's armies?" Isa asked, her brow wrinkled.

Were her own memories as slow to come back as mine? The first rush left my head with an ache forming, but smaller, less important facts still trickled back.

"Mostly. But me and mine are far from grunts. My father is the leader of our clan, so he was the High General here during the last king's reign. I'll be taking his place once Lucien is crowned."

And be married to that woman he told me about. The one his parents had chosen for him before he'd even been born.

"All of this was part of the curse?" I asked, turning my attention back to Lucien, then to Callum.

His appearance was similar to Lucien's, but his skin was more golden, and his eyes looked more like the depths of oceans than the blue of the sky, like his brother's. He didn't change much, just the tips of his ears, which were both now pierced with five gold and silver rings from lobe to tip.

I gave Lucien a sidelong glance, and he, too, studied Callum, frowning at the hoops, which earned him a sneer.

"Yes. The witch cast a second curse, along with the one that turned me into a beast. But not before she stole the Ruby, the source of my family's magic." He locked eyes with me. "I don't know how you found it, Belle, but thank you. With my power freed, I was able to shatter it. But..." He paused, shifting his attention back to Callum. "How did you escape it?"

Callum grimaced as if the question brought him physical discomfort.

"About that," he huffed out a breath, blowing up a displaced strand of blond hair. "There are some things we need to discuss."

I steadied myself. Those words never led to anything good. Lucien went as rigid as the stone beneath our feet as he read the expression on Callum's face.

This little reprieve of joy was about to be destroyed by whatever he had to say.

"Before your...curse...I was...trading...in the Onyx Court when Aamon found me. We've been pals for a bit. He knew about my vendetta against you and the old man and asked for my help, but he was playing some political game I wanted nothing to do with. He just shrugged when I said no and gave me a stone to keep on my ship, one that protected us from that curse. We were spared because of him.

"But, Luce, it's not just the Ruby Court that was cursed. All the Solar Courts were targeted by curses. They've fallen. One by one."

The wooden arms of his chair groaned under the pressure of Lucien's fingertips as he dug them in, nails carving crescents.

"Why were we cursed? To what end?" Isa asked, leaning forward in her chair and hugging her middle.

A muscle in Lucien's jaw ticked as his gaze slid to her.

"I don't know what their overall goal is." His eyes fell to the table, fingers flexing. "It could have been to destabilize us or to weaken us before they marched on our lands."

I had to search through the muddled mess of my memory for the information. The Onyx Court was in Hesnen, but that didn't help. They were part of the Lunar Courts, the worst of them. They held onto a centuries-long grudge and were always trying to find a way to create conflict, especially with the Ruby Court.

"Did Onyx act on their own? Or was it a collected effort by the Lunar Courts?" It was the bigger concern because if it was just the Onyx Court, then we could simply crush them, but if it was a collected effort.... If they were behind the curses, then it meant war was coming. None in the Solar Courts would let this slide. It would tear our world apart.

From my studies, the Ruby and Onyx Courts were matched in military might, but we'd been weakened for twenty years. Was this the plan? Weaken us, then claim a swooping victory? I chewed my lip.

"I don't know. I didn't care to ask. He didn't deem it necessary to tell me." Callum shrugged a shoulder and slumped back into his chair.

"You're sure all of the others have fallen?" Elie asked, fingers curling tight enough I would've sworn I heard the bones groan.

"How did every court fall prey to this? Even Eskea? They haven't let outsiders in their territory for centuries." Lucien rubbed a hand over his cheek.

Callum frowned at the slight disbelief. "Yes. For the past twenty years, every Solar Court territory has lived under a curse. I've heard rumors about the Lunar Courts' involvement up and down the Strait, but that's all they are – rumors. There have been whispers of the human Dark magic being used for them in the taverns.

"I haven't a clue who's behind it. But..." He leaned forward, forearms braced on the table and hands clasped together. "This is bad, Luce. Real bad."

What would happen if we went to war? How would the Onyx Court, the Lunar Courts, react to the news that we'd freed ourselves of the curse? My heart rate soared into my throat, the beat so loud I could hardly hear the conversation until Isa placed a hand on mine.

She didn't tremble at the news; she didn't balk or fear it. I squeezed her hand in mine, asking for just a little bit of the strength she held.

"If all of the Solar Courts are cursed, who's standing between the Lunar Courts and the humans?" Elie asked. He propped his head on one fist and drummed his fingertips on the table.

I cursed myself. I hadn't even considered what could have been happening to the humans this entire time.

"No one stands between them. Their only saving grace from our kind is that barrier. Aamon, Astaroth, and Erlik have yet to breach it."

"But they know of the curses?"

"Yes"

"That must be why the Daeva have been showing up on our lands," Elie said. "With our people forced to live as humans, I wouldn't doubt it if they were hunting them down this side of the barrier just to sate their taste for flesh."

Lucien placed a hand over mine. "Belle said they were looking for the Ruby, so that means when the witch cast her curse and stole the magic, she didn't take possession of it. If we're lucky, it's the same with the others." He gave me a small smile, and it eased the fear rapidly growing inside me just a fraction.

His throat bobbed as he strained to swallow, meeting Callum's gaze again. "Why didn't you stop them?"

Callum lifted a brow. "My only responsibility is to me and mine. And lest you forget, you lost the Ruby," he said with a shrug. "That limited my power too."

Lucien sucked in a deep breath and exhaled. "Tell me. Don't sugarcoat anything. What's the worst of what's happening?"

Callum studied Lucien's face.

"Have I ever?" Slyness gleamed in his eye. "The Daeva have

spilled into the other courts, setting up encampments as they hunt the cursed fae for sport. It's particularly bad in the north. They're not just contending with Daeva who've been left to roam wild, but beasts who've been corrupted by the Maliced Magick."

I grimaced as Lucien's fingers curled in on themselves, the tang of his blood drifting to me.

"We need to reach out to them, help them break their curses," he said. "We need to free the Solar Courts in order to stand against the Lunar Courts. We will need every player on the field to win in any war."

A memory pricked at the back of my mind. Another beautiful face. A man with a dark presence and twisted smile.

"It's impossible. No one can cross between the cursed realms," Callum paused with a smirk. "Well, no one except me and my crew, that is."

I dug at the memory, trying to surface in a pool of others; I trudged through the murk until it became clearer.

"Then make me a member of your crew." Lucien would do it, if that's what it took, without hesitation.

Callum's bark of laughter echoed off the stone walls of the dining hall. "As much as I'd love to see you on hand and knee scrubbing the grime off the decks of my ship, you have a realm to restore, Lucy."

Lucien fell silent, bristling because Callum was right. Our first priority was to our own people, to heal them and our lands. We didn't have time to galivant off to other kingdoms and involve ourselves in their problems.

"As of now, our armies are scattered to the gods know where," Elie spoke this time. "It will take time to call the banners of the Nov Fae." Elie dropped his hand to the table. "But the Afarit are different. I don't know where my father is, but when you ascend the throne, that mantle passes to me. All I need is a word from you, and I'll give the call to arms."

All of this was so much, so much planning, so much back and forth, weighing of our lives versus the lives of potential allies. It was too much. How could we go from peace throughout the lands to planning a war? But the die was cast twenty years ago, the day they cast the first curse.

The steady tap of Lucien's fingers on the table grounded me before I threw myself over the edge into that panic. Our kingdom may be in an even more vulnerable state now than before the curse broke.

"Give me a few months; I'll strengthen my court, then we'll sail to the Emerald Court and offer aid—if they haven't broken their own curse by then."

Callum slumped back into his seat with a sigh.

"Such a demanding king you are, brother." He shot Lucien a wickedly delighted smile. "Will your beloved be joining us?"

"It makes no sense." Elie cut in before Lucien could retort. "If Aamon was behind the curses, why did he show up and tell Belle about yours? It was almost like he wanted to help." His gaze shot to me, then back to Lucien.

"He gave her that cryptic message, too."

That was it.

The memory I kept pulling at the threads of.

"What message?" Callum raised a brow, looking from Elie to me.

"'The breeze from the East has shifted, and we need all the pieces back on the board,'" I answered.

The color drained in Callum's face, the knot in his throat bobbing. "You're certain that's what he said?"

I nodded. "Yes, why? What does it mean?"

Callum scrubbed his face with both hands and then raked them through his thick hair, leaning his elbows onto the table and mumbling something I couldn't quite hear.

"What is it, Cal?" Lucien asked. "I need you to tell us so we can prepare for whatever it is," Lucien said, his voice softening toward his brother.

Did he know what that message meant? What exactly was going on?

Callum shook his head. "I'm afraid we're focusing on the wrong enemy." He laced his fingers together and leaned forward. "You'd better call those banners, Luce. War *is* coming." The muscles in his arms and shoulders shifted under his shirt and I had to wonder how hard the grip on his own hand was. "And it's going to be a lot worse than we thought."

"What do you mean?" Isa, who had been quietly observing and taking all this in, finally spoke.

"I mean, our enemy isn't the Lunar Courts like we assumed." His knuckles turned alabaster white.

"Who's our enemy, Cal?" Elie asked with a tilt to his chin, golden gaze locked on Callum's every move.

He scratched at the back of his head.

"Fuck." He leaned back in his chair again. "An ancient one."

He stared up at the chandeliers sparkling with firelight.

"If we can't save everyone from these curses in time, they'll wipe us off the map completely this time."

I swallowed and hoped I was wrong. "The witch who cursed Lucien, she's not just a typical witch, is she?" I'd heard of witches, humans who made packs with the Nullifier for his dark magic.

"No, I don't believe she is." His eyes darkened as he lost that playful glint that always lingered. "If Aamon is trying to assist us, then there must be something far worse threatening not just the Solar Courts, but all of our kind."

"How do we fight them?" Elie asked.

"One step at a time," Lucien answered instead. "We free the Courts first. Then we worry about the witches."

"Once my ship is repaired, I'll sail with my crew to Dothya and find out what I can there." Callum raked a hand through his hair. "Princess Nerissa will be glad of the help."

"If we're lucky, we'll have time enough to break all the curses," I said, trying not to let that lead weight sink into my heart before I had a moment to enjoy the love I'd found.

"Before you go," Lucien held out a hand, palm up, as a sliver of the Ruby appeared in it. It was fashioned into a necklace, the chain glimmering with magic. "Take this. It'll allow you greater use of our magic and let us communicate."

Callum pinched the silver chain between his fingers and lifted the shard from Lucien's hand, studying it against the light shining through the large windows.

"Thanks. And by the way, Lucy – my boys and I need a place to stay while our ship finishes repairs. Since the castle is all but empty right now, how about you lend us some rooms?" The smirk on his face sent a shudder slithering down my spine.

Lucien considered him, lips etched in a frown. "You can use the barracks. I don't want their thieving hands on anything in my castle."

Callum clicked his tongue. "Now, now, Luce. That's no way to treat men who are about to embark on a quest for you." He slipped the necklace around his neck.

Lucien wrinkled his nose, but I spoke before he could, "You can have your old rooms back. And *you* can stay in the castle if you'll look after Isa." All heads whipped to me. Callum's lips curled as his eyes shifted to my sister at my side.

"I don't need someone to look after me," Isa hissed in my ear.

"I can't leave you alone in this castle, in good conscience, when the Daeva and Marid have been lurking around." I needed her to acquiesce to this because there was still one thing left I needed to take care of.

"Why would we be leaving Isa alone in the castle?" Elie asked with an arched brow, each word deliberate and slow.

"Because you and Lucien are coming with me to see my father and make sure he never does anything like this again." I didn't care if Lucien's magic made him the strongest man in the realm – the world. I wouldn't feel safe until I knew for a fact that my father—no, Henri—was out of the picture for good.

Callum and Isa stared each other down, having some silent battle with their eyes. "I can watch that one."

"I told you; I don't need you to watch over me." Her hands gripped the table again. "I don't want you anywhere near me."

Callum simply leaned onto a fist, amusement dancing in his eyes. "I really do think you'd be so much more fun if you said all that out loud."

I arched my brow at them, then to Lucien, who just shook his head.

"Did you not hear me the first time I told you to stay out of my head, *pirate*?" Every word was sharp enough to be a dagger thrown at him.

He placed a hand over his heart, dropping the smirk to feign hurt. "But you have such *enticing* thoughts, my darling *Isabelle*."

"Leave her alone, Cal." It was Elie's turn to give the warning.

Callum's gaze slid to Elie's. "You could always come to my bed instead. I've always wondered what it'd be like to fuck an Afarit."

I damn near choked, instinctively clutching Lucien's hand at the look passed between Elie and Callum and the now feral smile on Elie's face.

I was not prepared for what Elie said, and I'm not sure Lucien was either because his jaw dropped.

"We both know you wouldn't be the one doing the fucking, because I never give up being on top."

"That's really too bad." He splayed his hands on the table and pushed himself up. "If you'll excuse me, I need to go round up my men and see them to the barracks."

He turned his attention back to me. "Don't worry. I won't let anything happen to your sister while you're gone."

Before I could respond, he vanished in a blaze of fire that burned itself out.

Silence ensconced us in the absence of Callum's all-encompassing presence. I breathed out a small sigh until a different kind of fury took hold. I met Lucien's stare, then Elie's.

"It's time we go have a talk with my father." I didn't want Isa to be a part of this, and I didn't think she wanted it either.

CHAPTER

SIXTY-THREE

Arabelle

We would figure everything out with the courts and the curse breaking, but right now, the most pressing matter to ensure both Isa and I remained free of Henri was to go and deal with him directly. Isa told me he'd been staying with Louis, and even with the man dead, there was no way he'd go back to the cottage.

He'd worked with Louis to take me back, allowed him to treat Isa the way he did, and was the reason Callum came to harm Lucien—even if they were at an understanding now. The tension was still there when both were in the same room.

It was all unforgivable. And it was time to cut him off.

"Are you sure you want to go see him?" Lucien asked after escorting me back to my room.

My nails dug into the meat of my palms hard enough to draw blood, my knuckles white.

"He tried to steal me from you. He wanted you dead so he could take everything that's yours. He deserves nothing, and I will see to it that he gets exactly that."

451

Elie had already gone to change and get the horses ready. Lucien brushed the back of his knuckles down my cheek.

"I do not trust that man to let either of you go so easily," Lucien said.

"He won't. That's why I want the two of you there." I slipped into my room and changed into rider trousers and a tunic.

When I swung the door open again, Lucien waited on the other side, arms crossed over his chest, blond hair tied back, dressed in tight black riding leathers that nearly left me drooling when I caught the sight of his cut thighs through them. The white of his shirt sleeves stood out against it all.

He leaned against the wall; one ankle crossed over the other. He looked up at me through his lashes, his striking blue eyes like an arrow through the heart every damn time.

"Ready?"

A shiver rolled through my body at the sound of that voice, not as deep or rumbling as it was as a beast, but more steadfast and surer now that he was a man again. He held out a hand, and I took it, lacing our fingers together.

The moon was a jewel of silvery light in the dark sky with a backdrop of a billion tiny stars as Lucien led me to the stables. My chest caved as I remembered what he told me happened in there. My grip tightened on his. But Elie, that man was sent by the gods, I swear it, had two horses saddled and ready to leave before we even got close.

Two. I glanced to Lucien with the question burning in my eyes, and he answered, "We're riding one, and Elie will take the other."

Elie held the reins of both horses while Lucien mounted ours. He shifted in the saddle, removing his foot from the stirrup, and reached a hand down to me as he took the reins in the other. I grasped his forearm and used the empty stirrup to hoist myself onto the creature's back in front of Lucien. He pulled me tight against him, his front flush with my back, the warmth of him almost blustering in the heat of the castle grounds. Or maybe it was just me.

"Wait. If it's winter out there, why aren't we wearing cloaks?" It didn't cross my mind when we were leaving the castle, but none of us had them.

"Because they'd be too big of a risk. If it got snagged on a branch, it could yank you off the horse or, worse, break your neck. Don't want that, now do we?" Elie said with a wink.

He swung himself up in an easy, fluid movement, reins in his hand as he snapped them, and the horse jerked into a sprint. Lucien mimicked the motion and when our horse started its sprint, I could have sworn the hooves never even touched the ground.

"Will the horses be alright in the dark?" I asked as I stroked the dark mane.

"They'll be fine. If not, I can bring us home in an instant," he said into my ear, his breath warm and wet.

I opened my mouth to give voice to the question, but, like when I first came to the castle, the horse launched into a faster pace when it passed through the threshold of the gate. Wind whipped and pulled at my clothing, and I was glad I chose pants instead of a gown as I clutched the bridle for fear of falling off, even with Lucien's arms tight around me.

Everything was a blur of color, and the cold stung my eyes until I squeezed them shut, tears from the burn leaking out. Lucien's body warmed mine. He shifted so he was almost completely wrapped around me now. His thighs caged mine, his arms close to my torso, his chin on my shoulder.

By the time my mind and body settled into the speed, the feel of Lucien's body against mine, the horse came to a screeching halt, and had his grip not been so firm, I may have launched head-first into the brick wall.

Louis's manor was dark and quiet, similar to the way it'd been the last time I was here with Isa. I didn't even know if he had family. Did he have servants who knew of his death? Did anyone? I chewed my bottom lip. Elie's horse stamped its hooves as he waited for us to dismount.

"I'll go in by myself." This was something I should do alone. "I'm not sure if he's in there or not, but if I don't come out in five minutes, come get me."

I wouldn't take chances, and neither would Lucien. I'd be shocked if he actually waited that long. I slid off the horse and stepped back as he gave me a nod, eyes focused on nothing but the house in front of us.

"What'll you do if he is?" Elie asked, arms folded into himself to keep warm.

I hadn't thought that far ahead yet. The only thing in my head was to make sure he left us alone. I stared up at the clear night sky, the full moon a beacon of brightness that outshone even the hottest burning stars.

It didn't matter what lies he'd weave or how he'd try to explain away his actions. I reined in the rage that whispered to break his face with a brick for what he'd done, but it was the least important thing right now.

"No clue. Guess we'll find out." I pulled the door open and went inside.

"Belle? You've come back to me."

My eyes settled on the man who was on his feet the moment I walked through the door. I forced ice into the glare I threw his way.

"Did you escape from the beast? I'm glad to have you home, my child." Henri took a couple of steps toward me, but I reeled back.

"I'm not here to return to you. You are no father of mine after what you've done." I shifted so I was out of his reach.

"What are you talking about, Belle?" The fake smile plastered on his face made my blood turn from ice to hotter than the magma flowing through the veins below our feet. "All I've ever done is take care of you."

"Selling me to the highest bidder is hardly taking care of me. *I* took care of me, of us. While you schemed and weaseled your way into the good graces of awful men like Louis."

"You are home. *This* is our home now."

"No. This isn't my home. My home hasn't been with you since I left to save Isa from you bartering her away to save your own skin." His eyes flinched the slightest bit, that fake smile faltering a fraction.

"That's right, he told me everything. How you stole from him, and to save yourself, you agreed to give him one of us." I spat at my father's feet. "I'm done with you. Isa will stay at the castle with me. And you will get nothing."

Henri's lip twitched. "You really think you can come into *my* home and keep *my* daughter away from me? Did you think I'd let that happen? She's going to make me rich again. The deal's been made. I've already sold her to the Cordevaux family. They're the lords of these lands." The façade finally dropped, showing the true face of my father.

"I won't let you," I growled through my bared teeth. If I had to tear his throat out, I wouldn't hesitate to do it.

"It's already done." He heaved a sigh, bringing his palm to his forehead and massaging his temples. "And here I went to the trouble of getting rid of that godsforsaken monster who held you prisoner."

Bile forced its way up from my stomach, and I swallowed it back down with rage-fueled will. My nails bit at my palms until hot blood trickled between my fingers and dripped onto the carpet below. The muscle in my jaw ticked with every heartbeat.

"The only monster here is you."

"Ah, ah, Arabelle. That's no way to speak to your father. I taught you better than that." He wagged a finger at me, one I wanted to rip off and jam in his eye. He took a step closer.

"I told you, you are no father to me. Fathers love their children. They don't sell them or trade them for their own sakes." I stepped back. "I'm leaving. Don't ever come looking for me again."

"You really think it's that easy? I know where the castle is. And this time, there's no beast to protect it. Or you."

"What a shitbag you are, threatening your daughter like that." Elie's voice had never sounded so beautiful to me. My knees seemed to agree as they threatened to give out.

His large frame took up the entirety of the entrance. His fingers dug into the wood, burn marks arched under each one.

"Who the hells are you?"

"Name's Elie." He stepped into the room, his presence soaking up the atmosphere like a damn sponge. The foyer suddenly seemed a whole lot smaller with him inside it.

"You're one of those bloodthirsty Afarit." Henri spat at Elie's feet.

"Bloodthirsty? Is that what you think?" Elie howled with laughter. "Hear that, Luce? He thinks we're just some battle-hungry brutes."

"Careful, Elie, you're giving the bastard too much credit."

Lucien stepped in from behind his friend. "I doubt he does much thinking at all."

He cupped my face in his hand, dragging his eyes over me. "I could smell your fear from outside and decided you were taking too long."

"How dare you come into my house uninvited," Henri snapped, but he stepped back all the same.

"Is that how you speak to your king?" Lucien shot him a glance over his shoulder, hatred burning in the blue.

"K-king?" Henri sputtered. "There's been no king in these parts for years. Only the ruling lords."

"The Cordevaux are some of my courtiers. To think they'd step in to rule in my absence." He turned his full attention to Henri, then spoke to Elie. "I think they should be the first invited back to court so we can...discuss their decisions."

"Who are you?" Henri's voice lost its edge.

"Lucien Beaumont."

Henri's face went pale at the mention of his name. "B-Beau... did you say Beaumont?"

"There it is! You owe me twenty gold coins, Luce." Elie grinned from ear to ear, those fangs of his poking out over his lip.

Lucien ignored Elie. "I, indeed, said Beaumont."

"Beaumont. As in the *Nov Fae Lords of The Ruby Court,* Beaumont?"

"One and the same."

A smile split Henri's face, which made me want to vomit on the floor. I knew, without a word uttered, exactly what gears were spinning in that head of his. I knew, and I didn't like it in the least.

"Which one?"

"Pardon?"

"Which of them are you taking to bed? Or do you want both? Take them both if that's what you wish."

The muscles beneath the leather tunic rippled and strained

against it, and I could taste the disgust wafting off him at Henri's insinuation.

"It won't benefit you regardless, so I don't see why it matters to you." He gestured to me with his thumb. "Her and her sister at welcome at my home with me, and you're not going to come after us. If you do, I'll show you what it means to see a *real* monster."

Elie let out a low, long whistle.

"Forgot what it's like to see you like this." The grin on his face never faltered as he admired his king.

"You don't have the authority to keep them from me. They're mine." Henri flung his arm out, his eyes shifting from Lucien to Elie, then finally landing on me.

Lucien let loose a snarl that shook the entire estate, one more fearsome than any I'd heard from him as a beast.

Henri stumbled back a step—two.

"Arabelle is mine. Father or no, I will not tolerate another man calling her his."

My spine locked up at Lucien's words as if they'd leashed something in me and laid claim to it. My throat bobbed with the effort to swallow, and I studied the handsome profile of the man who'd stolen my heart away.

"If you come after us, if you set one foot inside my castle gates ever again...the gods will weep over the torment I bring down on you." His voice was low and full of every bit of the beast's temper that I'd grown to know so well.

"You can't take my children! They're mine! They belong to me!" He rushed at Lucien with an arm raised to strike.

"Ope, better take care of that," Elie said. He had come to protect us, but I thought he might be enjoying this a tad too much.

Lucien shot Elie a glare one moment, and the next, his claws flashed in a blaze of orange and yellow heat. The ground shuddered as Henri's body slammed into it. Lucien crouched over him with clawed fingertips that, gods, were on fire as they held Henri's face.

He dragged the points inward, leaving a trail of torn and cauterized flesh in their wake, a wound that would never heal.

"Do not, for one second, think that I am a merciful or forgiving lord. This is your final warning. The next time, you die."

I took a step forward. "We are not your property." I placed a hand on Lucien's shoulder. "Let's go home."

Lucien leaned forward and whispered something to Henri as Elie escorted me out, leaving the man curling into a fetal position.

The horses stamped their hooves on the cold ground as they waited for us to return. Warmth wafted off Elie, and I leaned into it. He was a living fire, given the shape of a man.

"Thank you for coming with me."

"Like hells I'd let you two go anywhere without me after everything. You'd end up getting yourselves killed," he said with the sigh of an old maid at her wit's end with the children she reared.

Lucien chuckled from behind and dropped his hand to my waist, shooting Elie an incredulous look. "I can take care of myself, E. The circumstances are different."

Elie snorted.

"Power or no, you've still never beaten me, Luce. Until you do, where you go," he paused, pointing a finger at Lucien's chest. Then he gestured to himself, "I go."

Lucien raised his hands in defeat.

"Fine. A bit clingy of you, but if that's what makes you happy." The warm smile on his face had my own lips wanting to twitch upwards.

Elie gripped the bridle of his horse and mounted, settling into the saddle for the ride home.

"You say that, but you wouldn't know what to do with yourself if I wasn't around."

Lucien shook his head with a smile and lifted me onto our horse, swinging a leg over. He held me much the same as he did on our way here.

Both Lucien and Elie snapped their reins at the same time, and the horses were off. Their speed halved on the way back to the castle.

SIXTY-FOUR

Arabelle

Relief flooded through my veins as we crossed over the threshold into the warm and balmy air of the castle grounds—kept in a perpetual state of early summer with Lucien's magic. The memories were slow to come back, but they did—even if it was a small one here and there.

The horses trotted side by side to the stables as we approached the castle. The moon gilded the stone in silver light and cast a shadow over the gardens to one side.

Elie slid off the back of the horse and ran a hand down the length of the horse, holding the reins in his other hand.

"Do you need to check on your sister?" Lucien swung a leg over the horse and handed the reins to Elie.

"No, I think she'll be fine until morning."

He grabbed my waist and lifted me off the horse, setting me on my feet in front of him. His hand splayed on my lower back as he held me close enough to smell the mint on his breath.

Elie only smiled and led the horses back to the stable without another word, giving us time to ourselves.

"Are you sure you're okay with leaving her alone?" Lucien

asked as he took my hand in his, leading me back into the castle, my home.

"She'll be fine," I said, covering my mouth when a yawn wormed its way out.

He laced his fingers through mine, leading me up the stairs and down hallways. The silence was only broken by our footsteps and the swoosh of sconces lighting as we passed. They shone brighter, chasing away the grim darkness that had seeped into every crevice before.

The dreary castle I walked into that first day melted away into rich colors and elegant décor. The dust and scarred stones were gone, and the paintings and portraits were back on the walls. "When did you have time to do all this?"

"Magic, Belle. With the Ruby back in my possession, I can do a great many things now. Including returning this castle to the once thriving place it used to be." He led us into the wing he once forbade me from entering and almost dragged me through the door to his chambers.

Lucien let go of my hand and spun to me.

"I was worried when you went into that manor alone." He held a palm to my cheek, tracing the line of the bone with his thumb.

I leaned into his hand. "I'm fine. I knew you wouldn't let anything happen to me."

I glanced around. "You said I wasn't allowed on this side of the castle, and now I've been over here..." I tapped finger after finger between us. "Three times."

There was a ghost of a smile on my face, but it was all to hide the fact that a monster made of claws shredded my nerves under my skin.

Dreams of his mouth, his fingers, his tongue, and that impeccable body emerged from the recesses of my memory, heating my blood. The things he'd done in those dreams brought a flush to my face.

He chuckled and backed me against his door, pressing his palms to the wood on either side of my head.

"That was then, this is now." He leaned down, hot breath in my ear, as he whispered, "We can't do all the things I have planned if I don't have you in my room."

I dragged my bottom lip between my teeth, suddenly grateful for the door supporting my weight because my knees would not. He moved back, eyes falling to where I chewed my lip, and a low growl rumbled from him.

He took my chin between his thumb and forefinger and tilted my face up to his.

"I told you, you don't know what this does to me." He tugged my lip from my teeth with his thumb. He brushed the tip of his nose down the length of mine in a move sending an electric charge to my tailbone and up my spine.

I wanted to arch into his touch but stood straight.

"I hope you know," he hovered his lips a hairsbreadth away from mine, "I mean to turn every last one of those dreams into a reality."

My heart thundered in my chest.

His eyes might have devoured me whole before his mouth ever got the chance to. I fought back a grin and sunk my teeth into the soft flesh of my lip again, daring him to do something about it.

His gaze dropped to my mouth and then moved back up to my eyes. He slid his hand behind the nape of my neck and pressed his lips to mine.

His kiss wasn't as gentle this time, giving way to the hunger building up within him until he caught my lip between his teeth and bit it. A soft moan slipped from me, and he answered it with a growl.

I pulled back from him and met his gaze.

"Show me your mark first," my words came out so soft I wasn't sure if he heard them, but it was his turn to take in a stuttering breath.

He took a step back, eyes failing to meet mine as a wave of pain washed over his face.

"The chances of us having the same mark are so extraordinarily low, Belle." He hooked his finger under the sleeve at his left wrist.

"So, you do have one." I hugged my arms around my middle, still using the door to brace myself up. "I want to...no, I need to see it." I needed to know.

"It doesn't matter. My feelings for you won't change." He squeezed his eyes shut, turning his head to the side.

The man had my entire heart, and I never wanted to bring him pain.

"Lucien, I never said they would. But I want to see nonetheless."

I stepped forward, holding his hand in mine and bringing it to my lips, pressing a kiss to his palm. A faded memory of wisps of blond hair flashed through my mind.

The breath he exhaled was a near sob as he lifted his free hand and tugged the sleeve of his shirt up to his elbow. I tilted his bare skin into the candlelight, and the burn of tears prickled my eyes.

Callum's words about the Ruby coming into my possession, my own memories, my very soul, all led me to believe that I was his.

A tear slid down my cheek as I took in the mark that stood out against his skin.

The room spun, and the air seemed like it was sucked straight from my lungs as the breath caught in my throat.

Tears burned hot as they continued to flow down my face and splatter against the stone at my feet.

My heart roared at the gold reflecting the light.

It roared in utter, pure rapturous joy because when I looked at the spot where his mark was etched into his flesh, it was a mark I'd spent so many years studying since the day a young boy saved me from the maze of a castle I'd never stepped foot in before.

The same gold-dusted red roses twining together.

I unbuttoned the sleeve over my left wrist and angled it into the light for him to see, lifting my palm to cup his cheek. When his eyes found the matching mark on my wrist, his tears fell onto my hand.

"H-how?" His voice was a rasp trying to die in his throat. "They're only supposed to appear when you've met your mate. Mine appeared long before you ever came into my life."

A laugh bubbled up from my chest.

"When I was a child, we were visiting the castle for some event or another, back when we were still of some importance. I got lost," I paused and dropped my hand to his chest, the thud of his heart against my palm.

"And this really precocious boy found me crying in some random hall. He took my hand and led me back to my parents. The next time I looked at my wrist, the mark was there."

Lucien held my arm and swiped his thumb over the marked skin as if it were some kind of illusion.

"I remember that. I was hunting down Elie when I came across this girl curled into a ball on the ground. Face red and covered in snot." He smirked. "To think it was you."

"I did not have—" I didn't get to finish before his mouth crashed against mine in a mixture of need and want, his fingers threading through my hair as he pulled me against him.

His tongue darted out and pressed to the seam of my lips until I parted them for him. He licked over my teeth and tongue in a slow and luxurious pace as his deft fingers worked the buttons on my tunic free until he could slide it from my shoulders and drop it to the floor.

My own were clumsy in comparison, fumbling over buttons and strings, which earned me a smile from him. He helped me remove his vest and shirt, breaking the kiss to pull both over his head.

I took a half step back to take in the glory of him, fighting back a potent need to run my fingers over the hard muscles of his chest, his stomach. I eyed the swirls of a scar on his left side. His father really didn't suffer enough.

My gaze caught on the V plunging below the waistband of his pants, and I pressed my hands together to my lips in a silent prayer to thank the gods for this beautifully flawed man.

His eyes softened from the edge of lust, and he took my cheek in his hand, tilting my head until I looked at him.

"Do you want this, Arabelle?" He lifted my left wrist to his lips and pressed a kiss to the center, where the two roses connected.

"Just because you share a mark with me doesn't mean you have to be with me. I know other realms force their mates together; it was done here. But you will always have the autonomy to choose with me."

I raised my hand to his cheek in a mirrored movement of his and traced my thumb along the plane of his face.

"I want you, Lucien. Every broken and scarred piece."

His breath was warm against my palm. He wrapped me in his arms and lifted me from the ground, spinning me back to his bed. I didn't have time to wrap my arms or legs around him before he dropped me against the down mattress.

My body heated from the way he stared down at me, his hands on the edge of the bed. His body leaned in, and gods, his eyes. The softness was long gone. The only thing living in them was the starving beast ready to devour his dinner. And that was me.

He yanked my boots off in a way that might have hurt had I still been human and shucked them into the floor with a thud. He crawled onto the bed, the ponytail he'd tied his hair into sliding over his shoulder as he moved up my body and straddled my hips.

The ends of his blond hair tickled my neck and collarbone when he leaned over, but all that came from me was the gasp when his tongue licked from the base of my neck, up my throat, and along my jaw until he reached my ear. He nipped at the lobe, leveraging his body so he didn't crush me into the bed. The feel of his breath on my skin sent a flurry of muddled thoughts through my head that I didn't even want to untangle.

His fingers pushed up the hem of my shirt as his warm hand slid up my side, inching the edge up and up as he pressed kiss after kiss along my throat until he got to the other side. Fingertips teased the sensitive skin at the side of my breast, and I arched my body into that touch.

"Ah, ah..." His whisper pulsed all the way to my core. "Patience, my sweet."

His tongue flicked out and licked the rim of my ear, and I could have melted from that alone.

"I'm not sure how much I have left."

I rubbed my thighs together as wetness gathered between them. I needed friction, any kind, I didn't care.

He shifted his weight down and trapped my thighs between his thick, powerful ones, preventing me from attaining that blessed relief.

"You can be patient for me, can't you?" He dragged his index finger over the tip of my nose, my lips and stopped at my chin, tilting it up to look him in the eye.

All the sound I could muster was a whine from the back of my throat that was met with a smirk. I hadn't forgotten about the hand he had up my shirt, but those damn blue eyes of his were almost mesmerizing enough to do it.

My eyes fluttered shut at the warmth of his palm over my nipple, his fingers digging into the soft flesh.

"Come now, Belle." He dragged the tip of his nose down my throat. "If I can wait for you for twenty years..." He lifted my shirt, and the cool air sent a rush of goosebumps over my skin. "You can give me twenty minutes."

If someone told me the heavens split open that second, I would have believed it because when his mouth closed over the peak of my breast, every nerve ending in my body sparked to life at once.

I wasn't prepared for the sounds coming out of me when he ran his tongue over my hardened nipple. It was warm and wet. When he pulled back and blew a cold breath of air against it, I arched and let the moan roll from my throat.

I grabbed his head, pulling him into me, wanting more, demanding more. My fingers threaded through his hair, skewing the neat ponytail. He grinned against my skin and pulled my blouse fully over my head, tossing it to the floor. He moved to my other breast, and *gods* he was going to end me here and now.

Why did the bastard have to have my legs pinned together? I needed to writhe. I needed to feel something. I freed one of my hands from his hair and reached for the ties of my own pants, but he grabbed my wrist before my fingertips even skimmed the laces.

"No. All of your pleasure belongs to me right now." There was that same command that caressed a claw down my spine and urged me to listen, to obey.

I did.

Lucien moved, finally freeing my legs, and settled himself between them as he placed slow, languishing kisses down the side of my breast, to my ribs, lower. He dragged the tip of his tongue down my stomach, fingers tugging the laces of my pants loose.

"I've wanted to taste you for so long." He hooked his thumbs into the waistband. "I've dreamed about it."

He peeled the last of my clothing off in a slow slide.

"I remember."

His smile was dangerous.

"Good." He trailed the tip of his tongue up the center of my torso, my chest. "Because I meant what I said about making them all real."

"I'm fine with that, so long as I get this, too," I bucked my hips underneath him with a wicked smile.

His teeth flashed. "It would be my pleasure."

He placed a hand on either knee, his thumbs traveling along the inside of my thighs as he pushed my legs further apart, moving dangerously close to where I wanted him. Muscles in my lower belly tightened with the anticipation of his touch.

A soft growl emitted from him, and his fingers dug into my skin, eyes locked on my lip where I'd dragged the bottom one between my teeth again. The corner of my mouth quirked up without letting my lip slip from its place.

"The more you disobey..." He dragged the tip of his finger through the wetness of my center and a sudden need to feel those fingers plunge inside me pulsated in my veins. "...the longer I make you wait."

I released my lip with a whimper. "Please don't."

Oh, gods. In a single, slow motion, he brought that same finger to his lips and opened his mouth wide enough for me to watch as he slid it down the middle of his tongue.

"I assume you remember how to beg."

Color rose to my cheeks. I wanted to feel that tongue on me— in me. I gripped the sheets at my sides, meeting his heated gaze with my own.

"Please don't make me wait any longer, Lucien. I need you. I need to feel you."

"How bad?" He slid his thumb through my slit in a slow stroke, groaning at the wetness he found and stopping at the apex just before the bundle of nerves.

I squirmed under his touch, the need almost at an overwhelming thrum in my head. "Bad. I might burst into flames if I can't have you inside me."

"We can't have that." And he slid a finger into me.

My toes curled at the small intrusion as he worked the digit in and out at a slowed pace. With each stroke, he moved deeper, twirling his finger, and curling it into the upper wall. A low hum built under my skin as my entire body scorched with heat radiating from where his genius hand worked.

"You're so wet for me, Belle." He slipped another finger in as he quickened his pace. "That's good: I need you to be soaking when I'm ready to fuck you."

He lowered his head and swirled his tongue over my clit in a move that made me see stars.

I gasped at the feel of his mouth on me, my body arching completely off the bed, my head pressing so far into the mattress it might have swallowed me. I wanted to grab him, claw at him, just to get more inside me, and like an answer to my silent pleas, he worked a third finger into me.

The world fractured in an explosion of color and bursts of light as my cries pierced the silence of the night. lightning rushed through my veins in a wave of blissful tingles crashing from my groin all the way to my fingers and toes and back again. Lucien kept working his fingers until I came down from the throes of my orgasm.

Words hadn't even fully formed in my head before Lucien was stripping his pants off.

"My turn." He crawled up my body and kissed me, hard.

I wrapped my arms around the back of his neck, pulling him closer, opening my mouth in an invitation that he greedily took, swiping his tongue over mine. He nudged my legs further apart with his knee, and I complied with the wordless demand.

Bracing himself on one arm, he reached down and guided the crown of his cock to my entrance but went no further.

Lucien pulled back and stared into my eyes, searching, waiting for me to change my mind and say no. I stroked my fingers down the side of his face.

"Your turn." I gave his words back to him.

With a gentle rock of his hips, he was inside of me, the burn of the stretch bottoming out my stomach in an explosion of fluttering wings. He held my gaze as inch after glorious inch of him sank deeper until he was fully seated. He dropped his brow to my shoulder and groaned from deep in his chest.

"Gods, you feel magnificent."

"I could say the same about you."

He tilted his head and kissed the side of my neck. "If it's too much, if it hurts, or you want to stop, say so."

I nodded and rolled my hips forward and his weight shifted him deeper inside me. His hands gripped my ass and held firm as he lifted his head to look me in the eye.

"I need you to say it." He refused to move, refused to let me move, not even to look away from him.

"If I need you to stop, I'll say stop."

"Good."

Without another warning, he jerked his hips, and my body rocked with the motion. A moan tore from my lips, and I dug my nails into the meat of his shoulders like I'd fall away if I didn't hold onto him. Another thrust and I wrapped my legs around his waist.

Each move of his hips came with an equally loudening sound from my throat until he swallowed them with a kiss. One of his hands braced him on the bed; the other cupped the back of my head so he could control how deep our kiss went.

That familiar buildup of tension started again, and in response, he moved faster, harder, with a bit of frenzy. He turned his head, his grunting and panting now in my ear, drowning out the sound of our bodies colliding together over and over again. His hand clasped onto my thigh, fingers digging in.

"I want you to come with me, Arabelle." His voice was ragged, his movements frantic and full of a need to find his own release.

He slid a hand between us, finding my swollen clit and rolling it between his finger and thumb until I barreled over the edge of ecstasy. I dug my nails into his skin, dragging them down his back as my orgasm shattered through me.

He slammed into me once, twice, three times before a deep, rumbling groan vibrated through his entire body. His cock pulsed inside me, spilling his hot seed in spurts until he collapsed on top of me.

I wasn't sure how long we stayed like that, in each other's arms, with Lucien buried inside me. He rolled to the side and wiped the back of his hand across his sweat-covered brow as he pulled me to him.

His fingers grazed over the dragon on the locket still around my neck. "You're still wearing this?"

I smiled, nuzzling into him. "Yes, I've grown rather fond of it and the little princes inside." The princes were Lucien and Callum, I'd since learned.

"It belonged to my mother. She had it commissioned not long before she got sick." His fingers caressed my skin in long strokes.

"Oh, I didn't know. It just appeared on the table next to my bed one day—"

"I put it there. While you were still asleep."

I arched a brow at him. "Why?"

"A desperate last hope that I might be freed from that curse."

We didn't say anything for the longest time, simply lay together, basking in each other, in the glow of what we'd just done. I traced lazy circles over his pectoral muscle with the tip of my finger.

"Lucien?"

"Yes?" His voice was husky. Sleep would take him soon.

"Do you love me?"

He caught my chin between his thumb and forefinger, holding my gaze, "An eternity of dancing through the stars with you would be nowhere near enough. All the stars in the sky and spirits living on our planet don't compare to the love I have burning in my heart for you. Should anything ever happen to you, I'll rip out my heart with my own hands and send it with you to the otherworld."

He stared at me with the same fierce eyes he had the first day we met, the eyes of my beast, my prince—my King.

CHAPTER

SIXTY-FIVE

Isabelle

The room Belle had taken me to was breathtaking in its beauty—the entirety of the castle likely was. I hadn't seen much of it yet, but the gardens out front were full of flowers I'd never seen before. Belle must have loved it. The garden at our cottage had given her so much pride. It was never something I enjoyed, but I understood the importance of it—it kept us fed.

I clutched a book in one hand as I gazed out of the window and into the blackness of night. I'd rummaged through the wardrobe until I found a thin nightgown. How they all slept in a place that never seemed to cool was beyond me.

A soft knock sounded at the door. I glanced at a clock setting atop a fireplace mantle. It was late. Was it Belle? I somehow doubted that. She would likely be too far gone in her Prince to come by tonight.

I glanced down at the book in my hand and frowned. It was probably the pirate again. I stomped to the door and whipped it open.

"What do you want—oh."

It wasn't the pirate.

The red-haired general smiled at me. What was his name again? That's right.

"Elie. I thought you were someone else."

"By the tone, I'm going to take a wild stab at it. Callum?" His eyebrows rose as he stared at me with those gods damned beautiful eyes.

"He was here earlier." I held up the book. "He gave me this."

He read the title and his eyes went molten, golden swirling like fire. "That book is..."

I gritted my teeth.

"Positively filthy. Just like the pirate." And I had never devoured a book so fast in my life. It made the fairy tales and romances Belle, and I shared look like no more than children's stories.

He had given it to me with that smug smirk he always wore, and his words set my face ablaze. *I think you should read this. We could have so much fun together, Isabelle.* If that wasn't enough, he pushed images into my head, images of the two of us entangled in each other. Images that made me want to take him up on his offer.

"Did he say anything else?" That golden gaze darkened a fraction, his shoulders tensing, the smile doing nothing to hide any of it.

"Nothing of importance." I didn't miss his eyes sweeping over my body, his gaze following the lines of my figure visible through the thin fabric.

"Did you come here for something? Or just to ogle me?"

I never thought the Afarit could blush, but his face turned a delicious shade of red and he snapped his eyes back to mine.

"I just wanted to check on you. See if you were okay." He shifted on his feet. "Or if you needed someone to talk to about everything."

"I don't know you well enough to talk about these things

with." Simon was the only person I ever fully opened myself up to before. I shared most things with Belle, but there were some that she just wouldn't understand.

He stepped closer, that deep flush of color nowhere in sight now. "You could let me in, and we can change that."

I let a flicker of amusement show on my face.

"I didn't want to fuck the pirate." I slowly and deliberately raked my eyes down and back up his body, watching every muscle tighten. "And I don't want to fuck you."

When I moved to shut the door, he caught it, fingertips burning into the wood. The damn thing wouldn't budge.

Heat radiated off him from fires he held in check by sheer willpower as he pinned me with a hard stare.

"I never said I wanted to fuck you." He leaned in, taking up all the space between us.

"Your sister will marry my best friend and become my queen. Unless you plan to leave, we'll be spending a lot of time together." His warm breath brushed against my neck and ear, making my toes curl. "Wouldn't you prefer it be pleasant?"

I tilted my head so that the tip of my nose skimmed his, staring up into those gold eyes that gazed back with such intensity that I thought my knees might buckle.

"Alright. Then let's have a chat."

He pushed off the door and strolled past me into the room. I shut the door and followed him to the small table by the window.

"How are you liking the castle?" He sat and leaned an elbow onto the table.

"It's fine, I guess." Was this really what he wanted to talk about? My feelings about the castle?

"And what do you think about Belle and Lucien?" He gave me a pointed stare, an expecting one.

"I don't know him well enough to form an opinion, but she loves him. And as long as she's happy, then that's all I care about."

Because she came so close to losing that happiness once, and it was all my fault. "You know them both. How do you feel about their relationship?"

He breathed in a sigh, and that golden gaze slid from me to the window beyond.

"I've never seen him like this with anyone. I've wanted him to be happy for so long; I honestly thought it would never happen. And then Belle showed up. Ready to kill him and run back home." His lips quirked up in a small smile.

I'd almost forgotten that she tried to stab him the first time they met.

"She's always been strong-willed and independent, much to our parents' dismay." I smiled at a memory of her in a torn dress after deliberately climbing a tree when she was told not to.

"What about you? You have a bit more fire in you than I thought." He held my gaze. Unlike others, he didn't back down from the steel I let show from time to time.

"You see what you want to see."

"Oh no, I don't believe that for a second." He propped his cheek on a fist. "I watched you during that meeting today. You may not have spoken much, but you followed every word. You weren't shaken like most women would be."

I straightened my spine. "Why would I be? It's not like women get a say in the wars of men."

Elie pressed his lips into a thin line. "While that is true for some realms, we aim to change that. Like it or not, these wars aren't just fought by men."

I didn't want to talk about this. "Tell me something about yourself."

He cocked an eyebrow. "Like what?"

"Something no one else knows."

His mouth twisted to the side. "That's going to be a tall order."

He leaned back in the chair and folded his arms over his chest.

"After seeing Arabelle and Lucien together, I've decided to break with my clan's traditions. I don't want to be forced into a marriage to someone I've never even met. I want to be with who I love."

I tilted my head in a way that had sent lesser men scrambling. "How do you know you won't find a love with her like they have?" I knew little and less about the traditions of the Afarit. But I knew about the arranged marriages their clans clung to.

"I don't."

"You should give her a chance. You never know what might happen."

He frowned at me, eyes turning icy. "And what if they try to trick me into it? Or force me to do it? Should I give up my chance at happiness?"

I studied him. According to Belle, he was a trained warrior, a general's son, and he was concerned he might not be happy with the decision his parents made. He had Lucien and Belle in his corner.

"Isn't Lucien king? Have him step in, make a decree that they can't force you to marry someone against your will."

He ran his hands through his hair. "He can't. The first king of Grienia agreed not to interfere with the way the Afarit chose to rule their clans. They answer to him on all other things, but our laws, our traditions cannot be altered by any king."

"All you can do is talk to your parents, then. Make them understand what you want." His situation was similar to the one Belle had been in, except he had no choice in the matter at all.

The laugh that came from him was void of any humor. We sat in silence for minutes.

"Your turn." He fixed his gaze on me again. "Tell me something about yourself that no one else knows."

Whether it was because he allowed himself a moment of

vulnerability with me or because the guilt was too much to bear alone, I told him my biggest, most damning secret.

"The fire that destroyed our home, that wiped out our wealth, wasn't an accident."

He went stone still.

"Louis hired men to set the fire because both Belle and our father refused his proposals." He opened his mouth to speak, but I pushed on before he could. "And I knew it was going to happen. I could have stopped it and chose not to out of anger and spite."

Rage burned in the gold of his eyes, making them look like molten ore. "What?"

I couldn't stop it once the words started. "Everything we lost, we lost because I was angry that my father wouldn't let me and my fiancé move up our wedding."

Why did I keep going? He would hate me. He'd tell the others, and they'd all hate me.

"It was all my fault."

It was a mistake to tell him.

Acknowledgments

The first person I would like to acknowledge and thank is my aunt. She not only provided me with a home when I was in need, but she was the first person to read my original work and encourage me to keep writing. Without her support, I wouldn't be the person or writer I am today. Thank you, Sheri! You'll never know how grateful I am to you.

The next person on my list is my best friend, Amy. She has been a solid support since I made the decision to pursue publishing. Not only has she been a supporter, but she's helped me improve my writing by leaps and bounds. She boosted my confidence with the craft and is one of the main reasons I am able to publish my work now.

To my friends in the art discord group (you know who you are), I couldn't have made it through writing this book without you. You all were my personal cheerleaders, hyping me up and going feral over scenes I shared with you. You guys will be some of my first readers and I wouldn't have it any other way.

Getting this book published was a whole learning process for me, including the search for an editor which was daunting. I didn't think I would be able to find one that fit within my budget that I vibed with. And then I found K. F. Starfell on Tiktok and they were an absolute dream to work with. From the time I finished writing the first draft, up until I sent my draft to them to edit, I felt like there was something missing. They helped me figure out what that was and how to fix it. Thank you so much for being amazing K. F. Starfell!

Another group that deserves acknowledgement is my Rebel Pack! They have been nothing but supportive and excited as I journeyed through the publishing side of this journey. So many of them have been eagerly awaiting the release of this book for months. Their excitement always fuels me to keep going, even when I wanted to toss in the towel because I have been over-whelmed. You all rock!

It wouldn't be a complete acknowledgement page without mentioning my family. Even though I don't expect any of them to read anything I write or publish, they have been supporting me nonetheless. My mom and dad, brothers, stepmom, and uncle. If you guys ever read this, know that all the small things you do to support me, whether I see it or not, it all means the world to me. Thank you.

And to wrap this all up, a big shout out and thank you to ACIE NEW who has gone on this incredible journey from start to finish with me. From the minute I said I was going to write a book in a month, all the way to publishing that book. Here's your acknowl-edgement Acie, I hope you're happy!

About the Author

J. D. Pierce is an emerging author of fantasy romance novels. She has loved storytelling for all her life. Whether it be in books, movies, television shows, anime, or video games. She decided to put pen to paper when she was 12 years old and write her first short story. Being encouraged by her 7th grade teacher, she continued to write.

Throughout middle and high school, it was fan fiction with her friends. But as she approached the end of high school, she wanted to give writing something original a shot. In 2012, she made the decision to pursue publishing and share her work with the world.

Whenever she isn't writing, she's usually reading and snuggling with her two fur babies, Mew and Ziggy. She enjoys a multitude of creative outlets, from drawing to knitting. She also enjoys playing video games, going to see movies, curling up with a new television show or anime.

NEWSLETTER

Sign up for my newsletter for early access, sneak peaks, and more!

Subscribe to Jewels of Asteria newsletter